A LADY WHO LOOKS GOOD WHEN SHE'S CRYING
SUNSHINE AND SPECTER PARANORMAL AGENCY #1

Dan Ackerman

Supposed Crimes LLC • Matthews, North Carolina

For David

Author's Note: A special thanks to Dane Terry for permission to use a line from one of his songs ("One More Name in Nightlife" from The Wild of Town) as the title for this novel. Find out more about Dane at @thedaneterry on Instagram or at **patreon.com/daneterry**.

February 4, 2016
Thursday

"Do you think she's gonna get out of the car?" Sunshine asked.

He and Felix had watched the green Ford Focus for about an hour now. They had followed it here from a motel and currently waited for their target, Robin Ingram, to exit the vehicle, or for someone to approach it.

"Maybe she's having second thoughts," Felix suggested.

"Second thoughts about what?" Sunshine asked. He scanned the plaza. A coffee joint, a dollar store, some kind of medical clinic, and one place that had been a nail salon and currently was for rent.

"Take a wild guess."

"Donuts?" Sunshine guessed.

"You think a seventeen-year-old runaway is having second thoughts about donuts?" Felix asked, each word tersely pronounced.

"It's what you've been staring at for about half an hour."

Felix rolled his eyes but spared him a smile.

"Go get something if you're hungry."

Felix punched Sunshine in his shoulder. "Come with me." He slipped out of the car without waiting for an answer.

Sunshine followed.

Felix shrugged further into his coat as he walked, glancing towards the hazy gray sky. He squinted at the smudge of sun like it owed him money.

The sky had been that color for the entire week they'd been in Wisconsin. It would probably stay that way for weeks after they left. Something about the unyielding, infinite sameness of the sky reminded Sunshine of Heaven.

Inside the coffee joint, Felix ordered a dozen donuts and then glanced back to ask, "You want anything, Sunshine?"

"A coffee."

Felix nodded and turned back to the cashier. "Large coffee, two sugars, no milk. And, uh." He snagged an orange juice from the fridge. "This."

"Anything else?" the cashier asked.

Felix shook his head, shuffled through his wallet, and handed over a few bills. He dropped his change and a couple of dollars into the tip jar, then shoved a donut into his mouth immediately upon receiving the box of donuts.

Old-fashioned and chocolate cake donuts, dense chunks of confection that might do something to quell the constant gnawing in the demon's gut.

Felix handed over his coffee.

Sunshine sipped it gingerly but burned his tongue anyway. He flinched and hissed.

"Stupid, you watched her pour it," Felix scolded.

"Stupid, you watched her pour it," Sunshine mocked under his breath.

Felix smacked his arm and devoured another donut.

"Pace yourself, Specter. You'll make yourself sick."

Felix scowled and headed back outside. A dusting of powdery snow, the kind that squeaked when trod upon, had fallen overnight. The forecast promised more.

Sunshine, personally, wanted to be indoors before that started.

He didn't want to spend any more time sitting in a car in a parking lot either. He liked his work, for the most part, but he'd never been fond of stakeouts. He shouldn't lack patience; he'd been made with it in droves. He could stalk a target for days. He could spend weeks standing perfectly still until the time came to spring a trap. God had created him as a perfect solider, except sometimes Sunshine thought the Almighty must have messed up.

Maybe the confined space of the car was what made him so antsy.

Felix made for the Focus with the box of donuts balanced in one hand. He rapped on the window of the car.

The girl inside screamed and flinched.

Felix pantomimed rolling the window.

She looked over him and shook her head. A fair assessment of the situation, really. Felix had always looked a little unusual with his shaggy white-blond hair and skin the color of milk. These days he looked a fright, his veins showing pale blue through his skin and heavy bags under his black eyes.

The demon crouched down and shouted, "Your parents sent us!"

That sent the girl into a tizzy. Her face contorted and she nearly started to weep.

Felix glanced towards the donut box.

"Oh, Specter, have a little class." Sunshine came close to the car. He nudged the demon out of the way and gave the girl his best beatific smile. "Forgive my colleague, miss. His manners need work. We're here to help you."

The smile seemed to do the trick. She cracked the window. Her tears had stopped, but her eyes remained red and watery. "My parents can't...they know where I am?"

"No. Not yet. We were waiting for you to get out of the car."

She drew in a breath.

"You are Robin, right?" Sunshine asked.

"I. Who are you?"

"Sunshine and Specter," he told her. He took a card from his wallet and passed it to her through the crack in the window. "Paranormal detectives. Your parents contacted us when they couldn't find you."

"I didn't...I just needed time to think." She rubbed her nose with her sleeve.

"Do you need someone to talk to?" Sunshine offered. It was plain enough that she did.

She shook her head. "I. I can't."

"You want a donut?" Felix asked.

She looked him over.

"Now or never, they'll be gone in a minute."

"No. Thank you."

"Well, we're here to help. Feel free to call our home office and check our credentials if you'd like," Sunshine offered. "We'll be in our car." He pointed to the Outback they'd rented.

"Don't tell my parents I'm here."

Sunshine nodded.

Felix opened his mouth, but Sunshine elbowed him.

They returned to their car to wait.

"You think that smile of yours is gonna work on everyone," Felix grumbled.

"Doesn't it?"

"Not on me."

Sunshine smiled at him.

Felix ate another donut. "Fuckin' angels," he growled quietly and indistinctly.

Sunshine passed the time doodling on his hand, enjoying the smooth roll of the pen over his skin. He wasn't an artist by any means, but he made a reasonable approximation of a few things.

Felix glanced over. "Why're you drawing shit on your hand?"

"It's not...it's that ice cream emoji."

"It's shit, Sunshine, not ice cream."

Sunshine licked his thumb and tried to smudge away the doodle.

"Oh, look here she comes," Felix said, pointing towards Robin.

She'd emerged from the Focus, bundled up in a red wool coat and a fuzzy pink scarf. She rapped on their window.

Sunshine rolled down the window.

"I think I do need to talk to someone."

"Let's take a walk," Felix proposed. He'd been staring at the donut shop again. He'd also been moaning about a stomachache for a while, too. He almost always had a stomachache these days.

Whether from overeating or hunger, or both, Sunshine could only guess.

Robin agreed, but her eyes stayed on Sunshine when she did it.

The three of them wandered the mostly empty streets. Most people had to be at work.

Robin walked with her head down and her hands in her pockets.

"Maybe give your parents a call, let them know you're okay," Felix suggested after ten minutes without a word from her.

She shook her head. "I can't until it's done."

Sunshine hadn't yet figured out what she'd run away from. Her family seemed perfectly loving and deeply concerned about her disappearance. The girl came from a warm, expansive coven of witches.

"Celtic Christo-pagans," they'd called themselves.

Her parents' home had cozied up their icons and crucifixes

with pentacles and sage bundles. He'd come across enough syncretism not to bat an eyelash at their mix of deities, but he'd decided to keep his divine nature to himself when he'd seen the collection of porcelain angels in their curio cabinet.

Mr. and Mrs. Ingram hadn't figured out what Sunshine was, but they'd known Felix for what he was right away. They'd assured him four times they weren't *those* kinds of Christians or witches and didn't hold any ill will against his father.

"We can only be the way God made us," Mr. Ingram had told Felix. He'd smiled genuinely and made eye contact.

Felix had squirmed.

Sunshine had really liked to see him squirm like that.

"It would break my mom's heart if she knew where I was," Robin said. "You haven't told them, have you?" She looked at Sunshine.

"They only know that you're safe," Sunshine said.

They'd felt obligated to share at least that much when they'd located her the other night. Her parents had feared the absolute worst.

She nodded. "That's alright. I don't know what I'm going to say when I go home. Or what I'm supposed to do about school! I've got to have a ton of work to make up."

"That's all manageable," Sunshine assured. "An education is important but less important than your wellbeing. People will understand."

She wrinkled her nose and shook her head at him.

"You know you need parental consent," Felix said.

She heaved a sigh. "A girl at school told me about this place. Said they'll do it without any paperwork. I've got the cash for it. Sean helped me get it."

"Sean's your fellow?" Felix asked.

"My cousin. He's the only one who knows."

"If you're sure about this," Felix began.

"I am," she insisted. "I don't even know if I want kids *ever*, let alone now."

Suddenly, Sunshine felt stupid. The pieces slid into place.

"Well, if it's decided," Felix said.

"I'm," she sighed. "I'm just scared, you know."

Readily, Felix offered, "We're here to help."

"You keep saying that. I know you aren't. My parents didn't hire some fancy New York detectives to help me. They hired you to bring me home."

"Oh, I very much intend to bring you home, but what happens between here and home is up to you."

He sounded so much like his birth father then, that slippery, insistent way of saying things that Sunshine had to look away for a moment. He liked Felix much better when he sounded like the parents who raised him, instead of the Devil. Sunshine had visited Hell, he'd met the Devil more times than he liked, and his skin still crawled at the thought of it.

He didn't hold any of that against Felix, of course. He couldn't hold anything against Felix.

"I just..." Robin sighed. "I don't want to go to Hell."

Felix glanced towards Sunshine. "That's his area of expertise."

Sunshine let out a breath. He never liked to tell someone what got people sent to Hell, since it was different for every person. "Well." He glanced at Felix. "Do you really think this is the right thing to do?"

"I don't know. I hope so. I think so. I just...I know I can't do this. I don't *want* to have a baby."

"Then you're probably okay. Don't worry about Hell now, it's a tricky place." Sunshine wanted to offer her more comfort, but the management of souls had never been within his purview. "But it takes so much more than one choice to seal your fate in either direction."

"Alright. Well. I figure. I figure I should do this."

"Do you want us to come with you?" Sunshine asked.

"Please. I don't know what it is, but I trust you."

"He's an angel, everyone trusts him," Felix said. He turned and set back towards the plaza.

Robin ogled Sunshine for a minute, but he kept his eyes straight ahead.

People always expected him to be a certain way, but no one ever seemed to have the same expectations. Righteous, gracious, kindly, stern, ethereal, splendid. He wasn't any of those things. He glanced at Felix.

There weren't many things to say while they checked in and waited. They sat quietly in the waiting room of the clinic, thumbing through magazines months out of date. The only other person had what looked to be a few broken fingers and spent his time hunched over his hand and groaning.

Every so often Felix would say something to one of them. He

told a few mild jokes or rattled off pointless facts about something in their surroundings. Something about lightbulbs. Sunshine didn't think Robin was paying attention, but she gave a small smile each time.

The wait took hours, but Sunshine could bear it better this time.

Felix struggled. He grew terse and cranky but managed to hide it for the most part. To anyone who didn't know him well, he just looked anxious. He viciously picked at his fingernails, but they'd be healed by tomorrow or maybe the day after if he really kept at it.

If Sunshine told him to get something to eat, he'd refuse.

Finally, the staff called Robin's name.

She stood and looked back at them.

"Do you want one of us to come with you?" Sunshine offered, not sure that was allowed but sure he could talk his way into it.

"No. But, uh, can you wait for me?"

"Of course."

She went with the nurse.

Felix watched her go and continued to tear at his cuticles. He hissed when he ripped a particularly large strip away.

At that point, Sunshine reached over and grabbed his hand. He touched him just long enough to separate his hands.

Felix flinched.

"You're going to hurt yourself."

"Oh, so better fucking burn me then?" Felix snapped.

Sunshine didn't sigh, but he wanted to. He hadn't touched him long enough to burn him. "If you're hungry, you should go eat."

"I'm not hungry. I mean...I am but it's not that."

"What's it about, then?"

Felix shook his head, shrugged, then leaned back in his chair. His legs, clad in black skinny jeans, stretched out in front of him. He crossed his legs at the ankle and clicked the toes of his boots together a few times. "You know how June gets chatty when he drinks?"

"Sure."

"So, we were drinking this one time. He starts telling me about how he met my mom."

"Where was I?" Sunshine asked.

"I think you were outside with someone. I think, uh, I think Kenya was throwing up. Anyway. June told me about how my mom, uh. How it was hard for her to decide if she wanted to keep me. He was never born, you know? I don't think he knew what he was really telling me. But I just, I can't help thinking about her right now."

"Oh."

"What she was like. What I'd be like if she hadn't died. Dad just says she was funny."

Sunshine licked his lips.

"Did you know her at all?"

"I." Sunshine sighed and rubbed his eyes. He didn't have a nice answer to give. He couldn't tell Felix anything about his mother except what her body had looked like.

"I know you didn't kill her, but we've never talked about the rest of it."

"Mercy was dead by the time I found the house. She'd handed you over to someone she trusted when she saw her family was in town. A vampire, I think."

Felix nodded. "Yeah, I think her name was Sarah. Dad told me about her once or twice."

"I'm sorry."

The demon sighed. "You were just doing your job."

"Yeah, so were the Nazis. I was going to kill a baby."

Felix grinned. "Ah, yeah, but I coulda been the antichrist, though."

Sunshine smiled back. He really wanted to hold his hand but settled for elbowing him. "Speaking of parents, you should send Hiram and Phaedrus a postcard."

"From Nowhere, Wisconsin?"

"You know they like getting them."

Felix nodded. "Fine."

The urge to hold Felix's hand had existed within Sunshine for decades now, but it had gotten stronger, more persistent in recent months. Felix had nearly died, though he liked to downplay the gravity of it. He said Sunshine had overreacted and Sunshine wanted to, but did not, point out, that Felix had kissed him, not the other way around. A near-death experience was enough to rattle anyone. It explained Felix's actions.

It had to explain them because Felix hadn't wanted to talk about it.

Sunshine had tried to bring it up a few times, gingerly broaching the topic. Felix always played stupid and got crabby on top of it. Sunshine didn't bring it up anymore. He tried not to even think about it.

What was one kiss, a desperate act born of fear and pain and adrenaline, in the face of so many years of friendship? Their friendship had outlasted relationships in either direction. It wasn't worth spoiling.

And besides, Sunshine reminded himself, nothing could ever happen between them. He couldn't even touch Felix for an entire minute without burning him. One kiss had made Felix bleed. Thinking about what would happen with anything more than that made Sunshine's stomach twist.

He couldn't think about it.

He stood and wandered aimlessly around the waiting room. He pretended to look for a magazine to read. He returned to his seat with an AARP magazine and feigned interest in an article about traveling on a budget.

Felix played on his phone.

When Robin emerged, looking a little shaky, they both stood and set to fussing over her. They offered her food, water, a ride home, tissues, anything they could think. She refused all of them, quiet and calm.

"I think I just want to go home. I'm tired," she said.

"Are you sure you don't need anything?" Sunshine asked.

"Something to tell my parents," Robin said with a small huff of a laugh.

Felix scuffed his toe against the floor and rubbed the back of his neck. "What about something to make them not ask questions?"

She frowned at him.

Sunshine frowned, too, because he had a much better idea of what Felix tended to do under circumstances like this.

"Just a little spell." The demon shrugged. "Sit 'em down for a cup of tea, slip it in, and..." He shrugged again. "You know. They don't ask too many questions."

She shook her head right away. "No. I couldn't do that."

"Mm. Well, you can think about it. You've got our card."

"Specter, we're detectives, not hypnotists," Sunshine reminded.

"No hypnosis involved, just magic. Anyway. We'll follow you home, just to make sure," Felix told her.

They parted ways in the parking lot.

Back at the Ingram home, Felix walked Robin up to her room while Sunshine stayed with her parents, arranged payment, and managed to talk them into giving her a few days to rest before they asked her too many questions.

On the way out, cash in hand, Felix said, "You can talk anyone into anything, can't you?"

"Perks of being an angel, I suppose."

"And how's that different than putting a spell on them?"

Ignoring the disquiet in his belly, Sunshine grinned at him and said, "I suppose it isn't, but I do look better doing it."

Felix pushed him.

Felix had unceremoniously hucked his bag through the door to his apartment then followed Sunshine into his. Currently, he lounged on Sunshine's bed, watching him unpack. Nothing interesting had happened between Nowhere, Wisconsin and the Weller building in New York.

Felix had sent a postcard, but Sunshine didn't consider that interesting

"Don't you have your own unpacking to do?" he asked.

"No."

"Liar."

"Have to do is not the same as should be doing," Felix corrected. His stomach growled. "I'm starving. Do you want to order out?"

They had already eaten on the plane and in the airport. Sunshine didn't think he could eat another bite without getting sick.

Felix read his face immediately. "Never mind."

"No, we could—"

"I just forgot we'd eaten."

How anyone could forget about four hamburgers and enough fries to choke a horse was beyond Sunshine.

Felix stood up.

Sunshine didn't want him to go. He also desperately wanted not to see him for a while. They had been hip to hip for over a week now, though that level of attachment only slightly exceeded their usual level. They worked together, lived next door to each other. They ate half, or maybe more, of their meals together.

"Tired?" Felix asked.

Sunshine knew Felix had given him an out. An easy way to ask him to leave. "No," he said. "Movie?"

Felix nodded.

They settled onto the couch, their thighs casually brushing against each other. He couldn't burn him through cloth...at least, he hadn't yet.

While they watched the movie, Felix ate two sleeves of rice cakes, plain, and gulped down a liter of water.

Sunshine knew better than to ask if his stomach hurt. He just paused the movie when Felix got up to pee, which happened with irritating frequency.

"Do you plan on going to work tomorrow?" Sunshine asked.

"Did you?"

"Maybe in the morning. For a little while. It'll be Sunday," Sunshine said. "You can sleep in. I'll call if anything needs your attention."

"You're a pal."

The credits rolled on the movie and they parted ways.

Sunshine took a quick shower to get the grime of travel off his skin before he went to bed. He also changed his sheets and shook out his comforter, just for good measure. After all, Felix had been rolling around on it with his shoes on. Finally, he set his radio to play quiet nature sounds. Too long away from this bed made him forget it was his and playing the same nature sounds wherever he slept made it easier to settle in.

For the twenty-plus years he had hunted the antichrist, he had been essentially homeless and the decades between then and now hadn't totally broken him of that rootlessness. Lots of the Fallen had struggled to adjust to Earth in their own unique ways and, though he wasn't officially a fallen angel, Sunshine figured it made sense for him to have his own difficulties.

Sometimes he lay awake at night thinking of those stridently aimless years, hunting something that couldn't be found. He thought of the times he had come close to finding his quarry.

He thought of the time he had found it, when the protection charm had been broken and he had sunk a knife into the accursed flesh of the Devil's most misbegotten son. The time he had stabbed a little boy.

He didn't know how Felix could even look at him.

Tonight, his thoughts blurred together, formless and strange. He focused on the sound of the meadow or the field or wherever this had been recorded, the little songbirds that would pipe. Always the same order. A blackbird, a robin, a house finch, the blackbird again, then a wren...He knew them all by heart.

Finally, he fell asleep.

He woke early and walked to the office. He made sure he had cash on hand before he left. It was a haul on foot, nearly five miles, but he liked to walk. The Weller was in spitting distance of Museum Mile and getting to the Village from there sometimes felt like traveling through different worlds. Today, he cut through Central Park just for the view and found Midtown relatively uncrowded, given the time of the year. He deposited money into the cups of the people he passed; after all, he was an angel. What else could he do?

On weekends, the office usually had one or two people catching up on paperwork, but today it was empty. He wished it wasn't. He could have used a friendly face.

He walked upstairs to the office he and Felix shared. Two desks, one meticulously tidy and clean, the other organized in its own haphazard way, occupied the room. Felix's desk faced the door and Sunshine's was off to the right, facing into the room and toward the window. Sunshine settled behind his desk and had to admit it wasn't as organized as it should have been. With a bit of envy, he glanced towards Felix's. Felix had been raised by an academic and that made him a little fussy about some things, paperwork being one of them.

Sunshine read through the case reports that had piled up while they'd been gone. He learned nothing he hadn't been told on the phone when he'd called to check in. He liked that. Smooth sailing, no surprises.

He thumbed through the file that Jen had left on his desk. She hadn't given much detail on either of it, saying, "I don't know, something about a missing bracelet."

A straightforward case. He looked through the papers for a number, found it, and spoke with a mage based out of SoHo who'd misplaced an enchanted bracelet. He didn't seem particularly distressed about it but said that it would be best to get it back before someone else found it.

"What kind of enchantment?" Sunshine asked.

"Uh." The mage hesitated. He cleared his throat. "You know. Standard Kavornian stuff, a few modifications."

Sunshine didn't know what that meant. Felix would have. He scribbled it down so he wouldn't forget to ask about it. "Nothing dangerous, though, right? Not cursed in any way?"

"No. Not dangerous," the mage confirmed.

"Alright, one of our agents will be in touch by Monday afternoon."

"Thanks. Thank you."

They had a brief discussion about payment rates and hung up.

Sunshine dropped the file off on the first floor, leaving it on Tate's desk. He also sent her a text letting her know she had a new case. She responded in typical fashion: no words, only an emoji.

He stopped at a deli on the way home and bought three sandwiches. Felix surely would have eaten by now, but the sandwiches would be a nice snack.

He rapped on Felix's door but got no answer. He allowed himself inside and found the demon still asleep.

He left the sandwiches in the fridge and returned to his own apartment. He ate his lunch, did laundry, and went back to check on Felix.

Still asleep. That wasn't like him.

And too motionless in his sleep, too.

He padded over to the bed, though he hesitated to touch the other man. Felix slept with a lot of skin exposed.

Sunshine gave him a quick pat on the arm, but that did nothing. He tried a shake and when that didn't work, he put two fingers to Felix's throat. His pulse came slow but steady. Not dead, thank God.

Sunshine touched him too long, though, and the demon jerked away from his touch with a shout.

"What the fuck!" Felix demanded. He gingerly touched the bright red burn that had come up where Sunshine had touched him.

"Sorry. You. You weren't moving."

"I was asleep!"

Sunshine felt so incredibly worthless and stupid. He plastered a smile onto his face, the brightest and kindest one he could manage.

Felix pursed his lips. "Don't do that."

"What?"

"That thing with your face."

"I don't know what you're talking about." Sunshine kept smiling.

"Ugh, stop." Felix reached over and squeezed Sunshine's face with one hand, gentle but firm.

It was an odd, uncomfortable experience to have the smile massaged off his face, but Sunshine tolerated it. It took less than a minute before Felix pulled his hand back.

The demon flopped back onto his bed.

"You should get up," Sunshine advised.

"I'm still tired."

"Didn't you sleep last night?"

Felix shrugged. "Eh. No. I ended up taking a bunch of sleeping pills."

"How many is a bunch?"

"Uh, enough to put me to sleep. Not enough to kill me." Felix waved away Sunshine's concern with a loose gesture. He yawned into the crook of his elbow. "Anything good at the office?"

"Not really."

Felix scooted over then patted the mattress.

Sunshine sat on the edge of the bed.

Felix nestled into his pillow and yawned again.

"I'm not going to stay and watch you sleep."

Into the pillow, Felix said, "You can if you want."

Sunshine shook his head.

"Or you could make me some coffee. Ten minutes and I'll be up. What did you come over for again?"

"Sandwiches."

"Mmmm. Yes. I'll get up for sandwiches. Ten minutes. Coffee." Felix pulled his covers up and seemed to immediately fall back asleep.

Sunshine did watch him sleep for a little while. Just a minute. Not long enough to be untoward, he hoped. He went to make coffee. Ten minutes ended up being half an hour.

Felix shuffled out of the bedroom, housed two sandwiches without a word, then leaned back in his chair. "Uh. Sorry I mushed your face."

"Don't worry about it."

"I think I was still a little looped."

"I assumed." Sunshine hadn't assumed. Felix did weird things sometimes and Sunshine took it in stride. Almost everything Felix did was harmless.

"So, no news at the office?"

"One case. A missing bracelet. Tate should be able to make quick work of it."

"A bracelet?"

Sunshine nodded. "Enchanted."

"Mmm. Look at it tomorrow, I figure. I might skip out early if it's slow. Stop by to get my comics."

"Might as well. You were jonesing for them all week."

Felix scowled. He grumbled under his breath and slurped his coffee. He snagged his phone and checked it. "You ever hear back from that girl? Vie? Vee?"

"Vee," Sunshine confirmed. "No. I didn't hear back from her."

"Your creepy smile probably put her off."

"It's not creepy, it's beatific."

Felix nearly choked on his coffee when he laughed. Once he settled, he said, "Dunno why you bother going on dates."

"The same reason most people do I suppose."

"Tryna get laid?" Felix asked.

"The need for interpersonal connection."

Felix blew a raspberry. "Just come out with me some night you wanna get laid."

Sunshine had gone out with Felix plenty of nights. Very rarely did it end in either of them getting laid. It usually ended with Sunshine herding Felix home as he stumbled and sometimes vomited as they walked back.

They hadn't gone out in months, not since before this business with the fairy curse.

"Maybe don't drink so much coffee," Sunshine suggested. "You know how you get with caffeine."

Felix paused just for a moment, then continued to pour himself another cup. "Listen, you come in here, wake me up, then tell me not to drink coffee. You're killing me with these mixed messages."

"Why couldn't you sleep anyway?"

"Uh. Probably the endless gnawing hunger that lives within the meat sack to which my consciousness is indelibly attached."

Sunshine had hoped he'd say he'd still been thinking about his mother or worrying about Robin, or something normal and easy to fix. "Maybe your father—"

"Fuck off about my father. What's it been? Fifty years and you don't want to talk about him and now you're bringing him up all the time."

"Closer to eighty."

Felix paused, his face screwed up in the way it did when he tried to think. "However many years. We've been in scrapes before, always got things sorted out. Let's keep not talking about my father. Let's keep things the way they've been."

Sunshine stirred his coffee though it had gone cold.

"Things have been fine."

Sunshine sipped his coffee and made a face.

"Right?"

"Hmm?"

"Did you hear me?"

Sunshine had heard him perfectly. "Coffee's cold."

Felix reached over and placed his hand over Sunshine's mug. A quick bit of heat rolled off him and into the mug. "I swear to God you've got fluff instead of brains."

Sunshine smiled at him. He couldn't crush the disappointment fast enough. It wasn't the insult. He actually liked it when Felix was mean to him. Not too mean, though.

Never too mean.

He'd only thought Felix might touch his hand or pat his arm.

Felix warned, "Stop with that smile again."

"You gonna squeeze my face some more?"

"I'm gonna take a shower. You want to go to the park after?"

Sunshine took a sip of his coffee and burnt himself. He'd forgotten Felix had warmed it for him.

Felix swigged the rest of his coffee and pushed himself back from the table. He made for the bathroom, yanking a towel off the back of his bedroom door as he went.

Sunshine washed the dishes while he waited.

They strolled to the park, both bundled in jackets, but also cozily encased by a bubble of heat that Felix had conjured. He threw magic around like confetti.

Sunshine had used to think it pretentious and wasteful, but once he'd gotten to know Felix better he'd realized how reflexive magic was to him.

Not too many people were out today, which suited them fine.

They looped around the park, a few yards behind a couple with a husky. They walked in silence while the couple bickered about plans one of them had made without consulting the other. They didn't like each other's friends.

They didn't stay out long. Just long enough for the husky to do its business. They argued whether to hail a cab, settled on getting an Uber, and left the park.

Once they were out of earshot, or close to it, Felix said, "Imagine that though."

"Imagine what?"

"Living like that. Everything's an argument."

"You overheard them for twenty minutes, you don't know they argue about everything," Sunshine said.

"Ah, it takes practice to bicker like that. They've been together for years and they'll stay together, but neither of them will like it," Felix decided.

"Whatever you say."

"Imagine if your girlfriend didn't like your friends."

Sunshine stayed quiet.

Felix glanced his way, an eyebrow quirked up.

Sunshine said nothing.

"What?"

"Kari didn't like my friends," Sunshine told him.

"Really? Who?"

"You, for starters."

Both of Felix's eyebrows raised this time. "I didn't like her either."

"Mm."

A grin spread over the demon's face. "Did you dump her 'cause she didn't like me?"

"No. We broke up for a lot of reasons. She thought I was insane, first of all."

"Hard to date someone with no Community connections," Felix agreed. "What else?"

"Just differences."

Felix groaned. "Come on, bitch with me."

It didn't take much goading. The break-up was relatively fresh and the complaints came easy. He'd seen Kari for a few months. They'd met at the party of a mutual friend, bumbled along together for a while, and broke up in mid-January. He hadn't loved her, but she had become familiar to him.

Felix offered all the opinions he had kept to himself for those months. He'd voiced his milder complaints, but given free rein to badmouth her, he dredged up problems with Kari from her taste in shoes to her opinions on healthcare.

Sunshine listened, pleased to find Felix had disliked her so much. He didn't know why, but he liked that Felix had paid enough attention to have problems with his girlfriend in the first place.

"And I bet she was a bad lay," Felix concluded.

"Mm."

"Well? Was she?"

The question struck Sunshine as odd. He and Felix talked about everything, certainly, and no topics were awkward for them, sex included. Something about the *way* he asked it felt strange.

Sunshine shrugged. "I don't know."

"D'y'mean?"

"We never had sex."

Felix stared at him, an odd look on his face. It wasn't the incredulity or snarky judgment which Sunshine had expected to come with the admission. It was a wide-eyed, pleased sort of wonder. Felix didn't demand to know why not or anything else. After a moment, he looked away, his eyes scanning over the park. He nodded towards a hot dog cart. "Hungry?"

"I could eat."

The vendor looked on in mild horror as Felix consumed six hot dogs in the time it took Sunshine to eat one.

"You should enter one of those contests," the woman suggested.

Felix paused mid-bite. He stared at the vendor with utter adoration. He shoved the rest of his last hot dog in his mouth, swallowed, and crowed, "But think about all those challenges! The big steaks! You get 'em for free, right? If you eat the whole thing?"

"Specter, calm yourself before your heart gives out."

"My heart's fine."

"You just ate your body weight in nitrates, even *your* heart might protest," Sunshine reminded.

Felix gave Sunshine's arm a push. "I'm gonna go home and make a list. This is what we're doing from now on."

"I can watch you stuff your face any day of the week, no need to make special plans for it."

"But how often do you get to see me do it for free?" Felix challenged.

Sunshine couldn't work up the right level of enthusiasm.

As they walked home, a strong wind came up.

Abruptly, the warmth around them cut out.

Felix had thrown back his head. Eyes closed, he spread his

arms and let the wind assail him. He grinned. The wind whipped pink into his cheeks.

"What are you doing?"

"Feels like sledding. We used to go, Bibi and Papa and me, all the time. There's a hill behind the school. It felt like flying." The smile slipped off his face. He opened his eyes. "But it's never the same, you know. How it was when you're little. You never get that back."

Sunshine had seen people sled, mostly in movies. "Never been."

"Never been sledding?" Felix clarified.

Sunshine shook his head. "Or little."

Felix squinted at him, then shrugged. "Huh."

At home, they put on a movie and Felix ate two bags of spinach. Not cooked or in a salad, just handfuls of plain leaves.

Casually, halfway through the movie, Felix said, "I've got a date tomorrow."

"Oh."

"Yeah."

Sunshine had to ask, "Like a date-date or...?"

"No, not a hook up. A date-date. I think. I don't know. He's picking me up at eight. So, you know, don't wait on me for dinner."

"I didn't know you were talking to anyone."

Felix shrugged and made a face. "We've, uh, mostly just been sending snaps. It's...Mostly about magic. He's a student at NY-AM. Grad student. I'm not *exactly* robbing the cradle." He sighed. "He just wants to meet, I guess. It's probably, well, you know how guys are."

Sunshine nodded.

A few minutes later, Felix had scooted a little closer to him. "What?"

Felix rested his head on Sunshine's shoulder. He had cocooned himself in a blanket, so ran no risk of getting burned. "I don't know why I bother."

Sunshine patted Felix's leg. "Nothing will ever be worse than the date you went on with Tina Powers."

Felix groaned. "At least there's that."

February 8
Monday

Felix looked over the case about the enchanted bracelet and seemed put off.

"What's that face?" Sunshine asked.

Tate warily watched them both.

Their most recent run of employees got a little squirrely around them. Sunshine hadn't figured out how to put them at ease. Or if he should put them at ease. Felix didn't seem to mind at all that everyone who worked for them thought they were involved in dastardly occult schemes and embroiled in underground societies.

"Weird enchantment for a bracelet." Felix handed the file back to Tate.

She took it gingerly.

Felix straightened up and slid off her desk. He shook his head and muttered again that it was weird. He continued muttering as he went upstairs.

Sunshine watched him go and ten minutes later, he watched him come back downstairs, approach Tate and say, "Try not to touch it."

Tate stared at him and nodded.

Felix went back upstairs and stayed there this time.

Dr. Love, to whom Sunshine had been speaking, cleared his

throat.

Sunshine returned his attention to the doctor. "Sorry. You were saying...uh. Zombies in Brooklyn?"

"Nah, ghouls, man. Anyway, that's what I figure. Didn't get to look at 'em too good, there was other people in the morgue. I'd keep an ear to the ground, just sayin'. Those fuckers get nasty. And quick."

"Thank you."

Dr. Maurice Love alone in the office addressed Sunshine so informally. After fifteen years in their employ, he stood on occasion for very little. He had no reason to, no longer worried about proving anything to his coworkers. At twenty-three, he'd maintained a purely academic air, especially around Specter, knowing his father ran a university.

Now, with several PhDs in additional to his MD and having nearly reached the age of forty, Dr. Love worried less about people knowing he was smart. He dressed impeccably every day, a perfect haven of immaculate fashion that seamlessly straddled formality and streetwear. Every color complimented the umber of his skin, the cut of each item flattered his form.

Sunshine didn't know how he did it. Maybe he had a PhD in fashion, too.

Dr. Love looked towards the staircase. "Specter doin' good?"

"Uh."

"I just. You know. He don't always look so good."

"Mr. Specter is well."

"Mhm."

Sunshine smiled his best smile.

Dr. Love smiled back. His smile spoke of uncomfortable suspicions and guilt of some manner. Too much teeth to be casual and too nervous to be plain concern.

"I have some work to do."

"Course. Yeah, sure. Catch you later, man."

Sunshine retreated upstairs.

Felix spent the better part of the morning refiling all his paperwork.

Sunshine watched.

"Stop staring at me," Felix demanded.

"Are you alright?"

"Yeah. Sure. Why?" Felix asked without turning around.

"You seem jittery."

"Too much coffee."

Sunshine frowned. He wanted to press but didn't. He wanted to help but didn't know how. He shuffled a few of the papers around on his desk, pretending to work. Normally, they had more with which to occupy themselves at the office, but things had been quiet of late. That was most of the reason why they had gone to Wisconsin themselves instead of sending someone.

That and when they'd brought it up, none of their employees had seemed keen on the trip.

It really had been kind of nice to get out of the city.

"We should go on vacation," he suggested.

Felix extracted himself from beneath his desk, where he had been fiddling with contents of the secret compartment. It housed items of mild danger and, though Sunshine had never gone through any of the papers, what he assumed were highly personal documents. That or blackmail.

Maybe.

"Vacation." Felix had emerged clutching a shriveled, waxy hand.

"When was the last time we went on a trip? Not a work trip."

"Uh. When we went to the Otherworld."

"No, that...that wasn't a vacation, not really."

Felix pursed his lips and went back under his desk. "It was something."

They had traveled to the Otherworld because Felix had been dating a fairy. Things had gone terribly sideways when she had invited him to meet her family. Sunshine had tagged along on Felix's invitation, which had upset the woman in the first place. She had considered it an intrusion.

Felix still hadn't parsed out all the details of what, exactly, they had fought about, but Sunshine knew it had involved Felix's heritage and her father's opinions of it. Many fey still brooded over the ancient troubles between Hell and the Otherworld. Sunshine didn't know if the woman or her father had cursed him.

"I mean a real vacation. Maybe somewhere warm. Somewhere sunny," Sunshine proposed.

"So I can eat my way through an entire island nation? Sounds fun."

"Don't be cranky."

Felix didn't answer.

Sunshine went over to sit on the floor beside the desk. "What about just a weekend?"

"What's got you so set on this?"

He shrugged. "I don't know."

Felix examined a pile of old sepia photographs. "Is Gordon Levi dead?"

"Has been for years."

Felix nodded and threw the pictures into the wastepaper basket. They caught fire on their way in.

Sunshine tried not to react. Felix would tease him, not mean, exactly, or at least, not mean in the right way.

Felix saw him watching the flames nervously anyway and caught his eye. He gave a half-smile.

Sunshine ignored him, took up some of the other things Felix had scattered on the floor, and examined them. A brooch looked familiar and sent a queasy feeling stirring in his gut. He had seen it before in the 70s, on a case when they'd gone to the Catskills to deal with a haunting. "You said you destroyed this."

Felix's smile shifted from teasing to guilty. "I say a lot of things."

Sunshine placed the brooch back among the collection. "How many other cursed artifacts did you keep?"

Felix didn't answer. He gathered up all the items and papers and put them back in the secret compartment. He checked his pockets and made for the bathroom without a word, sliding past Sunshine. He let himself brush against Sunshine as he went.

So many years of proximity had conditioned the demon to know exactly when and where he could afford to touch Sunshine. He would brush past him with ease but flinch every time Sunshine tried to hand him something too quickly. Whenever they went to the beach, he would stand stiffly and at least three feet off to the side. When shorts and short sleeves had come into fashion for men, summers, in general, had been hard for a decade or so.

Even now, Sunshine tried to stave off wearing more revealing clothing until he couldn't stand the heat. He relied on light cottons and linens. He hated when Felix avoided him; he didn't know if he missed those casual touches or if he hated the guilt that sprung up whenever he hurt him by accident.

There had to be a way to undo these wards.

And, of course, there was. Felix had already released him from being bound to the Earth and he could return to Heaven to have the spell removed.

The trick would be getting back to Earth afterward. The archangels would not understand why he had failed in his mission and why he wanted to return to work beside the monster he had failed to kill. Maybe it would be worse if they did understand.

So far, Heaven had not sent anyone to check in on him. They might have assumed him dead or kept captive by Felix in a meaningful way. Left chained in a basement, given over to the Devil, or something like that.

Heaven had sent other soldiers after Felix, but no one had been able to find him. The charm his father had created for him made him practically non-existent to the eyes of Heaven. Felix never removed the ring, a plain, worn band of electrum on his left forefinger. The inside of the band bore tiny, intricate rune work that had kept Felix safe for decades. The last sighting of an angel like Sunshine, one of the sixty identical soldiers the Almighty had created, had been five years ago and in Hong Kong.

They were safe here, invisible among eight and half million others, some of them just as unusual as the two of them.

Sunshine would make sure Felix was safe. He didn't like the idea of fighting one of his fellow angels, but he would do it for Felix.

Felix, who came back and poked Sunshine in the back of the head. "Come help me in the basement."

"What's in the basement?"

"Love just brought in a body. I saw him sneaking in through the bathroom window...I mean, he was sneaking in. I was looking out the window. He wasn't sneaking in through the window, he used the backdoor."

"Uh. Where did he get a body?" Sunshine asked.

"Let's go find out."

Dr. Love seemed surprised when they came downstairs and quickly twitched a sheet over the exam table.

Aside from paranormal detective, and sometimes regular detective, work, Sunshine and Specter Paranormal Detective Agency acted as a waypoint for the corpses of Community members until they could make their way to morgues and funeral homes that catered to the Community. No good ever came of mortal and mundane humans poking around dead creatures.

"Sup?" Dr. Love asked.

"Body?" Felix said, leaning in close to the sheet. He sniffed. "Old body. Very old."

"It's, uh. Bit of, uh." Dr. Love adjusted his tie. "Sort of a mummy."

"Sort of a mummy," Felix echoed. Without asking permission he flicked back the sheet and put his face much too close to the shriveled corpse. He lifted a hand.

"Wouldn't!" Dr. Love barked, "Wouldn't do that. Magic that is. Fucking…funny kind of mummy, is the thing. Uh. Three days ago, she was alive."

Felix's mouth formed an O for a second. "And where did you get this funny kind of mummy?"

Dr. Love sighed and looked towards Sunshine.

Felix made people nervous sometimes. He was a little too odd and slinky.

"I'd like to know as well," Sunshine said.

"My cousin, you remember Dontell?" Love asked.

"Dontell who got kicked out of NY-AM?" Felix straightened up and took a step back from the body.

"Yeah."

Felix cast his gaze around the room, eyeing corners and doors.

"He ain't here."

"Where is he?"

"Underground."

Felix frowned.

"Literally," Love clarified. "He's, uh, he's been living in the tunnels with, uh, you know, some other NY-AM dropouts."

"Dropped out or expelled?" Felix asked.

"Listen, I don't know them. And you know I don't mess around with the same kind of shit Dontell does."

"And yet there's a three-day-old mummy in my basement," Felix said.

"He's my cousin," Love insisted. "And he's real fucked up over this. Her name was Suzy and they were together. They got a kid together. What was I supposed to do?"

Felix sighed. "Tell your cousin to quit living with people who do illegal magic in abandoned subway tunnels to start with."

"You think I didn't?"

"What about the child?" Sunshine asked.

"Justice is okay, I think. Dontell said he was, anyway."

"Why don't you have him come in and we can make this a formal case," Sunshine suggested.

"He's hard up for cash."

"It seems as though this problem has landed on our doorstep regardless of payment arrangements," Sunshine pointed out.

Felix pursed his lips but said nothing.

"You're right. I'll call him." Dr. Love headed upstairs.

"How'd he even get this here?" Felix asked.

"You say that like you've never gotten a body through the city," Sunshine said.

Felix scowled and shoved his hands into his pockets. They didn't stay there for long. He crossed his arms, then a few moments later, raked his hand through his fine, blond hair, mussing it. "This is on your plate."

"Excuse me?"

"Necromancy. You know I don't mess around with that."

Sunshine knew. Felix had few lines, but the ones he did have, he refused to cross. Sunshine couldn't begrudge him this, either. Felix had, forty or so years ago, headed down to Georgia to clean up some trouble with a group who had set up in the abandon remains of his father's plantation. He'd been gone for weeks and hadn't spoken for days when he'd returned.

Hiram had gone to Georgia with him, but they had gotten separated at some point in a skirmish. He'd found Felix in the slave quarters when things had settled. He hadn't been able to get any answers out of him then and no one had been able to since.

"He wept, Sunshine. He collapsed into my arms like he was a little boy again," Hiram had shared when Felix had been asleep. "Please, keep an eye on him."

"Of course. You know I will. Of course."

Hiram had put his hand on Sunshine's shoulder and squeezed. A bit of beard did something to hide the youthfulness of his face but did nothing for the haggard, worn-thin look in his eyes. Sunshine had seen that look before, a bone-deep tiredness that lived in addicts and soldiers. Hiram was human and never should have lived half as long as he had. There was no end in sight for him, either.

Another thing the Devil had ruined, another life he had twisted.

Sunshine and Felix stood in silence, glancing at the body, waiting for Dr. Love to return. When he finally did, he gloomily reported, "I couldn't get a hold of him. Left a message though."

Sunshine nodded. "Well. I suppose you should look over the body, then. Let us know what you find out."

"And have someone stay down here with you," Felix advised.

Love nodded. "Will do."

Felix turned and hurried upstairs, taking the steps two at a time. He yanked on Sunshine's sleeve, jerking him towards the door. "Let's go for a walk."

Without pausing for jackets, they headed out into the gray afternoon. The wind barely had any time to bite before Felix conjured a warm bubble of magic. People eyed them as they walked, maybe at their lack of cold-weather gear or just their general appearance.

Felix had lost weight recently which, given his massively increased calorie intake, wasn't right. He'd always tended towards slimness, but he had never looked unhealthy. He had never had blue nails or dry lips.

Felix grumbled as he walked, hands shoved in his pockets and eyes narrowed at every person who dared to look at him. He stepped out into traffic and a car blared its horn at him.

Sunshine scampered after him. "Where are we headed?"

"I just wanted to walk."

"Do you feel alright?"

He didn't answer. He didn't even glare.

"Are you hungry?"

Again, he didn't answer.

"Specter—"

"Sunshine, can we just walk!"

Sunshine forced his mouth shut and trailed behind. He followed Felix all the way to Pier 45 and watched, uncomfortable and quiet as Felix stared out over the vast, bleak grayness of the Hudson. He kept his distance.

Felix stared for ages, shivering despite the warmth he had conjured. "I'm sorry I snapped at you."

"It's alright."

"I've got this awful headache."

"Too much caffeine," Sunshine suggested weakly.

Felix didn't even look at him.

He shouldn't have done it, but he had to do something. He put his arm around Felix and pulled him into an embrace.

The demon shifted in his arms and held himself stiffly.

"There's got to be—"

"I will throw myself into the river if you say another word," Felix warned.

"It won't kill you."

"But you'll have to jump in after me."

Sunshine reminded, "Won't kill me either."

"But you'll ruin your hair."

"In this wind? It's already ruined. Besides, I'm not the one who has a date tonight," Sunshine said.

Felix snorted and pulled out of his arms. "I must be a miserable date these days."

"What's this guy's name, anyway?"

"Kiernan."

"He's in grad school?"

Felix nodded. "Applied Elemental Conjuring."

"Oh, someone's an overachiever."

Felix laughed.

With a tug on his hand, less than five seconds, Sunshine guided Felix back towards the office. "So, Kiernan the Conjurer. Does he work?"

"Uh, yeah in Banefire's Dungeon of Wicked Elements, on Thirty-Third and Fifth."

Sunshine frowned. He had never heard of such an establishment and especially not in Koreatown.

"It's...You made him sound like some kind of DnD character."

"Ah. Well. Does he work?"

"Yeah, part-time. I think he, uh...does lab stuff at the Academy."

"Ah." Sunshine let a few moments passed. "Is he handsome?"

Felix shrugged. "I guess. Dick looks nice, though."

Sunshine's eyes widened and he tried to fix his face before Felix noticed. He didn't manage.

"Part of me misses dating before texting. You know, when a guy had to put effort into flashing you his dick. Corner you at a bar or something. Risk getting a drink thrown in his face."

The patter in Sunshine's chest quelled.

"Now they just flop it out wherever and send a picture like that's supposed to do something for me. I mean, Christ, maybe I'm just old-fashioned...What do you think?"

"Hmm?"

Felix held out his phone.

"Christ, Specter, you could warn a fellow," Sunshine grumbled. Just about the last thing he'd wanted to see was genitalia of the man taking Felix out on a date that night. Still, he couldn't help taking a second look. He took Felix by the wrist to steady the phone as he walked and squinted at the photo.

Felix took his hand back and returned his phone to his pocket. "So, does that eyeful send you wild with desire?"

"Not exactly."

Felix studied his face for a second.

"Must have worked, though, you agreed to go out with him."

Felix sighed. "Maybe I'm desperate. My dating pool is...well, you know, it's limited. I'm related to half the Community because my dad and his spawn can't keep it in their pants. Fairies are almost always not a fan. Werewolves hardly ever live in the city. Vampires usually bite and if I was into pain, I'd have let you bend me over fifty years ago."

Sunshine snorted. "Oh, are you back to bottoming?"

"Anything for you, sweetheart," Felix said in his very best impersonation of an elderly Long Islander. "You know I can't say no to a big strapping soldier boy like you."

"Try sending me a dick-pic, maybe then I'll be interested."

Felix rolled his eyes, but half a smile crept across his face. "Anyway. I still don't know about this Kiernan guy. I might need you to call."

"Dead pet?"

"He knows I don't have any pets."

"Sick grandfather?"

"C'mon, God died years ago. Don't you read Nietzsche?"

"Not if I can help it."

By the time they returned, they had decided Sunshine would call and say that there was a leak in the apartment, should Felix need an excuse to bail on his date.

Sunshine waffled between the hope that Felix would find someone and the worry that it would cut into their shared moments. Aside from Felix, Sunshine had made relatively few close friends. Acquaintances and business associates, he had plenty of those, but people got weird around him. He hadn't fallen so most people assumed he would be literally holier-than-thou. Nearly all angels that had fallen treated him like a child at best and like a very stupid, annoying child at worst.

Thank God June watched Manhattan. He, at least, could be bothered to give Sunshine the time of the day.

When they'd moved from Pickering, June had been the one to point them towards the Weller. He'd been the only one of the

Devil's Watchers that hadn't been openly rude or hostile towards Sunshine.

Dr. Love still hadn't heard back from his cousin by the time Sunshine headed home. Felix had skipped out early to pick up his books.

Sunshine took the train home alone. Sometimes he rode the train for hours, nothing better to do than suffer through whatever torture the MTA cooked up that day. He liked to people watch and hand out money to the performers. He arrived home after Felix had left for his date. He tried to pretend it wasn't intentional. He tried to pretend that the sight of Felix dressed up for someone else didn't bother him.

It didn't bother him, he reminded himself. Not exactly. It wasn't that it was someone else. He wanted Felix to be happy. To have someone.

Someone who could hold his hand.

He just didn't want it to be someone who wouldn't treat him right.

He stayed up watching true crime documentaries on Netflix, waiting for Felix to text him.

Around ten he got a text stating an address followed by *Come get me.*

Immediately, he stood up and called Felix on his way out the door.

Felix, of course, didn't pick up. He texted *I'm fine. Just come here.*

The restaurant wasn't far, about twenty minutes away. Sunshine made it there in fifteen, wishing he could have traveled through the in-between places. He'd lost the ability to do that when Felix had bound him. He didn't know if it was a side-effect of Felix's magic or if Heaven had decided to cut their losses when they'd realized he'd been compromised.

When he arrived, he tried to call again and got a text.

I'm in the bathroom.

Sunshine fed an excuse to the host and pushed, as politely as he could, through the people gathered at the bar.

It was, in fact, a nice place. Comfortable and stylish, but not too fancy. Busy but not packed. Cheerily loud but not deafening.

A really good spot for a first date.

He entered the bathroom. "Uh. Felix?"

"In here," came the slurred response.

He found Felix sitting on the floor in one of the stalls, his phone cradled in his lap. One arm flopped strangely at his side.

"Are you drunk?"

"I. Uh. I think."

Sunshine entered the stall and crouched beside him. He reached out to touch his forehead, though he didn't know what he thought that would do.

Felix weakly swatted his hand away. "I think I had a stroke."

"What!"

"Yeah. So. Take me home."

"Felix, you should be in the hospital!" Sunshine hissed.

"I'll heal. Just. Take me home."

"What about Kiernan?"

"He was a weirdo anyway," Felix said. His voice cracked when he spoke. "Please take me home."

Sunshine slid an arm around Felix's ribs and lifted him. Felix's arm draped across the back of Sunshine's neck, his skin clammy. They didn't make it out of the bathroom before Sunshine could actually hear the sizzle of Felix's flesh. The demon had his teeth grit so hard that Sunshine could hear that, too.

He leaned Felix against the wall. He kept his eyes away from the burn and evaluated Felix's outfit.

Practically, of course. He wasn't envious at all that Felix had dressed so smartly for Kiernan. He wore short sleeves, an honestly stupid choice given the weather, but that was it as far as exposed skin went.

"Did you bring a jacket?"

"It's at the table."

"I'll go—"

"Steal my jacket while he's sitting there?" Felix interrupted.

"I mean, honestly, Felix, I can just tell him you're not feeling well."

Felix let out a grunt.

"I don't know what the big deal is."

"Because he's a fucking creep. I don't want to see him again. I don't want to talk to him. I went out and bought a new goddamn shirt for this—"

"It is a nice shirt. I knew I hadn't seen it before. I like it."

"And he said it was *loud*."

Sunshine held his tongue. It was loud, a richly colored pattern of oranges and leaves on black silk. "I like it," he repeated after a minute. "It's like, ah, like a classy version of a Hawaiian."

Felix sniffed.

"And the oranges go with your boots."

Felix nodded. "I know." He rubbed his nose, or tried, at least. He couldn't move half his body or balance very well.

Sunshine wiped Felix's face with his sleeve, snot and all.

"He said he'd always been curious about demons. Said we had a wild reputation."

People regarded demons with hostility or curiosity. A lot of times that interest had sexual connotations, thinking the Devil's children would either be rapists or voraciously adventurous. Occasionally people believed demons craved human flesh but that was an old superstition, leftover from the Middle Ages. But to bring up something like that on a first date, well, it made Kiernan's expectations clear.

"Let's go home," Sunshine said.

He scooped Felix up and cradled him against his chest. It was easy to carry him; he was thin, and he curled up against Sunshine, tucked into the fetal position.

They got a lot of looks on their way out of the restaurant but fewer on the walk home. The whole time Felix weakly and incomprehensibly mumbled about dating and what a rotten bastard his father was.

Sunshine worried about Felix's health, mental and physical. Demons did sometimes lose their grip on reality, but not until they were much older than Felix. He didn't think he was going mad, but he did worry about just how unwell he was.

He carried him upstairs and had to set him down in the hall to unlock the door. He helped him to bed, making sure to hang up his new shirt instead of throwing it into the pile where he left the rest of Felix's clothes.

Undressing him was a tricky process, but he managed to inflict only minor burns.

Felix held out a pill bottle to him.

"I don't know—"

"I can't sleep otherwise."

Sunshine sighed and took the bottle. He studied the label. "You have Love writing you prescriptions for these."

Felix shrugged. "He doesn't ask questions."

"Of course he doesn't, they're all terrified of us."

"No matter how much you smile at them," Felix said.

Sunshine opened the bottle and gave Felix fewer pills than he requested; he refused to give him more, even when he whined or snarled. He pulled up the covers and gave his leg a pat. "I'll be in the living room if you need anything."

Felix worked his arm out from beneath the covers and Sunshine thought he was going to touch him, put a hand over his or something like that. Instead, he flipped him off.

Sunshine smiled. He headed out to set up the couch. He'd slept there plenty of times, whether it was to keep an eye on Felix or to sleep off a night out.

Quiet, still slurred, and to Sunshine's back, Felix said, "Thank you."

Sunshine didn't look back. If Felix had wanted to say it to his face, he would have. "You're welcome, Specter. Get some rest."

He left the bedroom door cracked so he would hear if Felix called for him. He nestled into the couch under a spare comforter.

Thursday

Felix spent Tuesday and Wednesday in bed. Sunshine asked a few neighbors to go check on him, too, which didn't thrill Felix. Sunshine ignored the complaints and made him stay home on Thursday, too.

Love came upstairs around noon. He rapped on the doorframe and poked his head in the door. "Uh. How's Specter?"

"Doing better."

Love nodded. "A stroke at his age, you know, wouldn't be unusual if he was human. Damn unusual for a demon, though."

"Mmm." Sunshine made himself put down his phone. He'd checked it nonstop all morning. "Any news from your cousin?"

"Uh. Yeah. He won't come above ground. Says if you wanna talk to him you can go to him."

"To the Mole People tunnels?"

Love shrugged. "Listen, he lives underground, he's not exactly got all his fucking pieces, you know. All of em down there."

Sunshine nodded. "Alright."

"Saturday work for you? I guess he's busy or something."

"Saturday is fine. I'm going to need directions to get there, though."

"Alright. Alright. Can...can you check up on the kid? I'm tryna talk him into letting Justice stay at my mom's."

"Sure, I'll mention it." Sunshine stopped himself from checking his phone. "I doubt he'll listen."

"Yeah, I doubt it too. Maybe you can do that smile."

Sunshine snorted. "Any updates on that mummy?"

"It's not a mummy exactly, it turns out. Dried out too fast. Empty on the inside, though, like a mummy should be. There's some magical traces on her. I'll let you know when I get more on that. Usually, I'd ask Specter but considering he'll have fuck-all to do with this and he had a stroke, he's off the table. I'll ask Tate, but right now she's out working on that bracelet case."

"Keep me posted."

"Will do, Sunshine."

Once Love headed back downstairs, Sunshine checked his phone. No news. Felix was probably still in bed.

The office stayed quiet for most of the day. They had just enough cases to keep people busy without making things hectic. Tate looking for that bracelet, Jim checking in with his contacts in the NYPD to find out more about the ghouls Love had mentioned, and Emil trying to find out who was selling hexed heroin up in the Catskills.

Normally Emil and Tate worked cases together, but things had gotten kind of hairy between them recently. It had something to do with the vampire with whom Tate hung around. Sunshine didn't know the exact details, but he didn't think the people involved knew exactly what was happening either.

Better to leave well enough alone.

He left at five and made it home by just after six. He let himself into Felix's apartment and called, "I brought you groceries. Your fridge was empty."

"He's taking a shower."

Sunshine's eyes snapped over to the couch.

Lounging with a book of crossword puzzles on the couch was James Kelly Rosenburg. He hadn't taken his pale brown eyes off his puzzle and tapped his pen against his teeth.

"Oh. I..." Sunshine stared. "Didn't know you were here."

"June sent me over to check up on him. He's so very desperately worried about his king's son," James Kelly explained. "And, well, you know how fond he is of Felix." The vampire smiled.

Sunshine unpacked the groceries. "How is he?"

"June or Felix?"

"Uh. Both."

"Felix is nearly full mobile and slightly tired. I brought soup, too, so he ate. June is busy in New Jersey. Something about...some actor...or maybe his wife. IVF issues. I don't know exactly, it wasn't anyone I'd heard of, so I stopped listening," James Kelly said. "He'll be by when he gets back."

Sunshine nodded. "I'm sorry if this inconvenienced you."

James Kelly was not a demon of any sort and had no loyalty to the Prince of Hell or his children.

"Don't be silly, Sunshine. He's a friend. And it gave me a reason to get out of the house. I'm afraid I'm a borderline shut-in these days."

"Oh." Sunshine shifted.

James Kelly still had not looked up from his crossword puzzle. After several long, quiet minutes, he said, "I'm auditioning for Jeopardy so that will give me something to do."

Sunshine grinned at the idea. "Let me know if you make it, we'll definitely watch."

"June's convinced I'll win so much he can quit his job." He set down his puzzle book on his lap and smiled at Sunshine. "Wouldn't that be something?"

"If anyone can do it, it's you."

James Kelly grinned. "Anyway, you're here now, probably about time for me to head out. Felix is probably sick of me."

"I doubt it. He's always excited to see you."

The bathroom door opened. "Sunshine, I thought I heard you. Any chance you want to take me out for dinner? I tried to talk James Kelly into it, but he's got plans, although watching Jeopardy doesn't count as plans if you ask me."

"It's studying," James Kelly insisted. He stood up, folded his puzzle book in half, and grabbed his jacket. "I'll talk to you both later. Call me if you need anything."

"But not between seven-thirty and eight," Felix said.

"Jeopardy airs at seven."

"You better hurry then!" Felix said with a grin.

James Kelly scowled, rolled his eyes, and left without saying anything else to either of them.

"You shouldn't pick on him," Sunshine chided.

"He likes it." Felix went into his bedroom and returned in jeans and a t-shirt a few minutes later. "You like it, too."

"No."

"Anyway, what's a girl got to do to get dinner around here?"

"Put on shoes."

Felix sat on the couch and started to pull on a pair of socks. "McDonald's has a pretty good dollar menu."

"I'm not taking you to dinner at McDonald's."

Felix shook his head. "I just need help getting there, I'm still a little shaky. I don't really want you to take me to dinner."

Sunshine hesitated, but asked anyway, "Why not?"

"What?"

"Why don't you want me to take you to dinner?"

"I know how much you get paid and how much your rent is; your bank account couldn't handle it."

Sunshine's bank account could handle a nice dinner. He insisted, "I make as much as you do."

Felix paused halfway through pulling on a boot. "I've also got the owner of a prestigious university, a best-selling author, and the Prince of Hell himself for parents, so my wallet has a little more padding. What do I owe you for groceries, by the way?"

"Nothing."

"Sunshine, don't be difficult." He finished putting on his boots, tied them, and stood with a stretch and groan. "You don't want to go to McDonald's?"

"Uh."

"Come on, we'll go somewhere else, then. My treat."

"You don't—"

"As a thank-you. You've been an excellent nurse, Sunshine, I owe you something," Felix said.

"You don't owe me anything."

Felix headed for the door, snagging his wallet and jacket as he went. He doubled back when Sunshine didn't follow immediately. He threw his arms around Sunshine and squeezed him. "Please."

How could he argue with that? "Fine."

They went for Italian. After an unforgivably long wait to get a table, Felix packed away enough food to feed a small army. After Sunshine had finished his entrée and dessert, Felix was still eating. Between bites, he kept up his end of the conversation and ordered more wine for Sunshine.

None for himself, though. Drinking with this new metabolism of his had gone disastrously. He'd gotten alcohol poisoning twice then swore off the stuff.

By the time Felix had finished, Sunshine's face had grown warm and his teeth felt slightly numb.

Felix paid the bill with a handful of cash he fished out of the inside pocket of his jacket. He often carried money that way, with little regard for how easily it could be misplaced or stolen.

Together they waddled home, Felix temporarily sated, even if it was just slightly, and Sunshine drunker than he should be on a work night.

They parted ways at the door of Sunshine's apartment. Before they entirely separated, Felix squeezed Sunshine's hand. Quick and wordless, but that was fine.

The next day at the office was quiet. Felix was quiet. And mostly calm. He spent most of his time with Tate trying to pinpoint the location of the missing bracelet. She'd narrowed it down to the right block but the sheer amount of magic coming off the thing muddled her senses.

Sunshine spent his day trying to figure out where he was supposed to go tomorrow to meet up with Dontell. So far it involved meeting someone at a Starbucks on Worth Street and from there they'd go to Foley Square. He had to follow this someone at a specific distance as they went to the entrance for the Chambers Street Station. Eventually, this stranger would give a signal, and Sunshine would be expected to follow them, somehow, from the Chamber Street Station to the abandoned Worth Street Station underneath the Federal Plaza Building.

The idea of it all made his stomach turn. He didn't fancy being underground and he disliked the idea of being underground and following a drop-out, off-the-grid mage through an abandoned subway station to an undisclosed location. He didn't know how far their little mole city even was from the Worth Street Station.

An inspection on Google Maps led Sunshine to believe that getting from the Chamber Street Station to the Worth Street station would involve no small amount of risk. He had no proof but strongly believed entire the underground railway system of New York had been designed using dark magic. Traversing the subway tunnels in search of a secret society of magical outcasts felt stupid. Felix had been right to wash his hands of it.

Still. A child was involved. Sunshine felt an obligation to go and at least examine the situation. God had hand-made him to be a soldier, he would be fine. He almost always was. The closest things had gotten to not fine had been years ago and had involved the Devil. That visit to Hell had terrified him and to this day the thought of returning made him sick to his stomach. On the handful of occasions when he and the Devil had crossed paths, he had all but fled the room.

The Prince of Hell had scared him badly enough that he had returned to Heaven and asked to be warded against the unholy beast himself. He had never anticipated that the wards would affect the Devil's children as well.

Felix had accused him of being dramatic when he'd found out all the details.

He barely registered the noises around him, not the voices from downstairs or the click-clack of the subway coming from the video on his laptop. It had happened over a hundred years ago, but the event remained fixed in his mind. He had heard the report of the child's soul trapped in Hell and the torture that the beast had created for it. Oh, yes, they all knew of the sickness of the Pit and its ruler, but to hear a firsthand report of what was done there, and to the souls of children, had been too much for Sunshine.

He had snuck down to the Pit with the intent to save that child. He had arrived too late. The boy's soul had already been corrupted.

Lucifer insisted that Sunshine had the details wrong, but did admit, with that awful smile of his, that he had taken a lot of pleasure in frightening Sunshine back to Heaven.

In the end, it had been that unauthorized trip to the Pit that had got Sunshine sent after Felix. He had glimpsed Mercy Specter and the archangels had hoped that would let him find her easier than someone who had not.

Nothing had worked out according to any plan, but it was better that way. It had been a stupid plan.

"What are you watching?" Felix asked.

Sunshine screamed.

Felix clapped a hand to his mouth. He turned away from Sunshine, shaking, trying to hide the giggles that wracked his body. Finally, he turned back. "I'm sorry. I'm sorry, I didn't mean to scare you." He patted Sunshine's curls. "What planet were you on?"

"I was just thinking."

Felix smoothed down the curls he had ruffled and perched himself on Sunshine's desk. "Thinking about what?"

Sunshine shook his head. "Nothing. I mean...nothing important."

"You get lost?" he asked, his mouth drawn.

"Sort of."

Old beings got lost in the maze of their thoughts sometimes. It took hold of different creatures at different ages. Sunshine hadn't been too troubled with such things, but he wasn't as old as some angels. He had been made to replace an angel that had fallen.

Felix wrapped a curl around his finger and lay it carefully. "You have the best hair, Sunshine. You really do."

"Thanks."

"We figured out that bracelet. I'm going with Tate to get it tomorrow."

Sunshine glanced at the clock.

"She's got some kind of doctor's appointment." Felix shrugged. "You'll be here tomorrow, too, right?"

"Uh. I can meet back here if you want." Sunshine hadn't planned on coming to the office.

"No, no, don't worry about it. I'll see you at home after. You sure you'll be alright meeting Dontell?"

Sunshine shrugged. "I can't imagine Love would lie about him not being dangerous."

"They're family, though. People have blind spots when it comes to that." Felix swung his legs, the toe of his boot tapping softly against Sunshine's chair. "So..."

"What?"

"Kiernan messaged me."

"Don't message him back."

Felix pressed his lips together and raised his eyebrows. "About that..."

"Specter, really—"

"No, no, hang on. He apologized."

Sunshine's eyes narrowed. "For what?"

"I guess he realized, uh, well that what he said about demons could be taken out of context."

Sunshine wasn't impressed. "And?"

Felix shrugged. "I don't know. We kind of talked it out." A small, embarrassed smile spread over his lips. "I said I was sorry for running out on him like that."

"What about your shirt?"

The smile faded. Felix stood up. "Anyway, he's coming over to have a look at the bracelet tomorrow after Tate and I pick it up. I think there's something weird about it. Kavornian enchantments are *not* for jewelry."

"What are they for?"

"Binding things. Dangerous things, usually. You'd normally see a Kavornian enchantment on a prison cell."

"Ah."

"And Kiernan is studying—"

"Kiernan the Conjurer. Yeah."

Felix scowled. "I just have a funny feeling about it. The mage who made it was sketchy on the details. I want to figure it out before I give it back to him. You know."

Sunshine understood.

Felix left the room without saying anything else, not an excuse or a destination.

They didn't eat together that night.

Sunshine left early and met his guide at the appointed location. He scanned the crowd, uselessly searching. No one had given him a description.

A young Korean woman approached him, a coffee in each hand. She held one out to him. "Hi, Kyle."

He blinked and frowned before he remembered that Dontell had assigned him a code name. He hurried to return, "Hey, Sylvie!" He took the coffee.

"Don't want to be late for the train." She headed out the door.

He didn't have enough time to commit her face, build, or outfit to memory. He followed her out the door, his heartbeat in his ears. He had to stay within three feet of her, which wasn't hard until a throng of tourists surged out of a building.

He shouldered through the crowd, irritated that they had tourists even in the dead of winter. It looked like a school trip, given the age of the crowd, and he couldn't imagine what kind of dreadful school would bring its students on such a trip.

He walked so close to Sylvie, or whatever her name was, that he stepped on her shadow. Normally, that sort of thing wouldn't have caught his attention but when his foot lingered too long on her shadow, it peeled away from where it met her body.

"Make sure you drink that coffee. You're gonna need it."

He slurped at it. Too sweet and too much hazelnut syrup, by far, but her voice had carried so much implication he had to obey.

She glanced back to see him making a face. "The hazelnut covers up the tonic, it's the only thing that works."

The coffee nearly gagged him. He managed, "What tonic?"

"He didn't tell you?"

Sunshine shook his head.

She rolled her eyes. "It just helps us get where we're going. Nothing dangerous. Besides angels are practically unkillable."

He didn't know who had told her that, but it was bullshit. Plenty of angels had died. Even the Devil died, though death didn't stick to him well.

By the time they made it to Foley Square, he had forced down the coffee and ditched the cup in a garbage can.

A tickle danced over his skin, though he couldn't tell if it was psychosomatic or not. He was, as Felix liked to point out, far too gullible for someone who had been alive since the Fall.

"You spent too much time up in that swimming pool," Felix had told him once. "It's the equivalent of being homeschooled."

Sunshine had bristled at the disrespect he'd shown Heaven. It was no common realm and it was *not* a swimming pool. He had snapped at the demon, the force of his emotions surprising even him. Felix hadn't spoken to him for six days after that.

Now, though, the memory of the hurt on Felix's face made his gut curl more than any slight against Heaven. Maybe he had spent too long away; maybe his tether to the place had withered. How close was he, really, to becoming one of the Fallen?

Sylvie had started to explain their route and he hadn't listened to any of it.

"What?"

She pressed her lips together. "If you fuck this up, you're going to get hit by a train."

"Oh."

"Just follow me. And run."

He nodded.

She grabbed her shadow off the ground and wrapped it around herself like a cloak. She blurred and it strained his eyes to look at her. "Get it on, otherwise people will call the cops when we jump."

He fumbled to pick up his shadow and it slipped between his fingers. He donned it. The world took on a grayish haze.

A train came and left.

As soon as it rushed past Sylvie jumped on to the tracks and began to run.

Sunshine kept pace with her but couldn't see her at all. He had to rely on the sounds of her feet and breathing to know where she was going. At one point, the roar of a train on another track drown out the sound of her running and he lost track of her.

"Sylvie!"

She didn't answer.

He stopped running and looked around.

He saw nothing.

Nothing but oncoming lights.

"Sylvie!" he cried, his voice rising up towards a scream.

"Over here!" Her voice came from somewhere to his left.

He bolted towards her.

"I told you to stay close."

"I can't see anything."

She grumbled something under her breath. She yanked on his coat sleeve. "Let's go before you get us killed."

They picked up a run again and he stayed so close to her she must have been able to feel his breath on the back of her neck.

When they arrived at the Worth Street Station, she leaped up on to the platform and he scrambled after her. She wasted no time looking around, though Sunshine paused.

He had been here before. He'd *used* this stop. To see it like this, dark and empty, jarred him.

Sylvie approached a patch of graffiti that Sunshine recognized as arcane runes, though not a script he knew well.

Not that he knew any of the runes well. Felix would have been able to rattle off which script it was, or what it was a variation of, at least. He would have spent ages staring at it.

He followed Sylvie through the doorway she created in the wall and into another tunnel, better lit than the one they'd just run through.

Small orbs of light studded the rounded ceiling, not uniform in size or color.

Sylvie peeled off her shadow and returned it to the ground. "Welcome to the Enlightened City," she announced with an arm wave.

"Are you all mages?" Sunshine struggled out of his shroud and didn't trust it not to stay stuck to the ground instead of his feet.

She shook her head. "Scholars of some sort, all academics, but not everyone works arcane magic."

"Ah." He shivered as his shadow dragged over the ground. "How long before this tonic wears off?"

"A few hours."

"And do I have to go back out through the tunnel?"

She shook her head. "Lots of ways out. One way in. Safer that way."

As they progressed through the widening tunnel, tents, shacks, and what Sunshine could only think to call hovels began to crop up. Finally, the small encampment swelled to a large room with arches and a domed ceiling. The remains of tile and signage speckled the walls, but mostly those had been chipped away and replaced with graffiti and mosaics. The place had a city center, complete with what appeared to a single general store and a restaurant that advertised "FOOD, HOT, FRESH."

In this denser area of population stood several campers and mobile homes. Magic must have played a critical role in getting those things underground, which meant they must have belonged to better magic workers. The tents likely belonged to those without such talents. Sylvie led him through the illuminated city center to an Airstream trailer that gleamed beneath the thousands of orbs that crowded the ceiling.

Sylvie pointed. "That's Dontell."

"Uh."

She gave him a small smile and walked away, hands in her pockets and her shadow flapping along behind her.

Sunshine approached the Airstream and tapped on the door.

"Who is it?"

"Sunshine, from Sunshine and Specter Detective Paranormal Agency. Maurice Love put us in contact."

Silence.

"Uh. Kyle?" he hazarded. "Sylvie brought me down."

The door opened a hair. A single black eye in a brown face appeared. It watched him.

"Listen, I've come down here to help. If you don't want help, I'll go."

The door closed.

Sunshine took in a breath. He took a step back, glad to head above ground. If he could never come here again, it would be too soon.

The door opened all the way. A man in his thirties stood there, whip-thin and dressed in a beautiful patchwork brocade robe with wide sleeves and dozens of pockets sewn into the lining. He wore the robe over a pale linen shirt and loose, rust-colored trousers that cinched in at the calf. His hair bloomed around his face in long, loose curls.

Without a doubt, Love's cousin was the most beautiful thing Sunshine had set eyes on in years. He stared at him so long that it took him a moment to notice the small boy clutching the man's trouser leg.

Sunshine cleared his throat. He smiled at them.

The boy smiled back. He glanced up at his father.

"Come in," Dontell finally said. He stepped away from the door.

The child continued to watch Sunshine.

"Have a seat." Dontell gestured to a couch with worn upholstery.

Sunshine sat, aware that he had sunk further away from the sky, even if by just a few feet. He rested his hands on his knees. "Maurice—"

"Maurice already said everything he had to say. You're supposed to be here to say something different."

Sunshine smiled. He wiped his hands on his pants, glad he'd worn something dark, sure that he would have left a mark on a lighter pair. "I. Well. My partner and I, we take on cases with unusual factors, ones for which an investigator outside the Community would lack preparation. Maurice has given me some details, but, ah, not many. Just that Suzy lived down here too. That you and she were together."

At that, Dontell put a hand on his boy's shoulder. He nodded. "Past couple of months, bodies like that have been turning up. Deeper into the tunnel. We...we live down here for a reason. But people don't always agree with what we do. Someone's bound to have it out for magic off the grid. Wouldn't be surprised if it was some university-type."

"Have there been people you don't recognize in town?"

"People keep to themselves. I don't recognize everyone."

Sunshine didn't know how much he believed that. This place wasn't easy to access, so a person had to know someone to get in here. That meant newcomers had to have a connection. And a man like Dontell seemed like he would keep an eye on everything.

"Has anybody been threatened? Or received any unusual communications? Been in contact with people at the universities?"

"We're all pretty cut off from the mainstream. They're keen on getting rid of us, we try to stay away from them," Dontell explained.

Paranoia peeked through, but then again, he lived in a secret underground city. "You said bodies, right?" Sunshine asked. "It was more than just Suzy?"

Dontell nodded.

"How many?"

"Seven, including Suzy."

Sunshine gripped his legs. He hadn't expected this. "We have Suzy's body. What about the others?"

Dontell shook his head. "I don't know. That's their family's business."

Buried or burned, Sunshine assumed. "Would the other families be amenable to speaking with me?"

"Don't know."

The boy piped, "Pharaoh says—"

"Shhhh," his father interrupted. "We mind our own business."

Sunshine had encountered that line of thinking before. It wasn't that Dontell didn't know what was going on, it was that he didn't feel someone like Sunshine had any right to the information. These people had learned not to trust people outside their community and learned it well.

The boy scowled at his father. Apparently, he hadn't learned to mistrust outsiders yet.

"Justice, right?" Sunshine asked.

Dontell's face tightened.

Justice grinned and nodded eagerly. He pulled away from his father and clambered onto the couch beside Sunshine. "Pharaoh says his grandma's been missing. She went out to the tunnel to look for her kitty," he confided in a highly audible whisper.

Sunshine glanced towards Dontell, who still scowled.

"You're gonna find who killed my momma?"

"I'm going to try."

"You find a lot of bad guys?"

"Uh. Sometimes. Usually, I, well, I just try to help people who need it."

"Not exactly help if you charge for it," Dontell said.

Sunshine shifted. "We don't ask for more than people can give," he said. It had always been like that. Felix pretended charitable work was just for good publicity, but Sunshine knew he couldn't turn away someone who really needed it.

"Daddy's been grumpy," Justice told him. He cast a look of perfect irritation towards his father, one that belonged on a much older face.

Surprisingly, Dontell's glower softened. He reached over to touch his boy's hair, fluffier than his father's and pulled back into a puff of a ponytail atop his head. "You sound just like your momma."

Sunshine hated having to ask. He couldn't imagine the mood he'd have been in if he was in Dontell's shoes. "Do you know what Suzy was doing in the tunnel?"

"No."

"Not even a guess?"

Justice began, "Momma was—"

"She'd been staying with a friend for a couple of days," Dontell finished.

"Ah." Sunshine nodded.

"Not like that," Dontell said immediately. "Ina's been sick. We all take turns helping out."

"And could I talk to Ina?"

"I can ask her. I don't know what she'll say." Dontell stood and made for the door.

Sunshine followed.

Justice scampered after them. He hurried to catch up with his father and climbed into his arms, still small enough that he rested easily on his father's hip.

Watching them, watching parents and their children, always stirred a hollowness in Sunshine. Childhood contained such an otherness to his life experience. He had never been small enough to hold like that; no one had ever cradled him. He had never grown or changed, he had always existed as he was, as he would always be.

He tried to focus on the homes around him instead, wondering how they'd gotten all these things underground in the first place.

"Magic," Felix would have said like it was the most obvious thing in the world. He might have called Sunshine oblivious or told him to use his brain.

Sunshine wished Felix, or anyone really, had come with him.

Dontell paused before a camper. "Wait here."

Sunshine obeyed. He stared up at the lights above him, trying to count them all. He made it to five hundred and seven before Dontell returned.

"She's not up to it today," the mage announced severely.

Sunshine rubbed his hands together. "What's, uh…What afflicts her, if it isn't too much to ask?"

"We don't know exactly. Ina did a lot of magic. That wears you out."

Nothing, really, that Sunshine could do to help. God had not made him to heal, so his powers in that regard didn't extend past what he would use during or after a fight. Open wounds, shock, pain, infection, those things he could help. Long term illness he couldn't heal. Not that he had tried.

"I'll spread the word around, see if anyone else wants to talk to you," Dontell offered.

"Thank you." He studied the area once more, marking the way he came in and the vast emptiness into which the lights faded. "Is that the tunnel?"

"I'd steer clear of it."

"I should take a look. I won't go in too far."

Dontell nodded. "Well. Alright. But you're on your own. When you're done head on over to the café. Someone there should be able to show you the way to get back up."

Sunshine had hoped for company but wasn't surprised that Dontell had declined. "Uh."

Dontell raised an eyebrow.

"Maurice wanted me to mention...Well. If Justice wouldn't be safer somewhere else."

"No. He's safest with me." He curled his arms around his boy.

Sunshine stepped back with his hands turned to show empty palms. "I told him I'd mention it. That's as far as I'll go."

Dontell nodded but didn't loosen his arms.

Sunshine headed towards the darkness. He kept his step light as he went, and his eyes peeled. Spiderwebs, the bones of small animals, garbage, and tents too shabby to inhabit. Maybe the encampment had reached further once, or maybe it was just more garbage. A few rats scuttled by and even a few pigeons fluttered through the space. Nothing extraordinary; even the tightness in Sunshine's chest and throat was nothing more than fear. He'd sweat enough to soak through his armpits and the small of his back.

He didn't go too deep. He couldn't. Within half an hour, he retreated to the city and sought out the diner. Inside, people glowered and stared at him, but when they realized he wanted to leave, the patrons gave him half a dozen ways to get out.

He returned to the surface via a precariously hung ladder and a manhole that brought him up to a small alley off Worth Street.

The dampness of his clothing demanded he go home, but he went to the office instead.

He found Felix, Tate, and an unfamiliar man laughing together. A bracelet lay on a piece of velvet on the table, surrounded by chalk runes. The trio looked up at him.

He smiled.

"I thought you weren't coming," Felix said.

"I, uh. Well. I wasn't going to. I wanted to make some notes. About the mummy case."

"Huh."

Sunshine hurried upstairs. His heart rate kicked up. He flopped into his desk chair and grasped his head in his hands.

"You look awful." Felix had followed him.

Sunshine looked up.

"You okay?"

"I. It's all underground."

Felix sat on his desk. He fixed Sunshine's hair. "We finished up with the bracelet. We were going to do happy hour."

"No, I..."

"Tate's coming too, it's not, you know, not a date or anything."

Sunshine sighed. "I'll be down in a minute."

Felix nodded, patted his arm, and went downstairs.

Sunshine scribbled a few haphazard notes, random thoughts, and postulations. He met the others downstairs.

"Uh. This is Kiernan." Felix nodded towards the man at his side.

Lean and blond, a rugged scruff of beard, and green eyes. Handsome and deeply aware of it. Kiernan offered his hand to shake.

Sunshine took it. "Sunshine. Nice to meet you."

"Sunshine," Kiernan repeated. "That's, uh...I think I knew someone with that last name. German extraction, right?"

"Maybe."

All through happy hour, Felix showed off. He paid for everything with haughty fistfuls of cash and laughed louder than the rest. He purred his words and flirted with everyone. Kiernan, the waitress, the bartender, everyone except Sunshine and Tate.

As an employee, Tate had immunity from his advances. Felix refused to take advantage of people like that, even when the other party made their interest painfully clear.

June and James Kelly swung by. June threw his arms around Felix, clearly elated to see him on his feet again. James Kelly chatted with Tate about something they'd both just read. June fretted over Felix and tried to convince him not to drink until Felix pulled June aside and quietly explained that all the piña coladas that he'd slurped down had not contained any alcohol.

It didn't stop June from fussing, but he fussed a little less afterward. After about two hours, James Kelly tugged on June's sleeve. "You about ready?"

"Uh." June glanced toward Felix, who was in the middle of telling Kiernan about the first time the Police had played at CBGB.

James Kelly laid his head on June's shoulder. "I'm sleepy. And we have Ben and Jerry's in the freezer."

June scolded, "Yeah, well, you shouldn't have been drinking wine. You know it makes you sleepy."

"I never drink...wine," James Kelly did his best Bela Lugosi impression, which wasn't very good at all. He buried his face in June's jacket.

"You drank four glasses of wine, I just watched you."

"It's happy hour, they're half off, so it's like I only drank two."

June kissed the vampire's temple. "Get the check, then."

Felix had already paid for their drinks, of course, and after they parted with the requisite hugs and cheek kisses, Felix slung his arm around Kiernan's shoulder, sagged against him, and sighed, "Could they be any fucking cuter?"

"Um."

"I could honestly die."

Sunshine warned, "Don't be maudlin, Specter."

Felix unwound himself from around Kiernan and came over to poke Sunshine in the chest. "I'm not being maudlin, I'm being sentimental. There's a difference."

Sunshine rolled his eyes. "Alright, fine, you're the smart one."

"Yeah, don't you forget it," Felix told him, his voice much sterner than the smile on his face.

Sunshine left early. He threw down some cash to cover his bill, though Felix protested.

Tate followed him out. "Mr. Sunshine!" she called.

He paused to look back. "Did you need something?"

"Just. You know." She shuffled and shrugged. "That bracelet is pretty dicey. I don't know how much they filled you in. Mr. Specter, I know he's been a little out of it lately. But make sure you get the details."

"Thanks for the heads up."

He went home and went to bed. He hadn't meant to, but it had called to him. He oozed into bed, on top of the covers, and closed his eyes. He didn't sleep, not for a few hours, but lay there in the dark, thinking about Hell and Satan, about the dried-up corpse in his office, about how green Kiernan's eyes had been.

He drifted off but jerked awake when something leaped on to his bed.

"It snowed!" crowed Felix from where he had landed. He pushed Sunshine. "Oh my god, did you sleep in your clothes? You're not even under the covers. How much did you drink? You were *definitely* not that drunk when you left. You didn't come home and drink, did you?"

"Jesus, Specter, what time is it?"

"Uh. Six, a little after six. But it snowed, Sunshine, get up. A lot of snow, too, mountains of it! Come on, up, Sunshine."

"Why?"

"Take a shower, we've got plans."

They had no plans that he recalled but got up anyway. A shower and coffee perked him up and made him aware of the energy with which Felix vibrated.

He practically danced as he dragged Sunshine out to the hall. He grandly gestured to the sled leaning against the wall. "Look!"

"You'll wake up the neighbors."

Felix sucked in a breath.

"Shh, don't, please!" Sunshine insisted.

The demon let out the breath quietly. "Get your jacket."

"Remember when you used to stay in bed to a decent hour after you'd been out all night?" he asked as he fetched his coat.

Felix grinned and let out a chortle. He hefted up the sled and made for the stairs. "So, you know I've, uh, not been drinking much. Tate got tipsy, told me how much she liked your hair about a thousand times. Kiernan, well, he drank too."

"And?" Sunshine took the back end of the sled, a heavy wooden thing suited to an old-fashioned Christmas card.

As they maneuvered down the narrow stairs, Felix continued, "So he got pretty drunk. Like not sloppy or anything but friendly. Real friendly." He shifted the way he held the sled a lot and his words came out fast and jumbled. "He's flirting, I mean flirting so bad, like I *bought it*, I would have...well, you remember that time up in Toronto when we had that case? The Jenkins case. The one with the dog? Big black dog, everyone thought it was an omen cause of those Harry Potter books. Anyway, I was telling him about that, and he started making these...implications."

"Specter, you didn't—"

"Date rape someone?" Felix asked.

"That's *not* what I was going to ask."

Felix grunted.

Sunshine stopped but kept his grip on the sled so that Felix had to stop, too. "Felix."

The demon glanced back with a scowl on his face. The scowl didn't cover up the hurt, though.

"You would never do that."

Felix tugged on the sled.

"You didn't start taking those pills again."

"I don't want to talk about it, Sunshine. I'm in the middle of a story, honestly. Anyway, you know how share-y people get when they drink. He's sharing, a lot, telling me about there's all these *things* he's wanted to try. How he just got out of a long-term relationship, that his boyfriend never wanted to try anything new. He's nervous he's not experienced enough. And I asked, 'experienced enough for what?' I'll bet you can guess what he said."

"For someone like you?"

"For someone like me!" Felix shouted.

They struggled through the front door.

"Someone like me, Sunshine, can you *fucking* believe it?"

"What'd you do?"

Felix huffed. "Put his ass in an Uber and sent him home. Blocked his number when he tried to text me at two in the morning. He's uncommonly apt at making apologies, I almost bought it again."

They lugged the sled to the top of Pilgrim Hill.

Sunshine watched as Felix climbed on.

He looked silly with his long legs bent up so he could fit on the sled. "You have to climb on behind me."

"Are you sure I'll fit?"

"Yes, of course, Sunshine. Bibi, Papa, and I all fit on one of these and the both of them are ridiculously tall. You're not even a little bit tall."

With great care, Sunshine climbed on behind him. He had to scooch right up against him, his legs around Felix's hips. With gloves, scarves, and hats, the chance he could burn Felix barely existed.

"Alright, hold on," Felix said, and with no more warning than that, shoved them down the hill.

Sunshine clung to him, his face pressed into Felix's shoulder and his eyes shut. His heart climbed up his throat.

Felix laughed the whole way down.

Sunshine remained pressed against him when they coasted to a stop at the bottom of the hill.

"Sunshine, if you squeeze me any harder, you're going to break a rib."

"It will heal."

"Don't be a baby." Felix wrapped his arms around Sunshine's arms and squeezed him back.

Sunshine couldn't see it, but he felt an isolated point of pressure against his inner arm. It could have been a finger, or Felix's chin or nose.

"Come on, help me get it back up the hill."

On the second ride down, Sunshine managed to keep his eyes open. He held on to Felix just as tight, but for different reasons. He understood what to expect this time and grinned. They raced back to the top of the hill, laughing and joking.

By the time children and parents arrived, he and Felix had exhausted themselves. The screams of children, the echoing calls of their parents ringing out over the snow, the barks of a few dogs. Sunshine threw himself onto a snowbank and gazed up at Felix, dark against the pale gray sky.

"What're you doing?"

"Breathing."

Felix scowled. "Aren't you some kind of super-soldier?"

"I'm a soldier, I belong to the supernatural community, that doesn't mean I don't need to breathe after running up a hill for three hours straight."

Felix dropped down beside him. He placed his hand on Sunshine's arm.

Children swarmed the hill now.

"What do you think about breakfast?" Felix asked.

"I think I want French toast."

"Then I shall make you French toast, Sunshine." The demon stood and began to walk away.

Sunshine hadn't known Felix could make French toast. He tried to remember if he'd ever seen him cook French toast before, then called "The sled!"

"Leave it, I'll buy another one."

Sunshine couldn't leave it. He hefted it.

Felix looked back, sighed, and doubled back to help Sunshine carry it. "Really, it didn't cost that much."

"Don't you care about the environment?" Sunshine asked. He didn't know why he couldn't leave the sled behind. At home, he stowed it in his closet, wedging it in beside the vacuum cleaner.

Felix rifled through his cabinets, taking out what seemed like every cooking utensil Sunshine owned. He shoved a handful of pills in his mouth, then started cracking eggs. He had his phone propped up so he could watch a video of someone else making French toast.

"You're going to have another stroke," Sunshine warned.

Felix didn't say anything. He didn't have to. He glanced up and his eyes said enough.

If Sunshine could have touched him, really touched him, he would have held him. He would have cupped his face and told him he would fix it. He'd seen people do that in movies.

Instead, he ate the mountain of French toast that Felix gave him. For the first time in months, he out-ate the demon. Felix barely ate anything.

February 16
Tuesday

Sunshine nearly threw up before he finished the conjuring spell. He worked himself into such a state that by the time he uttered the last words, he was out of breath and shaking. He stared at the chalk circle with his hands clasped together.

The Devil appeared. He looked around, frowning at first, and then smiling. "One of Daddy's pretty golden soldiers." His fingers lengthened to talons.

"It's me! It's just me, it's Sunshine."

Lucifer tilted his head. "You all look the same to me. Let me out of this." His claws returned to fingers.

He had to remind himself that the Devil couldn't touch him without hurting himself. He scuffed away part of the circle.

Lucifer stepped through the circle and seated himself on Sunshine's sofa. "So."

"I...I need help."

The Devil smiled. His face nearly split open with the grin. He looked different than he had last time Sunshine had seen him, although in most ways he looked exactly the same. Long black hair, skin as pale as snow, a tall, lanky body with spidery limbs. This version of the Devil had a femme sort of grace and posture to it but a shape that made any sort of gendering unclear.

"Felix needs help."

The smile disappeared. "In what way?"

Sunshine fumbled his way through the explanation of what had happened in the Otherworld. The girl, her father, and the curse.

Lucifer listened carefully, his elbow resting on his knee, his chin resting on his hand. When Sunshine finished, he said, "It can be fixed."

Sunshine dared to smile.

The Devil slunk over and put his finger under Sunshine's chin and tilted his face up. "Tell me why you're asking instead of Felix."

"He doesn't want to ask for help. You know he doesn't like asking you for help." His heartbeat sounded in his ears.

"Hmm." His finger began to blister against Sunshine's skin; he pulled his hand back to study the burn. He snaked an arm around Sunshine. "You've been in-between, so you know to hold on tight."

Unable to think past the awful dread that wormed around inside him, Sunshine wriggled out of Lucifer's grasp. "What are you doing?"

"Bringing you to get a cure for Felix's curse."

"Well...I don't see why I have to go with you."

Lucifer narrowed his eyes. "Because you asked for it and I'm giving it to you freely, nothing asked in return, no expectations except that you would plead Felix's case to the king of the Eastern Court. Fairy magic must be undone by fairies and you are in a better position to explain what happened to the king than I."

Sunshine blinked and licked his lips.

"Now come over here."

He obeyed.

This time, when Lucifer put an arm around Sunshine, he did it more gently. "Three, two, one," he counted softly.

Sunshine didn't even come up to his shoulders. He clung to him as hard as he could when the Devil brought them through the in-between place. As soon as they were through, he scrambled away as though he were the one who could be burned. He nearly stumbled and had to brace himself against a nearby tree to steady himself.

Felix would tease him for being dramatic.

"Christ, didn't your mother ever hug you?" the Devil asked.

"You know I don't have a mother."

"Fuck, well, neither do I but I don't flinch every time someone touches me."

Sunshine spat, "It's not everyone, it's *you*."

"Me? Heavens, what did I ever do to you?"

He glowered at the Devil.

"It's this way to the Court." Lucifer set off along a nearly imperceptible path. "I've done lots of things to lots of people, but you've got fifty-nine more of you out there, I never know which one of you is which."

"I'm the only one who lives on Earth."

"Mmm. How many of you were sent to kill Felix?"

"I...I don't know. I was the first one."

"So, you're the one who lives on Earth. The one who stabbed a little boy and ninety-odd years later calls me up to help that same boy. Lives next door to the life he tried to end, works with him...and what else do you do with him?"

"Felix is my friend."

Lucifer glanced back. "That or you are an absolutely *miserable* assassin."

They continued in silence. The path beneath them widened and the trees thinned. When the forest cleared altogether, Sunshine saw an enormous willow tree. Its branches created a veil around it, too dense to let through any glimpse of what lie beyond.

"It's best to kneel before a king," Lucifer advised as he began to undress.

"What..."

"Oh, fairies are funny about things." He handed Sunshine his bundle of worn silk and from nowhere produced a black dress with a long, chiffon skirt and a lace, open-backed bodice. He shimmied into it and placed a silver circlet upon his head, nestled atop thin, intricately woven braids. "They like pretty things here. Do I look pretty?"

The Devil looked wild and dangerous, but also somewhat like a runway model.

Sunshine nodded. Lucifer had been an angel once and God did not, as a rule, make ugly things.

He smiled, showing black teeth. He headed off towards the willow and slipped between the branches without waiting for Sunshine.

All too aware of the irony and a common turn of phrase, Sunshine hurried after Lucifer, not keen on being left alone in the Otherworld.

Felix had gotten cursed by them and he was far wilier than Sunshine had ever managed.

Immediately upon entering, Sunshine came face to face with a large white stag.

"I rode one of these once. Got me banned from the Eastern Court for a few centuries," Lucifer quietly confided, his hand on the neck of the stag.

The stag eyed Sunshine.

A few courtiers, colorful in skin and clothing, eyed them. One eyed Lucifer and leaned in to whisper to her companion.

Lucifer swept through the courtiers with his chin tilted up. He stepped out of the crowd and paused in front of a pale throne.

The man who sat upon the throne had dark hair, blue eyes, and pale brown skin. He was young, not just in the fairy ever-youthful sort of way, but young in years. He also wore blue jeans and a t-shirt with a fancy silver frock coat over it.

"Who steps before the throne?" the youth asked.

Lucifer glanced around. "Clearly I do."

"And who are you, my lady?"

"He Himself, the Prince of Darkness and Lord of Hell, who sits upon the serpent's throne."

The youth blanched. "Ah. Well. My lord, or...? Your Highness. What business do you have in the Eastern Court?"

"I came to speak with the king. A prince will do fine, though, provided he is one who can grant the favor I require."

"I..." The youth glanced around.

A dark-haired guard approached.

The prince leaned forward to whisper into his ear. When the guard left, he said to Lucifer, "My father will be notified of your presence, Your Highness. While you wait..." He gestured and someone presented a goblet to the Devil.

No one brought one for Sunshine. He had lingered by the edge of the crowd.

Lucifer took the goblet. He kept his eyes on the prince as he sipped. "Oliver, right?"

"Yes."

"I've heard about you. So many things."

"I've heard about you, too, Your Highness."

Lucifer grinned. "I liked it so much better when you called me 'my lady'," he said.

"Oh...I. Well, whatever you wish to be called—"

"You weren't so nervous then. They tell you such tricky things about me in the mortal realm."

"Your reputation isn't wonderful here, either," came a voice to the left. The man who spoke resembled the prince on the throne, but he had long, pale brown hair and eyes the color of summer wheat.

Lucifer grinned at him. He kissed the man's hand when he offered it, then the man kissed his, and Lucifer walked him over to the throne as though walking a date to her seat at a fancy restaurant.

The prince stepped aside and went to stand beside one of the stags.

The fairy king and Lucifer made polite conversation for a while, until finally the king asked what had brought Lucifer to Court.

"Ah..." Lucifer glanced over his shoulder and beckoned over Sunshine.

Sunshine went over and knelt, head bowed.

"Is this a matter that requires more privacy than we have?" asked the king.

"It wouldn't be unwelcome."

The king rose. "Come to my garden." He offered his arm to Lucifer.

They walked together, Sunshine and the dark-haired guard a respectful distance behind. Once in the walled garden, the guard positioned himself beside the entrance.

Sunshine went on following the two monarchs, listening to well-mannered small talk so devoid of open meaning and layered with secrets and insinuation that he couldn't follow a single thing they said.

"Truly now, what brings you to visit?"

Lucifer answered, "Couldn't it be that lovely smile of yours?"

The king smiled at him. "Have you told such glowing tales of me that you had to bring a friend to see me?"

Sunshine winced.

"Sunshine came to me," Lucifer said.

"As it comes to us all each dawn."

"Ah, no, sorry, Eri. *This* is Sunshine." Lucifer gestured to him.

"Your name is Sunshine," the fairy king stated.

"Yes."

The king grinned. "Marvelous. How did you come across such a name?"

"I, uh…" Sunshine hesitated. He hadn't been named in the same way as most people. "It's just what Specter called me. I guess it stuck, especially since I didn't have anything else to go by."

"Oh?"

"Well, when He made us after the Fall, He didn't bother giving us all our own names." *Or our own faces*, Sunshine thought bitterly. "So, when I met Specter, he…he was being sort of mean, really, calling me Sunshine, but it was the only thing anyone had ever called me."

"Like a stray cat," Lucifer noted.

With a bright smile, the king asked, "And who is Specter?"

"My friend."

"One of my sons," Lucifer added. "He's in a pickle, currently. Sunshine can explain it better than I can."

The king gave an expectant look.

Sunshine tried to start from the beginning but ended up rambling through more details than necessary. The words came up in a great rush. He told the king everything he did know and everything that he didn't, about Felix's health and all the pills he'd been taking. He finished with, "And I don't know what happened or why she did it, not really, but I do know…I know that this is killing him. He's wasting away and…" His throat tightened.

Lucifer smoothed a hand over Sunshine's arm.

"He's my best friend," Sunshine insisted.

They had stopped walking ages ago, standing beneath a tree as Sunshine spilled his guts.

The king reached up and plucked a fat, shiny plum from a branch. He pressed it to his lips and Sunshine wanted to smack him for eating at a time like this, but he only kissed the fruit. His lips left behind a distinct shimmering mark. "If your friend eats this, the curse will be lifted."

"Th—"

Lucifer squeezed Sunshine's hand so hard he stopped speaking.

"However, he offended one of my people, no matter the details. I cannot give things away so freely and maintain peace among my courtiers," the king added.

"I'm sure I have something suitable to offer," Lucifer said.

"There are a few things you…acquired that the Court would be glad to see returned."

Lucifer chuckled. "Pick one."

"The scales—"

"Oh, for a plum! The scales of Rideries, for a plum?" Lucifer scolded cheerfully. "What would I give you when I *really* want something?"

The king didn't seem to take offense. "What, then, will you give me to save your son's life?"

"Oh, it wouldn't kill him. Sunshine's just dramatic." Lucifer pushed his hand through the skin of reality and withdrew it clutching a sword forged entirely of metal so pale it was nearly white. His arm dropped as though it weighed far more than its size indicated.

The tip of the sword sunk half a foot into the ground, propelled by its own weight.

"Starsong," the king noted reverently.

"A fair price, we think."

"And there's some poetry to it," the fairy agreed. "Yes, it suffices." He handed over the plum to Sunshine. "Iko!" he called.

The guard trotted over. "Your Majesty?"

"Bring this to the armory. Somewhere safe."

The guard, not a small or slender man, struggled to heft the sword out of the ground. He had to carry it in both hands.

"Does this conclude our business?" the king asked.

"For now." Lucifer leaned in to kiss his cheek.

Sunshine cradled the plum. "I..."

The king waited.

"We're detectives. Specter and I. If you ever need anything detected, I'd...I would help if I could," Sunshine offered.

"I'll hold on to that offer, Sunshine. Best of luck with your friend. Tell him I love your name."

Sunshine nodded.

Lucifer took Sunshine by the hand and, as the king walked with his guard out of the garden, pulled Sunshine out of the Otherworld and back to his apartment. Once they returned, he didn't let go. He kept a hold of Sunshine's hand, watching his own skin turn bright red where they touched.

"Am I that unfavored in Heaven?" he asked quietly.

"I...No. It's only me."

Lucifer took Sunshine's arm in both his hands and wormed his fingernails under Sunshine's skin—no, not under his skin, but under the thin mesh of magic that clung to it. The magic expanded then snapped back against Sunshine's skin, just as hard as a rubber band would.

"You did this to yourself?" the Devil asked.

"I had it done to me."

"Why?"

"So you could never touch me again."

"Well, I mean...it doesn't seem to work that well, I'm touching you right now." The flesh of the Devil's hand started to crack and bleed. "You aren't the one I locked in that cell?"

"That wasn't even one of the soldiers."

"Hmm. Well." Lucifer released him. He leaned back against the counter.

Sunshine tossed the old silk clothes at his feet and put the plum in the fridge.

Lucifer watched him. "Aren't you going to ask?"

"No."

The Devil waited.

He didn't need to wait long.

Sunshine couldn't look at him, but said, "You can undo it."

"Sure."

Sunshine pretended to do something else. He tried to busy himself in the kitchen but only succeeded in making noise. "Aren't you going to leave?"

"Ask me."

"I already asked you."

"Here I was thinking you had all these hang-ups..." Lucifer hiked up his skirt and climbed onto the counter. He seated himself, cross-legged, and watched Sunshine mess up his kitchen trying to make a sandwich. "You aren't too proud to ask me for help. You did it for Felix."

Sunshine elbowed a jar of jelly onto the floor. It didn't break but it did vomit its contents all over the tile. As he scooped up purple chunks, he knew Lucifer still watched. He could feel his eyes, those hideous eyes on him.

"Aren't you going to ask me?" Lucifer prompted after Sunshine had cleaned the floor.

Shaking as he threw the mangled remains of the sandwich away, he asked, "What's the price?"

"You can owe me a favor," Lucifer proposed.

The idea terrified Sunshine. He shook his head. Felix wasn't his father, but his father *was* the Devil. He couldn't ignore that. Angels didn't make deals with the Devil and they certainly didn't owe him favors.

Angels weren't supposed to hurt people just by touching them. They weren't supposed to accidentally burn babies who happened to have a demon for a parent or make people bleed when they kissed them.

Life wasn't supposed to be about watching your best friend cry and being scared to hold him.

"Do it."

"You'll owe me."

Sunshine nodded.

"Two favors."

"You said one."

"That was then. This is now."

Sunshine hesitated.

"Three. Going—"

"Fine!"

Lucifer grinned. He offered his hand.

Sunshine stared at it.

"Or we can seal it with a kiss."

Sunshine shook his hand and wished he hadn't.

Lucifer slid off the counter. He pricked Sunshine's thumb with his nail. "It's done. Do you particularly like the clothes you're wearing?"

"What?"

"If you like them you should take them off."

Sunshine liked these clothes, but he liked the idea of being naked in front of Satan less. "Just do it."

"It will hurt. You've left this on for too long. It's stuck to you."

"Fine."

Lucifer dug his fingers into Sunshine's skin and ripped at the magic. At first, it didn't hurt so much as stung, but when the spell started to tear, he felt it. He felt it as though Lucifer ripped at his very flesh. The magic came away in pieces, not all as a single sheet, as it had been applied. The more Lucifer ripped it off, the worse it hurt.

The Devil's hands started to bleed as he tore at the spell. He lost finesse and started to scratch Sunshine as he grasped the mesh that had affixed itself to his skin.

Sunshine ended up shedding his clothes because it needed to be done to allow Lucifer to access the entirety of the spell.

As he peeled the magic off Sunshine's ass, Lucifer had asked, "What did you think I was going to do to you that you had this ward put here, too?"

"I had it put everywhere."

"Did you expect that we'd do some Greco-Roman nude wrestling on the battlefield?" Lucifer mused.

Sunshine grit his teeth and grunted as Lucifer ripped that piece off.

All in all, it took about an hour. They both bled.

Lucifer washed his hands and dried them on the shirt Sunshine had cast aside. "That should about do it."

The process had turned Sunshine's skin ruddy. He stung all over. He wanted to take a bath to get rid of the blood but knew that, hot or cold, water would bite.

Lucifer gathered the clothing in which he'd arrived. "Give Felix my regards."

"You're not going to see him?"

"If he wanted to see me, he would."

At that moment, Sunshine pitied him. He didn't trust him or have any idea what he'd ask for with those favors, but he said, "I'll say hi for you. I'll try to get him to call you."

Lucifer smiled and then left through the in-between.

Sunshine wanted to run over and wake up Felix, but he couldn't leave his kitchen spattered with blood.

He waited until morning. He went over as he had gone over so many other times. He made coffee, woke him up, and said, "I brought breakfast."

Felix rolled over and pulled the covers over his head. "Let's take the day off."

"Alright. Come eat breakfast."

Felix pulled down the covers on his own. He squinted and pushed himself up. He didn't say anything but followed Sunshine out to the kitchen. He frowned at the single plum Sunshine had put on his plate. "This is breakfast?"

Sunshine nodded.

Felix tried to rub off the shimmery smudge that the fairy king had left behind. It didn't budge. He sniffed it. "This reeks of fairies."

"It will fix your curse."

"Sunshine."

"Please, Felix."

"What did you do to get it?"

Sunshine flushed. "Your father says hi. You should call him."

Felix groaned.

"I didn't have to do anything more than go with him to get it. There's no strings attached, not from your father or the fairy king." Sunshine knelt beside Felix and placed a hand on his knee. "This curse is killing you and I don't know what I would do without you."

"It's not killing me," he scoffed.

"Please just eat it, Felix, get your head out of your ass and just eat the fucking plum. I'm begging you. I'm on my goddamn knees." Tears dribbled down his face, stinging his still-raw skin. He felt like he'd been scrubbed down with sandpaper; even the softest clothes he had still hurt.

"Alright, Christ, I'll eat it." Felix took the plum and dug his teeth in. Juice spurted over his hand and down his face.

As he ate, his whole body when slack. He melted into his chair as he devoured the plum with the reverence of someone in the ecstasy of a divine presence. He sucked every bit of flesh from the stone and panted when he finished. He slumped in his chair, eyes closed, breathing, lips parted, sticky.

Sunshine touched his hand.

Felix glanced at him, eyes half-closed. "Fuck," he whispered. He took his hand back.

"Are you alright?"

He nodded. He swallowed. "I..." He took in a slow breath and stared at Sunshine. "I need to take a shower."

"Should I stay?"

Felix shook his head. "No. I...I'll see you at the office."

"You're sure?"

"Yeah. I need..." He swallowed again. "Christ, I think I need to jerk off. What the fuck kind of plum was that?"

Sunshine giggled.

Felix laughed, too.

They dissolved into roaring laughter, out of breath and grasping their stomachs. Sunshine ached, he wanted to scream, but he couldn't stop laughing.

When their laughter died, Felix crouched beside Sunshine on the floor. He wrapped him up in a hug and breathed, "Thank you." He didn't hold him for nearly long enough. He tousled Sunshine's hair and kissed his forehead.

Sunshine almost started crying.

Felix didn't end up coming to work that day. He sent a text saying that he'd gotten in touch with his dad. He wasn't home when

Sunshine got back from the office, but there was a note taped to his door that said *In Hell. Back tomorrow night. xo – f.*

Sunshine pocketed the note, ordered Chinese, and fell asleep watching TCM.

February 19
Friday

Sunshine hadn't heard much from Felix. He hadn't spent much time at the office; he spent most of his days holed up at home reading comics. He'd been too out of it, either from the drugs or the curse, to stay caught up with his weekly subscriptions. Sunshine had visited him when he'd come back from Hell to find him organizing months of comics that he had bought and bagged, but never read and left in stacks around his apartment.

Friday night, Felix showed up as everyone else prepared to leave. He sprawled himself across Sunshine's desk. "Sunshine! Darling!"

"Yes, Tallulah?"

"We're going out tonight."

Sunshine raised an eyebrow. "Are we?"

"*Yes*, darling, of course. I know I've been absent of late, but you really did me a big favor there."

"It had to happen."

Felix sat up. "I was in such an awful place. I wouldn't have made it through without you."

He couldn't help but roll his eyes. "Specter—"

"No, I mean it, Sunshine, I really do. Please, take me seriously for once."

"I always take you seriously."

"Then why are you giving me such a look!" Felix demanded.

"You're flopped all over my paperwork wearing pearls and a beaded dress and you've gotten cigarette ash on my keyboard," Sunshine pointed out.

With a pout, Felix told him, "It's speakeasy night at the Black Diamond. I brought you a change."

A pout like that couldn't be resisted. "Fine. Get off my desk, though, I've got work to finish."

"Did Tate leave a package for me?"

Sunshine took a small paper parcel out of his desk and handed it over.

Felix stowed it in the secret compartment under his desk.

"What's that?"

"That bracelet. The guy's being sketchy. It's too small for an adult and I don't know what kind of child needs a Kavornian enchantment."

"Ah."

Felix shrugged and adjusted his stockings. "I don't know how Bibi ever wore these."

"You look lovely."

Felix blew him a kiss. "Would you be really mad if I brought you a dress instead of spats?" He asked the question as a joke, but beneath that joke lived a hint of uncertainty. It showed in his eyes.

He got like that sometimes. Even after everything they'd done together, he still acted like he thought Sunshine might finally say he'd had enough. Enough of what exactly, Sunshine hadn't figured out. He probably never would unless Felix told him directly.

He settled for saying, "I'd be disappointed if you brought me spats." Sunshine had come to Earth in a cuirass and leather skirt. Sometimes, he missed the airflow. Not to mention, he would have hated to be left out of one of Felix's escapades.

The answer made Felix grin. "Sunshine, will you marry me?"

"Yes," Sunshine said, "But only if you take my name. Sunshine Specter sounds much sillier than Felix Sunshine."

"Misters Sunshine and Felix Sunshine? No, I'll keep my name, thank you," Felix sniffed.

"Misters Sunshine and Felix Specter-Sunshine."

"Misters Sunshine Specter and Felix Specter-Sunshine," Felix offered with a grin. "You know my full name is Felix James Specter-Reinhart-Queen."

"It isn't."

"You're right, it's His Highness Prince Felix James Specter-Reinhart-Queen, most favored son of the serpent's throne."

"Most favored."

With his chin tilted up and wide smile, Felix said, "He only ever held two of us as infants and Elisa is not exactly in his good graces."

Sunshine finished up his work and changed into the dress and stockings that Felix had brought for him. The costume was so period-accurate that Sunshine had to ask, "Is this Bibi's?"

"Oh, they're so tall, we'd look like kids playing dress-up! Dad and I went thrifting."

"He won't be there."

"No."

"I look like Jack Lemmon."

Felix shushed him and hung a string of pearls around his neck. "Tony Curtis was the handsome one."

They left before a few of their employees and everyone stared at them as they walked out. Of course, they should have stared, really, because who expected their employers to come downstairs dressed like they belonged on the set of *Some Like It Hot*.

Emil stared the most and leaned over tell Tate, "Always up to something weird," in a voice he must have meant to be a whisper.

Felix helped Sunshine into a fur coat and shimmied into his own. "They're thrifted, don't worry!" he declared to their gawking employees.

They walked to the Black Diamond, which had started life as an actual speakeasy that catered to ladies, gentlemen, and others of certain inclinations. It had originally been known as Black Mama's after Clara, the woman who had owned it, but that name had fallen out of favor. The name, which started out as a strident affirmation of Clara as a woman, hadn't aged well.

Clara's granddaughter had rechristened it. She had said, "Anyone who knew my Nana knew she was more than just someone's mama. She was the rarest kind of gem in the world." Felix, ass that he was, had spent the night explaining that diamonds, black or not, were not rare at all and that the bar should have been called the Black Opal if they wanted something really rare. Sober, he'd written a long apology to Clara and offered to pay for the new sign.

The sign he'd bought still hung above the entrance and he paid to restore it every so often.

Tonight, when they passed under the sign, Felix smiled at it.

A few other patrons milled around, everyone in costume. Or, at least, in their best attempts at a costume. Sunshine reminded himself not to judge. He'd have worn jeans if Felix hadn't provided something for him.

"Don't let me get shitfaced," Felix said as they shed their jackets and approached the bar.

"I've never been able to stop you from doing anything."

"And don't let me go home with a scumbag."

Sunshine vowed, "You've only ever gone home with scumbags when I stayed home."

"It's that smile, Sunshine, it's like DEET for scumbags." Felix leaned on the bar and squinted at the drink specials. "Uh, two...well, the gin fizz, does that have egg whites?"

The girl behind the bar frowned. "Egg whites?"

"You know what, never mind, we'll have two, however they're made." To Sunshine, he continued, "How long has it been since you've had a gin fizz?"

When he received the drinks, he slid a card across the bar and asked the bartender to open a tab. He chucked Sunshine under the chin and said, "Whatever you want to drink, darling, it's on me."

Sunshine couldn't tell if Felix had spent too much time with his father or if he had really committed to this Tallulah Bankhead impersonation. With each sip of his drink and bite of food, he'd sigh and grin, happy as a pig in shit. He hadn't smiled like this in months and Sunshine wanted to taste that smile.

They sipped their drinks, nibbled on snacks, and watched the others. Sunshine liked to people-watch and he liked to hear what Felix had to say about other people. Felix didn't always have something bitchy to say, sometimes he liked something so much that he would approach people to compliment them.

A singer belted out tunes with varying degrees of accuracy to the Prohibition period. Specter rambled on about anachronisms for a while until Sunshine said, "They didn't even have Prohibition in Canada, what do you know?"

"I was alive."

"You were six."

"Not for the whole decade," Felix said.

Sunshine pursed his lips and took out his phone.

Felix yanked it out of his hand. "Don't google things trying to prove me wrong! I never went to a real speakeasy and the only thing I remember about the twenties is playing marbles and *you* stabbing me." He tossed Sunshine's phone on the table. "No, don't start pouting. Stop it."

"I'm not pouting."

"Looks like a pout to me."

Sunshine reached for his phone.

Felix slapped his hand. "Please be more present in the moment."

"Fine. How was Hell?"

"Weird, as always." Felix made a face. "But it was nice to catch up with Dad and Ira. He's got some kind of public works project going on in the slums. He was real proud of it. Ira seemed happy about it too. It's...unnerving how sweet he is to Ira."

Sunshine agreed. Seeing Satan wait hand and foot on his companion unsettled Sunshine. It didn't make any sense that the Devil could care about anyone that much, or why he would pretend to care about him, at least. Sunshine didn't think Lucifer cared about anyone except himself. Maybe putting on a show of his affections for Ira served some other purpose.

Felix took a big sip of his drink. "Christ. I don't remember anything tasting this good."

"Maybe have a water next."

Felix rolled his eyes but drank the glass of water when Sunshine placed it in front of him. He sighed after a sip. "Even *water*, Sunshine, even water didn't taste right. You don't think about it at all, you know, but I stood in the shower with my mouth open just drinking water this morning."

People on the dance floor attempted period-accurate dances. A few people managed it.

Felix nestled back into his jacket and then into Sunshine's arms. "Papa taught me how to waltz. What a useless thing to know how to do. And the polka and the two-step and the schottische. He said, oh...bless him, he said, 'Felix, you can't expect to properly court anyone if you can't dance, it tells you a lot about a man, the way he dances.' Nice coming from a man who married the first person he kissed. I told him that, you know, I said 'Bibi took you on a carriage ride and you married them. I didn't know you did any dancing on carriages. Must have been cramped.' Bibi thought it was funny. Papa not so much."

He continued rambling on about his parents and how lucky his father was and how lonely Bibi must have been for all those years. He worked his way deeper into Sunshine's embrace until Sunshine was cradling him against his chest while his legs sprawled across the rest of the booth.

"How lonely Bibi would have been if Papa had died like he was supposed to. I know...Sunshine, I know he's the Devil, I know he's a...bastard, you know, an absolute snake. He's got all these schemes and plans and he holds on to those favors like a goddamn hoarder." Felix paused here to finish his drink and rubbed his face on the sleeve of Sunshine's fur coat. "But he's so sentimental. He acts like he does things for himself, but...really, I mean. He saves Papa and makes it so Bibi won't be alone anymore. He brings me to them and..." He clutched onto Sunshine's arm and drew in a breath that came out shaky. He sniffled.

"Specter."

"No, I just...I love him so much, Sunshine. I do, he's my papa and he's so *old* and I know he's tired. I know he is."

Sunshine let out a breath, preparing himself for what came next. He had, since the moment Felix had sprawled himself over his desk, known this was coming one way or another.

"What would I do without him?" Felix asked.

At least, that's what Sunshine thought he said. It came out choked. He held on to Felix as he sobbed into his coat. "Oh, now, Felix, people pass away. Especially humans."

"But he won't, Sunshine, he won't. He's staying for us. I know he is..." Felix continued, though he became repetitive and incoherent and eventually just cried.

Sunshine did his best to comfort him, but nothing he said helped. Eventually, he stopped talking.

A staff member, not the same girl who had waited on them so far but a stocky man, approached. "Everything okay?"

Sunshine nodded. He knew the owner made a point of saying the Diamond was a safe space for everyone. The bathrooms had posters for mental health and domestic abuse resources and the bar partnered with a nearby clinic to get clients tested for free.

The man had his eyes on Felix, though. "Everything okay?"

Felix had his face buried.

"Felix." Sunshine gave him a small shake.

He sniffled. "What?"

"The gentleman wishes to know if you're alright."

He looked up, eyes red and shiny, his nose running. "Oh. I'm fine." He took a cocktail napkin and wiped his face. It didn't suffice. "For fuck's sake, Sunshine, letting me make a mess of myself like this in public." He crumpled the napkin and tossed it on the table. "Get me another drink. I'll be right back."

Sunshine watched him toddle towards the bathroom; two more staff members stopped to ask if he was okay. Sunshine didn't get him anything more than water.

Felix frowned at the water when he came back. "I want to get drunk."

"You are drunk."

"I mean really lit."

"You're safely there. Drink your water." Sunshine pushed the glass towards him. "Please."

Felix scowled but drank it. He slouched back into the booth.

"Are you ready to go home?"

"We didn't even dance."

"You barely made it to the bathroom, I don't think you can dance right now."

He pouted.

Sunshine patted his leg. "We'll go a different night."

"No, we won't."

"Yes, we will."

"We never go out anymore."

Sunshine smiled. "You're better now. We'll start going out again."

Felix eyed him. "You promise?"

"Of course, I promise. Are you ready to go home?"

This time he nodded. He sucked down the rest of his water, crunched a few pieces of ice, then made for the door without waiting for Sunshine.

Sunshine caught him, steered him back toward the bar to close his tab, then walked him home. He suggested getting a cab, but Felix wanted to walk.

"I want to feel things again, Sunshine, let me feel things."

"Of course."

"I wanted to kiss someone," he declared to the stars. "It's been so long since I *felt* a kiss. Tasted it. You don't know how much of it is that...the taste, the smell, of another person. Until it's gone."

"If you want to kiss someone you shouldn't spend your night in a booth with me."

Felix reacted as if Sunshine had said something cruel. He

wouldn't speak to him for half the walk home. He stumbled on a bit of ice and Sunshine caught his arm to keep him upright. Felix sagged against him after that and babbled about how hard it was to date.

Sunshine offered the correct platitudes. He helped Felix upstairs and into bed, then took his station on the couch when Felix insisted that he had to stay over. Felix had a comfortable couch and Sunshine didn't mind sleeping on it at all.

Late Saturday morning, a hungover Felix presented Sunshine with toast and a mug of tea. He set them down on the coffee table and pushed Sunshine's legs off the couch so he could sit, too.

"You tolerate me so well when I get in these moods," Felix said.

Sunshine touched his arm, then took the tea. "And you make the best morning-after tea."

Felix gave his leg a pat. "I need a shower. Oh!" He sprung up and grabbed Sunshine's phone from where he'd plugged it in. "You got a call, you slept through it. It's from the office."

Sunshine sighed and caught it when Felix tossed it to him. He sipped his tea and listened to the voicemail from Jen. He called her back, got more details, then went over to the bathroom. Over the shower, he called, "I have to go to the office."

"What?"

"I have to—"

"I can't hear you, just come in!"

A billow of steam smothered him as he went in. He flicked on the exhaust fan. "You're going to get mildew."

"Is that what you came to tell me?" Felix asked, his voice echoing off the tile.

"No, I have to go into the office. It's that tunnel case. I guess that Ina lady is feeling better. Good enough to talk to me."

"You have to go right now?"

"Yeah. I guess she...she doesn't stay lucid for very long at a time. It's kind of now or never."

Felix made some indistinct gurgling and sloshing noises, then let out a pleased, groaning sigh. "I can't believe you're going back down there. You got so worked up last time."

"I wasn't worked up."

"You were so sweaty!" Felix laughed. "You always sweat when you get nervous."

Offer to come with me, Sunshine pleaded. *Don't let me go alone.*

He stood and waited.

"That's what you get for fucking around with necromancers."

"I don't..." Sunshine sighed. "I don't even know if they are necromancers."

"Listen, do you know anything about what it takes to get kicked out of one of the schools of magic?" Felix asked.

"Uh, no? Not off the top of my head."

"There's a forty-five-page document called *Violations of Ethics in Arcane Magic*. It details dozens of minor violations like love spells, mind-altering potions, and hexes. Slap on the wrist type things."

Sunshine settled in for the lecture, seating himself on the toilet.

"I'd be lying if I said I didn't have my share of minor violations stacked up. Then there's major violations, you know, murder and shit like that. And then, right at the very end, there are the High Crimes. Automatically expelled, cut off from all resources, every library and lab, even the official publishers won't sell to you. Or buy from you. It's academic death."

"You sound like your father, you know."

"Everyone always goddamn says that. It's pure discrimination. We don't all sound alike or look alike. Or even look like him!"

"No, Hiram, you idiot."

"Oh. Well. Anyway." More splashing then the smell of soap, mild and herbaceous. "Necromancy, weapons of mass destruction, time tampering, extraction of innate magic...there's about ten more, if you really want to know them you can read the paper yourself. Papa co-authored it so it's a little wordy in places, but it's hardly the densest thing out there. If you want something dense you should read his *Treatise on Structural Reparations*. I didn't even make it halfway through, I just donated a hundred dollars for each page that was left."

The shower turned off and Specter stepped out.

Sunshine handed him his towel.

"My point was that people who get expelled aren't people you should hang around."

"I'm not hanging around. It's a case."

Felix toweled his hair and left the pale locks sticking out at wild angles. "Have fun with your sewer people."

Sunshine stood. He returned to his own apartment, to his own shower, then back to the coffee shop where he'd met Sylvie the first time.

Things proceeded as they had the time before, although he managed not to lose track of her in the tunnel this time. He started to sweat long before they went underground, and he knew it was because Felix had pointed it out.

Sylvie walked him to the camper he had visited before. He noted the gleam of Dontell's Airstream in the distance.

"She's doing good today, but don't stress her out," Sylvie warned.

"Just a few questions."

He knocked on the door of the camper and he heard the distinct jangle of keys and deadbolts being undone. When the door finally opened, before him stood a woman in her forties or maybe just over the cusp into her fifties. She wore a robe, not a beautiful brocade one, but a thin, ratty one of green terrycloth. She had hard eyes and a thin mouth; her salt-and-pepper hair was clearly dirty and tied back in a half-hearted bun.

She frowned at him and he wanted to run. Despite all the roughness of her appearance, she worried him, and it had almost nothing to do with the knife in her hand or the capable way she gripped it.

"Hi. I'm Sunshine, with the—"

"I know who you are."

Carefully, he said, "I hope this isn't too much of an intrusion, I just wanted to ask some questions."

"Just questions?" she asked. "Questions have never been dangerous, have they?" She smiled aggressively. Her voice carried a faint foreign lilt. Eastern Europe somewhere.

He smiled back, unable to stop himself.

For a moment, the hardness of her expression softened. He could see the handsomeness beneath the grime and anger, and intelligence instead of shrewdness. Then her eyes narrowed, and she shook her head. "Go."

"Ma'am, please."

"Before I make you, get out. I don't fuck with whatever you just did." She leveled her blade at him.

He put up his hands. "I didn't do anything but smile."

"You did something."

"It's just what happens when I smile, that's all. It's, uh...it's beatific."

She grimaced but didn't make any further threats with her knife.

"Literally. I'm an angel," he continued. "My friend always says that I think my smile's gonna work on everyone but, it's uh, it's like puppies, right? It's just the way they look, they can't help it. You know that dumb look that angels always have on their faces in paintings? That's me all over."

She snorted and lowered the knife. "Bullshit. Angels keep to themselves; they don't run around playing Hardy boys."

"Other angels, yes, that's very true. But, well...I was..." He narrowed his eyes, trying to think of the best way to undersell that Felix had held him captive with the intent of killing him. "Waylaid. On a mission. And things went sideways and—"

"Sure, sure. You got hurt, some pretty girl nursed you back to health, and pussy's the one thing they don't have in Heaven," she guessed.

"Uh. Well. Everyone's sort of...liquid in Heaven anyway, so you can't really have sex if you don't have a body. Before the Fall, angels used to sneak onto the Citadel—that's where God makes our bodies, so it's the only place you can use yours, but after He replaced the Fallen, He closed up the Citadel."

She crossed her arms, the knife dangling against her side.

He shrugged. "It's the truth. No clouds or harps."

"I know."

"You know?"

She parted the top of her robe to show a scar down her chest. "Congenital heart defect. Died during reconstructive surgery. Eight years old. Doctor brought me back."

He nodded. Most near-death experiences were bogus, projections of a desperate mind, but every so often, a soul did dip a toe into Heaven or Hell before its time.

"So, ask your questions."

He fished a notebook and pen out of his jacket pocket. "Uh, Suzy was staying with you right before she passed."

"Before she was killed."

He nodded. "Of course. Had she been in contact with anyone different around then?"

"She..." Ina paused. She shut her eyes hard. "She went to the tunnel for something."

"Do you remember what?"

She shook her head. "No. Just...she promised she would be right back. That tunnel, it's long and it's deep, it goes further than an old subway tunnel should. People never go more than a mile or so in."

"Do you know how long she was gone for?"

Ina again shook her head. "Not long. I know it wasn't long. It was...lunchtime. Maybe? Maybe breakfast, when she left. I don't know. But by dinner..." Here she scowled. "I got hungry. Went to ask for help. People knew it was Suzy's week to look after me so that's when they started to look for her."

Sunshine nodded. "Thank you."

Ina grunted.

"Is there anything else you might remember? Not just about Suzy, about any of the other people who've been missing?"

"I said I'd talk to you because I'm the last person who saw Suzy, but most days I can't tell you the day of the week. I couldn't even tell you who else is missing. I'm about useless."

He shifted, not sure what to say. "Thank you, again."

She huffed.

"If you can think of anything else..." He fished a business card out from his pocket. "Or if you talk to anyone who does."

She hesitated, then took the card. She put her hand on the door. "I'll hold on to it."

He stepped back, understanding that he had been dismissed.

As he walked back to the diner, a gaggle of children raced past him. One of them stopped dead.

"Shiny!"

"Sunshine," he corrected.

"Sunshine," Justice repeated. "You're back."

A taller boy, lighter skinned than Justice with hair in braids, came over and tugged on Justice's sleeve. The other children continued away. He made several quick hand motions.

"Pharaoh says his grandma's still not back yet. And no one's gone to look for her," Justice provided.

Sunshine looked at the other boy, who might have been taller but couldn't have been any older than Justice. Hoping memory served, he signed, "I will look for your grandmother."

Pharaoh stared, his head tilted. He finger-spelled grandmother then provided the correct sign for Sunshine.

Sunshine repeated the sentence with the correct sign. He'd done it backwards the first time.

Pharaoh told Sunshine, "She went to look for her cat. Everyone's cat has gone missing."

Sunshine hesitated. He didn't know how he should proceed.

His ability to sign was rudimentary and rusty.

Pharaoh signed, "You can talk out loud. Mute. Not deaf."

"Oh."

Justice said, "You gonna go now?"

Every fiber of his being demanded that he return to the surface. Instead, he said, "I'll start. I don't know what I'll find though. It...it might not be good."

Pharaoh signed, "I know."

Justice put an arm around his friend's shoulder. He touched his head to the other boy's.

Sunshine crouched in front of them. "I don't know if I can fix things. But I'll do my best. Promise you'll stay away from the tunnel, though. And always be with a friend or a grown-up."

The boys nodded.

"Tell your friends, too."

They nodded again.

He sucked in a breath and made himself stand. "Wish me luck."

"Good luck," Pharaoh signed.

"Be careful," Justice added.

Again, Sunshine headed into the tunnel, his face feeling slick before he'd even walked for fifteen minutes. He was desperate for a shower after an hour. He walked and walked, nothing to light his way but a conjured orb he'd plucked from the myriad within the city. Garbage, debris, small skeletons. Rats, mostly.

He checked his phone and had no service. He hadn't thought he would, but he'd needed to check.

Two hours brought him to a slope. It started gentle but soon enough he was struggling to stay upright as he made his way down. He'd also nearly sweat through his jacket. He'd have to wash it.

The slope evened out, though, after about a half-mile.

He nearly stepped on the corpse. He stumbled back, then crouched to get a closer look.

It was small and shriveled. Dry. Like Suzy's had been. Not too far away was a small, desiccated cat.

At least she'd found her cat.

He shucked off his jacket and wrapped it around her. He sucked in a breath, though it only brought the musty, cool taste of the tunnel air and the slight staleness of the corpse to his tongue.

The whole way back he breathed in that smell, the dryness of her death, the hint of sourness from the flesh that hadn't dried.

He brought her back to the city. He knocked on the first door he came across, but no one answered. He knocked on a dozen doors and called for assistance at each one. Finally, he gave up knocking and brought her to the diner.

He lay her down on the counter and left his coat covering her face. To the appalled waitress, he said, "I don't know her name. I'm pretty sure she's Pharaoh's grandmother unless you've got a lot of missing old ladies..." He looked around. "I, uh...I'll be back. To finish figuring this out." He wanted to rub his face but stopped himself. He didn't know what had gotten on his hands. He didn't know what had killed her.

He left via the same rickety ladder he had last time.

He made it home.

Of course, he made it home. There wasn't any reason why he wouldn't. Nothing had happened. That hadn't been the first corpse he'd found or carried. He hadn't even known her, let alone cared about her.

He stripped as soon as he stepped inside his door, kicking off his shoes and throwing his clothes in a pile.

He sat in the shower for a long time. He sat and sat, not getting any happier or cleaner.

The door opened and his heart nearly stopped. He grabbed at the bar and started to haul himself up.

"You've been sitting in the shower for a goddamn hour, I wanted to make sure you weren't dead," Felix said. "You better not go slitting your wrists or anything like that, you know we're grandfathered into the lease on these apartments together."

Sunshine sat back down, the porcelain squealing as he settled.

Felix had smoothed talked his way into their lease when they'd first lived here. He'd really laid it on thick with the owner, touting all his connections and his parents. Two rooms at a fixed rate, for as long as they both lived there. The original rent had been rather high, expected given the location of the building. They'd scraped by for a while with occasional help from Felix's parents, but decades later, they had the best deal in Manhattan.

"Hey, I heard you squelching around in there, don't ignore me."

"I'm not dead."

Felix stuck his hand in the spray. "Water's cold. Come on, get out."

"I have to wash."

Felix sighed and turned off the shower, plugging the drain so the bath would fill. He pushed the curtain all the way back, grabbed the bottle of shower gel and squeezed a huge dollop until the water so it frothed up. "I heard you throwing things when you got home."

"All these goddamn renovations and the walls are still like paper."

The water inched up Sunshine's body, freezing cold. He clenched his teeth to stop them from chattering. He shivered relentlessly.

"Yes. That. And-or maybe I have one or two...you know, one or two *minor* monitoring charms in your apartment."

Sunshine looked up.

"Public areas only—"

"It's my apartment, Specter, they're *all* private areas."

Felix waved his hand as though he could sweep away the privacy violations. "Listen, technically we're living in the safest time-period ever, aside from, you know, the climate change and mass destruction type shit. Lower levels of individual crime. Murders and shit like that. But that doesn't change the fact that people are awful, and we deal with sketchy people in our line of work. And anyway, they've been there for years and clearly, you never noticed them, so what difference does it make?"

"Is that why you always show up whenever I make myself something nice for dinner?"

"All your night-to-myself dinners involve searing meat. I can smell that from next door, no magic needed," Felix said. He turned off the water and then sat on the edge of the bathtub. He swung his legs in, legs bare since he wore only boxers and a t-shirt. "Christ, it's cold, look at you just sitting there like a fucking iceberg."

From around his legs, warmth spread through the water, slow enough that it didn't hurt. Soon, the water steamed, redoubling the scent of the body wash Felix had added. Felix waggled his eyebrows, as he did when he felt like he'd done a particularly nice bit of magic. He wiggled his toes. "I learned to do it with my feet."

"You put your feet in my bath." He'd stopped shivering.

"I frequently put things into your bath, this time it happens to be my feet." Felix looked around and snatched a cup from the shelf beside the tub. He dunked it into the water and dumped it over Sunshine's head with no warning but, "Eyes."

Sunshine closed his eyes in time.

A squirt of shampoo followed the water. "You're going to have to do that yourself because as much as I'd love to just sink my fingers into those curls of yours, I'd rather not sear off my fingerprints in the process."

Felix provided similar commentary and prompting throughout the rest of the bath until he flipped the lever to let the water out. He fetched a towel and threw it over Sunshine's head and vigorously toweled off his hair.

Sunshine pulled back. "You're going to mess it up."

"Oh, like you're going anywhere."

Sunshine dried himself and did his best to undo what Felix had done to his hair. He got the curls into a reasonable state of order.

Felix did play with them a little bit, though, and Sunshine allowed it. "Will you tell me what has you all..." He gestured towards Sunshine in general. "However you are."

He made for his bedroom where Felix threw himself on to the bed as Sunshine searched for the right pajamas. Usually, it didn't matter what he wore, but currently, he needed the right ones. When he had them on, he sat on the edge of the bed and explained, more or less, what had happened and his promise to return.

"Sunshine!"

"What?"

"Were you not going to tell me any of this?"

Sunshine shrugged. "You have your lines."

"Yeah, alright, but we're *partners*. And friends. What am I supposed to do if you get yourself killed in some stupid tunnel?"

"Someone has to help."

"Obviously! You know, you're...fucking fluff for brains. Next time tell me when you're going down there."

"I *did* tell you."

Felix scowled. He rolled closer to Sunshine and headbutted his thigh. "Next time tell me you need me to come with you."

"You could have offered, you know. For once."

Felix sat up. "I did offer."

"Bullshit."

"I did. I told you that you always get sweaty when you're nervous."

Sunshine stared. He tried to pretend he was Felix, to figure out any way that he could twist what Felix had said into an offer to accompany him. He couldn't manage it and nearly strained himself in the process.

"Sunshine," he whined.

"You're ridiculous."

"You *know* I'd go! You do, you've got to fucking know that. Honestly, if you were any stupider, we couldn't be friends."

"Honest to fucking God—" Sunshine began.

"But we are friends! You know we're friends, you know I'd crawl down any stupid tunnel you needed me to, why didn't you just ask me?"

"Because you told me a thousand times that you don't deal with necromancers and that it was my mess to deal with," Sunshine reminded.

"Well, yeah." Felix rolled his eyes. "But, you know, that's...that's just saying things. You know I'd do it."

"Clearly not." Sunshine started to stand.

Felix grabbed his sleeve. "You know I'll do anything for you. Even necromancers. But you have to tell me if you need help."

Sunshine wanted to be angry. He wanted to tell Felix that the way he dealt with people was fucked up and that normal people didn't act this way. They didn't monitor their friends' apartments or casually stash dangerous artifacts and blackmail in their desks or offer to tamper with people's memories.

He wanted to be angry, but he couldn't.

Quietly, Felix said, "I was going to have a look at the body tomorrow anyway."

Sunshine didn't answer.

"Love doesn't know what to do with it and he keeps asking all these idiots to come consult. Like Thomas Pierce would know what to do." His fingers tightened on Sunshine's sleeve.

Sunshine stayed quiet.

"So, let me look at the body first. So we know what we're dealing with better."

"Fine."

"I'll do it tomorrow."

"Fine."

Felix scooted closer to him. He pressed his head against Sunshine's shoulder, the cloth of Sunshine's favorite sweatshirt providing a barrier he didn't know was unnecessary. "Relax. Eat something. Maybe watch some *X-Files*, that always makes you feel better."

"Alright."

Felix pulled away, studied him for a moment, then left.

Forty-five minutes later as he sat on the couch watching anything other than what Felix had suggested, Chinese food he hadn't ordered arrived at his door.

He took it, tipped the delivery guy, and peeked next door. Felix hadn't poked his head out.

Just like he'd wanted to be angry, he wanted to throw the food away, but he hadn't eaten since breakfast and wasting food was a stupid, asshole thing to do.

February 21
Sunday

A sour sort of unkindness hung about Sunshine that morning. It started when he spilled his coffee and then intentionally dashed the entire mug into the sink. He left the shards and the spill and stomped to the subway. He sat with his arms crossed, glowering at all the people who bumped against him. He didn't offer to give his seat to any of the more deserving people around him.

He greeted no one when he arrived and continued his stomping upstairs. Something about pounding the ever-loving shit out of the ground made him feel better.

Felix hadn't arrived yet. *Perfectly like him,* Sunshine noticed with scorn so bitter he surprised himself.

On Sunshine's desk sat a fruit basket.

He glowered at it.

Before he could throw it into the trash, Felix let himself in and said, "Oh, I heard you clomping around! Come with me to the basement, we have things to discuss." He made a ghoulish beckoning motion with his hands.

"You can't just buy a fucking fruit basket and expect things to be okay."

Felix's mouth hung open, then closed. He made an odd face, his eyebrows raised and his mouth in a downturned expression of confusion. "I didn't buy you a fruit basket." He closed the door. "A true gentleman sends a much more personalized apology."

"Like Chinese food?"

"Oh, come on, I special ordered it with no cabbage and extra bean sprouts and everything. And those little pork dumplings you like so much."

Sunshine glared.

"And it wasn't an apology, I mean...I knew you weren't going to make yourself anything to eat and I know how you get when you're worked up. Quit looking at me like that. Who's the fruit basket from?"

No, of course, it wasn't an apology. Sunshine snatched the card and opened it. "Thank you for finding my mother. You have a friend in the Enlightened City. Zina."

Felix blinked a few times. "Oh, god, I forgot that's what they call themselves." He approached and peeked at the card over Sunshine's shoulder.

Sunshine shrugged him off. He threw the card on the desk. "What's in the basement?"

"Uh. Well. I mean, you don't have to come down to the basement. I can just tell you. I thought it would be cool with visuals—"

"People are dead, Specter."

"And visuals are still cool!" Felix snapped. "I want like four different kinds of holograms at my funeral and I want all of them to be overwhelmingly graphic. We're meat suits, Sunshine, no matter how long we stay fresh for, but I'm trying to figure out what turned that particular meat suit into a big old pile of jerky so that more people don't die and it just so happens, o divine epitome of grace and mercy, that you are a visual learner and not an auditory one, which means that everything I say goes in one ear and out the other but pretty pictures stick around better in that nothing brain you've got rattling around in your skull."

Sunshine stared. Felix could get mean and teased Sunshine a lot, but these sorts of vicious outbursts were almost never aimed at him. He thought about all the photographs Felix always took during a case, the detailed and carefully labeled diagrams he would add to their shared notes, and his insistence on making PowerPoints for staff meetings.

He labored over those PowerPoints.

"But maybe I'm wrong. What the fuck do I know anyway?

Clearly, I have no idea how to communicate with you!"

"Alright."

"Maybe I should just...just leave you the fuck alone and you should leave me alone because if you don't know by now that—"

"Felix."

"I'm not going to help people who don't ask for it, Sunshine, I'm not going to dance around pretending I know what people need like I think I'm hot shit, *deciding* that I know what's best."

Sunshine sighed. He approached Felix, who threw a file folder full of photographs at him.

"And you can't just expect me to know what you need!"

Sunshine looped his arms around him. "Take a breath."

"Get off me."

"You're getting yourself worked up."

Felix wiggled around in his arms.

"Hurry up and calm down." Sunshine squeezed him tighter.

After a few seconds, Felix relaxed into the calmness Sunshine projected and squeezed him back, then elbowed him away. "Before you singe me."

Sunshine put a hand on his shoulder. "I told you I think we need a vacation."

"We're clearly both frayed," Felix agreed.

"Somewhere warm."

"Yes, somewhere warm." Felix leaned in and patted Sunshine's cheek, then rested his forehead against Sunshine's. "You know I love you."

"Of course."

"Good. Come look at this dead body with me, please." Felix stepped back and rubbed his forehead. He took Sunshine by the hand, just for a little bit, and walked downstairs with him.

From the absolute silence that bloomed into hurried shuffling and stilted small talk, it was clear that not only had Emil and Tate overheard them, they had been listening intently.

Emil whispered something to Tate.

She responded with, "You know I'm a fucking lesbian, right?"

Maybe the discomfort between the two of them had not been about Tate's vampire friend after all.

Love waited for them in the basement.

Felix pulled back the sheet from the corpse with a flourish. He purred, "You think I'm being disrespectful, but Suzy and I actually got quite close this morning and she was telling me all these fun secrets—"

Without meaning it and forgetting that Love was there, Sunshine asked, "Did you fuck that corpse, Specter?"

"If I wanted to fuck a corpse, I would have bent you over ages ago."

"Why is someone always getting bent over in these scenarios? Why can't we fuck in a bed like respectable people for once?"

As he folded the sheet, Felix explained, "Because we conduct these things in secrecy so that our disapproving families don't find out. Hence, you and I, one of us bent over, likely in a broom closet."

"We could do it up against the wall," Sunshine pointed out.

"Not with all those shelves in there!"

Love shifted uncomfortably. "Uh. So."

"Right." Felix took up a thin metal rod that Sunshine recognized as the one Felix used to point at the PowerPoint during staff meetings. He pointed to Suzy's abdomen. "Organs removed, just like a real mummy, right?"

"Yes," Love agreed.

"Wrong. No incisions." Felix pointed to several sets of puncture wounds on the body. "Stab wounds, correct?"

"Maybe?" Love asked.

"Maybe indeed."

"They're curved, about four inches deep," Love provided. "Two sets. Centered around the abdomen. Perimortem, likely what killed her."

"Unlikely. A healthy, young woman like her killed by a few stabs?" Felix said. "They're not over any essential organs."

"She bled out from the stab wounds, I meant," Love grumbled, none too pleased at being corrected. Felix interrupted autopsies with a frequency that must have irritated the doctor. "I'm a fucking doctor, not a goddamn coroner."

"Being a doctor makes you much more qualified than most coroners, Dr. Love, and it makes you much more useful when living people require assistance," Felix said. "And don't sulk. I hadn't noticed but you helpfully pointed out that there was something *in* the puncture wounds."

"What is it?" Sunshine asked because he wanted to know and because Felix had paused intentionally for that question.

"I don't know!" he declared with delight. He tossed aside his pointer and took up a cotton swab in a vial. "But it is *drenched* with magic. You don't see radiation like this anywhere that isn't getting heavy-duty doses of arcane shit. Labs, workshops, factories." He smacked Love's arm.

The doctor flinched.

"Go on, tell 'em what you said."

Embarrassed, Love sighed, "Big Old Mutant Ninja Vampires."

Felix grinned. "Or like...a big fucking snake! Probably not a snake, though, snakes swallow things and she wasn't swallowed. But you know...maybe a big...vampire thing. Some kind of freaky mutant. Explains why she's all dried up."

"Vampires don't drain people like that," Sunshine said. "Even when they drink them dead, they're never fully, uh, exsanguinated. Or shriveled."

"Hence the big, freaky mutant part. But wouldn't a snake be cool?"

Sunshine stared down at Suzy's body. "Did you know Tate was a lesbian?"

"I do not date employees and therefore it has never been relevant to me to know if she is a lesbian."

"No, I mean, this weird vibe between her and Emil. Do you think..." Sunshine glanced towards Love.

"I don't snitch," Love clarified.

"Do you think Emil's giving her a hard time about something? Or like, making her uncomfortable?"

"Well, he's obviously making her uncomfortable, but I thought it was because he doesn't like that Hank guy she's living with," Felix said. "But, uh...well. I can attempt to speak to one of them about it."

"Talk to Tate. I'll bring it up with Emil. He likes you less."

"No, no, let's do the thing where we both talk to one of them at the same time. That always works."

"Y'all plan that shit?" Love asked.

Felix glanced at Sunshine. "Mr. Sunshine and I confer about all things that fall under the purview of the Sunshine and Specter Paranormal Detective Agency." He made a broad, elegant sweep of his hand.

"That is, of course, why it's called the Sunshine and Specter Paranormal Detective Agency," Sunshine told Love.

"Although there was some debate about the matter. Mr. Specter does tend for a little more flashiness. A little drama."

"I get it from at least one of my parents, I'm quite sure."

"Listen, guys, y'all done doing your weird Shining Twins thing?" Love asked. He had stepped away from them.

"That reference barely checks," Felix told him. "You're dismissed."

Love didn't need to be told twice.

Felix draped the sheet over Suzy's body and returned her to the walk-in refrigerator. He murmured something solemn to her before he closed the door. He passed by Sunshine as he made for the stairs and tugged Sunshine's earlobe as he did so.

Sunshine had every ability to control himself at that moment, but he had no desire to do so. He caught up with Felix from behind and wrapped an arm around him.

"Christ, Sunshine, what are you doing?" he asked without making any effort to step away.

"I think it's called a hug."

Felix reminded, "You don't usually come up behind people to hug them."

"Should I stop?"

Felix leaned back against him.

They didn't have any skin touching. Never anything more than hugs and pats, moments of hand-holding. A kiss. Just one.

Almost two. Felix had gone back into to kiss him again, his lips still bleeding from the first one.

"I have to go. I have to call Papa." Felix stepped out of his arms. "I told him I'd call ages ago." He rushed upstairs.

Sunshine sat down and stewed in his thoughts. He wished he had a father to call. He needed advice and desperately. He didn't know what he wanted with Felix; he had never allowed himself to think about it.

Except he had thought about that kiss. A lot.

Too much.

He gave Felix room to breathe.

Later, he asked how Hiram was doing. They discussed what to do about Emil and Tate and went over what they knew about the tunnel mummies.

After lunch, they called Emil up to their office. Felix seated himself at his desk. Sunshine stationed himself behind his chair, one hand resting on the back of it.

Emil entered the office and lingered with the door open.

"Have a seat," Felix said.

"Close the door," Sunshine added.

Emil did both.

"We have noticed some discomfort between you and Ms. Murray in recent weeks," Sunshine said.

"We worry it may lead to disruptions in the workplace."

"I, uh." Emil swallowed. He was in his fifties, gray-haired and blue-eyed. He was tall and lanky, but slightly soft around the middle. He had rough features, though not unpleasant ones. He glanced around the room, uncomfortable in a way not familiar to him.

"It had not gone unnoticed that you often have observations that you wish to share with your colleagues but not with us."

"We are always interested to hear what our employees have to say. Such things are always informative."

"She's just. Well. She's mixed up with the wrong kinds of people. Young people don't listen. You know that," Emil explained.

They waited.

He squirmed. "I know it's not...you're not supposed to say things like this anymore, I know, and she's given me a hard-enough time about it, but you can't trust a vampire. They're addicts. She thinks he's her friend."

"I trust a good deal of vampires."

"I trust all sorts of creatures."

Emil struggled to say, "It's different. Vampires are...it's an addiction."

"No, Mr. Zito, that's incorrect. Sleeping pills are an addiction. Speed is an addiction. Heroin and alcohol, those are addictions. A substance one's body requires for nourishment is not an addiction," Felix said.

"Explain to us the exact wrongness of this vampire without using the word vampire or addiction," Sunshine requested.

"He's using her."

"She feels this way?" Sunshine asked.

"No, but—"

Felix asked, "He holds something over her?"

"No."

"He's harmed her?"

"Listen, I just know—"

"Ms. Murray is a woman of, I believe, twenty-six years. Young, yes, but not a child. She has always proven capable in her work. Calm, conscientious, efficient," Felix said. "And while we encourage comradery and friendship among our staff, it is important to remember that this is a workplace."

"It is unfortunate when things become unprofessional. There are boundaries we must maintain."

Emil clenched his jaw. Continued to clench it, really, he had started clenching it a while ago.

"Please keep these things in mind," Sunshine requested. "And send up Ms. Murray when you return downstairs."

He rushed out of the office.

Sunshine came around the front of Felix's desk and leaned against it.

When Tate came upstairs, she peeked her head in.

They greeted her with a smile.

"How are things?" Sunshine asked.

"Good."

They continued to smile.

"A little weird," she admitted. She forced a smile in return. "Awkward."

"Have a seat, please," Felix gestured to the chair.

She sat and smoothed the edge of her skirt.

"We did just speak to Mr. Zito. The awkwardness has not gone unnoticed," Felix said.

Her smile faltered. "Listen, uh...Emil, he's..." She sighed. "I have this friend Hank; he happens to be a vampire. He's a really nice guy. He's like a big brother slash fun uncle. Emil found out we're living together and he just, he won't believe me when I say we aren't involved romantically. Which, first of all, isn't any of his business, and second of all." She shrugged. "I don't like boys."

Sunshine nodded. "I understand this is difficult and invasive. We have spoken with Mr. Zito. If you'd like us to do more—"

"No, no. That's fine. Emil's just, you know, he's an idiot, but he's worried about me."

"Please keep us appraised of any changes," Felix requested.

She nodded, then shrugged, and smoothed her skirt again. "He doesn't always have the nicest stuff to say about you two. Kind of like you're case-and-point why humans shouldn't get involved with creatures."

They glanced at each other.

"Everyone bitches about their boss but, there's bitching then there's being mean."

Felix nodded. "Thank you."

"Please let us know if you need anything." Sunshine motioned towards the door.

She gave another strained smile and left.

Sunshine settled himself more fully on Felix's desk. "Staff meeting?"

"Staff meeting."

Sunshine nodded.

"Outside consultant," Felix proposed.

Sunshine grinned at him. "Melody Blood?"

Felix returned his grin. "Melody Blood," he said with such joy and self-assurance that Sunshine wanted to laugh.

Felix called Melody Blood and set up a day for her to come in, then sent out an email to the staff announcing the time and date of the next staff meeting. *No exceptions*, warned the email.

Later in the day, Jen came upstairs to tell them that the mage whose bracelet they'd found had called several times and sounded irate.

"Put him through," Felix said.

He took the call and Sunshine delighted in watching him give this mage the run-around about the bracelet.

Sometimes it was the easiest thing in the world to know what he wanted and that was to watch Felix be a scamp for the rest of his life.

They would finish up whatever the Enlightened City case required of them and they would go on vacation. Two weeks, at least, somewhere warm and quiet. Somewhere with a beach so soft and white that Felix would blend in if he laid down. They would lounge around and swim and for the first time, he wouldn't have to keep a safe distance or sit around in pants on a ninety-degree day.

He started to look up plane tickets.

He started to think if he should tell Felix and how he should tell Felix that they could touch each other.

Casually, he decided. It had to be casual. Not a big deal, nothing changed between them. Friends, but now friends who could interact normally.

Felix peeked over his shoulder at one point while he browsed Airbnb and said, "I like that one. Is it right on the beach?"

"I think so."

He wrapped one of Sunshine's curls around his finger. "I'm going out to talk with this bracelet guy."

"Be safe."

Felix tapped the button on his jacket. "I think he might be trafficking creatures."

Sunshine looked up.

"I'm going to try to get him to let me in on it. If I can get him to say anything, I'll pass it over to the Academy of Magic. They know how to get in contact with the courts for stuff like this."

"Please be careful."

Felix gave him a small, half-hearted smile. "I really hope I'm wrong."

Felix usually was not wrong. Sunshine squeezed his arm. "I hope so too."

When he returned, he popped the button off his jacket and tossed it onto Sunshine's keyboard.

Sunshine had a passing familiarity with these button recorders. Felix had worked out the charm sometime in the sixties when he'd gotten sick of carrying around a tape recorder. He started to turn on the playback.

Felix said, "Don't. Not right now."

He put the button down in his paperclip container, where it wouldn't get lost.

Felix lingered by his desk. "You should do that thing."

"Hmm?"

"I think you called it a hug."

Sunshine got up and hugged him.

"Strange customs your people have. I think I could grow used to it, given enough time," Felix said into his chest.

He tightened his arms and kissed the side of Felix's face.

Instead of pulling away, Felix adjusted himself so his cheek rested against Sunshine's shoulder.

After a while, Sunshine asked, "You need anything?"

Felix straightened up but didn't go far. "No."

His face told a different story.

Sunshine barely moved.

Felix stepped back right away. "I can't fucking have this conversation with you right now. We both know how it ends."

"Felix, I—"

"Sunshine, please," Felix begged. He grasped on to Sunshine's hand. "Please."

The waver in his voice effectively took away any choice Sunshine might have had in the matter. They'd been not having this conversation for decades, but something had finally changed. Still, Sunshine changed the topic. "Do you want me to bring that to the Academy for you?"

"No, no, I'll do it. You wouldn't even know where to bring it." Felix waved him away and retrieved the button.

"I am capable of following simple instructions."

Felix shook his head.

"You could draw me a map."

That made Felix smile. He rolled his eyes like it wasn't funny. "Shut up. I'll see you later."

They spent the next few days quietly existing around each other. Not talking much but going about routines they had established so firmly that no words were needed to accomplish them. They booked flights and a small, beachside house.

Felix went shopping and Sunshine stayed home trying to find his sword.

They would be going back to the tunnel on Tuesday and he had no wish to go unarmed. Heaven had dispatched him to Earth with a sword and a knife. The knife he'd lost, but he kept its replacement beside his bed, just in case, but the sword he kept in the back of his closet.

At least, he could have sworn he kept it there.

He found it eventually but didn't recall putting it under his bed. He also didn't recall the last time he'd used it, so those two unremembered events likely coincided. He honed the edge and that of his knife.

Anything could have awaited them in that tunnel. Hopefully, it was something manageable.

A normal-sized mutant vampire.

Or even a slightly larger than average snake or two.

"You should wear your armor," Felix said.

Sunshine screamed, jumped up, and leveled his knife in his direction.

"You're very easy to sneak up on these days."

"I could have stabbed you."

Felix raised an eyebrow. He snagged Sunshine's sword off the floor and unsheathed it. He swung it around aimlessly and gracelessly. He wrinkled his nose and returned it to where he'd found it. "I meant it about the armor, we don't know what's down there."

"What about you?"

"Well, obviously, casters wear cloth and go to the back of the party."

Sunshine scowled and returned to honing his knife.

"Get some sleep tonight. Let me know if you can't."

In bed, Sunshine tossed and turned for a little while. He named the birds on the recording and that pulled him under.

Morning found him alert, but not exactly tense. He put on his armor but pulled a jacket on over it. Wearing a golden cuirass would draw a lot of stares and carrying a sword along with it would make him look like a maniac. He stuffed that into a duffle bag.

Felix talked the whole time they walked. He quieted once they met up with Sylvie and started whispering suspicions under his breath to Sunshine.

In the Enlightened City, a few people waited for them, including Dontell.

He carried a staff in his hand and Felix stared at him.

Dontell did cut a striking image, like something off the cover of a wondrous fantasy adventure novel, but Sunshine felt a funny twist of envy in his gut.

"Can I help you?" the mage asked.

Felix grinned. "I like your jacket."

Dontell frowned.

"Are you a wizard? Are we LARPing right now?" Felix continued, still grinning.

"Stop," Sunshine said.

"I didn't know we were wearing *outfits*. I would have worn an outfit."

Felix had very clearly already put together an outfit for this adventure. He wore all black, a long, structured wool coat, tight jeans, Docs, and a shirt with a standing collar. He looked sort of like a murderer; not a real one, but a cross between a TV vampire and the bad guy in a weirdly sensual thriller.

It worked on him, no doubt.

Or maybe it just worked for Sunshine.

While Felix harassed Dontell, Sunshine took out his sword and buckled on his sword belt. He felt stupid in a cuirass and jeans, but he would have felt even stupider in a leather skirt. He still had that, too, just as shiny as the cuirass.

God had designed his crop of soldiers with something distinctly Greco-Roman in mind. Like marble statues gilded and brought to life.

Sunshine had toured the Mediterranean once, seen the generic handsome faces and toned bodies, the same curls on every statue. A deep worthlessness had gripped him then because he had known, just known in his heart that he and the others had not even been cast from a lovingly made model. They had been lifted wholesale. Not an ounce of originality or creativity.

"What's your favorite dungeon?" Felix asked.

"Felix, please, let's not," Sunshine said.

Felix got in one more jibe but left it alone after that.

They sketched out a rudimentary plan. Stay close, stay calm, this signal for stop, this one for go.

In total, six of them set out down the tunnel.

Dontell conjured a light so they could see.

Felix conjured a fancier one.

Sunshine walked in front of them. Sylvie walked beside him; he didn't think it was his place to tell her she'd be safer walking with the others. She had a baseball bat over one shoulder and the definition in her arms suggested she could slug the shit out of someone.

"So," she said softly. "Mutant vampires."

"We don't really know. That's just a guess. It might have even been a joke," Sunshine said. "How far does this tunnel run?"

"Six miles until it's too small for people."

"This...this wasn't a subway tunnel, was it?"

"I think there's a reason they put up a wall between our space and the Worth Street Station. As far as we figure, they wanted to make a little underground shopping plaza off Worth Street. Those were kind of stylish for a while."

"There's one in Barcelona," Felix chimed.

"But this tunnel." Sylvie gestured to the area around them. "It's not the same construction as the area where we live. It's..."

"Older?" Sunshine guessed.

"Newer!" Felix said.

Sylvie glanced back. "I don't think I got your name."

"Felix Specter." He edged his way forward and offered his hand.

She frowned at him. "I...Do I know you?"

"You've probably seen me. I've done talks at NY-AM," he offered easily. "And a few other places, if that's not where you went to school."

"Who says I went to a school of magic?" she asked.

"The fact that you're living in a subway tunnel full of other dropouts," he answered gamely.

"I'm a witch," she answered.

"A witch? What's a witch doing living with these degenerates? I mean, I know witches have their, uh, taboos, but the Hag Councils don't usually exile people."

"I haven't been exiled," Sylvie told him.

"So you live down here for the fun of it?"

"It's not any of your business why she lives down here," Dontell said.

"Dontell, mind your business," Sylvie said. "I live down here because I like it. It's quiet and safe—"

Felix said, "Except for the freaky sewer mutants."

"It's not connected to a sewer," Dontell said.

"And no one cares what I do down here. People get nosy and that gets annoying."

Felix grinned. He sidled up to Sunshine and whispered, "You know what witches get nosey about?"

Sunshine pushed him away. "Honestly, Specter, this is why you haven't got any other friends."

"I have friends."

"So, wait, then what do I know you from?" Sylvie asked.

"Do you read much?" Felix asked. "Academic things."

"Not arcane stuff."

"Hmm. Alright. I guess it's a mystery, then. You were saying about the tunnels?"

"They're newer."

Felix beamed. "I thought so."

"Does he ever shut up?" Dontell asked Sunshine.

"No," Sunshine answered.

Felix scooted ahead of them in the tunnel.

So far, they had not gone deep enough into the tunnel that Sunshine expected anything dangerous, so he let him pass.

Some of the others chatted among each other, quiet and mostly worried speculation about what lay ahead.

They came to the slope and Sunshine called, "Felix!"

Felix glanced back.

"Come back with the group."

He glanced ahead then returned to the group. "What?"

"I found the body a little way up from here."

Felix peered at the slope. "It gets steep. You think she rolled down?"

"It evens out after a while."

"How far do we go?" someone from the back of the group

asked.

"As far as we need to," Felix answered.

Sunshine and Sylvie headed down first with the others spread out like a V behind them. Dontell's staff made a soft noise against the floor as they went, sometimes knocking into something.

No one spoke anymore.

They passed by the cat.

Sunshine loosened his sword in its sheath.

Quietly, Dontell said, "This is where we found Suzy."

They all murmured something vague and sympathetic.

They stopped around four miles in, passing around water and snacks. Felix dropped bits of orange peel on the ground as he wandered around, poking at bits of debris on the floor.

"So," he announced to the group.

They turned to look at him.

"I'm not, ah, uh, a bug expert or anything," he continued around an orange slice, "But I think spiders don't usually come in bright green." He had his eyes fixed on a heap of garbage.

"Not that I'm aware of," Sunshine agreed.

"What about bright green and the size of, let's say, a women's size eight shoe?"

Felix tossed Sunshine his orange, crooked fingers on both hands, and entered into a slow, controlled crouch. When he stood, he had a large, green spider encased in a small forcefield.

The spider skittered around.

"Are the mole people familiar with this kind of spider?" Felix asked, displaying the spider more clearly for them.

Everyone shook their heads.

Dontell moved his light closer to the spider and it flipped out, scurrying and leaping around. He moved it back and as the light faded, the spider calmed. He repeated the process.

"Probably why you haven't seen them in Lightning Bug City," Felix guessed. "I'd really like to touch it."

"Why on Earth—" Sunshine began.

"Because I can't examine it through a forcefield, obviously. But like, I don't know, bright green spider, corpses laced with magic radiation...Sounds like good odds to me."

"It's a big spider but Suzy...she wasn't a pushover," Dontell said.

"Spiders smaller than this have killed people," Felix said. He peered at the spider. "But, uh, doesn't exactly explain the size of the wounds on the body."

Felix released the spider and watched it skitter away.

They all watched it scurry deeper into the tunnel.

"We should follow it, right?" Sylvie asked.

"Seems like it." Felix snuffed out the light he'd conjured. He stood. "Uh. You all should hang back and keep your lights dim. Sunshine and I should be able to see if you do that."

"You want it dark?" Sylvie asked.

"I feel like yes," Felix confirmed.

Sunshine didn't agree. He wanted to flood the tunnel with light, or better yet, leave. He followed along when Felix tugged on his sleeve. He linked hands with him. "Are you sure about this?"

"Go big or go home." Felix took his hand back.

They picked along in the dark, both of them able to see better than their human companions would have been. Sunshine counted the humans lucky. They didn't see the shriveled-up rats, cats, and pigeons that littered the ground. He tried his best not to step on them but every so often felt bones crunch beneath his feet.

It took about fifteen minutes before Felix grabbed Sunshine's arm and put up his hand to tell everyone else to stop. The sound of footsteps behind them stopped. Dozens of bright green spots dotted the walls, ceiling, even the air in front of them.

Something much larger loomed further back. At least the size of a trash can; not the lid, but the entire trash can, and that was just the body.

"Let's really hope these are the kinds of spiders that eat their mates," Felix whispered, close enough that Sunshine could smell his breath, still citrusy. "What's the plan, soldier boy?"

"We should fan out and try to pick off the smaller ones. Quietly. Without disturbing them. Deal with the big one last."

"I'll go tell the others." Felix turned back.

Almost as soon as he turned around someone behind them screeched.

Sunshine whipped around to see that a spider had descended from the ceiling to dangle right in front of one of the tunnel dwellers.

Sylvie batted the thing away from her.

All the other spiders exploded into action, crawling and scurrying everywhere.

"Lights!" Felix cried, throwing up his own orbs.

More orbs illuminated the scene, showing the thick strands of webs that delineated the spiders' lair.

Some of the small spiders fled. Others skittered towards the group.

Sunshine drew his sword and stabbed the first one that came close enough.

The big spider in the back stayed still. Not motionless, though. Just...still.

Sylvie swung at and missed another one and Dontell squashed one with his staff. The other two, Sunshine had never caught their names, made their moves.

Felix, of course, was tossing fireballs and conjured darts like an absolute showoff.

He did look good doing it.

He'd brag about the darts later if anyone so much as mentioned them, saying that none of the other demons he knew had figured how to do it. "Oh, sure," he'd say, "Demons who can conjure glass always turn a little profit making it into baubles and conduits for mages, but this is more fun."

Sunshine hacked a few more of the little spiders in half but kept an eye on the ones retreating.

The more that retreated, the more the big spider moved.

It began to descend, one thick, spiky leg at a time. Its eyes, the size of saucers, glinted as it approached, the glow of Felix's fireballs lending them an eerie glow.

"Incoming!" Sunshine warned.

Everyone else turned to look.

Despite its size, the thing didn't move slow. It barreled right towards the closest intruder, which happened to be Sunshine.

He scurried back, hoping for better ground.

The spider lashed out a few times and he parried its legs with his sword.

Felix hurled a shard of glass the size of a hand at it. The glass sunk into the spider's side and it turned towards Felix.

Sunshine took the chance to slash at it, slicing one of its legs.

"Move!" Dontell cried.

Felix and Sunshine both scrambled away towards the group.

Dontell twirled his staff, called out a chant, and swung towards the spider. It sent a crackling, explosive blast towards the creature, effectively taking off two more legs and making the thing stumble.

Felix let out an excited cry. "Wow! Oh, holy shit, what was that! Is that what you got kicked out for!"

Dontell scowled at him. "I can only do it twice before the staff breaks."

"Aim better this time, then," Felix advised.

Sunshine got the feeling Dontell might turn the staff on Felix before he turned it on the spider.

Dontell pulled in a breath, closed his eyes, then repeated the spell.

This time he caught the spider squarely in its side. The exoskeleton burst, spending out a spout of goop that thankfully didn't spurt onto any of them.

Felix let out another crow of delight.

Dontell tossed the shattered staff onto the ground.

"Hot damn," Felix said. He picked up the pieces and immediately began to examine them.

Sunshine skewered one more spiderling. "We should get these little ones cleaned up."

The group, except for Felix, spread out and did their best to eliminate the remains of the spider nest.

They didn't know how many had gotten away but agreed that patrols would come down here to check things out more regularly to make sure that a new nest didn't crop up.

Felix rattled off a few compliments on the spell and asked to keep the staff, apparently ready to make friends with Dontell.

Dontell snatched the pieces out of his hands.

"I bet I could get it to go three times," Felix declared quietly.

"Oh yeah? And you'd do that with real magic or just the demonic shit living inside you?" Dontell asked.

Sunshine started wiping the blade of his sword on a kitchen towel he had brought expressly for this purpose.

The others took time to breathe and recover. No one had been hurt by the spiders, but Sylvie had accidentally wailed another tunnel dweller in the ribs during the fray. Someone had tripped and skinned an elbow.

Felix scowled. "It's all the same magic."

Dontell snorted.

Felix made a face. "Pullman lays it out pretty clearly in *Examinations*, it's all the same energy, it's just how you tap into it."

"One of them takes skill and discipline and knowledge. The other shit is just...wild. Unmanageable."

"The last statistics report shows that mages, not witches or innate magic users, are three times more likely to engage in magic that harms both themselves and others."

"And who publishes those?" Dontell challenged.

"The World Commission on Magical Studies?"

Dontell smirked. "You don't think those so-called reports might be biased? Everyone knows that the Commission's been taking bribes from the Hag Councils and Hell for the past three decades. And we all know that the university in Pickering won't say shit against demons, considering how far up that demon's ass the owner is. Anything that comes out of there is worthless."

Felix's eyes widened. He opened his mouth, closed it, then gently informed Dontell, "That's like...Zionist conspiracy theory level paranoia."

Dontell opened his mouth.

"No, that's...I don't argue with crazy people, there's no dignity in it," Felix cut him off.

Dontell seethed but didn't push the matter any further, especially not after Sylvie shook her head at him and said, "Not worth it."

They trudged back to the Enlightened City in awkward silence.

Before he left, Sunshine tried to say goodbye to Justice and Pharaoh but all he managed to do was wave before Dontell placed himself between Sunshine and the boys.

"You know how to get out," Dontell reminded. His eyes stayed on Felix as he spoke.

Sylvie put a hand on Sunshine's arm and walked him towards the ladder. She confided, "Listen, Dontell can get a little outspoken, you know, we're not all that..."

"Aggressively prejudiced towards inhumans?" Felix supplied.

She sighed. "Anyway. Thanks for the help."

Felix started to climb the ladder without another word.

Sunshine stayed a little longer. "I hope things are safer now. You guys will want to look out for whoever's letting off all that magic. Things like that don't happen overnight and where there's radiation, there's bound to be complications."

"More than just enormous spiders?"

He nodded.

She thanked him again.

Once they reached the surface, Felix said, "As if Hell would bother to bribe the Commission."

"I know."

"This is why I hate conspiracy theories, you know. People think they're all silly nonsense, but like…people actually believe them."

"I know."

"It's fucking racist."

Sunshine snagged his arm as he started to walk away, not to stop him but to stay by his side. "We're going on vacation."

"That doesn't fix it."

"Three more days. Private house, white sand beach."

"And you know, you can't tell a black guy he's being racist because, well, obviously, but like shit! I don't know a better word for it. It's…I mean, it's not institutionalized in our broader society like anti-black racism is but it's certainly pretty present among the people who know about creatures. I mean, fucking…Europe purged us a few hundred years ago!"

"Europe does like to purge things," Sunshine agreed.

"What do you say to that?"

Sunshine tried to think of a good answer, but could only settle on, "Maybe just tell him it hurts your feelings."

Felix wrinkled his nose.

"I mean." Sunshine shrugged. "He'd probably understands what it's like to be considered dangerous without someone getting to know him first."

Felix snorted, but then the harshness of his expression softened a little. "Yeah. And his girlfriend just died a pretty horrible death…"

"People lash out when they're hurting," Sunshine agreed.

Felix sighed.

"You're pretty good at that," Sunshine tried to joke.

Felix let out a moan.

Desperate to have him look a little happier, Sunshine said, "We're going on vacation."

Felix grunted.

"Waves crashing on the beach. Moonlight on the water. Sunset with tropical drinks and…and scallops."

"Ugh, scallops, are you going to give me food poisoning again?" Felix demanded.

"Little tiny toothpick umbrellas."

"Reading in a hammock," Felix added.

Sunshine knew he hadn't erased the hurt Dontell's comments had dredged up, but he also knew he probably couldn't. The Community had its rifts just like the wider world, but that was why people like Melody Blood existed. Maybe this staff meeting would ease just a little of the sting.

February 26
Friday

They both packed light, a few changes of clothes and toiletries. Sunshine wore jeans and a sweatshirt. Felix had dressed for their destination in itty-bitty shorts, a tight tank top, and a Hawaiian shirt he wore unbuttoned over the tank top.

Before they even got out of the apartment building, he'd run back to pull a pair of sweatpants over the shorts.

By the time they got to the airport, Sunshine had surrendered his sweatshirt.

Felix's warming spell worked, but it was a spell, not a miracle.

Felix yammered excitedly the whole drive to the airport and as they waited to board. Within twenty minutes of take-off, he fell asleep, hood up and slumped against Sunshine.

Sunshine watched a movie but mostly thought about how these two weeks would go. Should he tell Felix right away? Or wait until they had both unwound? How could he even start a conversation like that?

If he said, "We should talk," or "I want to tell you something," Felix would be on high alert, sick with worry. He'd have to just say it, casually, without preamble, at some point. Over dinner, "I had the wards removed," or while they were sunbathing, "I can touch you now if you need help with that sunscreen."

He tried not to think about how Felix would react. Hopefully, something quiet and understated, something like, "Good, can you get my back for me then?"

The bustle and mild confusion of getting from the airport to their house broke the endless cycle in Sunshine's mind.

Felix stripped down to his original outfit as soon as the plane landed. It drew looks, for sure. He peered eagerly out of the taxi window, pointing out the clear blue of the sky, the palm trees, the chickens roaming the streets.

The house they'd rented had two bedrooms, both mostly taken up by the bed, a tidy kitchen, and a small sitting room, as well as a bathroom and a porch. The whole thing had been decorated in pale neutrals with the occasional pop of blue. Comfortable, clean, but nothing luxurious.

Felix dropped back, poked around, and asked, "Is there much of a nightlife here?"

"I didn't check."

"Of course, you didn't."

"What's that supposed to mean?" Sunshine asked.

"It means you treat dating like a chore," Felix said, "And you treat sex like...Well. Like I don't know what. But it's certainly something." He took his bag and went to unpack. He emerged fifteen minutes later and said, "Like an afterthought."

Neither description was inaccurate.

"You should get back out there. Been more than a month since you and Kari called it quits."

Sunshine shrugged.

Felix checked the cabinets and fridge, found them empty, and started making a grocery list. He leaned against the counter to do this, bent over at the waist and resting on his elbows. He had one leg bent and the other bearing most of his weight. He glanced up after he'd penned *eggs, bacon, butter, bread, vodka, orange juice.* "Maybe you..." He pursed his lips then returned to his list.

"Maybe what?"

Felix shook his head.

"Don't do that."

Felix sighed, turned around, and crossed his arms. He shrugged. "I don't know, you've always been pretty amenable to, uh, you know, when I want to dress up, or you'll come with me to clubs." He licked his lips. "Maybe try dating a guy."

Sunshine stared. "I..."

"No, I mean. Just an idea. We've always...You know. There's that tension. I'm not saying that you're not or that you are, but if..."

Felix did not usually mince words concerning an idea like this. He'd never skirted around the topic of sex and sexuality. With parents like his, how could he?

Sunshine couldn't watch him flounder, it was painful. Like watching a fish flop around on the floor. "It doesn't go any better with men."

"I don't mean just hooking up, straight guys do that all the time," Felix dismissed his confession out of hand.

"I haven't been deeply embroiled in a same-sex relationship that definitely violates the boundaries of friendship for the better part of a century because I'm in denial about liking boys, Felix."

Felix shoved the list in his pocket. "Yes. Well. We can't. And I don't even think I'd want to. So, you should find someone else who can."

"What if—"

"Help me find my wallet. I need to eat, and I need alcohol. And to not talk about this. We're supposed to be on vacation, *don't* make it weird."

Sunshine helped him find his wallet.

They walked into town, acquired both food and alcohol, and walked back.

Sunshine made lunch and Felix made drinks. They consumed both, then finally went down to the beach. They spent the afternoon in the water, returning to the house only to make more drinks or food.

Sunshine lounged in a hammock watching the sunset over the ocean.

Felix stood beside him. He'd been talking for ages, one hand on his hip, a drink clutched in his other hand.

Sunshine had tuned him out, he didn't even know what he was talking about. It could have been Hiram's newest research paper or the plot of a book.

"It really is beautiful here," Sunshine told him.

"Don't interrupt me."

"You should watch the sunset."

"I can see it."

"No, you should watch it."

Felix huffed but turned his eyes towards the sunset. He stopped talking. He swayed. His eyes drooped.

"Come lay down."

He shot Sunshine a dirty look.

"Just for a minute."

"Fine, but I'm not getting up, you are." Felix put his glass in the sand and crawled into the hammock with all the grace of someone made entirely of elbows and knees. As soon as he'd settled, he fell asleep.

He smelled like sweat and salt, and a little bit like vomit. He must have gotten sick one of the times he'd gone up to the house to make more drinks.

Sunshine decided to get up early to make him breakfast and tea.

The decision took him nowhere. He fell asleep, too, lulled by the sound of the waves and the sway of the hammock, by the smell of Felix, even if it was a little sour, and by the sticky warmth of his body. They both remained in the hammock until the sun roused Felix.

Felix, upon waking, slapped Sunshine on the chest. "What the fuck!"

Sunshine squinted and raised an arm to fend off further attacks.

"What the fuck, Sunshine!" Felix ran his hands over his face and arms, checking for the burns that should have been there. According to everything he knew, last night should have killed him. He pressed his hand against Sunshine's chest, skin against skin, and waited for the burn.

It didn't come.

They stared at each other.

"How?" Felix demanded. He pressed harder against Sunshine's chest.

"When I warded myself, I didn't know what it would mean."

"How. Did. You. Undo. It."

"I made a deal."

Felix screeched. "He's the...Fucking! Sunshine, he's the Devil!"

"I know."

Felix sighed, sat back, and rubbed his face. "A deal for what?"

"Favors."

"Plural?"

"Yes."

Looking like the answer might make him vomit, Felix asked, "How many?"

"Three."

"Three!" Felix shouted. He climbed out of the hammock, tripped, and nearly dumped Sunshine out as well. "Three!"

Sunshine got up and followed him as he took off towards the house. "I had to do something."

"You'd have been better off going back to Heaven at this point."

"If I went to Heaven, I'd never make it back to Earth."

"Just because he's my dad doesn't mean he'll be nice to you. It was stupid. He can make you do anything. And he does, you know. He *makes people do things.*"

Sunshine followed him through the door he'd slammed. "Felix, I had to do something."

"Just...really stupid." Felix sagged into a chair at the kitchen table. He rubbed his eyes.

"I'm sorry."

"Shit."

"Felix."

"Don't...don't say you did it..." Felix sighed and ran his hand through his hair. "You know, this doesn't mean. I'm not going to."

Sunshine sat at the other chair. "It doesn't mean anything except that I won't burn the ever-loving shit out of you anymore. Everything else is already there. Or hasn't happened yet."

"I'm not going to fuck you."

"I don't think I asked you to."

"No, I mean, you don't get it. Like, this isn't an adjustment period type of thing. It's not going to happen. Ever. Just because I kissed you once doesn't mean...it doesn't mean anything." Before Sunshine could say anything, Felix got up. "I need to take a shower."

Sunshine let him go.

Of course, he let him go, what was he supposed to do? Follow him? Stop him from leaving?

He made breakfast and tea. He had to rifle around through Felix's things to find the herb packets for the tea, but they had gone through each other's things plenty of times.

Felix emerged from the shower looking soggy and frowned when he saw the contents of his bag strewn on the couch.

"I'll clean it up later," Sunshine offered.

"I'm still mad at you." He began to pick up.

Sunshine went over to help.

Felix snatched a Ziploc bag out of his hand. "Could you try not to handle my personal items?"

Sunshine frowned and eyed what Felix had snatched from him. Just lube. Felix knew the spell to conjure lubricant popular with most in the Community, but he'd freaked out enough human dates with it that he used the regular stuff with those partners. The fact that Sunshine knew those details meant such items had long since lost any private connotations.

He picked up a few of the other items and placed them in his bag. "I made breakfast."

"Good for you."

Sunshine rezipped his bag. "Can we at least talk?"

"About what? I told you I wasn't going to fuck you."

"That's what I want to talk about."

"Why? I don't owe you an explanation."

Sunshine said, "No, of course not. I just wanted to know why you think that's what I'm after."

"Uh, because you're a man."

"I'm an angel."

Felix snorted. "Fine, man, angel, whatever you are, you've got a dick. You think one kiss means I'll let you do whatever you want."

"No."

"And I won't you know, I don't...I don't even. It's none of your business. Things were fine the way they were, Sunshine."

"Our relationship was fine. *Is* fine. You're my best friend and I don't care if anything between us stops there. But I don't want to hurt you anymore. Warding myself was a stupid, fearful thing to do but I'm not the person I was then. I haven't been for a long time."

Felix stared at him warily.

"It had to be done."

"I suppose it did," Felix admitted sourly.

"Please come eat breakfast."

"I threw up in the shower."

Sunshine made a sympathetic face. "I made tea."

"Thank you."

"I'm sorry I went through your stuff."

Felix snorted. "It's fine. Not like we have any secrets, anyway. I mean, other than you making ill-advised deals with my father."

As they settled down to breakfast, Sunshine offered, "You know he had to, like, physically rip the magic off my skin."

"Oh."

"Everywhere."

"Oh." Felix's eyes widened. "Everywhere?"

Sunshine nodded.

"My dad touched your dick, didn't he?"

Sunshine nodded. "And he did that smile. You know. The weird one. And I thought he was going to bite it off. Like I'm standing there in my kitchen, we're both covered in blood, he's holding my dick like it's a, a used tissue and he just...smiles. And I thought he's gonna bite my fucking dick off."

Felix cackled.

When they'd eaten, Felix slumped back in his chair and stretched. His feet bumped against Sunshine's; he let them linger. He usually did for a little while. He smiled, but it didn't last. He sat up slowly.

"What's wrong?"

"I'm so used to letting go before it starts to hurt. I never even had to think about it anymore, I got so good at the timing." Felix dragged his mug of tea over and drank the last little bit. "I didn't think you'd ever undo it."

Sunshine wanted to take his hand.

"I always thought you kind of liked it. That safety net between us. We'd flirt or you'd let me put you in costumes, but you never had to worry that I'd try to make a move on you. I didn't know if it was because I'm a man or a demon or what, but I knew you wanted that net."

"You're really giving me mixed messages here."

"Well, clearly, Sunshine, I'm confused and overwhelmed and..."

"And?" Sunshine prompted.

"Scared." Felix scooted back in his chair, pulled one foot up onto the seat so his leg rested against his chest. He placed his forehead on his knee for a while. "Eighty years is a long time to tease someone. All those...those stupid things I'd said. A lot of build-up to a pay-off I'm not willing to give."

"Ah."

"I'm sorry."

"So, you're telling me..." Sunshine began, debating the merit of what he intended to say, but soldiered on, "Is that your mouth has written a check that your ass can't cash."

Felix's head jerked up. He stared in abject horror. "Are you fucking kidding me?"

Sunshine smiled at him.

Felix swiped at him from across the table. Sunshine easily dodged that, but Felix got up and came around the table at him. "Are you *fucking kidding me?*" the demon demanded as he lunged.

Sunshine laughed even when Felix smacked him repeatedly. Eventually, he grabbed Felix's wrist and dragged him closer, circling his arms around him to hinder any further attacks. "Don't get worked up."

"My nerves are so delicate these days," Felix agreed wistfully as he fainted into Sunshine's lap, wrist against his forehead. He peeked an eye open. "I can't believe you said that."

"I can't believe you thought I was straight."

Felix snorted.

"I'm honestly wounded."

"I never thought you were *straight* just...not...open? Willing?" He sighed. "I don't know. I don't. You only ever date women."

"Well."

"Well?" Felix pressed.

"Don't start smacking me again."

"I promise."

Sunshine admitted, "Frank Cantamesa. But you hated him so much that I never told you about it."

Felix straightened up like he'd realized something. "Oh! I knew there was something *weird* about you two, ever since that case in Auburn. Oh my god, was that...? When you two were always going to that atrocious bar to get beer? Christ, I thought he had a drinking problem and you were cleaning up after him."

"I mean, he did have a bit of a drinking problem."

"So, what happened with you two?"

Sunshine shrugged. "It was just...he wanted to get out of the city. And he hated working cases. He wanted to focus on a 'real career.' I think he's a plumber now. I mean, shit, he might be a retired plumber by now."

They sat together for a while.

"Do you want to do something today?" Sunshine asked eventually.

"I'm going to read in a hammock. You?"

"I think I'm going to swim for a bit."

"Mmmm."

They parted ways on the beach, Sunshine towards the waves and Felix to a hammock. Around noon, Felix started drinking.

Sunshine sloshed his way out of the water. "Are you sure you should do that?"

"I'm on vacation, Sunshine."

"At least drink some water."

"At least drink some water," Felix mocked and slurped his drink with intentional loudness.

Sunshine went inside to make lunch. He goaded Felix into eating and Felix pouted until Sunshine had a drink.

They spent days like this, doing nothing except swim and lounge and walk on the beach. If they walked far enough, they encountered other people on vacation in houses similar to their small one. They would wave and Sunshine would wave back.

If they walked really far, they left the private section of the beach and encountered tourists who stayed in hotels and resorts and flocked to the beach *en masse*. Felix started to refer to them as 'commoners.' The lofty way he said it suited him.

At first, they walked apart, ambling beside each other, barefoot and sweaty. Always sweaty. By the third day, Felix seemed to have embraced some aspects of their revised situation. They walked hand-in-hand almost everywhere.

Six days passed and Sunshine could not believe he'd have to leave this place behind in eight more.

"We should do this more," he told Felix as they sat out on a jetty.

"I don't know, the rocks are kind of hot. It hurts my butt."

"I meant go on vacation."

Felix squinted at the sun, then the sea, then at Sunshine. "I don't know. It's a little quiet."

"There's things to do. Restaurants in town."

"Mmm. Maybe."

"I'm sure there's a nightlife somewhere on the island. We could find a club," Sunshine offered.

Felix shook his head. "I don't think this is *that* kind of island."

"Oh."

Felix shrugged.

"Well." Sunshine stared out at the sea. A wave lapped against the jetty and splashed his legs.

"Not that I don't like it! It's a nice trip."

"But...?"

Felix didn't answer.

Sunshine didn't ask again.

Things still hung over them. Heavy, uncomfortable questions that no one wanted to bring up.

Sunshine dipped his feet in the water. "I've been thinking."

"Mmm."

"You don't have to tell me."

"I probably won't."

"It's more than just you thought I only dated women."

"Yeah," Felix answered, his eyes on the sky.

"Is it because I stabbed you?"

"No."

"Will you tell me why?" Sunshine asked.

They were both staring at other things now, the sea and the sky, as if that made anything easier.

A long time passed. Long enough that Sunshine had given up on an answer.

"People have these expectations of me. That I'm easy, that I'll do anything, that I'll sleep with anyone, anywhere, any time. I always knew that at least even if you thought so too you could never expect me to carry through with anything."

Sunshine looked at him.

"People thinking I'm a slut is better than them knowing the truth."

"What truth?"

"I only flirt because I don't know how else to get people to look at me. So, I say all these things to get their attention and get mad when they want what I said I'd do. I'm a tease, an insecure tease who can't even..." He sighed. "It's just better that we don't try anything. I don't want to...it's this cycle of disappointment and accusations and trying to make up for things. I don't want that for us. It gets too ugly."

Sunshine climbed up to sit next to him. "But you like me?"

"No, not at all. Obviously, I hate you. That's why we've been doing this Odd Couple bullshit for eighty years."

He rested his chin on Felix's shoulder. "I like you, too."

"You wouldn't for much longer."

He wrapped his arms around Felix's torso. "I don't think that's true, Felix." He nuzzled into the crook of Felix's shoulder. "But I won't push things if you're not comfortable."

"Couldn't you be an asshole about it?"

"Uh...I thought demons were all sex maniacs?" Sunshine attempted.

Felix giggled. "I really liked the conviction. You ever consider being an actor?"

After a while, he smacked Sunshine on the thigh. "Come on, before these rocks burn a hole in my shorts."

They disentangled and Felix stood.

Sunshine watched him. "What shorts? All I see is these little things." He went to snap the fabric of Felix's very tight swim trunks.

Felix swatted his hand. "Come on. I'm hungry." He took off.

Sunshine followed happily after him, satisfied with the conversation they'd had. It was unlike Felix to talk about things like this and while he by no means owed Sunshine an explanation, Sunshine liked that he would talk about it at all with him.

March 9
Wednesday

Sunshine fell asleep in a state of absolute bliss. He was lightly drunk, freshly showered, and well-fed, not to mention exhausted from a day of frolicking about the beach and waves. He could have, at that moment, died with few regrets.

He woke in a panic, at first thinking he'd had some awful dream, but soon realized that something, someone crouched over him. One foot on either side of his waist, their face close to his.

"Are we awake?" the Devil asked

Sunshine screamed.

The Devil immediately pressed a hand over his mouth. "Yes, we are awake, then." He removed his hand but remained crouched over Sunshine.

"What the fuck are you doing here?" he demanded.

From within the folds of his shapeless, black garment, Lucifer produced a manila envelope. "You are a detective. I have something for you to detect." He dropped the envelope on to Sunshine's chest.

"Sunshine!" Felix called.

A light turned on in the hall.

"Find her," Lucifer said, then disjointedly climbed off Sunshine and into nothingness. He made eye contact the whole time.

Felix ran into the room. "Sunshine, what was that? Are you alright?"

"I..." Nothing but a few wrinkles in the sheets suggested anyone else had been in the room. He pushed himself upright and examined the envelope.

Felix snatched it from him and growled when he saw the seal on it. "Was he here?"

"Yeah."

Felix grunted and sat on Sunshine's bed. "I thought you were being murdered."

"Makes two of us."

"Well, he's fucked if he thinks I'm leaving early." Felix tossed the envelope on the bedside table. "Are you alright?"

"I think so."

Felix studied him.

"Rattled, I guess," Sunshine admitted.

Felix scooted further back into the bed. He waved a hand towards the hall and the light shut off. "I was having a marvelous dream, Sunshine, you wouldn't believe it."

"Try me."

"I was on the moon with Jane Fonda," he began.

"Ah, one of those dreams."

Felix lay his head on Sunshine's shoulder. "Don't be jealous, you were there, too." He wiggled up to him, hooking a leg over Sunshine's. He wiggled up to people like that a lot, draping over them at clubs, twining all around them when they danced. His hand rested against Sunshine's chest.

Sunshine put his hand over Felix's. "So, what were we doing, you, me, and Barbarella?"

"Rolling around naked on shag carpet on a space shuttle."

"That does sound like an interesting prospect."

Softly, Felix said, "We did other things." He swallowed. "I could show you."

"You don't have to," Sunshine assured with quiet sincerity. He still felt unsettled and he didn't know that he could handle anything more than cuddling right now.

Felix twisted his hand and laced their fingers together. "You'd believe me if I said I was confused and overwhelmed by all this still. You'd understand that I don't want to...to do anything."

"Of course."

Felix let out a sigh followed by a yawn. "If I closed my eyes...Or should I go?"

A strident *No!* leaped to mind, but Sunshine said, "I wouldn't mind the company."

Felix yawned again. "I really don't know what he was thinking. He's so bizarre. Think how much weirder I'd be if he'd raised me." He tucked himself under Sunshine's arm and fell asleep.

Sunshine didn't drift off so easily.

He woke with Felix still glued to him. He didn't doubt that he woke in no small part because of how glued to him Felix was. When he shifted, Felix loosened his grip and rolled over.

A few minutes later, Felix sat up and looked around. "Sunshine."

"Mmm?"

"Tell me that I came into your room in the middle of the night because you were screaming."

"That's why," Sunshine confirmed.

"Alright, good, I wasn't sure if that was a dream or if the other thing was."

"What, you weren't sure if we were on the moon with Jane Fonda or not?" Sunshine asked.

Felix blushed.

"What do you want to do today?"

"I need a shower." Felix left and took Sunshine's sheets with him. The shower started almost immediately.

"No, that's fine, I don't need my sheets," he called.

He got no answer. He puttered around until Felix finished, then took his turn. Over breakfast, he asked again, "What do you want to do today?"

"I think I need to dry out, honestly, we've only got a few days left and I've been continuously buzzed for more than a week straight." To himself, Felix added, "And I make foggy fucking choices when I'm drunk."

Sunshine couldn't argue.

When the dishes had been washed, Felix dried his hands and paused in the middle of the kitchen. "Was my father here last night?"

"Yes."

"What did he want?"

"I don't know, to scare the shit out of me?"

"Sounds like him. He does like to pick on people," Felix said.

Sunshine had stowed the envelope with his luggage. He

couldn't very well find anyone right now and he doubted that Lucifer's timing had anything to do with Sunshine's current location. The Devil's grasp on time and space ebbed and flowed; he always seemed surprised to find out what year it was on Earth. On the occasions he'd visited their office, he'd looked around each time and asked, "Same place then...?" with true doubt.

Despite his decision to stop drinking, Felix made them drinks with lunch.

"I thought we were drying out," Sunshine said when he was handed a drink.

"Yeah, well, I found half a bottle of vodka in the freezer and we can't bring it back with us," Felix said. "Besides, that's like...a quarter of a bottle each. And one bottle is like sixteen shots so its four shots each, which is basically like not drinking at all if you spread it out enough."

"That's some sort of logic."

"I could drink it by myself if you don't want any."

Sunshine kept a grip on his drink. "I don't really want you to drink half a bottle of vodka."

"Why not? You can touch me now."

Sunshine frowned. "So?"

Felix slipped an arm around his waist and pressed close. Very close. Closer than he usually did. A lizard grin crept across his face but didn't last as he met Sunshine's eyes. "I suppose you can more effectively hold me over the toilet while I barf my brains out." He released Sunshine. "I'll be on the beach."

Sunshine followed him. He didn't have much of a choice, there wasn't anywhere else to go. He sat by where Felix had parked himself in the sand. "You haven't tanned at all."

Felix glanced down at his arm. "I'm almost human-colored now, I don't know what you mean."

He still looked white as milk to Sunshine.

He must have noticed the doubt on Sunshine's face because he pulled the waistband of his shorts to show the nearly ghastly whiteness of his skin in contrast to that which had gotten sun. "See?"

"Are you really that fucking pale?"

Felix nodded. He held out his arm for Sunshine to examine. "Look how bleached my hair got."

Sunshine peered at the hairs and found them paler than usual. He put his own arm next to Felix's. His skin had deepened in color, bronze instead of gold, but still just as shimmery.

Felix's eyes raked over him. "You ever think about how God made sixty of *you* and people still think He's homophobic?"

"I don't think..." Sunshine's face warmed.

"You don't think God made you sexy on purpose?"

"I think God is an asexual, genderless being who prefers to be a liquid."

"That's not how Dad makes Him sound."

"Maybe He's changed," Sunshine offered with a shrug. "People do that. He may have some aesthetic preferences. I wouldn't know."

"Mmm."

Sunshine shifted, then finally said, "Besides. God barely made me. I'm probably just a copy of whichever Greek statue He saw first."

Felix glanced at him, pity on his face.

"I don't even know which one I am. Like...did He make us one at a time? Was I last or third or thirty-eighth? Or did He make us all at once? Did He just...pick a random statue? Or was it a person? Did some man walk around with this face at some point?" Sunshine continued. "I don't know. He never told us. We were all the same to Him. He never really *talked* to any of us. Not like He talked to the first angels."

"Sunshine."

Unexpected and unwelcome, Sunshine's throat tightened. He shook his head. "It doesn't matter."

"Sunshine." Felix slid his fingers into Sunshine's hair. He leaned against him. "It matters. And it hurts. We are what our parents make us; they send us into the world with the best they could do. You were sent here with nothing."

A thousand useless thoughts rolled through his mind, one after another, questions of doubt and fear, of longing, of the useless, horrible need to love something, to be loved by someone. In Heaven, *alone* didn't exist. He hadn't felt the emptiness of everything he didn't have. No one else had had them either.

"You've done really well, Sunshine. Beautifully." Felix pressed his lips to Sunshine's cheek.

Sunshine put his arms around Felix.

"Close your eyes."

Sunshine closed his eyes.

"Relax, your face, your shoulders, arms. Breathe, listen to the waves."

He did what Felix said, but also pointed out, "I'm not having a panic attack."

"I know. But you don't have to be in the throes of desperation to relax. Listen to the waves, hmm? Smell that sea air."

"All I can smell is vodka."

Felix snorted then pulled back. He still had his fingers in Sunshine's hair, knotted there. He tightened his grip just a smidge. "I guess He didn't send you with nothing at all. You do have a fabulous head of hair."

His scalp tingled and that feeling trickled down his back and settled, warm and fluttering, in his gut. "Maybe He thought that's all I would need."

Felix gave a little tug, let go, and took a sip of his drink. "Did you see on Facebook that Chrissie had her baby?"

"I did. A girl, right? What was her name?" Sunshine couldn't think right.

"Uh, Annabella? Isabella? Something like that."

"I think it was Annabella," Sunshine confirmed. "Cute."

"Itty-bitty baby," Felix murmured. He took another sip. He traced shapes in the sand between them. "You think Tom's gonna propose?"

"I don't know, you think he'd have proposed some point between getting her pregnant and her giving birth."

"Yeah but imagine looking down at that widdle-biddy face. Might change your mind."

"Maybe," Sunshine agreed.

Felix drew a stick figure family, two tall figures, a short one, and a cat. He pointed to the cat. "That's Jangles. She died before I kidnapped you."

"You used to talk about her sometimes."

"She was a good cat. A good friend to me."

They sat for a long time, sipping their drinks and staring at the sea. At one point, Felix started muttering a song by The Cure.

After two drinks, Felix nearly talked Sunshine into walking into town to get more alcohol. Sunshine managed to dissuade him by reminding him of the time he'd had to fly home hungover. They migrated from sand, to waves, to hammock several times, but stayed on their small beach, away from others.

Sunshine had gone to the hammock to nap.

Felix had followed and wedged his way in, making a nap impossible.

"Do you think things will be different at home?" Felix asked.

"It's only two weeks."

"No. Us."

Sunshine debated what to say. Felix had fixated on this, obsessively worried about what it would mean, but declined to say what he was really worried about. Something other than his race's reputation as promiscuous and his self-admitted status as a tease. Sunshine had no idea what to do to soothe his worries or how to convince him that he was worrying over nothing.

He didn't know how to do any of that, so he turned his head and blew a raspberry into the side of Felix's face. He made it as loud as possible.

Felix elbowed him. "What's wrong with you?"

"Just another of my people's strange customs."

"Fuck off."

"The Angelic Tongue is impossible for earthly creatures such as yourself to comprehend, but in your language, it roughly translates to 'stop worrying, we've already tried to kill each other, it doesn't get worse than that'."

Felix tried to scowl, he really looked like he was giving it his best effort, but he just sighed. "Did you hate me then?"

"As a concept, maybe. As an extension of your father, yes. As a person? No. You were just...something I had to get rid of. Does a lumberjack hate trees? Or is it just his job?"

"I hated you. I hated your fucking guts."

Sunshine leaned in to blow another raspberry. Felix pushed his face away, so Sunshine blew the raspberry into his palm instead.

"You're straight-up awful," Felix told him and dried his palm on Sunshine's chest.

"The absolute worst," he agreed.

"I'm never going on vacation with you again."

"I wouldn't let you. Worst two weeks of my life."

"I've heard good things about those European river cruises," Felix replied.

"Yeah, yeah, Jen was telling me when I was booking this. She went on one last summer. She said she loved it. I think she did, uh, like Norway and stuff."

"It's supposed to be beautiful up there."

Sunshine adjusted himself so they were comfortable again. "Maybe in the fall?"

"Two vacations in one year? Who are we, the Kennedys?"

"Fucking yolo, man. Before climate change kills us all."

Felix grimaced. "Shit, well, we can always move somewhere else. Hell maybe."

Sunshine suggested, "What about that, uh, that weird city-state dimension where they're like...subterranean bug people. They lay eggs?"

"Oh, yeah, I know the one you're talking about. They're a little xenophobic, at least, that's what Bibi's heard. And, well..." Felix shrugged.

Sunshine chimed in so they spoke in unison, "They know what is said, not what is true."

Felix grinned but it slid off his face. Within moments, he looked absolutely miserable. He began to get up.

Sunshine sat up. "Felix."

Felix paused but said, "God, I hate it when you say my name like that."

"Mr. Specter."

"I don't know if that's better," Felix said.

"I know you're worried. And I know how you get when you're worried. I want you to promise me something."

"No." Felix fidgeted.

"Promise you won't pull away from me. If you need space or time to think or you want to, you know, just digest, that's fine and I respect that. But don't pull away. Don't think that I want you in my life any less, or that I expect anything more than what we've had. Okay?"

"You know I'm irrational. I can't promise that."

Sunshine nodded. He did know. He squeezed Felix's hand. "Maybe I just needed to know you heard it."

"Fucking Christ, Sunshine, you've really got this good guy act down pat. You've got all of us fooled with that smile and those big orange eyes of yours. One of these days I'll figure out what you're getting at," Felix said.

Sunshine didn't take offense. Felix didn't mean a single word, he knew. He just couldn't say anything nice to someone's face without the circumstances being precisely right. His mood, the other person's level of need, how rotten he'd been lately, and perhaps even the position of the stars themselves played into Felix's ability to look someone in the eyes and say, "This is hard for me. Thank you for understanding. I appreciate it."

It didn't matter because even though he couldn't say it with his voice, he said it with other things. His eyes, the set of his lips, how hard he held someone's hand.

Although, it was entirely possible that Sunshine had deluded himself into believing that. Maybe Felix spoke true and everything else was Sunshine projecting his own hopes and beliefs on to him.

Felix took his hand back, stood up, and announced, "I'm going to go drown myself."

"Scream if you need me."

Felix snorted and walked away.

Felix did not drown himself. He stood in chest-deep water for a while, then floated on his back for a while longer.

They ate out that night since they hadn't so far, and it seemed wrong to spend two weeks on vacation without going out to eat at least once. Felix eyed the other diners the whole time and they eyed him back.

"What?" Sunshine asked.

"I think those are Canadians," Felix whispered. He slung his eyes towards a straight, middle-aged couple who had been staring at them all night.

"And?"

"You know how Canadians get."

Sunshine assured, "It's been years since anyone's bothered you."

Felix grunted.

"First of all, they'd have to be," Sunshine put up his fingers to list the reasons, "One, Canadians, two, Community members, three, interested at all in talking to you."

Felix bared his teeth.

"No, there's nothing in your teeth," Sunshine said.

Felix growled.

"I kind of like it when you growl at me like that," he said. "Maybe pull my hair a little bit, too."

Felix's eyes widened a hair. "Don't do that."

Sunshine grinned.

"Finish eating so we can go."

Sunshine resumed eating but didn't hurry.

The possibly Canadian couple asked for their check and paid. Before Sunshine had the chance to say, "See? No one cares," they slowed on their way out and paused beside their table.

The woman cleared her throat. "Um. Excuse me...I."

"We just wanted to ask," the man began.

Felix set down his fork and gave them his attention. "Yes?"

"Phaedrus Queen is your father, right?"

"No. Phaedrus Queen is not my father," Felix answered with careful dictation.

The woman began, "Oh. There's...there's this writer, he's pretty famous—"

"They are," Felix said.

"And he wrote this—"

"They wrote," Felix interrupted again, "A trilogy of books. It did very well. A couple of the Pickering University students made a documentary about them, which included interviews with Dr. Queen's family. Papa was so very proud and screened it at the University at the inaugural Pickering Film Festival."

The couple stared at him. They stared with the wide-eyed terror at the breakdown of polite society that only Baby Boomers understood.

The man asked, "So you are...uh, well, you...You are the son, aren't you?"

"Yes. You two are, what? Mages?"

"Oh, no, no. Mage adjacent. My sister was always the smart one. Well. Duncan dabbled a little," the woman said and gave the man an affectionate pat on the stomach. "But our nephew *loves* those books. An absolute fanatic. He's praying they'll get made into movies."

Felix forced a smile. "Well. Glad to meet a fan of Bibi's."

The three of them stared at each other.

Felix raised his eyebrows and glanced towards the door. "Anything else you wanted?"

The woman twisted her hands. "Just. Well. Let your father know—"

"Phaedrus Queen is not my father. They are not a man. Please."

The man shifted and looked at his shoes.

She visibly grimaced, though if it was at being corrected or that she was embarrassed she'd needed to be corrected, Sunshine couldn't tell. "My nephew was in a really hard place. Those books helped. A lot. Let...let *them* know." She gave a small smile.

"I'll let them know."

Her smile widened a little.

Felix softened. "I really will. Bibi loves to hear when they've helped someone."

"Sorry to bother you," the man said.

Felix shrugged. "No problem. Have a nice night."

"Thanks, thank you. You too," the pair chorused.

Felix waited until they'd the restaurant. "Some people."

"I know."

"Bibi really does like knowing, though. I'll have to call them."

Sunshine suggested, "You should send—"

"I sent two postcards already."

A sheepish smile made itself at home on Sunshine's face.

The following days flew by and before Sunshine knew it, he was on a plane home. While Felix once again slept through the flight, Sunshine sifted through the materials Lucifer had delivered.

He had asked Sunshine to find a young girl, fifteen years of age, and last seen in her hometown of Tinsville, Pennsylvania. Her parents had been murdered in what the police had called a botched breaking-and-entering. She hadn't been seen since that night four months ago. At this point, according to police reports that Sunshine didn't think had been acquired through favorable means, police assumed her kidnapped.

Kidnapped young girls ended up in a limited number of situations, none of them good. Dead, trafficked somewhere, tied up and brutalized in some basement.

The case had gone cold and the file was thin.

It didn't surprise Sunshine at all to see so little information.

Lucifer had included a few photographs of her, most of them family photos. Father, mother, daughter, all of them even-featured and dark-skinned. One photo showed them in front of a red brick rowhouse with a floppy-eared mutt.

He put everything away. It didn't help to stare at things for too long. He'd be back at the office soon and he had more resources available to him there.

If Lucifer had brought this to him, it meant of all the people who owed him favors, he thought Sunshine was uniquely positioned to find this girl. Regular human cops and detectives must have owed the Devil, too, so the fact that he had turned to Sunshine meant that finding her required something paranormal.

Or Satan was just a dick and liked to pick on people.

Or possibly both.

Probably both.

March 15
Tuesday

Smiles didn't work over the phone and convincing secretaries to give him information about young girls who had gone missing was hard if he couldn't smile at them. He hung up and crossed out the school he'd called. After a lot of sweet-talking and bullshitting, he'd convinced the secretary to tell him whether a Sarai Robinson had ever attended their school. It was the last high school within an hour's drive of the girl's home address.

The documents he'd been given indicated nothing about the girl's schooling and listed her parents' jobs as *homemaker* and *self-employed.*

He'd just come back home, and he really did not want to go to Pennsylvania. A vast chasm separated the delight of vacation and the soullessness of traveling for work.

Felix had sent about ten thousand emails so far that morning. It sounded that way, at least, because he'd been typing and clicking away nonstop since they'd come in. It had something to do with that trafficker he'd turned in, but he'd been too grumpy to share more details.

At noon, he stood up and Sunshine started to stand too, anticipating the question before Felix asked it. "Lunch?" or some variation thereof. Not always the same time, but always from the same deli, as long as they were both at the office.

Felix hesitated. "Uh. I'm. I actually have an appointment. It was the only time she had."

"Oh." Sunshine frowned. He tried to think of Felix mentioning something about an appointment. He couldn't even guess what kind of appointment it might be, work-related or personal.

"I didn't want to make a thing about it." He grabbed his coat and picked a few bits of lint off the wool. "You know, make it weird after all the shit we talked about. I just need someone who's not as close to the situation."

"Oh. Of course."

"You get it."

Sunshine didn't get therapy at all, but he understood that it helped Felix in a way that he needed. "Yeah. Sure. Are you gonna eat? Do you want me to grab you something?"

"Uh. Yeah. Yeah, thanks. Maybe soup? Whatever the special is."

"Sure."

They stared awkwardly at each other.

Felix pulled on his coat and left, eyes on the floor.

Sunshine waited a few minutes, couldn't get the idea of lunch out of his head, and made his way downstairs.

He and Tate tried to be polite letting each other go out the door first but just made things weird.

She laughed.

"You headed to lunch?" he asked.

She shook her head. "Coffee. I'm struggling."

"There's a little deli on the corner a few streets down," he offered. "If you're interested."

She quirked her eyebrows as if she wasn't sure he was serious. "Yeah. Alright. Sure. I was just going to go to Dunkin but it's all the same, right?"

"I read your write up on that last case. The Himmel bird?"

She laughed. "Yeah! Easy peasy. Sassy bird though! I mean, I know parrots can talk but that one had a mouth on her. She did *not* want to go home, started cussing out the Himmel lady as soon as they saw each other."

"You did a nice job on it. The case and the write-up."

"Oh. Thanks. I, uh, I did have Dr. Love give it a read for me first." She smiled and tucked a piece of dark blonde hair behind her ear.

They walked a few more steps.

"You guys had fun?" she asked.

"Hmm?"

"On vacation."

"Oh, yeah. Yes. Beautiful island. I think we needed it."

"After those spiders, I bet!" she agreed. "Oooh, god, I couldn't have. Ugh."

A bike whizzed past them at a red light and dipped its way through traffic.

"I swear it's like people want to die," she muttered.

"Hubris," he guessed.

He ordered his sandwich and Felix's lunch to go. Tate clutched her coffee in both hands while they walked back. Before they reached the office, he said, "I know we haven't asked you to travel much for the agency yet."

They had never sent her more than a few hours' drive away from the city and never anywhere she'd need to stay overnight.

She stopped blowing into the mouth of her coffee.

"You've been with us three years now?"

She nodded. "Yeah, in December."

"Would you be comfortable traveling more?"

"Yeah, I mean. Maybe. Depends on the case. Not that I wouldn't! Everything new is weird, right? It was weird being a psychic detective, but I'm pretty used to it now!" She blew into her coffee a little more. "You have something in mind?"

"I might."

The complications with the trafficking ring had Felix busy and worked up. Sunshine had thought about asking him for help finding the girl but didn't want to overburden him. Or take him out of town if he'd started seeing a therapist again; finding a good therapist could be impossible, everyone seemed to need one, and getting an appointment could be just as hard.

"Yeah?"

"For overnight trips, it's standard to give twenty-four-hour notice. Does that work for you? I know Shay has children, so she needs more of a heads up."

"No, that's fine. Perfect. Hank'll be home so Couscous will be fine."

He couldn't imagine that Couscous was the name of a child.

"My cat," she provided. She took out her phone and found a

picture so fast it almost gave him whiplash. She beamed as she showed off an unremarkable brown tabby.

He agreed about the handsomeness of the cat and the sweetness of its face. They parted ways at the stairs. He began to eat his turkey and swiss on rye in the overwhelming silence of the office. After a few bites, he had to turn on music because all he could hear was himself chewing.

Felix returned a little after two, hung up his jacket, and warmed up his soup with just a touch.

"Not going to use your feet?" Sunshine asked.

"Who gave you permission to speak to me?"

"Forgive me, master, I am but a worm before you."

About halfway through his soup, Felix said, "I have to go down to the police station later. Meet with this detective."

"What for?"

Instead of answering, Felix stared at his spoonful of soup.

"Specter?"

"Uh." Felix cleared his throat. "That mage is squirrely. The one I told the Academy about? He won't go for any of the decoys the cops have set up, but I had to get kind of cozy with him to get him to say what he was doing in the first place. I mean, how else do you get a guy like that to talk?"

Sunshine uneasily recalled the times Felix had played into the darker stereotypes about his kind to get close to someone. No one ever doubted that a demon would be involved in black magic or ritual murders. He'd infiltrated a cult that supplied hexed drugs, worked his way into a secret society that had been assassinating bankers, and he'd even had an in with Risalda Timberton before she'd died.

"They think he'll bite if I get back in touch, ask to trade the bracelet for a...well. You know. A sex slave. That's what the guy implied before anyway."

Sunshine's stomach decided at that moment to take issue with his lunch.

"So, I've got to go down and talk to the detective that handles this kind of bullshit. He's Community adjacent and knows how to get this guy to, uh." Felix waved his hand. "You know. Wizard prison."

Sunshine had intended to tell him he might have to go to Pennsylvania but that could wait. "Do you need help with anything?"

"I don't know. Do you know what kind of sex slave I want to buy? I guess people are pretty specific about that kind of thing."

"Maybe go home."

Felix shook his head. "I'm talking with this guy and if I have to read about this shit at home too, I think I'll just about kill myself. I can't eat this, do you want it?"

"Save it for later."

Felix replaced the lid and stowed the soup in the mini-fridge behind his desk. He stared at the fridge for a while.

Sunshine couldn't watch him like that. He retrieved something from the locked drawer of his desk and brought it over to Felix.

"Don't, whatever it is, I'm emotionally fragile."

Sunshine placed a wrapped box on his desk. "I was gonna give it to you for your birthday."

"Sunshine, don't do it."

"Mmmm, just open it."

With a sigh, Felix eyed the box and eyed Sunshine. He opened the top and pulled out a brick of Styrofoam. He parted the halves carefully to reveal a bookend of a deathly pale man with a mop of black hair. The other bookend showed a woman with the same coloring.

"I thought they'd look nice on that shelf next to your bathroom," Sunshine suggested.

"They are a little empty." Felix touched the face of the male bookend.

"Do you feel better?"

"About ten times worse."

"Oh. I'm sorry. I thought..."

Felix shook his head. "It's fine. I get it. I do like them, I really do."

"Uh. They're signed." Sunshine pointed to the signatures in Silver Sharpie on the backs of both pieces. "I, uh, I sealed it, they should last pretty well. Bibi pulled a few strings for me."

"This is really sweet, Sunshine. It is." Felix smiled at the bookend. He glanced around the office, eyeing a shelf. "What about there?"

"Hmm?" Sunshine followed his gaze. "They're yours. Put them wherever you want."

Felix placed them on the shelf to the left of their door. He touched each of them once more. He flicked a pencil off Sunshine's desk as he walked past it to return to his own.

Sunshine decided to pursue this case from the office for another day. He sent Tate an email telling her that she might be coming with him to Pennsylvania on Thursday afternoon.

Wednesday afternoon, when Specter had come back from another meeting with the detective, he said, "I have to go to Pennsylvania."

"How far?"

"Out near Pittsburgh."

Felix grimaced. "I, uh…"

"I know you can't come. I'm having Tate come. I think her powers will be useful in this case."

"What case?"

"The one in Pennsylvania."

Felix frowned.

"Missing girl."

"Ah. Well. Better find her. Missing isn't a good way to be," Felix agreed. "Do you have a file on this? I don't remember taking a case about a missing girl."

"I'll update you when I have something worth sharing. So far, I don't know shit. I'm hoping being on the ground will shake some things loose."

"Alright." Felix pelted him with a balled-up scrap of paper. "You're bringing Tate?"

"Mmm."

"We've never sent her that far before."

"Well, I'm going with her. She'll do okay, I'm sure."

"Hope so. Make sure you're back by Monday. Staff meeting."

"Staff meeting," Sunshine agreed. "We'll be back. Shouldn't take more than a day or two."

Felix lapsed into an agitated quiet.

Sunshine gave him space and went downstairs to update Tate. He started by asking her to meet him at a car rental place, to which she said, "We can take my car."

"Your car?"

"Yeah, definitely! Better than renting something. I love a chance to take her out."

Sunshine considered it. They did have a standard mileage reimbursement agreement with their employees. "What do you drive?"

Tate grinned and rattled off a series of numbers and letters that might have been a year and model number but meant nothing to

Sunshine. He understood only, "Mercedes," and didn't ask for more. The lack of understanding must have shown on his face. "She's a sedan, plenty of legroom. Don't worry."

"Very well. Can you bring it here for noon tomorrow?"

"Absolutely! I have to go call the garage, though, they get a little fussy about taking her out without notice." She slipped her phone from the waistband of her leggings. "I'll be right back." She bounced off to the front of the office, which had much better service.

"That's a lot of car for a kid like her," Emil mentioned from his desk, which faced Tate's.

"There's a staff meeting on Monday," Sunshine reminded.

"Yeah. I got the email. What about? Email didn't say much."

"I'd think you'd be able to extrapolate based on your conversation with Mr. Specter and me. If you can't, I'm sure you'll find Monday enlightening."

"Bet I will." Emil grunted and adjusted the way he sat with more noise than strictly necessary.

Sunshine had never disliked Emil, but he felt the sentiment stirring. He made himself smile. "As always, Jen handles human resources if there's something that concerns you."

Emil gave him a look that bordered on dirty.

"Is something bothering you?" Sunshine asked.

Emil never got a chance to answer.

Tate came back to her desk. "All set with the garage!" She flashed a smile at Emil. "Tell Sunshine what a good driver I am."

Emil rolled his eyes. "Try not to kill him, the other one would probably go nuts without him," he muttered.

Tate turned bright red and looked up at Sunshine, eyes wide. "I...I'm sorry. Emil, jeez! Could you not?"

"What? It's not..." Emil sighed.

Sunshine didn't know what to do. He knew what he wanted to do but also knew it would not be appropriate as an employer. "Is there something you wanted to say?"

"No."

The others in the area had sent awkward glances their way.

"Then I suggest that you stop muttering. It makes it seem like you have something you want to say."

Emil shifted uncomfortably. He rubbed his mouth and grunted again.

"And that which you are unwilling to say clearly and to my face are likely words best left unsaid altogether."

Emil stood up. He was taller than Sunshine and tried to use that height.

Tate grabbed him by the arm. "Cut it out, Emil, really."

He yanked his arm out of her grasp, but she seemed to have dislodged whatever thought he'd had rattling around in his head. He walked out of the office.

Tate let out a long breath, looking absolutely mortified. "I'm sorry, Sunshine. Really. He's...I don't know what's wrong with him. He's got stuff going on at home, I think."

"You're certainly not at fault."

She shifted.

"I'll see you tomorrow. Twelve o'clock."

"Yeah!" She hesitated then followed Emil outside. Faintly, he heard her call, "What the fuck was that shit!" before the door shut.

Sunshine made a note of the whole interaction in his phone; it helped to have records on things like these, just in case things escalated. Ruffled feathers he could soothe, but prejudices could be hard to manage. The best Sunshine hoped for at this point was teaching Emil to keep his mouth shut and not having to fire him.

Tate texted him when she'd pulled up in front of the office. Sunshine gathered his things and hesitated in front of Felix's desk. "I'm heading out."

"Drive safe."

"Call me if you need to talk."

Felix glanced up. "Yeah. Same. I know the missing kid cases can be rough." He leaned across his desk and grasped Sunshine's hand for a second. "See you soon."

Sunshine squeezed back, then headed downstairs. He put his duffle bag with Tate's in the backseat and climbed into the passenger side with his backpack.

"Ready?" Tate asked.

"As I'll ever be."

"Got everything?"

He nodded.

She squinted at him. "You sure?"

"Pretty sure," he said, no longer sure at all.

She nodded and pulled away from the curb. "Alright. I'm gonna get on seventy-eight unless you know a better way."

"I'm indifferent."

"See, thank you! Emil always gives me shit no matter what way

I go. Like, honestly, what's the difference between the Holland Tunnel and the Lincoln Tunnel? Like he thinks just cause he grew up here...!" She sighed and shook her head. "Always something with him these days. Anyway, I don't want to talk about him and if you let me get started, I'll do it for the six hours between here and Tinsville. Tell me about this case."

He slid the file out of his backpack and read her all the notes he'd been given and what he'd accumulated since then.

Tate listened, fiddled with the music a few times, and when he'd finished asked, "Does that all sound as bad as I think it does?"

"There's a lot of gaps here so I'm hoping that whatever we find to fill them in will point to this girl being alive and well. Or, at least, alive. I can't imagine how well she'll be."

"Yeah, that's really rough. The whole thing."

Sunshine hummed his agreement and stared out the window.

"So."

He glanced her way.

"You have any pets?"

"We travel too much."

She nodded. "Yeah. Makes sense."

The awkwardness became nearly painful. "So you have a cat, right? Anything else?"

She told him no, but she'd been thinking about getting another cat lately. She debated the merits of getting one with little input from Sunshine for about forty-five minutes; the debate included several tangents on animal welfare and how awful it was that people didn't take care of their pets better.

They chatted about banal things like that, pets and family and childhood. Sunshine could make few contributions; everything he had to share either involved the lack of something in his life, revolved around someone who had died or moved away or included Felix. If Tate hadn't worked for them, he would have shared more readily.

She did her best to compensate for his lack of input and did it with grace.

Finally, she asked, "You cook much?"

"Yes!" He'd answered with too much enthusiasm, but cooking was a safe topic. "I try to make dinner every night."

"Better for you. I should cook more, but..." She shrugged. "You know. The struggle is real."

"We used to have people over for dinner a lot, you know, not too many people but a few friends. I think dinner parties have sort of fallen out of favor, though. No one's much interested in staying in, or when they do, they're not in the mood to entertain."

"Who's we?" she asked.

"Hmm?"

"You keep saying we. We travel too much, we had people over," she said. "Not that it's my business."

"Ah. Well." No point in lying. No shame in admitting the truth. "Specter and I."

She grinned triumphantly, a knowing look in her eye. "That's kind of what I thought."

"Not like that."

"No?"

She was an employee, he reminded himself. He had to keep a certain distance, keep things professional. "Not exactly *not* like that either," he said anyway. "We aren't dating."

"Oooh, is this drama?"

"Things..." He paused. "Things are both complicated and extremely simple. On the one hand, I'd struggle to define exactly what we are to each other in a way that other people could understand. Business partners doesn't cover it. Friends doesn't exactly either. Companions makes it sound like one of us is an old man and the other one is a faithful dog."

She snorted. "So, what's the simple version?"

"Are you familiar with *The Symposium*?"

"No."

"It's one of Plato's works. Anyway, very abbreviated, in it, there's this idea that people used to have four legs and four arms and two heads. Zeus cut them in half because he wanted more tribute and hated how happy and strong they were. Once halved, the humans were miserable."

"I can imagine."

"Apollo sewed them up but not back together. They were still halved, but you know, not gaping monstrosities anymore. They would always long for their other half. If they ever met again, they would know each other without words, there would be unspoken understanding between them. They would be happy again."

"That doesn't sound simple at all."

"No, and it didn't happen. Humans never had four legs, it's just a myth, but the idea, well..." He shrugged. "Specter's my other half."

"Okay, but I'll never get the image of you two as a four-legged monster out of my head."

"I'm terribly sorry if it gives you nightmares."

She chortled becomingly. "So, where'd you learn to cook? We always had someone who cooked for us, so I never really got a chance to learn." In a perfect transatlantic accent, she said, "One does not learn from the help, it is in poor taste."

He raised an eyebrow.

"Oyster Bay," she admitted with an eye-roll, albeit an embarrassed one. "But anyway, I've talked your ear off. Where'd you learn to cook?"

"Through many unfortunate accidents and *Mastering the Art of French Cooking*. Although tastes have changed a lot since then. I try to stay relevant but sometimes you just want cassoulet."

"I struggle with grilled cheese so honestly, whatever you make would impress me."

"It's all practice."

She let out a small breath, appeared poised to say something until a flamenco version of *Killing Me Softly with His Song* came on, at which point she cried, "Oh, hot damn, this is my jam!" and turned up the volume of her music.

She belted out the song with no hesitation and some degree of adherence to the notes of the song.

He appreciated her enthusiasm and that she had felt comfortable enough in front of him to do it. Maybe unease among their employees had its root in their employees' unease with them. Things had not always been so uncomfortable, but workplace culture had changed since the founding of the Sunshine and Specter Paranormal Detective Agency. People had different wants and needs, different expectations. Especially a young woman like Tate. She was their youngest employee and, in that sense, their most vulnerable.

And really, what harm did it do to hand over a few small, personal facts in exchange for her comfort?

Not to mention, keeping up his half-answers and lingering silences would have made the six-hour drive intolerable.

March 17
Thursday

Darkness enshrouded the rowhouse in Tinsville. Not just the sordidly lugubrious mood of the place that rolled off it like mist, but literal darkness as well. They had arrived there well after nightfall, having checked into their hotel first. He'd booked them separate but neighboring rooms. They'd freshened up, much needed after six hours with only a single bathroom break, then headed to the Robinson home.

Tate stared at the house and pulled her jacket tighter around herself. "Are we allowed to be here?"

"It's not an active crime scene, I alerted the police to my intentions, and I spoke with the family of the deceased to gain permission to enter, so yes, technically, we are allowed to be here."

"Technically."

"The brother of Mrs. Robinson said, word for word, 'do whatever you want with the place, I don't care,' which is technically permission," Sunshine said.

He couldn't pinpoint the year, let alone the day when he'd started using words like technically. When he'd first come to Earth, wiggle room had not existed. He either could do something or he couldn't; moral ambiguity hadn't existed either. He was either following orders or he wasn't.

He made his way up the steps and slipped a key into the lock. It was not the key that belonged to the house, but a blank purchased at a hardware store and enchanted to work in the first lock into which it was inserted.

Instead of the usual bit of wiggling that usually accompanied the use of such a key, the lock fired the key out across the street. It left a trail of red light in the air as it went and singed the grass where it landed.

Sunshine had seen keys do that enough times that he'd known not to stand directly in front of the door.

He'd neglected to warn Tate and shot her an apologetic look.

"Was it supposed to do that?"

"No." He watched the twisted remains of the key cool on the grass. "But it fills in a gap."

"Which one?"

"The key was enchanted."

"Mages?" Tate guessed.

He nodded, glad she'd reached the conclusion on her own. Tate had not been born into the Community nor known of its existence until her teens; she'd lived most of her life thinking her psychic abilities made her uniquely and freakishly alone.

A related depressive episode and persistent suicidal ideation had brought her to a behavioral health center. There she had met a vampire working as an orderly—Sunshine assumed this was Hank—who had taken pity and clued her into the existence of a wider world. Her admission to the center had also brought her to the attention of a friend of Felix's, who kept an eye out for such things.

Upon finding out she was a New York native and in possession of some serious, if untrained, psychic skills, they had driven out to offer her a position at their agency upon her release from the center.

They hadn't heard from her for years, but she had found their way back to them eventually with a shrug and the sheepish admission, "College isn't for everyone."

She nudged the key with the toe of her sneaker. "Well. Any other tricks?"

He eyed a loose chunk of rock, but the situation didn't call for broken windows yet. He stepped off the porch, surveyed the face of the house, and asked, "How comfortable are you with me helping you onto the roof?"

He'd boosted Felix in similar situations dozens of times. If he'd been alone, he could have hauled himself up without much trouble, but he'd also ripped the gutters off roofs more often than he liked.

"Uh. Awkward but willing."

"Good. That window looks open." He pointed to the window above the porch. "Can you pull yourself up?"

She squinted up. "For sure."

"You'll have to go through the house and open the front door."

"I'm a big girl, I can handle it."

He boosted her up and once she was on the roof, she called, "It's open. I'll be right down."

Lights came on within the house. Not five minutes later she had the door open.

He stepped inside to the overwhelming scent of cleaning products. The house hadn't been aired.

They combed through the house, treading delicately around the scattered items and eyeing places on the carpet or walls that looked *too* clean. Books littered every room and not a single bookshelf had gone untouched. Biographies, romance novels, encyclopedias, classics of American and British literature, a handful of novels in French.

Sunshine peered into closets and under beds; he checked cabinets and dressers. Those places had been disturbed but not ransacked like the bookshelves. The jewelry box in the master bedroom hadn't even been touched.

He glanced at Tate.

She stood at the top of the stairs, staring down at the landing. Staring, breathing, not moving.

He edged closer, careful not to disturb her.

After several minutes, she tucked a piece of hair behind her ear. She glanced at Sunshine and expressed no surprise at seeing him there. "The girl came home. They came in right behind her. Lots...not lots. More than two. Less than five. She screamed and ran." Tate pointed to a room.

The room through which she had entered the house. The room with the open window.

He waited for additional revelations.

She shook her head. "That's it for now."

He nodded and headed to the room she'd indicated. Clearly a child's room, posters decorated the walls and the twin bed had dinosaurs on the comforter. The books had been tossed here too, dozens of YA novels about fairies and witches, a slick of National

Geographic magazines across the floor. A copy of *Jurassic Park* had made it to the bed.

Spiral-bound notebooks fanned out and a glimpse of neat, slanted handwriting made him stoop. Arcane runes mixed with notes in English. He crouched and flipped through the notebooks, which started to feel a lot like homework. Questions about *To Kill a Mockingbird*, math equations he couldn't follow, a quick diagram of a plant cell.

No class, no teacher, just that slanted handwriting that leaned back covering page after page. Math book, science book, and there was *To Kill a Mockingbird*. A history book about West Africa.

He checked the notes again. She *was* studying magic. The runes took up pages.

He looked around once more.

No books of magic. Not a single arcane text. He had never gone to school, but he'd seen Felix's apartment and Hiram's house and based on those locations, he assumed people who studied things usually had books on what they studied.

"Things are missing," Tate said. She had her hand on the white and green speckled desk against the wall. "Things were taken...not by the girl, either. She went that way." She pointed towards the window. "Just a bag." Tate squeezed her eyes shut. "There's too much magical interference here. It's like bad CCTV. She ran. They took stuff."

Sunshine gathered up the notebooks and combed through the books on the floor.

Not a single text on magic in the entire house. Highly unusual for a family with an enchanted lock and a daughter that studied magic.

"Do you know if she made it away?"

"If she died, it wasn't here," Tate confirmed.

He did one last sweep of the house. He glanced over his shoulder at one point to see Tate with her phone out. "What are you doing?"

"Snapping this girl I've been talking to. She thinks crime scenes are sexy."

He spun through about a thousand emotions in a second.

Her face fell and she turned red from ears to cheeks. "Specter told me to take pictures."

He settled on a single emotion: a warm kind of appreciation tinged with embarrassment. He held in a smile.

"That was a bad joke, I'm sorry."

He shook his head.

They finished their final look at the house and headed out, closing the window and locking the door as they went. Tate didn't say another word.

"I'm sorry about what I said. It was uncouth of me," she said once she'd driven them about halfway back to the motel.

Sunshine had made far more uncouth jokes in far more heinous situations. "I understand."

"Just...you know, it was unprofessional."

"Ah. Well. Such things happen."

"I just. I know we have that staff meeting and it's kind of been a hot topic around the office." Her voice wavered at the end of her sentence.

"Oh, well." Sunshine tried to think of something to say. "There is tasteless humor and then there is harassment of coworkers."

"Harassment?" she asked. She took her eyes off the road for too long to stare at him.

He nodded towards the street in front of them. "Eyes forward, please, Ms. Murray."

"Sorry, sorry. Just. Harassment, that's heavy."

"We'll discuss it more on Monday. I've always found Melody Blood to be most illuminating when it comes to such things. She's a wonderfully compassionate speaker," he assured her. "No one at the agency is in trouble."

"Not even Emil?"

Sunshine couldn't help but smile. "Not yet."

She laughed nervously. "He's not a bad guy, I just really think something's going on at home."

She said nothing else and he changed the topic to a late dinner.

They stopped at McDonald's and brought their food back to the motel. He snapped Felix a picture of the bag, to which the demon responded with an emoji vomiting and the words *never again.*

Sunshine shoved as many fries in his mouth as he could, took a selfie, and snapped it to Felix with the caption *Look I'm you.*

A video call came through a few seconds later and he answered it, struggling to chew everything he'd put in his mouth.

"How'd it go?" Felix asked.

Sunshine rested the phone on his chest as he lounged against the headboard.

"Sunshine."

"I'm chewing," he garbled. He swallowed, then said, "It went pretty good. Kind of had to break in. Figured out they're mages. Tate says the girl didn't die in the house, so that's good news."

"Mmm."

"I'll send you my notes in a little bit. I didn't get the chance to write anything up yet."

"Yeah, whenever. No rush. I'm kind of busy."

"Still that mage?"

"Yeah."

"What's his name again?"

"Goes by Lodger, which I doubt is his real name, but whatever." The audio of Felix's sigh crackled through the speaker. "Fucking whatever. I got your mail."

"Anything good?"

"Four different misspellings of Sunshine. You've been preapproved for two credit cards. And something from Lisa Munroe. Looks fancy."

"Did you open it already?"

"No, but I'm dying to know. People only send like…three things in the mail these days. It's not Christmas, so what's Lisa sending you?"

Sunshine had no idea. He and Lisa had met through a friend and dated her for about six months. They had broken up mutually and amicably when she'd moved to Vermont and remained in touch through social media. Occasionally, she called for advice on a case, though she was more a bounty hunter than a detective. She tracked creatures that had gone rogue and risked exposing the entire Community. He had not laid eyes on her in six years.

She had always described Sunshine as "Exactly what I need right now" which he assumed meant that following the abusive stalker she'd previously dated, she appreciated that Sunshine neither stalked nor abused her. He had been unoccupied at least two evenings a week, courteous to her, and about as sexually aggressive as a panda.

She had been uncomfortable during anything more than kissing or handholding, pulled away if he moved in too suddenly, and flinched at raised voices. She had also been funny, kind, and overwhelmingly normal, which had been a nice contrast to work and Felix.

"Open it," Sunshine said. He turned the phone so they could see each other and bent his leg so he could rest the phone against his thigh.

Felix held up the envelope. He struggled to open it with one hand and resorted to using his teeth. Finally, he shook a piece of paper out of the envelope and held it up to the camera.

"You put it over the camera, it's all gone dark."

Felix pulled it back.

Sunshine scanned the wedding invitation. He'd known Lisa was engaged, but he'd had no reason to expect an invitation.

Felix said, "RSVP by April first. Oh, Sunshine, you were on her B-list. Thursday night wedding, no wonder people aren't going."

"Anything else in the mail?"

"No."

"Alright." He fished out the hamburger from the McDonalds bag. "How are you?"

"Alive."

"We'll be home by Saturday night."

"How's Tate doing?" Felix asked.

"She seems fine."

"Good, don't do anything to make her quit. Psychics are hard to come by and most of them are looney."

Sunshine's phone notified him that he had low battery. "Alright, well, I have to charge my phone. I'll email you in the morning."

"Like I said, no rush."

"Bye."

"See you soon."

Sunshine hung up and went to find his phone charger. He combed through his backpack and his duffle bag but couldn't find it. He asked Tate for her car keys and checked there, too, but came back empty-handed.

She offered to lend him hers, but they had different brands of phones. He sent Felix a quick text to appraise him of the situation and turned off his phone to conserve what battery he had left.

He'd have to buy a new charger in the morning; they were cheap enough at dollar stores.

Without his phone, he couldn't play his sounds. He tried to settle into bed. Sometimes he didn't need them.

Tonight, he did.

He tried, really tried, to sleep, but gave up and worked through the night, typing up notes, sending emails, and sorting through the photographs that Tate had already uploaded to a secure file-sharing website. The kinds of photos they took in their line of work did not need to be available to any inquiring minds with reasonable computer skills. They had learned that by proxy; vampires had nearly achieved public recognition through photo sharing.

It had taken a lot of grease, the combined efforts of all their government infiltrators, and a good cover-up story to send the undead back into the shadows. The BDSM community had taken an awful hit, which was a shame since they'd already had issues with misrepresentation in recent fiction trends.

The world at large had barely been ready to recognize mermaids and a lot of people still considered the discovery a hoax; what would the world do with more exploitable creatures? Zoos, experimentation, reservations, mutated super-soldiers, magically produced nukes...the list went on.

Thankfully, most people did not want to believe in anything that made them uncomfortable, be it demons, their partner's infidelity, or things much worse than those. Easier to duck your head and pretend you hadn't seen Uncle Jeff coming out of little Sammy's room late, late at night. Bad things belonged in the shadows.

Tate rapped on his door on Friday morning with a grin and a plastic package dangling from her finger. "Stopped at the dollar store on my coffee run. That's the right kind, right?"

He nodded. "Yes, thank you."

"I had a feeling." She handed over the charger, paper bag with a Danish, and a cup of coffee. "Two sugars? I can never remember which one of you drinks it which way."

"No supernatural intuition there?"

She shook her head. "You two are..." She snorted. "Never mind."

"We're what?" he asked as he followed her to the car, hands full.

"You two get fuzzy sometimes. It happens with people who spend a lot of time together. Little details get mixed up. Telepathic people, uh, they have a really hard time with it. Family, close friends, spouses, the telepaths end up not being able to keep their thoughts on lockdown anymore. Theirs slip in, yours slip out." She made a weaving gesture with her hand. "You two are like...retirement home couple level fuzzy. Like codependent mother-daughter fuzzy. Like an orange you forgot about in the back of your car for six months fuzzy."

He slid into the passenger seat and set down his coffee. He started to pick apart the stiff, stubborn plastic casing of the charger. "Is that too much fuzz?"

"Hell if I know. Never been with anyone long enough to get fuzzy. I think it's, you know, to each their own. Some people like bleu cheese, some people don't."

Sunshine tried not to dwell on the comparison to fermented, mold-laden dairy. When he had his phone plugged into the car and charging, he dropped his shoulders and loosened his back. He hadn't realized the stiffness until just now.

Probably the lack of sleep. He didn't require sleep on a nightly basis, but without sleep, he couldn't relax. His body assumed that if he didn't have time to sleep, he must be in the middle of some battle or campaign.

Felix had tried to get him to meditate. A lot of demons did that if they weren't up for prowling the night and didn't care for videogames, Netflix marathons, or the hell that was three a.m. television since their biology required less rest than a human. Before the advent of the internet and especially when the broadcast day had had an end, demons had tended towards restlessness in the wee hours.

He turned his phone back on and checked his texts.

Nothing.

Satisfied, he turned his attention to the Danish Tate had procured. "Where are we going?" he thought to ask as he got the last bit of icing off his fingers.

"I had a dream about a pawn shop. A little research told me that there is a pawn shop in town that deals in books. A little more research led me to believe that this might be the kind of pawnshop that would be interested in acquiring books of magic."

Sunshine did not usually base his investigations around dreams, but he hadn't come up with many ideas.

"I mean, it's weird to burgle a joint and not take jewelry. It's easy to carry, easy to pawn, but books are big and heavy and unless they're like, famous first editions, they're not worth much," Tate continued. "Even if they didn't pawn them here, the brokers might be able to point us to someone who would want them. A collector or an academic, probably."

Sunshine didn't say anything.

Tate glanced over at him. "Right?"

"Sound reasoning."

She gave him a nervous smile.

He realized she was trying to impress him. They had never worked together this closely before.

"My grandfather collected books."

"Ah."

She parked across the street from the pawnshop and said, "I should go in alone."

"I don't know if that's smart."

"Yeah, but if two of us go in asking for questions and they're selling things they know are stolen, they might get squirrely. And you look so..." She glanced him over. "Sunshine, you look so nice. They might not talk."

"Sometimes it helps," he said.

"You're the boss."

They got out of the car. She hung back and entered the store a few minutes after he did. He browsed the collection of books on display and made a show of comparing them to something on his phone. He sighed and frowned.

The woman working the counter came over. Without an ounce of warmth, she asked, "You looking for something in particular?"

"I am. I'd sort of heard this place sells special books but, I, I don't really see what I'm looking for."

The woman glanced at the books. She crossed her arms. "Well. What are you looking for?"

"Uh, my, uh." He gave a practiced smile, sweet and sheepish. "My boyfriend. His birthday's coming up next month and I really wanted to get him something he'll love. He's had such a rough few months and I just...He collects books, but they're kind of hard to find. Like. Really hard to find."

Her face softened at his story and his smile. This time, she spoke more gently, "What kind of books?"

"I, uh, I think he calls them arcane books? Something about magic. I don't really know much about it, but he can..." Sunshine glanced around. "Well. He kind of does magic." He made sure his smile looked excited but a little embarrassed. "It sounds crazy. He makes these beautiful nightlights."

"You're looking for magic books?" the woman clarified.

"I know, it sounds nuts. His sister said this might be a good place to check, though."

The woman looked him over, lips scrunched off to one side. "We have a few special collections. I don't know about *magic* though. I'll get Barry, he's worked here longer." She beckoned for him to follow.

"Thank you. So much. It means a lot."

She nodded.

Tate, who'd been browsing the jewelry, caught Sunshine's eye and gave him a small smile.

The woman went into a back room. Not too long later, a tall, broad man in a crisp polo and khakis approached Sunshine. He looked him over, his eyes a foggy gray that made Sunshine wonder if he could see. To Sunshine's general direction, he said, "I hear you're interested in one of our special collections."

"Yes, I—"

The man's hand darted out towards Sunshine, his aim too accurate for a man who possibly couldn't see.

Sunshine knocked his hand away, stepped back, and settled himself on an angle to the man. He waited but didn't relax.

"What are you?" the man asked.

"Excuse me?"

"Ashley knows how to keep a secret and she's meaner than a rattlesnake. There's no way she'd come get me for anything other than an approved buyer. So, what are you?" He turned his eyes on Sunshine's face now.

Sunshine put up a hand to block the man's eyes from meeting his. It felt somehow incredibly important that their eyes not meet. Those eyes could see right inside of him, tear out all his secrets if he'd had any secrets to keep.

He fixed his eyes on Barry's mouth. "You're a telepath, right? I'm an angel—"

"A demon."

"No. An angel. I am not one of the Fallen."

"Fine. What are you doing here?"

"Exactly what I told your coworker. I'm looking for arcane texts."

"For your boyfriend?" the man asked with enough of a sneer in his voice that Sunshine almost made eye contact.

He checked the urge to stare him down. "Sure. You do sell arcane texts here, don't you?"

"Not to anyone who walks in."

"And what about buying them? You buy them from anyone who walks in?"

Barry grunted. "You a cop or something? You got a badge?"

Sunshine peeked away from the man's mouth and smiled at him. "Would you really want a cop poking around here? I just want to know what kind of books you have. If you've gotten any new ones lately."

The searing intensity of the man's eyes softened at Sunshine's smile. He shifted, then said, "We don't sell books to anyone who walks in. Not my call to sell them either."

"Whose call is it?"

"Owner's. She handles all that spooky shit."

Still not fully meeting the man's eyes, Sunshine asked, "If I leave a card, can you pass it on to her?"

"Figure I can."

Sunshine handed over a crisp card the color of bone. The small, neat letters gave the necessary information on the agency. "Thank you."

"Mhm." The man eyed the card and turned it over in his fingers.

Sunshine headed towards the door. Tate followed right after and they leaned against the side of the car, eyeing the pawnshop from across the street.

"That seemed sketchy," she said.

"It was a pawnshop. They tend to get that way."

"He didn't like you."

"He doesn't have to like me. He just has to give that card to the owner."

Tate sighed. She scuffed the toe of her shoe against the ground. "Well, that was my idea. Zilch."

They lingered for a while longer, since they had no other destination in mind.

Sunshine checked his email. Once he'd read through the pertinent ones, he told her, "I'd like to go back to the house. I've asked Specter if he knows a way to clear up the magical interference. He made some recommendations."

Felix had recommended a few spells, but he'd also known Sunshine wouldn't do the spells. He'd written as much: *I know you won't bother with any of those because it might take too much effort to learn a few runes.* He'd sent the address of a reputable shop in the area which could sell them a smudge stick meant for exactly this purpose. Witches cleaned up after themselves better than mages. Sunshine also thought they tended to have better manners, toward certain members of the Community at least.

"And once we get rid of the interference?" she asked.

"Ideally, we would find the girl, if she can be found."

Tate scrunched up her face. "Sounds dicey. What if she's, uh, you know, what if dangerous people have her?"

"We'd contact the appropriate liaison within the police department. This city seems to be a Community city, or at least, it has a sizeable Community element. They'll have officers we can work with."

"You're the boss." She made for her side of the car, jangling her keys in her palm.

"Tate."

She paused.

"I would not bring you knowingly into danger."

She grimaced. "I, you know, you're used to working with Specter. I'm not a demon, or an angel, I'm human. We're a lot easier to kill."

"Humans are surprisingly hardy. People survive tremendous falls, car fires, awful diseases," he began, then stopped when he saw the look on her face. He amended, "I won't bring you anywhere unsafe, Tate. You have my word."

"Great. Thanks."

"Do you regularly feel unsafe during work hours?" he asked.

"Um. No. Not really. But I don't usually work these kinds of cases, do I?"

Sunshine had failed to consider that. "No, I suppose not. If it makes you feel better, I was handmade by God to be a soldier so I can protect you from most things."

She leaned against the trunk and looked him over. "Were you really? I mean. I know you are what you say you are. I believe you. But, well, I guess believing you aren't lying or believing in Specter's dad is one thing. He actually shows up places. I've seen him. I've seen you. I've seen the goddamn Devil but, I mean. Believing in God just seems like a step too far."

"Faith isn't made with your eyes, nor your heart or mind. It comes from your soul."

"Oh."

"Even the Devil requires faith. He cannot do anything to you unless you believe he can do it," Sunshine assured. He assured most people of this because factually it was true. Practically, though, the Devil could do almost anything because the greater human consciousness that acknowledged him believed he could.

She let out a breath. "Let's not dive too deep. I guess religion kind of comes with the territory, but I don't know if I'm ready for this talk."

"Most people never are."

"Where are we headed?" She gave her keys another jingle then unlocked the car.

He gave her the address of the shop.

The smudge stick worked exactly as the witch who'd sold it to them had promised it would. Once the magical resonance from the home dissipated, Tate sat on the front porch for a long time. Sunshine sipped at long-cooled coffee and wished someone was there to warm it up for him. He tried not to stare at Tate too much. It would have unnerved him to be stared at while he was trying to work.

He checked his phone several times. Probably too many times. Thousands of years without it and now he couldn't go for a few hours.

He looked over the comments Felix had added to his notes. Most of them useless ramblings as far as Sunshine was concerned, but they meant something to Felix.

If Tate couldn't get a read on the girl, they would have to cast a locator spell. Or, more accurately, Felix would have to come here and cast a locator spell. Sunshine couldn't cast basic magic and a locator spell was outside the grasp of most practiced mages.

Movement on the porch caught his eye.

Tate had stood. She started down the steps, her movements heavy and clumsy. She walked and he knew better than to ask her where she was going. She would lose the trail and it would be next to impossible to get back.

Psychic energy got fussy and more than that, it got picky. Sunshine knew more than a few psychics who said it even got huffy. Better not to offend it and stay quiet.

He followed behind her but hung back a few feet.

Tate inched along and before each turn she stopped and stood still for minutes, staring at nothing.

Or something only she could see.

She brought them out of the quiet, clean neighborhood of rowhouses into areas that became more rundown the farther they went. These neighborhoods were less quiet and more silent, punctuated here and there by sirens, raised voices, howling dogs, or crying babies.

People watched them from cars and windows. No one looked hostile, just somewhere between interested and concerned.

They passed over a set of rails and the boarded-up, dilapidated buildings and filthy sidewalks made Sunshine assume they had found the literal other side of the tracks.

He started to think about turning back.

Tate led him to a building in an abandoned factory yard, a ramshackle and rusted shack made of corrugated metal.

He put a hand on her shoulder before she could get too close.

She sucked in a harsh breath and recoiled from Sunshine's touch. She pulled in shallow gasps and stared at Sunshine, eyes the size of the moon.

"Tate."

She clenched her jaw and her fists, her whole body shaking.

"Fuck," he breathed. He called up a bit of calm and placed his hands on her shoulders, letting the feeling he'd conjured seep into her.

She, thankfully, let him. Her breathing calmed and her body relaxed. She rubbed her face. "I'm sorry."

"No, I..."

"I was in it too long, I'm sorry. I know better than that."

"Do you feel alright?" he asked.

"Uh. Yeah. I." She glanced towards his hands on her shoulders. "I feel fine."

He took his hands back.

"What was that?"

He shrugged. "Angel stuff."

"Angel stuff."

"I have some sway over emotional states. Sometimes on the battlefield people get too riled up or see something too awful. I can take the edge off."

"Handy."

"It helps..." He stopped himself. He'd almost told her it helped with Felix, which it did, but that was too personal. "It's handy."

"I bet." She turned around to look at the rusted building. "That place is one big blank."

"Wards?"

She nodded. "Or a portal to one of the Otherworlds, which I

doubt."

Sunshine surveyed the building and believed that it might be a rift that led to Hell. "I supposed we should go in."

Tate tapped a piece of debris with her shoe. "Try knocking."

He raised an eyebrow.

"It's polite. Haven't you got manners in Heaven?"

"There aren't any doors in Heaven."

"Not a single one."

"Not that I ever got to use. God sealed the Citadel to almost all of us."

"The Citadel?" she asked.

"The one place in Heaven where we can use our bodies. I'm sure there must have been doors there." He reached out and rapped on the sagging door of the building; he'd rather face whatever lie within than have this conversation.

No answer came from inside.

He knocked again and tried to peer inside through one of the rusted-out holes in the metal. He thought he saw movement. "Hello?" He waited a few seconds, but his hail went unanswered. "My name is Sunshine. I work with a detective agency."

He heard a voice but didn't understand the language. He recognized it, for sure, and stepped back before the door blew off the hinges. He caught the scent of ozone and yanked Tate back and to the side before the door, or the bolt of lightning could hit either of them.

A small figure darted out of the building. Short legs, so not very fast. Sunshine asked, "Tate, are you alright?"

"Yeah, yeah, thanks."

The glimpse he'd caught of the girl resembled the pictures he'd been given of Sarai. Dirty, wild-eyed and hollow-cheeked, her hair in disarray and her clothes ragged and baggy, but he'd seen the familiar, even features.

Even after she had run for a full five minutes, Sunshine could have loped after and caught her easily. He didn't want to dodge any more lightning bolts.

"You have the office number, right?" he asked Tate.

"Yes."

"If I get knocked out, call the office." He jogged after the girl and called, "Sarai Robinson! I'm not trying to hurt you, please stop running."

She did not stop running. She did start to chant, her breaths coming short between the runes.

"If you don't stop trying to cast that spell, I will stop you," he warned.

She didn't stop. She did try to run faster, though.

Sunshine didn't know how long it would take to cast that spell and he didn't like the gasps as she chanted. She could easily foul up a spell that way, which could hurt her as much as it hurt him. He lengthened his stride and grabbed her, wrapping her up in his arms and pulling her off her feet.

She thrashed in his grip and tried to bite his hand when he covered her mouth.

He uncovered her mouth as soon as he'd interrupted her spell. "No more magic."

She screamed and kicked at him. "Put me down."

He complied but kept a grip on her. "Don't run."

She threw her head back and hit him hard on the chest.

"I won't hurt you," he assured. He tried to calm her as he'd calmed Tate, but she didn't relax into it. He urged the aura into her a little more and she stopped thrashing. He loosened his grip.

She wrenched out of his arms but didn't run.

"No magic," he warned.

"What the fuck!"

"Are you Sarai Robinson?"

Her eyes narrowed.

"If you are, I've been hired to find you."

"By who?"

He hesitated. The truth wasn't exactly comforting. "I work for a detective agency in New York. We specialize in cases that involve the Community. My associate," here he gestured towards Tate, "is a psychic and tracked you here from your home."

She took a step back.

"I am here to help."

"Then why'd you chase me?"

He raised an eyebrow. "Why'd you run?"

She tightened her hands on the straps of her backpack. "You aren't the only one looking for me."

He had not expected to find this girl so easily. If she had been a relatively short walk from her home, then the Devil should have been able to find her without help. He put his hands in his pockets and considered what to tell her for a while. How to explain things and how to proceed from here escaped him.

"We're staying in a motel. Why don't you come take a shower, at least? Have a meal," he offered.

Tate had approached, but not too close. She waved. "Hi."

Sarai eyed her without returning the greeting. She took another step away from them.

"You've been in there for a while. That little shack?" Tate said. "That's a long time to hide."

"I didn't have anywhere to go."

"No friends or family in the area?" Tate asked.

"Three of my father's *friends* broke into our house," she said, "And killed my parents."

"That's really rough." Tate came a little closer. "I'm a detective, too. Did he tell you?"

Sarai nodded. "Psychic."

"Yeah." Tate smiled. "So, you know I can feel things, that energy. I can feel how scared you are. How angry."

The girl glared at her.

"It's not gonna get any better hiding out in that shithole," Tate said. "And if I could find you, someone else can do it too."

"I have that place warded."

"From spells, right?" Tate asked.

"I'll do better next time."

"We can bring you to a safe house," Sunshine offered. "You can ward that if you want. Or call your uncle."

"No."

"We can talk about that later. Come take a bath. You've got to be dying for one," Tate tempted.

Sarai glanced at Sunshine.

He smiled at her.

Her shoulders sagged. She rubbed her face and wiped her nose on her sleeve. She sniffled.

He took a business card out of his jacket and handed it to her. "This is our office. You can call to make sure we're legit."

"Cause no one's ever printed fake business cards before," she huffed. She stared down at the card. She rubbed her nose, then narrowed her eyes at the card. She turned it over then back to the front. "You're Sunshine."

He nodded.

"Who hired you to find me?"

He pressed his lips together. He had to bring this girl to the Devil; he owed Lucifer favors and he couldn't negotiate how or when Lucifer called them in. If he told her the truth, she'd flee. If he lied…Well, he didn't like to lie. He did it, but he didn't like it. But the truth, it would bother the girl, it would bother Tate, it would probably bother the whole office.

She stared at him, right into his eyes. She had dark eyes, so dark he couldn't see her pupil.

Felix had eyes like that, except in the sun his eyes took on an unholy red glow. Hers warmed marginally, the brown shining through. Her gaze didn't soften as she stared him down.

"A minute, Tate?" he asked.

Tate frowned.

"Please."

Tate went, heading back towards the shack.

Sarai repeated, "Who hired you?"

"Lucifer told me to find you."

She looked less impressed and terrified than he had expected. "Yeah, did he say it, or did you hear it from the neighbor's dog?"

He hadn't expected disbelief.

"I'll take a pass on the bedtime stories. You really want to help, get me a ticket out of this place. As far as I can get."

"Alright." He had no other way to get her to come with him. "Wherever you want to go."

She nodded, her lips tight.

Without another word, they headed towards Tate.

Tate persuaded Sarai into coming back to the motel with them by promising they'd get her a room of her own and whatever she wanted to eat. She also agreed to wait until morning to go anywhere, given how long it had taken to walk back to the car.

As soon as they handed over the card key, she disappeared into the room with a bag of fast food.

Tate followed Sunshine back to his room, arms crossed.

"What?"

"You know I trust you."

"Okay."

"But what are we doing with this girl?"

Sunshine shrugged. "Hopefully, getting her out of harm's way. Maybe finding out who killed her parents."

"She seemed to know who did it."

"Maybe we can get her to talk to the police. Or maybe you can at least," Sunshine said.

"Just…" Tate sighed. "Tell me this isn't something sketchy."

Blessedly, at that moment, Sunshine's phone rang. He fumbled to answer it and ducked inside his room. "Hello?"

"You sound sweaty."

"How does someone *sound* sweaty, Specter, honestly?"

"I don't know, but you're managing it. Wonder why He made you so sweaty. You think He's into it?" Felix mused.

"Did you call for a reason?"

"I wanted to hear your voice."

Sunshine sat on the edge of the bed. He was not prepared for that or the melancholy way Felix had said it.

"I'd really like a hug, too, but you're in Pennsylvania on a case we never actually took."

"I–"

"Save it, Sunshine. I trust you." Felix let out a breath. "I'm meeting with that guy tomorrow night. He's..." His voice caught.

"You don't have to tell me."

"I can't tell anyone else."

Sunshine would have traded everything he possessed to be by Felix's side right then. Every knickknack in his apartment, the very clothes off his back. "What is it?"

"He's bringing the kid with him. I have to meet him somewhere that he'll tell me like twenty minutes ahead of time. I have to go fucking pick up this kid."

"That's..."

"They've been calling him Theo. Lodger says I can call him whatever I want."

Sunshine flopped back. "But the police are going to grab Lodger then?"

"I think so."

"And they'll take the kid, too. Won't they?"

"Yeah. Try to find his parents."

"That's good at least," Sunshine said.

The line went quiet. Sunshine thought Felix had hung up or the call had been dropped. He checked to make sure they were still connected.

"Specter?"

"I wish you were here."

"I'll be home by tomorrow."

Felix sighed. "I understand Dad a lot more on days like this. How could we let such awful things happen? Not just one or two sick fucks but a whole world that lets it happen? We all deserve to go to Hell."

"You don't mean that."

"Don't tell me what I mean," Felix growled toothlessly. "Tell me about something else. I need to think about something else."

Sunshine told him about the pawnshop and the trek through Tinsville. He told him about finding the girl in the building and how she'd run away.

"She ran?" Felix asked.

"I mean, I would run if I was her."

"No, I mean, she's *alive?*"

"Oh. Yes." Sunshine smiled. "She's alive."

"At least one good thing happened today." Felix let out a huff of a laugh. "Can we get ripping fucking drunk when you get home?"

"Is that your solution to everything?" Sunshine asked.

"I mean I do have a fairly explicit history of substance use and at this point, it's not a solution so much as it is another problem."

"You're not..."

"I'm high functioning, but that doesn't mean I'm not an addict."

Sunshine rolled onto his side. It didn't feel like a conversation they should have over the phone, but it might have been something Felix couldn't stay to his face. "Are you still taking those pills?"

"I'm...It's not the day-to-day bit, you know. I don't need anything. Not yet. I just want it. It's the...the now-what times. No case, nothing on TV. No one to hang out with. Or when I kind of feel. Well. You know."

Sunshine knew.

"And I shouldn't get this way. You know, nothing bad ever happened to me really. I have friends, a job I like, great parents, and a pretty normal childhood. Or, at least. A happy, stable one. I wasn't always like this. I don't know what changed."

"I'm sorry."

"Why, have you been doing something to me?" Felix asked with feigned suspicion. "Sometimes I think...You know, never mind. Just forget it."

"Please."

"No, some other time. When we can talk."

"We're talking now," Sunshine pointed out.

Felix heaved an excessively loud sigh.

Sunshine could imagine him sprawled dramatically across his couch with an arm draped over his eyes.

"I think I was sheltered as a child. Bibi and Papa kept me so away from what the world really thought of me. Even Dad danced around it, in his own way. I think all these years finding out who I really am to people...and what people expect of me. And what I can't give them."

Sunshine tried to think of something to say.

"Or what I give them anyway. Things I thought I couldn't." Felix went quiet again.

"Felix?"

"Hmm?"

"You know they're wrong about you."

"I wish they weren't," Felix mumbled.

"What do you mean?"

"I mean I wish I was what they think I am." After a beat, he added, "I mean, not like a flesh-eating rapist, I'm not that fucked up. I just wish...Jesus, Sunshine, listen. Can we talk about something else? Literally anything."

"I might need to put a locator charm on this girl."

"Sketchy!"

"I know."

"I'd pay ten dollars to watch you try to do a spell."

Sunshine huffed. "Are you going to help me or not?"

"I bet you'll get extra sweaty!"

"Don't be a bitch."

"Say please or I won't help you," Felix pouted.

The way he said it made Sunshine shiver. He knew that pout, he knew the risqué hint of physical contact that would have come with it. He put a lot of feeling into his voice when he asked, "Please, Felix."

Felix let out a startled cough. "Uh. Have you got a knife?"

"Yes."

"Ok. Get it? What shoes are you wearing?"

Sunshine went to retrieve the knife from his duffle bag and glanced at the shoes by the door. "My brown boots?"

"The Clarks?"

"Uh, no, the waterproof ones."

"Mmm, the Chelsea boots. Never mind. What jacket did you bring?"

"What does that have to do with anything?" Sunshine asked.

"What jacket?" Felix repeated.

"The green one."

"Green?" Felix demanded. "That corduroy blazer you've had for a thousand years?"

"Olive," Sunshine corrected. "With all the pockets."

"Ah. Right. Alright. Get your jacket."

Sunshine retrieved his jacket. "Now what?"

"Are you sweaty yet?"

"No." He wasn't nervous, just annoyed so far.

"Turn the jacket inside out."

"Stop fucking around."

"Turn the jacket inside out. Look at the bottom of the sleeves. Like...the under part. Not the cuffs."

Sunshine sighed and if Felix had been there, he would have shot him a dirty look, but did as he'd been told. He found nothing. "What am I looking for?"

"It should be like a little lump."

He found the lump, no bigger than a penny, along the seam of the jacket near the armpit. "What is it?"

"It's a tracking charm. You can probably pop the insole out of her shoe and hide it under there."

Sunshine cut the charm out of his jacket and poked at the spot where it had been hidden, checking for damage to the fabric. There was not. Felix had been careful. "Do the words 'invasion of privacy' mean anything to you?"

"I've never *used* it."

"Still."

"Don't act like I'm stalking you! It's for *emergencies*. Jesus. Things go sideways all the time."

"I think your parents let you read too much pulp fiction."

"Bad things happen, Sunshine, I'm not about to let them happen to you, too. What if you'd gotten lost in that stupid spider tunnel?"

Sunshine sighed and rolled the small charm around in his fingers. Just a small disc of glass; Felix had probably conjured it himself.

"It's not any different than tracking your cell phone."

"It's different," Sunshine said.

"Are you mad?"

"No. Just concerned." Even the concern barely registered, though. He had at some point surrendered himself to Felix's invasive brand of affection.

"I just worry."

"I know. But you didn't have to do it in secret. You could have asked."

"I. Well. I. You know what! You're the one trying to put this thing on a little girl," Felix declared. "Talk about invasion of privacy. You don't even know her."

Sunshine rolled his eyes. He had no argument in his favor and knew if Felix hadn't brought it up, he would have agreed that placing a tracking device on a child was decidedly sketchy. "I didn't eat yet."

"I had some grapes."

"You should have a real meal."

"I had a lot of grapes. Like half the bag. I don't think I could eat a real meal."

"Fine. Take care of yourself. I'll be home tomorrow."

"Yeah."

Sunshine wanted to say something. He didn't know exactly what. Something to make Felix feel better. "I'll make dinner. Carbonara."

"And daiquiris."

"They don't really go together, but sure. Carbonara and daiquiris."

"It's a date," Felix said and hung up before Sunshine could say anything else.

Sunshine considered his food options. He eventually went next door to get Tate and asked if she wanted to eat somewhere that didn't have a dollar menu.

They debated what to do with Sarai, but when they went to tell her they were going out, she didn't answer. Tate put her hand against the door and said, "I think she's asleep."

They slipped a note under the door and went out to find something marginally healthy. They ended up with salads at a chain, which was better than fast food, but less than ideal. Tate asked a few questions about the case and Sunshine gave unilluminating answers simply because he didn't have any good ones.

She examined a piece of lettuce. "You ever get food poisoning?"

"No."

"I did once. Thanksgiving at Marnie Torrance's house. We stayed overnight cause she was from like Jersey, but like deep Jersey, by the Pine Barrens."

"Oh." He picked a piece of cucumber out of the salad and

examined it.

"You don't like cucumbers?" Tate asked.

"Mmm. Not really."

She took the slice off his fork with her fingers. "Marnie got it first, booked it to the bathroom. I, well...there were no empty bathrooms at that point."

He winced. "That's awful."

"I literally shit the bed. I thought I was actually dying. It was the mushroom soup in the green bean casserole. It was expired as fuck. Normally I don't touch that shit but Marnie was going on about how it was so good, so I ate it to make her happy."

"I hope you learned something about peer pressure."

"I learned something about what several gallons of vomit and diarrhea does to a relationship," she said.

"I've had mixed results."

"I think it has to do with how long you've been together," Tate said. "I think long-term people tough it out."

Sunshine didn't agree, but he also didn't feel strongly enough about it to disagree. "Some people are just squeamish," he settled on. He hunted down a crouton and crunched it happily. "We'll leave in the morning."

She nodded. "Quick trip."

"We found what we came here for. At least, some of it I guess."

That night, Sunshine slept, but poorly. He wanted to be home and done with this case. Felix's business with Lodger left a terrible feeling in his gut and made him wonder what the Devil wanted with this girl. People did such awful things to children and of all the people Sunshine knew, Satan might be the worst.

Saturday morning, he waited by the car for Tate to retrieve Sarai. He'd given the job to her since the girl responded to her better. With good reason, of course.

Sarai gave him a withering look when she emerged from the motel.

"Where's that ticket to?"

"I want an uber to the bus station and enough cash to get me to New York City," she said. "I'm not going anywhere else with you."

Tate tried to hide a smile. "What's in New York City?"

"New York Academy of Magic. My mother has. Had a colleague there."

"Who?" Sunshine asked.

"It doesn't matter," Sarai answered but sounded like she was lying.

"I know the diversity committee chairperson," Sunshine said. "So I might know your mother's colleague too. Or at least have met them in passing."

"Who's the diversity chair?" Tate asked.

"Ashton Rasp," Sunshine asked. "They also teach, uh...metaphysics and arcane theory. Incredibly smart. You should see them and Specter when they're together, it's like watching two black holes try to rip each other apart."

"The bus station?" Sarai asked.

"You really think you're safer on the bus than with us?" Sunshine asked.

"I been safe this whole time without you."

"You were living in a shack."

"Cause I didn't have any money and I wasn't about to go around trying to make any," she said. "I'll take my chances on the bus, Berkowitz."

Sunshine struggled to believe this was the girl who's room had been littered with fairy tales, who'd still had a dinosaur blanket on her bed.

"Come on, kid," Tate said. "You're like, thirteen. Why do you think they'll even sell you a bus ticket? There's rules for unaccompanied minors."

"I'm fifteen."

"Oh, sorry." Tate rolled her eyes with supreme big sister energy. "You're still an actual child though. I feel like we should have called the cops already anyway."

"Don't. I don't need the cops. I have shit to do. You promised me a ticket anywhere I wanted."

"Let us help you get shit done," Sunshine offered. "You want to find out who killed your parents—"

"I know who killed my parents."

"A detective company is a pretty good bet," Sunshine continued as though she hadn't snapped at him. "We know the Community."

"No."

Sunshine nodded. "Alright. Fine. First, you tell me who your mother's colleague is, then you can go. Cash and all."

"Gwen. Her and my mom worked on stuff together."

"Gwen what?"

"Gwen I'll figure it out when I get there. How many Gwens can there be at one school?" Sarai asked. She put out her hand.

He pulled out all the cash he had. It wasn't much. He wondered if Felix had sewn any emergency cash into the lining of his coat. He didn't hand the money over yet. "So you find Gwen. Then what?"

Sarai reached for the money.

"Our agency has safe houses. Resources. Connections with the legal system and in the Community. We can help you."

"Honestly," Tate said. "I know you aren't supposed to go with strangers, but we're not the bad guys here."

"And I only have thirty-two dollars," Sunshine said. "Which won't get you to New York."

She snatched the cash out of his hand. "Fuck you. You're a scumbag."

"Let us drive you," Tate said.

"Do I have any fucking choice in the matter?" she demanded. She threw the money at him.

Tate and Sunshine exchanged an uneasy glance.

"We really won't hurt you," Tate assured. "Scout's honor."

She rubbed at her eyes. "Can we just fucking go?" Her voice came out thick and strained.

Sunshine really didn't want to see her cry. He opened the back door for her.

She climbed in.

He and Tate looked at each other outside the car. He bent to pick up the money she'd thrown.

"Is this as bad as it feels?" Tate asked.

"I hope not."

"Should we bring her to the bus station?"

"I don't know."

"I mean. She's just a kid. We shouldn't put her on a bus to New York, right? I mean, I'd hate to be a kid with no money and no friends in the city."

Sunshine nodded. "I think this is right."

"It kind of feels like kidnapping."

Legally, Sunshine wasn't sure they weren't kidnapping her. He sighed. "We'll figure it out."

Tate tugged on her ear, made a face, then got into the driver's side of the car.

Sunshine climbed in and buckled up. He drew in a breath.

"Here we go," Tate announced with false cheer as they pulled out of the motel.

The car stayed silent.

Sunshine had to turn on the radio. In the rearview mirror, he could see Sarai with her knees pulled up to her chest. When they had to make a pit stop, he tried his best to be nice to her. He didn't get anything out of it; she glared and scowled at every turn. He deserved it.

He texted Jen and asked her to get one of their safe houses ready. The agency had a few small apartments scattered throughout the city for situations such as this. Ditching a teenager in an apartment didn't feel right, but it was better than living in a shack.

Had to be.

Traffic turned a six-hour trip into an eight-hour one. By the time they reached the apartment on Katonah Avenue, Sunshine wanted to lay down on the floor and melt into a puddle. If he never sat again it would be too soon.

Jen met them outside the apartment and walked them up to the one-bedroom, one-bathroom apartment that Sarai would call home for now. It was clean and safe, if not a little shabby.

"I put some groceries in the fridge already. Any allergies?" Jen asked Sarai.

"Kiwis."

"I'll keep that in mind. My name is Jennifer González," she shared her name without a single concession to anglicization. "I manage the office side of things for Misters Sunshine and Specter. Anything you need for the duration of your stay, or anywhere you need to go, you can arrange through me." Jen extended her hand to Sarai.

Sarai eyed the woman.

If anyone in the world had a face that said 'trustworthy' more than Jen, Sunshine had yet to see it. Short and curvy, with a bright smile and eyes that practically twinkled, Jen exuded warmth. She calmed the world around her, brought energy to exactly the places that needed it.

She was also the only one in the office with better hair than Sunshine and he had gladly ceded the title of "most fabulous ringlets" to her when Felix had hired her from the reception desk at a Marriot.

Sarai shook her hand.

"Nice to meet you."

"You too," Sarai answered sullenly.

"Jen is going to get you all set up and settled in. It's been a long drive. Why don't you get some rest?" Sunshine suggested.

"I want a computer."

"There's one inside," Jen assured. "It's a decent place, modern amenities. There's a phone—a landline—if you need to make any calls. Come on up, honey, we'll get you all set."

Sarai glanced at Tate and received an encouraging smile. The girl sighed, adjusted her backpack, and consented, "Fine."

"I'll check in tomorrow," Sunshine said.

"Don't come here. Call or something."

He nodded. "Of course." He wouldn't set foot inside the safehouse if that made it feel less safe to her. "Oh, put up whatever wards you like, but first check the ones that are already there. There's a list taped to the inside of one of the cabinets. Jen knows where it is."

"Yeah." She glanced towards the apartment door and Jen. "Bye."

He gave a small, awkward wave, then turned back to Tate. Before she brought him back to the Weller, he asked her to stop at a grocery store.

Felix didn't text him that he was on his way home until nine and didn't slump through the door to Sunshine's apartment until almost ten.

Sunshine glanced over, intending to greet him and perhaps offer a word of comfort if he looked particularly miserable. Instead, he cried, "Your hair!" then immediately covered his mouth.

Not only was his hair much shorter, clipped close on the back and sides and distinctly longer on top, it was purple. Not soft lavender or subtle lilac but bright and vibrant amethyst.

Felix shrugged and ran his hand through the tousled length on top. "Yeah." He looked at the floor instead of Sunshine.

Sunshine approached him. "Oh my god."

"I know."

"It's so purple," Sunshine enthused.

"It washes out. I just...I went for a haircut, but Kim was on maternity leave so I went with some new girl and she asked all these questions cause she thought I was bleaching it then we talked about if I'd ever colored it and I haven't and, well. You know I'm impulsive."

Sunshine skated his fingers over the fine fuzz at his temple.

"It was stupid, I look like—"

"You look *amazing*," Sunshine insisted.

Felix shrugged.

Sunshine raked his fingers through Felix's hair. "The whole thing. The color, the cut. You look really good."

Felix smiled. "It was getting kind of long."

"I love it."

Felix shrugged again but he still had a smile on his face. "I thought you were making me dinner."

"Mmm." Sunshine moved in closer and slid his arms under Felix's and around his ribs.

Felix let out a breath. It was such a small noise, barely there. A half-whispered, "Oh," followed by him putting his arms around Sunshine's shoulders. He nestled in close.

Sunshine pulled back. "Come have a seat." He nodded toward the stools by the kitchen island.

Felix sat.

"As you requested, milord." Sunshine set a daiquiri in front of him. "I'll get started on dinner."

Felix sipped the drink.

Sunshine pulled over the guanciale and started to cube it. "All's well that ends well with that kid?"

"If by that you mean Lodger sold me a six-year-old he called 'still fresh' and a SWAT team stormed the brownstone we were in, then sure. All's well." Felix flashed a sharp, tight-lipped smile.

"Yikes."

"Big yikes," Felix confirmed. "But I don't want to talk about it. Or think about it. New topic."

"I need to get in touch with your dad."

"That's an even bigger yikes. Besides, you know how to summon him."

"Yeah, but it feels so rude. And last time he thought I was one of the other ones and he did that thing with his hands. Can you, you know, call him or something?"

"I'll give you his number." Felix fished out his phone and began tapping at the screen. "Has he called in a favor already?"

Sunshine nodded.

"Quick. Normally he holds on to those."

"Well, he got three out of me."

Felix snorted. "Normally no one's dumb enough to give him that many. Especially not all at once."

"Nobody but me, I guess."

Felix snorted. "Do you think that makes you the dumbest?"

"You've always reminded me that I am," Sunshine said mildly.

Felix cleared his throat. He took another sip of his drink. "Someone's got to keep you humble."

"Mm."

Felix fidgeted with a few things. He checked his phone and sipped at his drink. He cleared his throat again. Finally, he set down his phone with a clack. "You know…"

Sunshine glanced over. He had moved to the stove during Felix's silence and currently tended the frying pan. "Hmm?"

"Dr. Reza thinks I lash out at you."

"Does she?"

"I told her it's not like that. I said it's just teasing."

Sunshine shuffled the guanciale around in the pan and waited.

Felix moved a few more things around and cleared his throat again. He sighed and twitched. He squirmed in his seat and finally said, "You know that, right?"

"Of course, I know, Specter."

"That's what I told her," Felix declared with quiet triumph. "You're a good sport about it, too, you don't get bent out of shape. Some people get so sensitive."

"You aren't this mean to other people. Not unless you really don't like them," Sunshine pointed out. "You're kind to Tate and Jen, to most of our employees. You're kind to your parents. Sort of a bitch, but kind in your own way."

Felix stared. "What's your point?"

Inspired by the two daiquiris he'd had while he'd waited for Felix to come over and by the third he'd started drinking when Felix had shown up, Sunshine explained what he normally would have left unsaid, "Sometimes I think you do it because you haven't got any other outlet for how you feel about me. You're verbally, emotionally aggressive towards me because you can't be physically aggressive."

"I don't want to hurt you!"

"There's more than one way to be physically aggressive," Sunshine pointed out.

"I don't want to fucking rape you either, Jesus Christ. You've been watching too many serial killer documentaries."

"I didn't mean sexual assault. I didn't mean anything non-consensual, but there is an aggressive element to sexual intimacy. It's a consensual act of violence, but still. All that grabbing and dragging. Penetration. There's a lot of overlap. It's a pretty common sociocultural theme. I mean, think about horror movies. Those weird perfume ads with men standing over naked bodies that might be dead," he concluded. As he did so, he decided that he must have mixed the drinks too strong. It would have been unlike him, but everyone made mistakes. He must have been more than just tipsy to say all that.

"You watch too many documentaries."

"See what Dr. Reza thinks," Sunshine suggested.

Felix snorted and drained his drink.

Sunshine placed another daiquiri in front of him. He paused and leaned across the counter. "I think that's part of it. Repression and a lot of it. It started with dislike and tension, then turned into some kind of affection."

Felix leaned back in his chair with his drink held strategically in front of his face. "What's the other part?" he mumbled as he took a sip.

Since he'd already said too much, Sunshine figured he might as well say, "I think you know I like it."

"Jesus Christ," Felix breathed. His cheeks turned pink.

Satisfied, Sunshine stepped back and returned to cooking. "I got wine; I really don't think daiquiris go with carbonara. I thought about Pinot, but I know you like Chablis, so I went with that. It doesn't really make a difference."

"Jesus fucking Christ," Felix muttered to himself. "I'm gonna go sit on the couch."

"Go ahead."

Felix migrated to the couch and turned on the TV, but minutes later he was back at the counter, leaning against it and watching Sunshine cook. He yammered on about inane things and Sunshine listened contentedly.

They ate at the island counter and Felix allowed Sunshine to pour him wine instead of another daiquiri. They finished the bottle of wine on the couch watching conspiracy theory documentaries that Felix debunked in real-time. He sat with his feet on the arm of the couch and legs over Sunshine's lap.

Sunshine placed his hand on Felix's thigh. Mostly near his knee. Mostly.

"You know when I said it's a date I didn't mean—"

"If you're going to talk over the show, at least say something productive instead of explaining common idioms to me," Sunshine suggested.

"Then stop trying to feel me up."

"Have I profaned this holy shrine with my most unworthy hand?" Sunshine asked.

"Shut up."

Sunshine took his hand back.

A few minutes later, Felix asked, "You really like it when I'm mean to you?"

"Would you really have kept being mean to me if you thought I didn't like it?"

"I don't know, I am kind of a bitch," Felix admitted. He sat up and arranged his legs Indian style. Or...what was it Tate had called that position the other day? Crisscross applesauce, that was the one. He'd have to remember that. "You have a plus one to that wedding."

"Do I?"

"Come on, you know I love weddings."

"You love open bars," Sunshine corrected.

"And dancing!"

"Do you want to be my plus one?"

"Yes."

"I'll send the RSVP on Monday."

Felix pecked his cheek. He pulled back as soon as he'd done it. He crossed his arms and settled deeper into his corner of the couch.

An hour later when Felix announced his intention to leave, Sunshine suggested, "Sleep here."

"I'm not too drunk to walk the two yards between your door and mine."

"I wouldn't mind the company."

"I'm not going to fuck you."

"Of course, you're not, we're too drunk. Sleep here."

Felix squinted at him. "Fine." He headed into the bedroom without waiting for Sunshine.

Sunshine cleaned up and headed in a few minutes later to find that Felix had already buried himself deep in the covers and taken up the middle of the bed. Sunshine climbed in beside him and tugged at the blankets. "I'm gonna need some of this."

Felix grunted and unwound himself.

Sunshine settled in.

Ten minutes later, Felix got up to use the bathroom, came back to bed, announced, "I used your toothbrush," then wormed right up to Sunshine.

"That's gross."

"You're trying to put your dick in me but you're worried that I used your toothbrush?" Felix demanded, mostly of Sunshine's ribs.

"Maybe I'm trying to put your dick in me," Sunshine suggested pleasantly.

Felix snorted so hard Sunshine felt the snot spatter against his skin. "Good fucking luck with that, I can't even get hard half the time." He started to pull back after a second.

Sunshine tightened his arm around him so he couldn't go.

"I should leave."

"If you want to talk—"

"I don't want to talk."

"Then let's get some sleep," Sunshine said. He scooted down so he lined up better with Felix and wrapped his arms around him. He kissed his hair. "Your hair smells like grape bubblegum."

Felix pressed hard against him. "It's the dye, it's still fresh. I'll probably leave a stain on your pillow."

March 21
Monday

Sunshine placed a Tupperware full of cookies in the middle of the table. Everyone gathered for the staff meeting watched him do it, nearly a dozen pairs of eyes. Emil, Tate, Dr. Love, Specter, Jen, Rollins, Yang, Hernandez, Bossley, and their guest, Melody Blood. He peeled off the cover to reveal perfectly round and golden cookies studded with chunks of dark chocolate and pecans, drizzled with a touch of salted caramel.

"I made cookies," he uselessly told the room.

Felix took one first and shoved it into his mouth. He didn't look at Sunshine when he spoke.

He'd avoided him all day on Sunday, claiming a bad hangover. Believable, they'd had a lot of wine.

Sunshine thought it had more to do with what they'd talked about. It was easier to talk when they'd been drinking. It was much harder to wake up sober in the morning and look at each other. He didn't know what Felix had done all day, but Sunshine had baked to avoid thinking too much.

He'd also texted the Devil that he'd found the girl and gotten a perfectly normal answer in return. He didn't know what he'd expected; maybe blood seeping out of the seams of his phone or the whole thing bursting into flames, but Lucifer had answered *I'll be by.*

Thank you.

Melody Blood stood at the front of the oblong table at which they held staff meetings. She wore high waisted navy trousers with a cream-colored blouse and with nude heels. The heels had rose-gold spiked studs, which did not make her seem aggressive, but only emphasized eerie danger implied by her unnaturally pale blue eyes.

Her dark red hair wrapped around her head in a braided crown.

She usually wore her hair up. Neat, but not straight-laced.

Sunshine had always wanted to take down her hair and comb it. It was entirely inappropriate, although not exactly sexual. It felt much closer to subservience than desire. He heeded her mildest suggestions without thinking, handing her pens or getting her a glass of water before anyone else could move. Her ease of command and his nature as a solider quietly and comfortably settled together.

She smiled at him, her teeth even and white against her red lipstick.

He smiled back.

"Mr. Sunshine."

"Ms. Blood. How are you?"

"I'm well. Thank you. How are you?" she asked.

"I'm doing fine, thank you."

She looked towards the Tupperware. "Still baking, I see." She did not take a cookie. "They look delicious."

He placed a cookie onto a napkin and handed it to her.

Her eyebrow barely raised.

"They're vegan," he confirmed.

She took the napkin. "Thank you, Mr. Sunshine."

"You're welcome." Dismissed from the conversation, he took his seat beside Felix.

They always sat together at staff meetings.

Felix fidgeted with the clicker that controlled the PowerPoint. Today, he was not in charge of the slideshow, but he had not yet ceded control to Melody.

The last person hurried in and took her seat; the treacherous black magic of the MTA had delayed Shay yet again.

Sunshine pushed the cookies towards her.

Felix cleared his throat. "It has come to our attention that some discomfort has taken root among our staff. It is our intention today to discuss your rights as workers and the boundaries required of you legally, as well as the agency's internal professional expectations. This meeting in no way represents disciplinary action towards anyone, but we do hope that it will alleviate some current tensions, prevent escalation, and help us avoid future such situations. Mr. Sunshine, anything to add?"

"Ah." Sunshine set down his coffee. "Thank you, Mr. Specter. To help us, we have Ms. Melody Blood. Many of you know her. She is proficient in matters regarding discrimination and harassment, as well as the nuanced ways in which things that are legal, but not appropriately sensitive, can impact protected classes of citizens. Furthermore, Ms. Blood is highly recognized in her field for her knowledge of the dynamics within the supernatural Community with whom we deal regularly in our line of work and of which some of us are members."

"Thank you, Mr. Sunshine. You always introduce me so accurately."

"I try. Ms. Blood, the floor is yours." He took the clicker from Felix and passed it towards her.

She smiled at him again.

He couldn't help but smile back.

Maybe it was sexual, that pull he felt towards her. He didn't honestly think so but couldn't explain the compulsion in any other way. The world conflated attraction, sexual desire, and enjoying people's company in so many directions that Sunshine couldn't keep track of what half of it meant. When the hormones kicked in, it confused him even further.

"In front of you all, you have two pieces of paper. What you write on them is private, I assure you. On one piece of paper, I'd like you to write something you've heard in the workplace, or out in the field, from a coworker or supervisor that made you feel uncomfortable in any way," Melody began. "When you've finished writing you can turn the paper over."

Everyone took up their paper and scratched out their answers. As soon as they'd finished, they immediately set the paper face down.

She brought them through a series of explanations and activities that started with federal and state regulations, then moved into the policy of the agency. She talked about race and gender politics, disability, the position of parents and pregnant women in the workplace, queer and trans rights.

Certain people participated, like Tate, and others nodded along.

Emil offered answers a few times. Most of his answers made the cut of basic human decency.

Shay shared the time when she'd been asked to cover up her pregnancy while she worked.

Everyone had something to add, whether comfort for a coworker or a story about how they'd been treated or something they'd seen, whether at this agency or a previous place of employment.

Things stayed civil right up until she turned to the slide labeled "The Supernatural Community".

At that Emil snorted.

Felix glared at him.

Sunshine placed his hand on Felix's arm.

It did not soothe him. He glared at Sunshine, too, so Sunshine slung his eyes towards Melody and raised his eyebrows.

It all happened in a few seconds. No one else noticed.

Melody continued her rundown of who comprised the Community and fielded questions about what, exactly, was the difference between a witch and a mage, or a vampire and a ghoul. She explained persons of mixed supernatural heritage and how the term 'coldblood' made some of them proud and others uncomfortable.

She supplied short recordings of various Community members voicing the ways in which the world had treated them poorly. Vampires who had been kidnapped and dumped in the desert, werewolves who'd had blood dumped on them when neighborhood pets had gone missing, a witch who'd had Bibles tied to bricks flung through her window, a fairy who'd had iron filings thrown at him while he rode his bike by a school.

Between each one, she opened the room for discussion and asked questions.

Sunshine did his best.

Felix shredded his cuticles.

The room grew hushed and people volunteered their comments less willingly. Melody never faltered but did grow a little impatient when no one spoke after a vampire spoke about how he'd nearly died from restricting his blood intake after being told it was an addiction.

She stared out into the room, waiting for someone to answer her question whether a biological need could be an addiction.

Finally, Sunshine had to say, "If it will kill you not to have it, it's not addiction."

"Alcoholics die in withdrawal," Emil pointed out.

"If they detox right, then they won't," Felix reminded sharply. "But a vampire can't live without drinking blood."

"If you can't live without draining people, maybe you shouldn't live," Emil suggested.

"That a vampire must take a life is a misconception," Melody said, "The amount needed is manageable if there is a responsible system of donors in place."

"Donors," Emil scoffed.

"It's not any different than giving blood," Tate said. "It's safe and—"

"It's just another way to sell yourself," Emil interrupted. "A whore's a whore, call it what it is."

"Do you need to excuse yourself for a moment?" Melody asked.

"And vampires are killers. I don't care what bunch of strung-out dopes they set up to feed on, they all crack. They all go back."

"Excuse yourself," Felix said.

Emil didn't go. He turned to Tate and insisted, "Tate, you listen to enough of this garbage you're gonna end up dead in some alley."

"Don't start," she groaned.

Sunshine stood. "Emil, take a walk with me."

Emil stood forcefully enough to jostle the table. "Don't bother." He stormed out.

Tate stared after him and began to stand.

"Let him go," Sunshine said.

She pressed her lips together.

"He's in no state to talk."

She nodded. "Yeah."

Melody did not dismiss them but did lead them through some stretching and mindfulness exercises for a quarter of an hour. They wrapped up by returning to the impact of vampire's restricting blood intake based on the idea of addiction.

No one was happy, but no one else walked out.

The last thing she did was say, "Take your other piece of paper. This one's private too, I promise. Write down something you've said that would have impacted someone in one of the ways we've talked about today. Something that hurt someone. Even if you didn't think it would."

Everyone hesitated. They looked at each other.

"It's not always big things. Think about the environment you create for others and the one you want for yourself," she suggested.

She waited until everyone had scribbled their answers.

She took one last cookie as she bid them farewell.

Felix rose to walk her out. As he did, he tucked his second piece of paper into Sunshine's shirt pocket.

"That's lunch everyone," Sunshine announced to the room. "Take your hour, no rush, and then back to your cases. Thank you, to everyone who participated and thank you even more to those who shared. Remember, Jen handles human resources and you can always come to Mr. Specter or me with any concern."

Everyone murmured an agreement or a farewell.

They trickled out.

Sunshine went up to his office and fished out the note Felix had slipped him.

You've got a dick and you think one kiss means I'll let you do whatever you want.

Sunshine put the note in his drawer, tucked into a small day planner with a folder pocket. He didn't know exactly what Felix meant to communicate by it, but he knew it meant something.

When Felix returned to their office, he said, "Aren't we going for lunch? What are you waiting for?"

"I kind of want sushi."

"The deli doesn't have sushi."

"We could go somewhere else."

Felix shook his head. "We'll do sushi for dinner."

Sunshine hesitated.

"Oh, I know, I know, you don't like to eat out on weeknights, but honestly, I think we earned it. Sushi for dinner," Felix promised. "My treat."

"Fine."

Felix tossed him his jacket. "I think we have to fire Emil."

"I don't know about that."

"I think we need to give him a written warning and some kind of disciplinary action."

Sunshine agreed, "Sure. I also think we need to hire more creatures. They're all human, even the ones who are part of the Community, except for us. They spend all day seeing the darker side of the Community. They need exposure to the good parts."

"We don't need anyone right now."

"Maybe someone part-time."

"Mmm."

"What about an intern?" Sunshine asked. "Jen would love an intern."

"I'll think about it," Felix said without sounding pleased in the slightest.

Over lunch, they chatted stiltedly about work topics unrelated to the staff meeting and Emil. They talked about their friend's baby, whether Sunshine had remembered to RSVP to the wedding, and where they should get sushi.

Finally, Felix balled up his napkin and threw it on the table. "I don't want to hire any creatures."

"Uh."

"It's not." He raked his hand through his hair. "It's not a good place to work."

Sunshine opened his mouth but didn't know what to say. "I...Is something bothering you about how we've been running the company?"

"No, it's not...well, you know. They're all human. They all work cases where the things that go bump are real and sometimes worse than you imagine. They don't like creatures."

"I don't..." Sunshine frowned.

"They like you better. You're clean and shiny, normal, for the most part. You put a vamp or a fairy in with them and it'll be..." Felix sighed and shook his head.

"Felix, are people—"

"You know they are. You hear what they say just the same as I do."

"The things they say about us are just...stupid rumors. Idle prattle, products of overactive minds."

"The things they say about me, Sunshine. Not us." Felix stood. "Let's go." He left the deli.

Sunshine swept up their trash and tossed it in the garbage as he went after Felix. He had to jog to catch up with him. He snagged him by the elbow.

It took Felix by surprise and he pivoted towards Sunshine. He looked beautiful in his surprise, his eyes dark wells, his hair falling disheveled over his forehead. "What?" he demanded.

Sunshine stared at him. Not down at him or up. They were the same height, less than an inch of difference and some of it was Sunshine's hair. He stared into his eyes.

"*What?*" Felix repeated as he stepped out of Sunshine's grip.

"I love you."

Felix frowned.

"You're a good person, it doesn't matter what other people think."

"It hurts."

Sunshine had not expected that answer. "Sorry?"

"My feelings, you idiot. It hurts my fucking feelings. And I don't want to bring anyone else into a place that feels like that," he explained.

Not knowing what else to do, he slid his hand behind Felix's head and kissed his forehead.

Felix gripped the collar of Sunshine's jacket.

"Trust me."

Felix let out a slow shudder of a breath. "Fine."

They resumed their walk back to the office and found a small, gray cat stretched out in front of their door. It was a scraggly thing with a paunchy belly. It glanced lazily up at them with green eyes.

Felix sighed. "Dad," he addressed the cat.

Sunshine raised an eyebrow.

"Nobody likes it when you hang around like this! It's creepy as fuck."

The cat appeared unimpressed. It stretched.

"What are you even doing here?" Felix glanced back at Sunshine. "Did you call him?"

Sunshine admitted, "He said he'd be by. I don't know when."

Felix huffed and opened the door to the agency.

The cat eyed the door.

"Well, go on," Felix urged the cat.

The cat went in.

"You look like shit."

The cat scampered away from them, tucking itself beneath Jen's desk. It wrapped its tail around its body and watched them.

Felix frowned. "What are you doing?" He approached the cat and went to grab it.

It hissed, swatted at him, and ran to another dark corner.

"I think you let a stray inside," Sunshine said.

"No, he does this cat bullshit all the time," Felix assured.

"I know. I think it might just be a cat, though."

"What are you guys doing?" Tate asked, poking her head out of the room with her desk.

"Specter let a stray cat inside."

"It's not a stray, it's my dad."

Tate stared at them. "What?"

Sunshine pointed to the cat hiding under the table on which they kept their photo printer.

Tate peered at it. "It looks kind of…sick. Is that cat sick?"

"It's my dad," Felix said.

"Is your dad sick?" Tate asked.

Felix grunted. "Whatever. Leave him." He headed upstairs.

Sunshine stayed downstairs and waited for Jen to come back from her lunch. He spoke with her about the possibility of getting a part-time office assistant. She liked the idea but didn't seem to understand why they'd need one.

He shrugged. "I just thought it would be nice."

"Oh, I'm sure it would be," Jen said. "There's some filing and organizing that I could use a hand with. Or chores that need to get done. I can only be in so many places at once."

"Mmm. I'll keep you up to date. Have you heard from Sarai? I called but she didn't want to say much."

"She's alright. Getting settled. She wants to find someone at the university."

He nodded. "Thanks." He turned towards the stairs.

"Uh. What's going on with this cat?"

"Oh. Specter thinks it's his dad."

Jen tilted her head. "Alright. I'll just leave it alone, then."

He gave her an apologetic look and headed upstairs. He tossed aside the idea of an intern and drafted a job posting for a part-time office assistant. It would be good to have a familiar, friendly face in the office. A Community ambassador of sorts. He'd send the posting around to various Community social media sites and the handful of newspapers that still circulated.

A small commotion came from downstairs and the cat came streaking up the stairs to wedge itself under the free-standing storage cabinet in the corner by Felix's desk.

Felix looked over with a scowl, then glared at Sunshine.

Sunshine looked back at his computer screen and tried not to say anything.

About twenty minutes later a burlap sack dropped onto his desk without a single word of accompaniment.

He startled and looked up to find the Devil looming above him and wearing an oversized black linen dress with half-sleeves.

Felix let out an exasperated groan, one that belonged to a

teenager, not a man over a century old.

The Devil said, "You found her."

"Yes."

Lucifer gestured towards the bag. It contained not just coins and mixed bills but mixed currency.

Sunshine picked up a coin. "Is this a doubloon?"

"It's an écu."

"What's it for?"

"Payment," Lucifer informed him as though he suspected Sunshine might be simple. "For services rendered."

"I...no." Sunshine stared up at him. "That was. That was a favor."

"No. That was detective work."

Felix had gotten on all fours to look under the cabinet. He stood up and brushed off his hands and pants. "It is a stray."

"Hello, Felix," the Devil said. He smiled at his son, broad and genuine, without a hint of ravenous intent.

"Hi."

"I like your hair."

"Thanks."

They stared at each other.

"It was a favor," Sunshine insisted weakly.

"No," Lucifer told him. He sat in the chair across from Sunshine's desk. "Is she well?"

Sunshine could only answer, "I think so. What do you want with her?"

"It will all come together," the Devil assured.

"Dad, what do you mean it's not a favor?" Felix asked.

"A favor is a favor. That was work. I've paid."

"Dad."

Lucifer gazed at his son. "You may be mine but you know nothing of favors, little one. The bargain was not yours and so neither is the concern."

Felix gave Sunshine a piteous glance. He turned back to his father and jabbed a finger in his direction. "Don't do anything to him."

The Devil did not smile.

"I mean it. Leave him alone."

His face smooth, Lucifer said, "The bargain was not yours."

Sunshine peered into the bag, a feeling of dread worming into his stomach and up through his chest.

"A moment, Felix," the Devil requested.

"Are you kidding!" Felix demanded.

"Let him stay," Sunshine whispered. The words got stuck in his throat. "Please."

Lucifer rose. He came around Sunshine's desk and cradled Sunshine's jaw in one long, thin hand. "You are so frightened of me."

Sunshine didn't dare to look up, didn't say a word. He almost didn't breathe.

Felix stared at them. He'd taken half a step towards them but even he didn't dare come any closer.

"What have I done for you but help?" Lucifer asked. "It was you who came to my realm, who turned a weapon against me, who sought to steal one of my souls, and when you asked I helped."

Sunshine glanced up.

Never had Lucifer indicated that he knew Sunshine had been the angel who'd gone to Hell with the idiotic notion of freeing one of the more tormented souls.

The Devil tipped back Sunshine's head and gazed down at his face. "What have I done but help?"

"You're the Devil."

"What have I done?"

The tears burned Sunshine's eyes and scalded down his cheeks. He pulled away.

"The first favor—"

"What are you going to do to her?" Sunshine asked.

"Nothing, presently."

"I won't hurt her. Or anyone."

Lucifer brushed his fingers through Sunshine's hair. "You will if I ask you to."

"I won't. I'll break the bargain before I do."

"Do you know what that means?" Lucifer asked.

Sunshine couldn't answer.

One finger lifted Sunshine's chin. "Do you know what it means, angel, to break a bargain with me?"

He nodded.

"As long as you understand." Lucifer seated himself on the edge of Sunshine's desk. "The first favor is to keep her safe."

A new dread settled over Sunshine at those words. It had nothing to do with the task and everything to do with the weight of the magic that bound their bargain. "That's all?"

"That's all. Keep her safe until I release you and your favor is fulfilled."

Sunshine swallowed. He didn't understand why Lucifer would use a favor on such a frivolous thing unless something or someone awful pursued this girl. Of course, her parents had been killed. Maybe Sarai was still a target.

Lucifer produced a handkerchief and wiped the streaks of tears off Sunshine's face. "Are you too long away from Heaven, sweet thing, or did He make you of something more delicate than a soldier deserves?"

"Leave him alone," Felix said. He'd edged closer but regarded his father with caution.

Lucifer tucked away the handkerchief into his dress. He stood.

"Dad, please."

The Devil came around the desk and embraced his son, a foot taller than him. For now at least. Sunshine had seen him get much taller than this. "You know that business is different. There are rules I cannot bend. Not even for you."

"I know."

"I'm meeting with the Watchers later."

"I'll be home tonight. Don't go without saying goodbye."

Lucifer squeezed Felix and kissed the top of his head. He smiled at Sunshine on his way out.

For dinner, Sunshine no longer wanted sushi. He no longer wanted anything. He went home, even when Felix tried to talk him into going out.

He was embedded deep in his couch when the door to his apartment opened.

Felix entered carrying a plastic take-out bag. "I brought you something."

"Thanks."

He approached and set the bag down on the coffee table. He took out packets of soy, little containers of ginger and wasabi, and plastic containers containing rows and rows of beautiful sushi. "I know you said you weren't in the mood, but I said I'd get you sushi."

"Did you get the cat out of the office?" Sunshine asked. He stared as Felix took the lid off the containers and released the clean, smooth smell of their meal.

"No. But I bought a litter box and cat food."

Sunshine shook his head.

"Can I sit?"

"Of course you can."

Felix didn't sit. "Can I say something? It's not about my dad, it's about Saturday night. What I said. But I'll wait if you're not up for it."

"Go ahead."

Felix didn't speak right away. First, he fetched plates and doled out Sunshine's half of the meal. He handed the plate over, took up his own, and finally sat. "It's not medical, you know. I mean. Physically. I'm healthy and everything. It's not, uh, it's not exactly psychological either. It gets worse if I'm anxious or stressed."

"Alright."

"But I've just sort of..." Felix shrugged. "Eat something."

Sunshine put a piece of food in his mouth and chewed.

"I've always been this way. Sort of. Slow to get going. Or, you know, sometimes I can't. Even if everything is fine. Even if I'm into things."

Sunshine wished he hadn't put anything in his mouth. He didn't know what to say, but he knew he shouldn't spew rice and fish while he did it.

"Dr. Reza said she could give me a prescription for it. Everyone always wants to give me a prescription for it, as soon as they came out with those little blue pills." Felix tapped his chopsticks against his plate. "I've tried them. They work but it's not how I...it's not how I want things to be. It sucks sometimes not getting it up when I really wish I could, but it's almost worse to take them just because someone else thinks I should. I want it to be me, not just a chemical reaction."

The half-conversations they'd had about sex recently clicked into place better for Sunshine.

"Things really do get ugly sometimes. People take it personally if I can't get hard, or they get irritated with waiting. I try to find ways to make it up to them. I do other things, let them do other things to me." He shrugged. He'd kept his eyes on his plate this whole time. "I just...Well. There's types of sex I don't like, either. I flirt and imply and then it gets weird when I don't put out. Or when I do put out and I can't even look at someone after. It's just that...I'm a hot mess, Sunshine. I am."

"That's okay."

Felix shoved one chopstick through a piece of fish. "I don't want to ruin things. Or make you resent me."

"Felix, it doesn't matter to me. It doesn't matter if you don't want to ever have sex or if you want to try, or if you say you want to try something but you change your mind. Or if you tease me for decades and never put out. I want to love you the way it's right for us to love each other, however that is."

"People say they don't care a lot. It's never really true."

Sunshine set down his plate and took Felix's too. He hugged him for a long time, Felix's throat against his cheek. He held him without worrying. There were things he could have said, but he didn't think anything would be right or helpful.

Eventually, Felix pulled back. "Eat your sushi." He pushed the plate back into Sunshine's hands. "Put something else on, I hate this narrator."

Sunshine ate another piece of sushi and put on a David Attenborough documentary.

Felix remained fidgety and didn't look at Sunshine much while they ate.

Part of him wanted to share something similarly difficult to reveal but couldn't think of anything in particular that he wouldn't tell Felix. Surely, something existed, but nothing came to mind. He took their plates and trash to the kitchen and returned to the couch. He took Felix's hand.

Felix glanced his way but didn't say anything. He checked his phone constantly. After about an hour, he took his hand back and said, "My dad's on his way up. I told him to stop by."

"Okay."

Sunshine followed him to the door when he stood and lingered at the doorway. "Thank you for coming over."

"Yeah. I felt bad about not letting you get sushi for lunch."

"And thank you for sharing with me. I know it isn't easy."

Felix pressed his lips together.

"I appreciate it."

"Don't make it weird."

"It's been weird."

"Don't make it worse!" Felix scolded.

They both looked over when the hall door opened. Lucifer ducked his head to get through the doorway. He ambled towards them. "Hello, you two."

Sunshine shrunk back into his doorway.

Felix touched his hand before he moved toward his apartment.

Lucifer paid no mind to where Felix headed. He oozed past

Sunshine into his apartment. "Felix, you redecorated. I think." He frowned. "Did you? Is this...it *looks* familiar."

"It's my apartment," Sunshine said. He'd shrunk away from Lucifer.

"Dad, come on."

The Devil didn't heed his son. He opened the refrigerator and peered inside.

Felix sighed and trudged into Sunshine's apartment. He pressed his keys into Sunshine's hand. "How are the Watchers?"

"No business, this is a social call. Bring Sunshine inside."

"I don't think he wants to spend time with you."

"I don't care if he wants to spend time with me. Bring him in. What's a game that three can play? Old Maid, right?"

"Go ahead." Felix urged quietly Sunshine towards the other apartment.

"No, it's almost worse to have him here without me," Sunshine confided, just as hushed.

"Stop whispering, come inside."

They went inside and sat where the Devil indicated they should sit. He dealt a hand of cards and said, "Ira sends his regards, love."

"How is he?" Felix asked.

Lucifer kept his eyes on his cards. "Tired."

Sunshine sorted through his hand, evaluating what he had.

"But it isn't, you know, dangerous? Right?" Felix asked.

"We don't think so," the Devil said.

Sunshine glanced between them and finally had to ask, "What happened to Ira?"

"He's been having convulsions," the Devil shared. "We don't know why."

"Oh." Sunshine felt bad for asking. He tried not to ask any other uncomfortable questions as he fumbled his way through a game of rummy.

He lost every time.

Felix and his father chatted about other topics, most of them outside of Sunshine's ability to participate. They spoke of people he didn't know and magics he couldn't understand. They did, for a while, talk about which sweetener hurt their teeth the worst and Sunshine contributed to that.

The Devil shared how he liked to torment graverobbers and unethical archaeologists, and how he had plagued the explorers who had opened Tutankhamen's tomb just for shits and giggles. It was, honestly, a funny story, and Sunshine chuckled a few times despite his deep unease.

He also mentioned a few nice houses without occupants in Hell.

Felix rolled his eyes. "Dad."

"What? You live on a trash island in the middle of a climate crisis, you might want to think about other options."

"You're so dramatic."

"Alright, but when you're up to your knees in melted ice caps and you need a place to stay, you'll wish you listened to me. The guest bedrooms have a lot of cat hair."

"I'll just go back to Canada."

Lucifer looked a little wounded.

"What? I can't bring Sunshine to Hell, they'd tear him to shreds," Felix said. "Literally."

Lucifer's eyes slid towards Sunshine. "A big strong soldier boy like that can't take care of himself?"

"He's not even six feet tall."

"I'm right here," Sunshine reminded.

Lucifer ignored him. "They look relatively well built, these soldiers. Good physique. Muscles but not too many. Statuesque, really."

Sunshine flushed.

"But you know those statues..." Lucifer glanced over Sunshine with a little knowing smile on his face. "They're a little..." He waggled his little finger towards Sunshine.

"Oh, shut up, Dad. You're so fucking weird."

The Devil grinned hideously.

It was the smile and not the insinuation that made Sunshine uneasy. He shifted around and couldn't get comfortable suddenly.

Lucifer reached out and patted Sunshine's hand, an unexpectedly warm gesture. "He knows I'm teasing. Don't you?"

"No." Sunshine shook his head.

Genuine hurt and confusion flickered over the Devil's face. "What did I *do* to you?" he asked with real concern and curiosity, as though he might have forgotten. And he might have. He forgot a lot of things.

Sunshine could never tell him. He could never tell anyone, probably not even Felix. He had acted without permission and made the trip to Hell in secret, carrying a poisoned blade and the hope of saving a child's soul. He and the Devil had scuffled, and

Sunshine had landed all the blows. Lucifer, though, had known somehow that Sunshine came as a rogue and he had whispered quiet, assured threats into Sunshine's ear. He had pressed himself close and refused to let go. That much most people knew.

He had murmured, "If He finds out, He'll do to you what He did to me. He'll send you here and you'll be mine, too, and it has been *so long* since I've been bad," except it hadn't stung like a threat, it had ached like a vow made between desperate lovers. It had promised violence and pain and ecstasy that had sent twists of terror and hunger through Sunshine's guts.

Sunshine had fled.

Lucifer's eyes bored into Sunshine's, gloomy and ancient with knowledge that bordered on madness. He knew without Sunshine needing to say anything. "You might still be mine someday." He tightened his hand over Sunshine's arm, not painful, but as a gesture of comfort. "You could pray to me."

"Dad, you're scaring him," Felix scolded.

Lucifer withdrew his touch. He scooped up the cards. "I should go. Stay in touch, darling." He squeezed Felix's shoulder. He glanced towards Sunshine. "You too, angel. We have business."

Sunshine nodded.

Lucifer left, passing through the skin of reality without any further farewells.

Sunshine walked Felix to the door when he started to head that way.

"I'll see you tomorrow," Sunshine said.

"Don't get me for breakfast. I have an appointment first thing in the morning."

"Oh, it must be really bad if you're getting up early to go to therapy," Sunshine teased. Felix didn't sleep much but he did not, as a rule, like to be awake between the hours of four and eight a.m.

Felix snorted. "Goodnight, Sunshine."

"Goodnight."

Felix hesitated, sighed, and rolled his eyes then leaned towards Sunshine like a twelve-year-old leaning in to kiss his least favorite grandmother.

"Don't do it if you're going to be like that about it."

"Fine. I won't."

"Good. Don't."

Felix flipped him off and headed towards his apartment.

Sunshine slapped his ass as he walked away.

He spun back, his mouth hanging open, beautifully scandalized.

Grinning ear-to-ear, Sunshine said, "Dream about me tonight."

"Don't fucking push your luck," the demon growled. He stalked back to his apartment but glanced back with a smile before he went inside.

April 13, 2016
Wednesday

Sunshine had not set eyes on Sarai since he'd dropped her off at the safe house. It felt wrong, especially given his charge to keep her safe. He called every so often, but she never wanted to talk to him for more than a minute.

Yesterday she had asked Jen for more groceries and Sunshine had decided to bring them to her.

He wouldn't even go inside the building if she didn't want him to, but he had the awful need to set eyes on her.

He gathered up the cloth bags of groceries from the seat beside him in the back of the Uber, thanked the driver, and headed out into the rain. He hurried towards the overhang of the apartment building and jammed the buzzer as he huddled as far out of the rain as he could get.

Into the speaker, he said, "It's Sunshine. I have your groceries. I'll wait here if you'd rather come down."

Sarai buzzed him up without a word.

He rapped on the door to her apartment.

She barely opened the door. "Just leave them outside."

"I need the bags back."

"What?"

"They're reusable. I need them for my groceries."

She groaned and opened the door all the way. She grabbed one of the bags out of his hands and left the door opened behind her. She started unloading the bag.

He did the same. "How have you been?"

"Fine."

He glanced around the apartment. It was messy but not disgusting. "Jen says you haven't been able to find your Gwen."

She pursed her lips.

"If you'd like, the agency can help you."

"I don't need you to help me."

"I can send Tate over," he offered. "She's good at finding things. Or Specter has a lot of connects with the academic world. Even if the person you want isn't at NY-AM anymore, she might be at a different university."

He folded up the bag she'd emptied and placed it inside the bag he'd emptied. He put them both in his backpack. He took out the notebooks he'd taken from her house. He'd scanned the ones about magic but didn't have any need for her notes on character arcs. He placed them on the counter and said, "These are yours."

"So you're stealing things too?"

He crossed his arms. "Would you rather be living in a shack right now? Was that great for you? Cause all the shacks and hovels I slept in kind of sucked."

"Don't be facetious."

"Beg pardon?"

"You were never homeless, your parents never got murdered, you don't know what I've been dealing with. You don't know anything about me other than 'the Devil' told me to find you."

He uncrossed his arms. The posture was too aggressive; so had been his tone. "I was homeless for twenty-six years."

He hadn't thought of himself as homeless; he hadn't had the concept of an earthly home at that time. He'd understood the purpose of buildings for shelter and warmth, but not for anything more. He wondered sometimes if he'd still be out there a hundred years later, prowling the world look for an antichrist to eliminate, if Felix hadn't held him captive.

If he hadn't had a meaningful interpersonal encounter for the first time in his life.

"I still have a hard time sleeping at night sometimes. It doesn't feel real. My own bed, safety, consistency. Every so often I get this flash that...that it's so unreal. That past and this present."

Her face softened.

"You've been under extreme stress. You've been isolated and traumatized. Anger is fine, it's normal, and you're right, I don't know you. And you don't know me. But I can help you."

"Twenty-six years? What, are you like...thirty?"

"Much older than thirty. I was created a few thousand years ago. But I was sent to Earth on what should have been a quick mission."

She shook her head and started to put away the groceries. "Sent to Earth. Right. Forgot you were crazy. Where, exactly, were you sent from?"

"Heaven."

She laughed, harsh and loud. "Fucking okay."

He kept his face neutral. "You're a mage but you don't believe in the Community?"

"The Community? You mean those nut jobs that bite people or say the Devil banged their mom? No. I don't believe in them. They come hanging around mages because they think magic will get them whatever weird shit they're after."

"So you believe in magic, though?"

"I don't have to believe in magic. I've seen it. I've used it. You don't *believe* in the sun or air or water. Besides, people call it magic but it's just another type of energy," Sarai said.

Sunshine had never met a mage who didn't believe in supernatural creatures before. It was possible; somewhere out in the world existed a scientist who didn't believe in climate change or vaccines or platypuses, but that didn't make it normal. "What if I could prove it to you?"

"What?"

"Prove to you that creatures are real. That I'm not some lunatic."

She looked him over. "So either creatures are real and the Devil is real and he sent you to find me, or you're a nutjob. Great options, there. You really know how to sell yourself."

He decided to table the issue. "Regardless. I have resources available to help you in whatever way you desire."

"Great. Thanks. You done?"

He studied her. "Are you sure you should be alone?"

She wrinkled her nose and curled her lip. "You trying to keep me company?"

He held back a sigh. "Let us know if you need anything."

"Yeah. Bye."

He took his things and headed back into the rain.

At the office, he sifted through the handful of applications that had filtered into his inbox and did a cursory search of NY-AM staff, faculty, and alumni for women named Gwen. It was not illuminating.

Maybe Gwen was a nickname or a middle name.

Felix returned with lunch and a can of wet cat food. He set it out on a plate for the stray he'd let in and sprinkled in a crushed pill.

"What's that?"

"It's got worms."

"Ew."

"Don't say ew, she's sick."

"Specter, if I get worms, I swear..." he began.

Felix waved a hand to silence him. He set out the plate of food near the cabinet where the cat liked to stay. "Be quiet."

"Mmm."

Felix came over to inspect the things he'd laid out in an attempt to organize this case. Lucifer had said nothing about it, and Sarai didn't want his help, so it wasn't exactly a case, but he didn't know what else to do.

"Why don't you start with the mom?" Felix asked. "This Gwen is her colleague, right? Might be good to start there."

"You're so smart."

"You're smart, too," Felix offered.

Sunshine glanced up.

"Dr. Reza said I should try it. She also said that constant, unrequited sexual tension is probably not healthy. I said it's not as bad as it sounds. I also said I'd try."

"Oh."

"So you should probably just let me blow you or whatever," Felix suggested wearily.

"Oh my god, Specter, I do not think that is what your therapist had in mind *at all*."

Felix sighed and put Sunshine into what probably should have been a hug but felt like a half-hearted headlock, given that Sunshine was sitting and Felix stood.

"Come here, come sit," Sunshine said after a few seconds of having his face in Felix's armpit.

Felix sat on his lap.

"What's wrong?"

"I don't know. I'm sad maybe? And I still kind of want to fire Emil."

"You can when he eventually fucks up this 'not being racist to creatures' probation we put him on," Sunshine soothed.

"Can I tell him?"

"Of course you can tell him."

Felix nestled against him. He dragged over Sunshine's keyboard and placed it on his lap. "So what's this lady's name?"

"Gwen."

"No. The mom."

"Oh. Uh. Danielle Robinson. But, hang on." He struggled to snag the case file. "Maiden name is Moore."

"E?"

"Yeah with an e."

Felix pulled up the website for NY-AM and found his way into a list of thesis projects and dissertations through some kind of academic search engine. After a minute, he said, "Sunshine, spell Gwen."

"G-w-e-n."

"Try again."

"G-w-e-n-n?"

"N-g-u-y-e-n."

"Oh." Sunshine's heart sank. "That's not pronounced 'Gwen'."

"No but imagine if you were a fifteen-year-old who'd only ever heard your mom say it in passing," Felix said. "Nguyen was Danielle's thesis advisor for her undergrad, it looks like. I think, uh...the title makes it seem like she tried to make synthetic blood for vamps. Or tried to recreate one? Hmm."

"That's weird."

"Why? Synthetic blood is a pretty common aspiration, it's kind of like lab meat."

"No, I mean, Sarai doesn't believe in creatures."

"Ooh, that is weird," Felix agreed. He returned the keyboard to the desk. "You gonna email Dr. Nguyen?"

"In a little while."

Felix remained on Sunshine's lap. "Your sandwich is on my desk, but I don't want to get up."

"You're okay."

Felix took out his phone and read for a while. A cursory glance showed that the article seemed to be related to Shay's current case, which involved a witch who thought she was being poisoned by her husband.

Sunshine read job applications.

The cat eventually crept out from beneath the cabinet and scarfed down the food.

"What's your plan with that?" Sunshine asked as the stray made unappealing gobbling and smacking sounds while it ate.

"Should probably take it to the vet, but I don't want to traumatize it."

"You could put it to sleep."

"Jesus, Sunshine!" Felix scolded, sitting up and glaring at him.

"I mean literally, not euphemistically. A spell."

Felix settled back into his lap. "Oh. That makes sense."

Jen came upstairs to find them like that, eating a late lunch. It wasn't easy to eat with Felix on his lap, but he managed.

She paused at the doorway. "Should I come back?"

"Oh, I don't imagine things will get any more normal," Felix said. "What did you need?"

"There's a package downstairs, I need someone to bring it in."

"Sunshine, you're up," Felix said. He moved off Sunshine's lap with all the grace of an eighty-year-old with a bad back.

Sunshine set down his sandwich, went downstairs to bring inside a huge box of printer paper, and asked, "Do we need this much paper?"

Jen gave a sheepish grin. "I might have put an extra zero in the order somewhere by accident."

"Ah."

"Thank you."

He nodded. "I emailed you a couple of phone numbers. Can you give them a call and set up some job interviews?"

"Sure, of course."

"Thanks," Sunshine said. He returned upstairs and found that Felix had gone back to his desk. "You don't have plans Friday."

"No."

"Do you want to go out?"

Felix shrugged. "I'll let you know."

"You have to come to work."

"I don't have to do anything."

"There's an interview set up on Friday, I need you to be there for it," Sunshine lied.

Felix grunted. He shuffled through some case writeups. "Do

you remember when we actually worked cases and didn't just read about them?"

"We still work cases. Don't get restless," Sunshine soothed.

Felix grunted again and made a lot more noise than reading paperwork required.

Sunshine left it alone.

Uncomfortable energy had vibrated off Felix for the past few weeks and mentioning it tended to result in Felix becoming borderline erratic. Over the weekend, Sunshine had mentioned that he seemed uncomfortable and Felix had first smashed his drink onto the floor and freaked out when Sunshine had cleaned it up before he could, then spent the right of the night waffling between cleaning unrelated parts of Sunshine's apartment and apologizing.

The next day they had flushed all the uppers in Felix's possession down the toilet.

Sunshine became aware that Felix made increasingly disgruntled sounds. "Something wrong with that report?"

"Yeah, it's not done. It's shit. I've written better reports shitfaced."

Sunshine came over and held out his hand.

Felix gave him the papers.

Sunshine skimmed it and found it not just incomplete but rife with typos. He checked the name on the front. "I'll talk to him."

"You better because if he says one word to me, I'm going to lose my shit. If he fucking looks at me—"

"Felix."

"I know!" He shoved himself back from the desk. "I know!"

"Go for a walk."

Felix shook his head.

"Then come here. Let me help."

"I need to learn how to self-regulate. You can't just squeeze the crazy out of me when I get upset."

Sunshine didn't necessarily agree with that. He also doubted that Felix would ever learn to effectively self-regulate. He'd seen a lot of therapists over the years and gotten a lot of different types of counsel. He went through these spikes of manic distress in the first few months, which likely came from unpacking all his problems instead of just burying them. He would, without fail, act up, get his shit together, then even out for five to ten years.

Occasionally less than five years. Sometimes it only stuck for a year or a few months, but that only happened when he couldn't catch a break.

"Why not?" Sunshine asked.

"Because you won't always be there. And it's not your job to take care of me."

Ah, that again. "Then go ahead and regulate. You know how to meditate; you know how to calm yourself down."

"But I want *you* to do it. That's what...I'm not saying it's your fault or that it's causal, but I get...I get like this and you help me and I want that. I want you to take care of me like that and it's not..." Felix gripped his hair, which had started to fade, but remained purple. "I need to, to figure out which parts are healthy and which parts are a crutch. Like, what's normal boyfriend stuff and what's toxic codependent stuff."

Sunshine made a face, a weird, twisted grimace. He didn't mean to and if he had wanted to make a face, he would never have made this one. He fixed his face and did not repeat the least important part of what Felix had said. The word echoed in his mind. *Boyfriend, boyfriend, boyfriend.* He forced himself to say, "I've told you before, I don't mind helping and I'm here if you need me."

"I know."

"I'll talk to Emil about this report."

Felix stretched out his hand.

Sunshine took it.

With his fingers tight around Sunshine's, Felix said, "Thank you."

He squeezed back, then went to speak with Emil.

As soon as Sunshine approached his desk, Emil started to shift and look guilty.

"Hey," Sunshine said as amiably as possible.

"Hi," answered Emil, his eyes both squirrely and buggy. "You. Uh. You need something?"

"I just had a few questions about your writeup on the Bell case."

"Oh. Uh. Okay. Yeah. Shoot." Emil had straightened up.

He'd taken his probation hard and, it seemed, seriously. He had expressed desperate concern bordering on fear at the prospect of losing his job.

Sunshine handed it over. "Why don't you take a look at it?"

Emil's eyes darted over it and his face paled. "Oh, shit. Shit, shit, I'm sorry. I...I finished working on it at home, I must have sent the draft instead of the final copy. I'm so sorry."

He seemed so earnest and genuinely worried that Sunshine said, "Alright, just get me the final copy."

"I'll find it right now, I promise."

"It's alright. Mistakes happen."

"I'm really sorry, I just, I've been trying to be home more but I'm not good with computers..." Emil gripped the papers in his hand. "Shit."

"You can feel free to bring your office computer home with you, if that would be easier," Sunshine offered. "We do have a fairly lax policy on working from home."

Emil frowned and looked at him.

"It's in the employee handbook."

Emil opened his mouth.

"Most people never actually read it," Sunshine admitted, "But it is in there. If you need to be at home and you can still get your work done, you can do that as long as you come to the office at least once a week and attend all staff meetings."

"Oh. I might need to do that. My wife—"

"You don't have to tell me unless you want to," Sunshine said.

"She's sick."

"I'm sorry to hear that, Emil," he said with as much kindness as he could muster.

He didn't like Emil, but more than that, he disliked the effect Emil had on Felix and office morale in general. But the unpleasant changes in demeanor were recent, less than a year, as Sunshine recalled.

"Is there anything we can do to help?" Sunshine asked.

"I...I don't think so."

"Let me know if that changes."

"I will."

Sunshine took a step back.

"Thank you."

"Of course."

Emil had the complete report in by the end of the day.

On Friday, Emil worked from home, but not before sending two emails making sure he had permission.

As they headed into the conference room just before lunch, Felix said, "I don't know why you wanted to schedule another meeting. The last one went so well."

"Just a follow-up. It's good to check-in." Sunshine opened the door for him.

Felix entered the room to a chorus of "Surprise!" from all present members of the agency.

He flinched physically from the noise then clapped his hands over his mouth. "Papa!" He rushed into the room and threw his arms around his father. He nearly bowled over the tall, thin man, a human with curly, brown hair and a close-cropped beard.

Hiram embraced Felix and kissed his cheek. "Happy birthday."

Felix's eyes scanned the room and lighted on the green-skinned figure a few feet away from his father, previously in a conversation with Tate. "Bibi."

Phaedrus approached and hugged their son. "Happy birthday."

"You didn't have to come all this way…"

"Oh, of course, we did," Phaedrus scolded.

Sunshine hadn't known what else to do; any other gift ideas had eluded him. He'd thought to invite a few of their friends, then it had occurred to him to invite Felix's parents. He'd also known Felix would sniff out a surprise party a mile away and he'd never expect Sunshine to interrupt the workday with one.

Late and showy as always, Lucifer stepped through the nothingness practically on top of Hiram. Both the Fallen in the room dropped to the floor; Phaedrus knelt, and June dropped to both knees and touched his forehead to the floor.

"Rise," the Devil said right away. "Happy birthday, Felix."

James Kelly gave Lucifer a bit of a look.

June rolled his eyes and slung his arm around the vampire. He nuzzled into his throat. "Don't be grumpy. It's a party."

"I'm not grumpy," James Kelly said. He kissed June.

Sunshine smiled, satisfied with himself, with the happiness on Felix's face. Those gathered fell into conversation. Lucifer and two witches Felix knew gathered on one side of the table, chatting about cats. The witches gave both the Devil wide-eyed and rapt attention, though they probably didn't know who he was.

James Kelly, a werewolf that Felix had once dated before she'd realized she was gay, and Felix discussed a TV show they all watched.

June and Hiram stood and looked awkwardly at each other. They had not seen each other in years; decades for June, but nearly two centuries for Hiram. Not to mention, Hiram's family had once held June captive.

Finally, June pulled the mage into a hug and asked, "How the fuck have you been, Hiram?"

The employees of the agency regarded their supernatural guests with some uneasiness.

Except for Phaedrus and Tate. Presently Tate had Phaedrus's hand in hers, examining an intricately woven silver ring. "It's gorgeous," Tate raved.

"I stole it," Phaedrus shared proudly.

Ira came to stand beside Sunshine. "Nice party."

"Oh. Thank you."

Bags stood out against the dark gray of the demon's skin. "It was sweet of you."

"I didn't know what else to get him."

"He looks happy."

Sunshine looked over Ira.

"I look like shit, I know."

"No, no," Sunshine assured. "How are you, though?"

"I get tired sometimes, but really, I'm alright. Lu's worrying a lot more than I am. But he does tend to worry," Ira said. "Besides I can't die, so I'm not really worried about it too much if it does turn out to be something bad."

"Ah."

"Well...maybe I can die. But I won't stay dead, I guess." Ira grinned up at Sunshine. He was by far the shortest person present. He waved to Lucifer when the Devil glanced his way. "Been up to anything fun?"

"Mmmm. Oh. We went on vacation," he said, "This lovely little island."

Ira listened patiently to Sunshine's rhapsodizing and shared the last trip he had gone on to a cabin in the mountains of Hell.

They chatted until the pizzas arrived. After pizza, Sunshine brought out the cake he'd baked yesterday and snuck into the office early that morning.

Felix gasped at all the candles Sunshine had placed on top and gave him a playful smack. "You're *not* supposed to say how old a lady is," he scolded. He blew out the candles after everyone sang to him, then threw himself into Sunshine's arms and kissed his cheek.

People stared.

Hiram and Phaedrus exchanged a look.

The werewolf Felix had dated let out a small whoop and everyone laughed.

Everyone stayed for cake.

Employees trickled back to work, except for Tate, who seemed to be ready to mingle all day. She spent a lot of time talking with Lana, the werewolf, and ended up with her number by the end of the night.

Slowly, their guests headed home. Phaedrus and Hiram made plans with Felix for the following day, since they would be in town all weekend.

Lucifer stayed and helped clean up, then brought himself and Ira home.

Felix sat on the table and watched Sunshine wiped down the table around him. "So do we know *any* straight people?"

"Birds of a feather," Sunshine said.

"I like it better this way."

Sunshine let out an amused breath through his nose.

"I'm ready to go home."

"Go ahead," Sunshine said.

"You should walk me home; this city isn't safe for a girl on her own."

"Then help me take out the garbage."

They brought the trash out and headed home.

Felix stopped walking as they passed a tattoo shop, eyeing the flash art displayed. "I've kind of always thought about getting one."

"Then let's go."

"No, I can't."

"Why not?" Sunshine asked.

Felix shrugged.

"Why not?" Sunshine repeated, giving the demon's hand a tug.

Felix dug his heels in. "I'm too scared."

Sunshine rolled his eyes. "No, you aren't."

"I am, don't be mean."

"Let's just go in and look."

Felix consented to that. They looked through the generic collections of art, spoke with an employee who said they did have openings and bickered back and forth about what to do. Finally, Felix began to insist on leaving.

"Come on, if you want one, do it."

Felix gave the flash books a pained look. "I can't."

"Do you want me to go first?" Sunshine had never considered getting a tattoo before, not even in passing, but suddenly it seemed he would without hesitation.

He bit his lip, then nodded. "You don't mind?"

"Of course not."

Sunshine picked out the first tattoo that appealed to him and an hour later had a bumblebee the size of his thumb permanently inked into the skin of his inner bicep. The artist questioned the design initially because apparently women tended towards tattoos of bees. Sunshine didn't understand the reason and had him proceed anyway.

Felix watched anxiously the whole time and nearly chickened out of his at the last minute. He didn't say anything, but Sunshine saw it in his eyes. He selected what he'd deemed a "Halloween kitty", which was a silhouette of a black cat with an arched back, and had it done just below the elbow on his inner forearm.

He held on to Sunshine's hand so tight that by the end his fingers had gone numb.

Sunshine insisted on paying for both, even though Felix grumbled, "You already got me a birthday present," afterward.

Sunshine ignored him.

He walked Felix back to the door of his apartment. They lingered outside of it, chatting without any real purpose. They had spent hours in this hall, trapped in the space between their apartments, just talking. People expected it by now.

"You might as well come in," Felix said after half an hour.

"You sure?"

"Mmm."

Sunshine followed him inside. They did basically nothing for hours, but they did it together. He slept at Felix's that night, both of them without a single drink in them. That had never happened before.

Felix never went to bed this early, not unless he was sick or drunk or exhausted from something else.

They stood on opposite sides of the bed and stared at each other.

The window let in a steady stream of cool night air and rattled the shade.

"Just get in," Felix finally said but made no move to do so himself.

Sunshine sat on the bed.

Felix made turning back the covers and sheet a long process, but also eventually sat on the bed.

"Do you want me to go?" Sunshine asked as Felix perched on the very edge of his own mattress.

"No."

"Do you need a Xanax? Cause you look like you're about to have a nervous breakdown."

"No."

Sunshine grabbed him by the arm, hauled him over, and locked his arms around him. "You've been captured, Mr. Specter."

"But I'll never talk. You'll never get the formula."

"We're two rational men. I'm sure we could negotiate something that would make us both happy."

"I'd rather die than betray my country."

"Then I suppose you shall have to die, Mr. Specter. Such a shame. But you will be such a beautiful corpse. All of Canada will mourn you."

Felix let out a nervous giggle. He twisted out of Sunshine's arms and burrowed into the bed. "They're going to ask me about it tomorrow."

"Your parents won't care if you have a tattoo."

"No, about us, stupid. That kiss. They'll know you can touch me now."

"You didn't tell them?" Sunshine asked.

"It didn't seem relevant."

"Well, it was only a kiss on the cheek. I'm sure no one thought that much of it."

Felix sighed.

"Do you want them to?"

"I don't know."

Sunshine lay down beside him and put a tentative arm over his ribs. When Felix didn't tense or pull away, he snuggled a little closer. "You said boyfriend the other day."

"Well."

"That's not exactly accurate."

"No. But nothing is. What am I supposed to call you?" Felix shifted around, getting comfortable, and pressing closer to Sunshine.

"We could make it accurate."

"What? After three-quarters of a century, we move up to 'boyfriends'? That's a step backward practically."

Sunshine pointed out, "You did propose."

"Don't be a shit, Sunshine, it's my birthday."

"What about bosom friends?"

Felix groaned. "It doesn't matter."

"No," Sunshine agreed. Any term or title they bestowed on

each other would benefit other people's understanding of their relationship, but it would do nothing for their own. "How about—"

Felix elbowed him.

Sunshine kissed the back of his neck, and then his shoulder. "Happy birthday."

April 19
Tuesday

Felix had gotten restless around three a.m. and texted Sunshine *u up? come over* which had felt an awful lot like a booty call. Sunshine went over, made him a cup of chamomile tea, and surreptitiously checked the apartment for drugs.

"I'm not high."

"Can you blame me for checking?"

"No."

Sunshine sat next to him on the couch and sipped the tea he'd made for himself. "So what's got you worked up?"

"I couldn't sleep."

"You're never asleep at this hour."

Felix sighed. "I know. Sometimes I wish I could sleep through the night for once."

"Yeah, but your body just runs different."

"I get bored."

"Maybe you need a new hobby," Sunshine suggested.

Felix ignored the suggestion. He stirred his tea, rhythmically tapping the spoon against one side of the mug, then the other. He did this for at least a minute.

Sunshine started to doze off, lulled by the warmth of the tea in his belly and the quietness of the apartment. A few floors down, someone played slow, thoughtful jazz and three doors down the Bashirs' new baby cried for just a few minutes, no longer than it would take to pick her up and make a bottle.

He became vaguely aware that Felix had taken the mug of tea out of his hands and set it on the table.

"I'm sorry I woke you up."

"Mmm." Sunshine kept his eyes closed.

"Are you awake?"

"Mhm."

"I kind of wanted to tell you something."

"At three in the morning." Sunshine nestled deeper into the couch, his face turned into the cushions on the back.

Felix smacked his leg. "Take this seriously."

"I am," Sunshine promised into the cushion. "I am. I'm just keeping my eyes closed."

"I think we need to spend less time together."

Instantly, Sunshine was awake. He pushed himself up. "Why?"

"Just because. We do everything together. We work together and eat together, we hang out together and go on trips together, and it's just not healthy."

"Is that how you feel?"

"What do you mean?"

"Is that how you feel? Or is it just what your therapist said?"

Felix stood up and paced between the couch and the kitchen.

"Specter."

"I don't know. She didn't say it. She just...I don't know. She asked me something that made me think. And I think I..." He pulled on his hair. "You said to let you know if I need space. And I do. I need to think and figure out what I want because I want it and what I want because I'm scared to lose you."

"You won't."

"I know. I know." Felix came back to sit next to him. "But that's why I need to figure it out. That way in ten years I won't have done all these things just because I thought I should or wonder if that's the only reason why I did them. I need to know that whatever happens between us is, is mutual and consensual and not coming from the wrong place."

Sunshine nodded.

"And I need to not think about this. I see you and I start worrying and you know that I get irrational. I need to not see you for a little while. Not see that stupid perfect fucking face of yours or smell your goddamn skin or feel how *fucking soft* your hair is. Cause I can't think straight and I'm afraid to lose you and I know," he held up a hand to stop Sunshine from speaking, "I *know* I won't, but I don't want to fuck this up. I don't want to blame you for something you never said or did, that I inferred or got worked up about. So just. Say you understand."

Sunshine didn't understand. He didn't worry like Felix did. Their relationship, to Sunshine, felt straightforward: they cared about each other and enjoyed each other's company. Together, things were right, whatever it was they did together. But he didn't have Felix's strained relationship with sex; matters of attraction and libido, whether they waxed or waned, had never concerned him beyond the initial heady confusion of trying to figure out what the fuck his body was doing the first few times he'd become aroused.

They didn't teach sex ed in Heaven.

"If it's important to you, then do it," Sunshine settled on saying.

"You mean it."

"Of course."

"Because I'm going back to Canada for a while."

Sunshine's stomach hurt immediately. "Okay."

"I spent the weekend with my parents and things felt...they felt normal. I didn't think about what the fuck was going to happen with us. I didn't worry. It'll be a reset." Felix put his hand on Sunshine's knee. "You'll have time to think, too."

Sunshine didn't need to think. "Okay."

"You're not mad, right?"

"Of course not."

"I'll still work on cases from Pickering. You know. Work stuff is okay."

"Sure," Sunshine agreed.

"And I just miss them."

"Makes sense," Sunshine said.

Felix went to visit his parents fairly regularly; it was a perfectly normal thing to do. Sometimes, Sunshine had tagged along, other times Felix had gone alone, or brought someone else. But one of Felix's visits home had never felt like being left behind before. He'd never thought he'd driven Felix away.

Like an absolute idiot, he thought of the wedding invitation affixed to the front of his fridge. May fifth, a Thursday night wedding in Vermont. Nothing special, his heart hadn't been set on going, accompanied or otherwise. "What about Lisa's wedding?" he asked.

"I...I'll meet you there. Okay? And we can come back to the city together. It's the first week of May, isn't it?"

Sunshine nodded.

Felix took Sunshine's face in his hands. "Don't look so fucking sad. I'm not going away forever. And I'm not running away from you. I'm just clearing my head."

"No, I know. I get it."

Felix hugged him. "Come get some sleep. I'm sorry I woke you up."

"You don't want me to go?"

"You're already here." Felix shrugged. "Might as well stay."

Already Felix seemed calmer as if the act of revealing his plan had helped. Maybe he'd expected a poorer reaction from Sunshine. Maybe he'd gotten too worked up thinking about it. Maybe it had finally gotten late enough for him to be tired.

Sunshine followed him to his bedroom.

This time Felix climbed in right away and snuggled up to Sunshine once he lay down. Quietly, he said, "You know how I get."

Sunshine had never thought of Felix as particularly vulnerable. Sensitive, irrational, fickle, yes, but he'd never thought he had to protect Felix from anything other than his own whims and tendencies. He'd never seen himself as something from which Felix would need protection.

"Don't take it personally," Felix insisted, still quiet.

How could he not?

Felix squeezed him half to death.

Sunshine squeezed back just as hard.

Felix squeaked. "Christ." He giggled.

In the morning, he went with Felix to the train station under the guise of carrying one of his bags for him. He stood to the side, agitated, as Felix argued with the ticket kiosk under his breath. He walked him to the platform.

"Take a breath," Felix advised.

Sunshine obeyed.

Felix rubbed his arm. "You know I'm coming back, right?"

Sunshine took another breath.

Felix set down his bag and took the other bag out of Sunshine's hand. He didn't really need help carrying anything. "You know I'm coming back," he said again with a funny smile on his lips. Amused and affectionate.

"I'm going to have so many leftovers," Sunshine admitted weepily. He could never manage to cook for less than two people.

"You'll be fine. I'll see you soon. May fifth, right?"

Sunshine nodded. "They're going to make my fridge smell."

"Try using less garlic."

"Do you think I use too much garlic?" Sunshine asked, actually on the verge of tears.

"No." Felix rolled his eyes good-naturedly. "You're being ridiculous. It's like two weeks."

"I know."

Felix put a hand on his shoulder. "You've got like ten minutes to tell me what's bothering you."

"I just hope you have a nice time with your parents." He wiped his eyes before any tears could run down his cheeks.

"Okay." Felix patted his cheek. "Maybe this time I'll send you a postcard."

Sunshine let out a sniffling laugh.

Before he boarded the train, Felix gave Sunshine a long hug and repeated, "I'm coming back."

Sunshine hugged him hard. "Have fun. Be safe."

"I won't do anything you wouldn't try to talk me out of," Felix promised. He pecked his cheek, grabbed his bags, and climbed aboard the train.

Sunshine went to a bakery, bought a dozen cannoli with the intent to bring them to the office, but he ate three and then gave the rest to a homeless person who'd asked him for spare change. He also handed over a twenty.

At noon, he made his way to the NY-AM campus in Brooklyn, as he'd scheduled a meeting with Dr. Nguyen for the afternoon.

He regretted the cannoli. They sat heavily in his stomach. Or maybe that was just whatever mélange of emotions this experience had produced.

He tried to put all of it out of mind as he wandered through the Davidson building of the Academy of Magic, trying to locate the right office. He stopped a passing undergrad and asked for directions.

The youth directed him to the third floor.

He found the office and rapped on the door, just as nervous as he would be if he'd failed an exam.

At least, as he imagined he would be. He'd never taken an

exam, except for the one to get a driver's license. He had taken that one multiple times, not because he'd ever failed but because every so often the DMV caught on that his apparent age did not at all match the from on his birthdate.

"Come on in," called a voice.

Sunshine entered the office and waved at a woman in her sixties. "Dr. Nguyen?"

"Yes, yes. Mr. Sunshine, correct?"

He nodded.

They shook hands and Sunshine had a seat.

"I have to say, I'm a little confused," Dr. Nguyen began. "You think I might have something to do with Danielle's death?"

"Oh, no, I'm sorry. I didn't mean to give you that impression at all. I'm simply trying to speak with people who might have an idea of where to start. I don't have much else to go on. The police have sort of...let things fall to the wayside. They didn't have any leads either."

"I haven't seen Danielle since she finished her Master's and by then we weren't...we weren't as close as we had been."

"Can you walk me through things?" Sunshine requested with a smile. He took out his notebook and tried to scribble in it as unobtrusively as possible.

Dr. Nguyen smiled back at him. "I met her when she was a sophomore. She took one of my classes and I was impressed. I think everyone who met her was impressed with her. She was smart as a whip, applied herself on top of that. She produced excellent work. She had this charisma. This confidence that just filled up a room."

Sunshine nodded.

"So when she asked me to advise her thesis, I agreed. I was delighted to work with her. I knew she'd have a wonderful career in front of her. Did you read her thesis?" Dr. Nguyen asked.

"Ah. No, but I had a friend fill me in on the gist." Sunshine had tried to read it but the technicality of it had baffled him and he'd needed to call in Felix for help. "Synthetic blood, right?"

Dr. Nguyen nodded. "Yes. During her graduate courses, she worked in a lab we have on campus for, uh, as part of her scholarship. She worked under Dr. Hauer. They had mutual interests and continued to pursue the formula she'd researched. Blood is complicated, but she'd made good progress trying to isolate which parts are vital to the vampire metabolism."

Sunshine knew her tone would change by the slight downturn

of her mouth.

"Unfortunately, there was an accident at the lab. It..." Dr. Nguyen sighed. "A vampire came in, he'd volunteered to undergo some basic testing and evaluations. Apparently, he took a liking to Danielle and started seeking her out in a more personal way. Things escalated; the two of them got into an altercation. We never were able to tell if the vampire had...Well. We never knew what his intentions were towards her. Sexual or predatory."

Sunshine almost asked, "What's the difference?" but kept his mouth shut.

"She was never the same after that. She lost some of that confidence. Her work quality slipped. Eventually, she changed programs. She didn't want anything to do with her previous research. When she met Thomas Robinson, another grad student, she seemed a little better. Happier, calmer. But she also...The two of them ended up in a few unpleasant discussions with faculty members who belonged to the Community. It's a shame, what happened. All of it," Dr. Nguyen concluded.

"Thank you."

"Does that help?"

"It makes tremendous sense," Sunshine said. "Do you have any idea what Danielle might have been pursuing presently?"

"We only spoke a few times over the years. I think she had started to focus on, uh..." Dr. Nguyen looked almost embarrassed here. "It's not something widely accepted in academia and certainly not here at NY-AM, but she was doing some research into containment enchantments."

"What do you mean?"

Carefully, she explained, "Uh, think of it as keeping the more dangerous elements of the Community isolated from the wider world. It requires a subtle touch since the difference between humans and supernatural creatures can be small. And sometimes, of course, some genes are recessive. One might spend one's entire life unaware of any supernatural heritage. I think, hmmm. I think it was five percent of the general population had some supernatural heritage without anything to distinguish them from a normal human."

"Oh. Like a Kavornian enchantment?"

"Not quite. Kavornian enchantments work on a single, defined space or an isolated object. This would have broader applications."

He nodded like he understood what that meant. "Thank you,

again. Do you mind if I get back in contact with you if I have more questions?"

"Not at all. Despite everything, I always was fond of Danielle. I hope you find who did this."

"So do I."

They shook hands and Sunshine returned to the office to make note of everything he'd learned. What good it did him, he didn't know, but it explained why Sarai didn't believe in the Community.

The last thing he did that day was interview a half-fairy who'd applied for a job. He'd interviewed half a dozen people so far but hadn't quite found what he'd wanted.

As soon as the fairy came in, though, Sunshine knew.

He arrived a few minutes late, flustered and apologetic. He didn't look any more than twenty and it must have taken him all those years to grow the midnight blue braid that hung down his back. "I'm so sorry, I am, but I just, I *can't* ride on the subways, there's so much iron and I get so sick!"

"That's alright."

"I'm Rose."

"Sunshine."

"Rosewood McAuliffe, actually. But, really, call me Rose."

They shook hands, both of them beaming at each other. Rose stood a few inches shorter than Sunshine. He had gentle features, somewhat unusual for a fairy, and a soft slenderness to his build.

"Uh, have a seat." Sunshine gestured to the chair across from his place at the conference table. "Why'd you apply for this job?"

"I...Well. I need the money, first. Second, um." He flushed, turning his periwinkle skin slightly purple. "I'm so sorry, I'm trying to hard not to say the first thing that comes to mind, but I'm not very good at it! This place sort of has a reputation in the Community."

Sunshine thought of their prickly employees and didn't want to know what their reputation was.

"Everyone says the two of you, you and Specter, that you're...very open-minded. And I need that. I can't keep working at some Starbucks with a manager who doesn't like my nail polish or which bathroom I use. I've never worked in an office but...You know. I'm really hoping."

"Do you need a glass of water?"

"Please!" he said with an embarrassed giggle.

Sunshine got him water and watched with fascination as he

guzzled the whole thing and seemed to breathe for the first time since he'd come in the door.

"I figured people would be better about it in the city, which they might be, but I haven't lasted at a real job for more than a week. It's the whole...Not being good at lying thing."

Sunshine glanced at the interview questions he'd prepared. "Uh. You've never worked in an office?"

"No."

"Uh, how are you with computers?"

"I'm good with phones."

Sunshine tried not to grimace. "How about, uh, things like copies and faxing? Or filing papers?"

"I can learn. I learn quick. Honest."

"How are you with people?" Sunshine asked. This boy had to have some redeeming quality, something that could let Sunshine hire him with a defense stronger than, "I liked him."

"Uh. As long as they use my pronouns, we'll be fine!" he said with a nervous smile. "I make friends pretty easy...I think people feel bad for me honestly."

"What are your pronouns?" Sunshine asked. "Mine are he/him."

"Mine too!" Rose practically gushed. He said it with such affirmation and pride. "Uh. It's been a bit of a journey, though."

"You're certainly welcome to share if you want," Sunshine said, "But don't feel obligated. People will address you appropriately here regardless of how much you tell us."

"I..." Rose smiled. "I kind of like to talk about it. Is that weird? A lot of people don't, I don't think. But I got top surgery a few months ago. I'm still kind of stiff sometimes, but I've...I've never felt happier. I swear to god, it's...well, it was a literal weight off my chest, but I feel like I can breathe for the first time in years."

"I'm glad this turned out well for you," Sunshine said. He scribbled a few things on his piece of paper. "How are your ties to the Community?"

"My dad tried really hard to keep me connected after my mom went back to Court. You know, he didn't want me to feel isolated or anything. So, I, uh. I've kind of got one foot on either side."

That. That was exactly what Sunshine had needed. Everyone else he'd spoken to had been too firmly rooted in one world or the other. "Uh. Well. We don't have gendered bathrooms or a dress code other than...you know, a general smart-casual vibe. Fridays are more relaxed. Jeans, t-shirts, just nothing vulgar."

"Huh?"

"The position is twenty hours a week, for now. It pays eighteen an hour. Does that work for you?"

Rose stared.

"There is room for, ah, improved wages and more hours eventually. But let's think of this as a probation period. If you're interested."

Rose squinted. "So I have no skills and no experience and you're going to hire me at significantly above minimum wage?"

"If you're interested."

"I. Is there some kind of angle here? Fine print I didn't read or something?"

Sunshine caught the suspicion. "I don't expect anything other than office work and, uh, assistance in helping to shape relations between our office and the larger supernatural Community."

"What's that mean?"

Sunshine shrugged. "Mostly, I think, it will mean being yourself and being present so that people will get to know a better side of creatures."

"Tokenism, I get it. Are people going to give me a hard time about being fey?"

"I want to say no. I'm honestly not sure. But something needs to change around here, and you seem like the person to help."

Rose snorted. "First time I've ever heard that."

"So do you want the job?" Sunshine asked.

"Uh. As long as I don't need to work nights. I, uh...I work another job then."

"No nights. How's...ten to two?"

"Perfect."

Sunshine offered his hand and Rose shook it.

"I appreciate this a lot," Rose said. "So much."

Sunshine stood and brought him out to talk to Jen. He turned Rose over to her to handle the paperwork.

Sunshine and Tate left at the same time.

She looked lonesome.

"You doing okay?" he asked.

"Emil stayed home again today."

"Oh."

"No one to talk to." She shrugged. "No one at home either."

"No Hank?"

"He's at his girlfriend's."

Sunshine contemplated a night alone and considered the boundaries that should exist between an employer and employee. "You want to learn to cook?"

She glanced at him. "What?"

"I was going to make stir fry, but I always make too much. And I wouldn't mind someone to talk to."

"Uh...Yeah. I guess. Sure."

He smiled.

She smiled back.

"My train's this way," he said with a nod up the block.

Tate spent a lot of the night talking more than cooking, but Sunshine really had wanted company more than he'd had any aspirations of becoming her cooking instructor.

Rose started on the twenty-eighth, a Thursday. A nice two-day week to ease him into things. Sunshine showed him around the office and made introductions. Jen, he already knew, and Tate took right to him, which he'd known she would. The others responded similarly: polite but hesitant.

Sunshine brought him to a desk adjacent to Jen's larger one. It had a laptop and a few other office supplies. "This is your area. Feel free to personalize."

Rose ran his hands over his clothing and spread his arms. "This is okay, right? I wasn't sure if it counted as smart casual or not. I had to google what that even meant."

He'd worn dark khakis and a blue sweater over a white button-down with brown boots.

"That's fine."

Rose gave a small smile. "I've never had a job with a dress code that isn't a uniform before. At least, not one where I'm not getting paid under the table."

"You'll get used to it."

Rose ran his hands over his pants. "Good, I'll just get these in like, five more colors."

"My office is upstairs. The door is usually physically closed, but it's metaphorically open."

"Thanks."

"I'll let you settle in," Sunshine excused himself back upstairs.

He gave Sarai a call, just to make sure she wasn't dead. He felt compelled to do that every few days. At least once a week, a dreadful need to see her overcame him so he brought her groceries. She continued to refuse any help, even when he told her he'd found her mother's colleague or offered to bring her to an aunt or an uncle, a grandparent. She didn't want anything but to add to the piles of papers she'd created without his aid.

Rose took to the office like a duck to water, for the most part. He filled his desk with knickknacks, learned how to brew a perfect pot of coffee, cleaned the dishes that inevitably got left in the sink every day, and learned how to use most of the office machinery without too many egregious errors. He picked up everyone's names and the relevant details about their lives in a blink.

He talked non-stop, to himself or someone else.

Sunshine had considerably less luck with the stray cat that had taken up residence in the upstairs office. It rarely came out and when it did, it either scarfed down its food or sat, unmoving, for hours, on Specter's office chair. If Sunshine moved too fast, it bolted back under the cabinet, even if he hadn't been anywhere near the cat.

He fed it and gave Rose the unfortunate job of cleaning its litter box. He fully intended to make Felix take back that responsibility when he returned.

Sunshine stayed obsessively busy to keep from thinking about Felix's absence too much. They still communicated through emails, mostly about work, and a single phone call, where Felix had wanted to confirm the time and place for the wedding.

For a while, no one asked about Felix's absence or when he would be back, except for Jen, but Sunshine wondered if that was more for office reasons than out of any personal interest.

By the first of May, though, more people had casually broached the topic and did seem relieved when Sunshine told them Felix had just gone to visit his parents.

Sunshine tried his best to keep from reaching out to Felix. He'd wanted space, time to think, so he worked all his personal statements into work emails.

Here's the update on the Berhart affair. Hope you're having a nice time.

Shay got some good photos of that hex lab. Say hi to Hiram and Phaedrus for me.

Rollins figured out those dog thefts. See you soon.

He brought in a lot of food to the office, brownies and cookies. He even brought some to Sarai on his weekly grocery drop off.

Jen asked a few times if he was okay and he assured her he was.

He just had more time on his hands without Felix around, which was mostly the truth.

He missed him, of course, but more than that, he could only binge TV and cook and pester his other friends so much. People had lives, jobs and significant others that meant they weren't free on weeknights to simply waste time with him. He kept his weekends and Friday nights busy, at least.

May 5
Thursday

The shuttle booked specifically for the wedding took Sunshine from the hotel to the outdoor chapel where the ceremony would be held. On a hill overlooking a beautiful wooded valley, the site offered a breathtaking view.

Sunshine couldn't appreciate it.

Felix would never be late for a wedding; his parents had raised him better than that. And he wasn't late yet. The ceremony didn't start for half an hour.

Sunshine smoothed his tie, buttoned and unbuttoned his suit jacket, and looked around desperately for someone else he knew. He couldn't find a single familiar face. He likely only knew Lisa and her limo hadn't pulled up yet.

A green Chevy sedan pulled up and Sunshine watched it like a dog watched a bone.

An elderly couple exited the car.

Sunshine made himself look away from the road. He fixed his eyes on the view, then tried to name the types of trees and flowers he saw. He heard bird calls. Those he could name; it took the edge off.

He thought about texting Jen to see how things were going at the office.

Before he could reach for his phone, someone leaped on to his back.

He yelped loud enough that everyone turned to look at him and his assailant.

Felix giggled. "It was too easy, I had to." He released Sunshine, his shoes tapping against the pavement.

Sunshine turned around.

Felix had dressed in an all-black three-piece suit, the tie and shirt black as well. A hint of color showed in subtle gray floral pattern on his vest, a dark gray flower in his lapel, and a silver ring on his right middle finger. Sunshine recognized it as the one Phaedrus had stolen. His hair, now deep fuchsia, made up for the darkness of his suit. "The purple was all faded and I wanted it to look fresh. I tried to do red, but this was what I got."

"It's lovely. You look fantastic."

Felix reached out to smooth the lapel of Sunshine's jacket. "You look like James Bond."

Sunshine glanced down at himself. A light gray three-piece suit, white shirt, and charcoal tie, with black shoes. "You think?"

"Yeah, straight up Sean Connery."

"I was going to do a different colored vest, you know, but I didn't want to be too much. You never know what people are going to wear to a wedding anymore. There's a little bit of a pattern on the tie."

Felix nodded approvingly. "You look sharp." He adjusted Sunshine's tie ever so slightly. "Very sharp. Shall we?" He nodded towards the seating.

They approached together and were seated on the bride's side.

Felix slipped his hand into Sunshine's.

Such a small thing, but it relieved Sunshine enormously.

"How are your parents?"

"Wonderful. Papa's doing, he's actually doing really well. Not so worn out as he's been. They send their love."

"Did you have a nice time?"

"No place like home," Felix sighed.

The ceremony was thankfully brief, lighthearted and sweet. Lisa glowed with happiness and her groom beamed at her the whole time. People shed tears.

Felix sniggered a little bit at the smudged eye makeup of one of the bridesmaids. He made quick work of two drinks during the cocktail hour.

"Pace yourself," Sunshine warned.

"Why, you need me conscious for something?"

"Yeah, walking up the stairs to our hotel room. It's historic, it doesn't have an elevator."

"That's not ADA compliant," Felix said.

"They might just give people with handicaps priority on the first floor."

Felix made a face then took out his phone. He asked a stranger to take a picture of them and sent it to his parents. Several minutes later, he said, "Bibi thinks you look like James Bond, too."

"That makes you a Bond girl, then, doesn't it?"

"Maybe I'm the villain."

"Are you going to tie me up later?" Sunshine asked.

"Only if you do something to deserve it."

The MC interrupted any further discussion as he asked them to return to their seats. Felix peeled away to grab another drink and he returned to their seats with two Manhattans.

"That's a bit much, don't you think?"

"One's for you, Jesus, I'm not an alcoholic yet." Felix set the drink in front of Sunshine.

The MC announced the bridal party and Felix said, "Oh, good, she fixed her makeup," a little too loud. People at the next table shot him looks.

He tittered and covered his hand with his mouth to stifle the sound.

"You're awful," Sunshine told him.

"Oh, shh, they're going to dance."

When the first dance and obligatory parent dances had concluded, the MC opened the dance floor to the rest of the wedding. Felix sort of watched, barely interested, which was unlike him.

The first note of "Take Me to Church" played and the demon seemed to stand on instinct rather than of his own volition. He looked at Sunshine, a little desperate.

Before he could ask, Sunshine took his hand and led him out to the dance floor.

"I thought you were going to make me beg," Felix murmured.

"What?"

"You didn't even ask me to dance."

"Since when do you wait for me to ask you to do anything?" Sunshine placed a hand on Felix's waist and kept a hold of his other hand.

"Since I'm trying to tell you what to do less." Felix kept trying to lead Sunshine and eventually asked, "Listen, can we switch?"

They switched and Felix led much more easily than Sunshine could have.

"I don't mind being told what to do."

"It's not very nice of me."

"I find it helpful," Sunshine said.

Felix rolled his eyes.

They stayed on the floor for ages. Felix promised to teach him how to waltz, which he had been promising for at least fifty years. People around them came and went, but Felix never wanted to leave except to get a drink.

When the food came out, he conceded that they should eat, especially since the MC turned down the music. The bride and groom came over to greet and thank them.

Lisa smiled at the two of them. "Saw you guys dancing up a storm out there."

"Felix likes to dance," Sunshine offered mildly.

"Who gave you permission to use my Christian name?" Felix demanded.

Lisa chuckled. She looked between the two of them and asked a few carefully worded questions about what they'd been up to.

Sunshine answered as simply as he could, since what they'd really been up to felt ridiculous, untruthful, and dramatic. He mentioned their vacation and asked about her honeymoon plans.

Felix chimed in every so often, but mostly he fussed over Sunshine's hair. "I just. There's just this one that won't play nice with the others," he fretted.

"Would you leave it alone?" Sunshine asked.

"Impossible. It's the only thing I like about you."

Sunshine gave Lisa an apologetic smile and pushed Felix's hand away from his hair.

"Explains a lot," she said finally. "I always wondered why you were so, uh. Patient. With me."

Sunshine didn't know what to make of that and didn't bother to ask for clarification. He took an overlarge bite of salad and said, "Food's great. Make sure you eat, too."

She thanked them for coming again and made her way to the next set of guests.

After dinner, and more drinks, Felix pulled Sunshine back to the dance floor. They remained there for the rest of the night.

There was nothing else to do, really; Sunshine didn't know anyone else. And there wasn't anything else he wanted to do.

The songs slowed as the night wound down. They swayed together, circling the same spot as Eric Clapton, Etta James, and Elvis played. All the wedding classics he'd heard at nearly every wedding he'd attended.

Felix had placed both his hands on Sunshine's hips and Sunshine draped his arms over Felix's shoulders.

"Can You Feel the Love Tonight" came on and Felix murmured, "You know this is a waltz."

"Are you falling asleep on me?"

"No."

"You sound pretty sleepy."

"I'm not tired. I..." Felix sucked in a breath and straightened up a little. "I'm just kind of sad."

"Why?"

Softly, Felix shared, "Because society is standing on a precipice of madness and revolution and things might get really bad really soon."

"Oh." Sunshine wanted to offer that they had made it through Nixon and Reagan, but so many people hadn't survived those administrations. They had lost friends. He said the only thing he could, which was, "We'll be together, at least."

Felix looked up at him for a little while, his face solemn, thoughtful. He seemed to be on the verge of saying something profound. He took in a breath and declared, "Fuck it."

"What?"

Felix didn't repeat himself. He kissed Sunshine instead. Slowly, but not carefully. He was savoring it, not holding back. "We should do this."

"Do what?"

"Whatever we want. No matter what it is."

Tension Sunshine hadn't realized he carried slid out of his shoulders. He grinned. "Fucking finally."

"Excuse me?"

"Fucking finally," Sunshine repeated. "What's the point in being so goddamned smart if you can't figure out that some things just can't be figured out? Embrace the unknowable for once, Felix."

"You're going to make me change my mind."

"That's gonna suck for you, cause I'm the one with the hotel room and the car to get back home."

"I'll go back to Canada."

Sunshine nipped his ear. "I thought you were going to tie me up later."

"You're awful."

Sunshine kissed him, warm and exploratory, something he'd wanted for so much longer than even he'd known.

The song ended and the MC wished everyone a goodnight.

Felix stepped back first. He'd turned pink and couldn't quite look at Sunshine. He grabbed his hand. "Come on, you said there's a shuttle."

They gathered their jackets. Felix stole a centerpiece and smuggled it back to the hotel room under his jacket.

He swaggered into the bathroom and emerged half-undressed in trousers and an undershirt. Wonderfully disheveled, he swooned onto the bed like a concubine in an Orientalist harem painting from the nineteenth century.

Eyes closed, one arm draped above his head, a hand resting on his stomach, he asked, "Are you going to make love to me now?"

Sunshine stared at the strip of his stomach exposed between his rucked-up undershirt and the waist of his trousers. "I don't make love. I fuck. Hard." He barely managed to say it with a straight face.

Felix peeked open one eye but when he saw Sunshine's face, he dissolved into giggles.

Sunshine shed his clothes, placing them more neatly than how Felix had strewn his shirt and tie about the room. He knelt over Felix, one knee on either side of his body. "If you want to reenact bad movies, I'd rather do *Trolls 2*."

Warily, Felix looked up at him. "Which one is that?"

"With the popcorn?"

"Where are we going to get that much popcorn at this hour?" Felix demanded.

"The hotel has a pool; if it's open, we can do *Showgirls*."

"Christ. I don't know if I can *physically* do that."

Sunshine slipped Felix's shirt over his head. He unbuttoned the demon's pants and stood so he could tug them over his legs.

Felix stared, his chest moving shallowly and flushed pink all over. He went almost perfectly still when Sunshine came back to his side.

Sunshine circled one arm around him to lift him out of bed and onto his feet, threw back the covers, then nudged him back towards the bed.

Felix sat and watched Sunshine circle around to the other side of the bed. His eyes narrowed when Sunshine snuggled under the covers.

"Aren't you tired? You've been on your feet for hours."

Felix lay down like he thought the bed might be full of snakes and eyed the covers when Sunshine tugged them over him.

Sunshine scooted a little closer, resting his hand on Felix's hip.

"What's your deal?"

"Hmm?" Sunshine asked. He pressed a kiss to the other man's shoulder.

"You're not even going to try to fuck me, are you?"

"Don't get yourself worked up. What was the point in doing all that thinking if you're just going to start worrying again?" Sunshine asked. "Relax."

"I just wish you would tell me what the fuck is going on in your head for once."

Sunshine paused to evaluate his own thoughts.

"So I don't have to guess. When I have to guess, I start guessing all kinds of things and I'm usually pretty far off base."

"Yeah, you're usually jumping to the worst conclusion possible." Sunshine had thought it respectful to keep his own desires to himself, but he could see how Felix couldn't handle that. "I don't have any expectations, nothing I'm assuming you will or won't do for me. Those limits are entirely yours to decide and adjust. Other than that...Uh." He trailed off.

He didn't know how to say what he wanted. He'd never needed to with anyone; he'd gone along with whatever they'd wanted because it had all had value to him.

What did *he* want and what did he want from Felix, specifically?

"Hey," Felix said, pulling him out of his thoughts.

"Tonight," he began, thinking it must be best to start with the situation at hand, "Is not a good time to do anything we haven't done before."

"And after tonight?"

Words that had come out as teasing, as jokes, felt much harder to say if they might come true. "I like it when you're mean to me. And when you pull my hair. I think about that sometimes. I think...I think I'd like it if you hit me. Or, maybe if you did tie me up."

"Oh."

"Or if you told me what to do for you."

"But in a sort of mean way?" Felix guessed.

"I've never really done that. But I think I'd like it."

Felix slid closer and knotted his fingers in Sunshine's hair. He tightened his grip. "Like this?"

Sunshine's stomach clenched. He swallowed. "Yeah."

Felix studied his face as he pulled even harder. "You're not kidding, are you?"

"No," he breathed.

"I don't know if I could hit you, even if you liked it." He loosened his fingers. He placed a kiss on the tip of Sunshine's nose.

"That's okay."

Felix kissed him once more. "There's a big ass bathtub in there."

"I noticed."

"What time is check out? Cause I'm gonna be in it right until we have to go."

"Sunday at eleven."

"Oh, Sunshine, this place has got to be really expensive!" Felix exclaimed quietly. "You can't—"

"Your dad paid me in literal gold coins. I think I can splurge a little."

Felix huffed and rolled his eyes. He hooked one leg around one of Sunshine's and aggressively made himself comfortable, mashing the pillow into a shape that pleased him better. "Night."

"The light is still on."

With a flick of his fingers, Felix turned off the lights. He yawned, then tossed and turned, elbowing and kneeing Sunshine as he did so, but finally settled after an hour or so.

Booking the hotel for the long weekend had been a gamble and Sunshine had made sure that he could trade the room for one with two beds, just in case. He hadn't known what Felix would decide after his trip home, but he'd feared the worst.

An end to any romance between them wouldn't have been bad, or even unexpected, but Sunshine had almost convinced himself that Felix would want him gone entirely. He would want to excise Sunshine from his life the same as Sunshine trimmed out brown spots from apples with which he intended to bake.

He made himself stop thinking about that immediately. He wasn't some rotten corner of Felix's life and feeling that way wouldn't help anything.

He slept fitfully, waking now and then when Felix moved or when some half-remembered anxiety showed its face in his dreams.

Felix woke him up at just after eight by tickling his lips with the end of a croissant.

He grunted and swiped at whatever attacked him.

Felix poked a little harder. "Come on, I got us breakfast. It's continental," he said with a strange inflection that sounded both swanky and ghoulish. He sat down hard on the edge of the bed.

Sunshine rubbed his eyes and took the croissant.

Felix wore a bathrobe open over short, tight trunks. Sleep had ruffled his hair and he'd done nothing to tame it.

"Did you scar any children in the process?"

Felix flipped him off. He snagged a piece of melon from the plate he'd brought up. "What, exactly, are we supposed to do all weekend in this lovely haven of nothingness?"

"I thought we could reenact *The Shining*."

Felix raised an eyebrow and did not say any of the various innuendos that could have come from that film, though clearly, it required effort.

"Mostly I didn't want to drive all the way back yet."

They picked over the plentiful, but hodgepodge breakfast Felix had selected and wasted about half an hour trying to flick Cheerios into each other's mouths.

"The bathtub," Felix declared as he stood and brushed crumbs off himself, "Might be big enough for both of us."

"Should we investigate?"

"We are detectives."

The bath held them both comfortably. Felix used an entire bottle of hotel body wash to make it sudsy and stretched out so his feet, crossed at the ankle, rested on Sunshine's chest.

"Am I supposed to enjoy this?"

Felix peeked open one eye. "You tell me. You're the kinky one."

Sunshine ran one finger against the sole of his foot.

Felix jerked away. "Don't!" Felix swatted at him. "Be rude." He settled back into the bath with his feet tucked under one of Sunshine's thighs this time. "Does it go both ways?"

"Hmm?"

"Your newly confessed predilection for consensual bedroom acts of violence. Does it go both ways? Do you wish to inflict as well as receive?"

Sunshine could not, ever, imagine Felix consenting to being restrained or wanting someone to strike him in any manner. He could not conceive of doing that to him, either. "No."

"Good." Felix played with a floating island of suds. "What about regular stuff?"

"Whatever you want."

"That's not what I asked."

"Well, 'regular stuff' is not descriptive."

"Hands and mouths I'm fine with, pretty much anywhere...Uh. Well." Felix winced at some thought he didn't share. "Not always the whole hand. Sometimes just fingers," he clarified. "But I don't like to bottom."

Sunshine pulled his thoughts back; he'd started thinking about lunch. Apparently somewhere around this hotel was a restaurant with a Michelin star. "Okay."

"I've tried. A lot. All different ways. And I'm just...it's. *Not* my favorite," Felix insisted with the same tone that someone might use to recall a restaurant that had given them food poisoning.

"That's fine."

"And topping is...well, it's not always physically an option for me. And I kind of suck at it. Are you paying attention? Do you think you could at least manage to be disappointed with me?"

"I think I'm still hungry," Sunshine admitted. "Cause you said topping and immediately I was like, damn I want some sprinkles and caramel sauce. And why would I be disappointed?"

"I don't know, because I'm fucking...sexually dysfunctional?" he demanded.

"Shhh, relax. We can figure it out."

"Am I just supposed to spit on you and call you a faggot in bed? What are we *doing* here?"

"Don't call me a faggot," Sunshine requested softly.

Felix's whole demeanor changed. "No, I won't. I wouldn't. I'm sorry."

Sunshine sat up. The bath felt too hot suddenly. He wanted to get out.

Felix sloshed forward and grabbed his hand. "I'm sorry."

"No, it's—" Sunshine tried to pull away, but Felix wouldn't let go, so much stronger than his frame suggested.

"It's not! Tell me, Sunshine, tell me that hurt you. Hold me goddamn accountable for my actions. Because if I'm going to...if I'm going to do this with you, then you need to tell me when I go too far, or in completely the wrong direction."

Rational. Responsible, too. Unlike Felix, except that it was so like him to do this for someone else and not himself. "I didn't like that." Saying it felt sullen and weak.

"Alright, we're going for, uh, like some light BDSM here, not abuse. And I don't think either of us knows what we're doing, despite being older than the fucking Chrysler building. We need to be careful with each other."

Sunshine nodded.

Felix took Sunshine's face in his hands. "I want to do this, but I want to do it right. Okay?"

"Okay," Sunshine managed.

Felix kissed him.

They kissed for a long time, sweet and without anything more than lips and tongue; their hands did not wander any further than to wrap around each other's torsos. Honestly, it was the best thing that had happened to Sunshine in years. He could kiss Felix for hours.

Or at least until the bath got cold.

"We should actually bathe," Felix suggested at one point.

"Mm. Why? Do you have plans?"

"I'm a little worried my skin might slough off if we stay in here too long. I'm deeply wrinkled."

Sunshine released him.

All the bubbles had fizzled out, leaving the water cloudy.

Felix leaned over the side of the tub and dragged over Sunshine's toiletry bag. He riffled through and returned with a small metal case from which he extracted a bar of soap. He offered it to Sunshine. "I can't believe you haven't used this yet."

Sunshine sniffed it and sighed. "It's so nice, I didn't want to waste it."

"No one makes you buy cheap body wash, Sunshine, you're an adult."

Sunshine mockingly repeated what he'd said as he lathered up the bar and started to wash.

During the rest of their bath, Felix gave a rundown of the things in the area he'd decided they should do. Apparently, he'd been up for hours before Sunshine.

He climbed out, dried off, and announced, "I don't have a change of clothes."

"What?"

"I forgot. I had all my stuff shipped back home because I didn't want to have to worry about it."

Sunshine took the towel he held out. "You can borrow something of mine."

"Sunshine, I love you deeply, but if I had to dress like you, I'd slit my wrists." Felix patted his cheek and walked away.

"What's wrong with the way I dress!"

"Oh, god, all those warm tones and earthy neutrals? They work for you, but, well. There's fashion and then there's style."

"Maybe not everyone wants to look like goddamn Dracula all the time!"

Felix reappeared in the bathroom doorway. "That's racist and inaccurate. I do not dress like Dracula."

"No, you dress like your father."

Felix's eyes widened. "I. Do. Not. None of his clothes *ever* fit him and they're all falling apart. Take it back."

"You dress like your father, you spooky boy. Go put on my jeans so we can go to the stupid sheep you wanted to see."

"They're not going to fit. I have a longer inseam and a smaller waist."

"Go get dressed."

Felix huffed but went. He tore through Sunshine's bag until he found the clothing he deemed most acceptable. He pulled on a pair of jeans without any underwear; they rested dangerously low on his hips.

"Maybe—"

"No, you've made this fucking bed, Sunshine. You have to take me out in public looking like this." He pulled on a pair of socks and the same black dress boots he'd worn last night; he cuffed the jeans so his boots showed more prominently. He dragged a burgundy sweater over his head and tucked it into the jeans.

He looked in the mirror, sighed a lot, and eventually hiked up the jeans and belted them high on his waist. "This is...it's actually not that bad, right?"

"You look fine."

Felix stared at himself in the mirror for a long time, adjusting and preening.

Sunshine found clothing for himself, another pair of jeans and a Henley in one of the earth tones Felix apparently disliked so much.

Felix scowled at him. "I want to get clothes while we're out."

"Yeah, whatever. But you do look exceptionally adorable presently. Like...uh. Like, I don't know, like you're giving me...queer modern European goatherd. Like your papá sent you out to tend the flock but you didn't know such a handsome stranger would be traveling through the mountains today. You've always been warned away from outsiders but this one...You want to be nearer. You can't control yourself." He intentionally glazed over his eyes and stared past Felix.

"Alright, well now I feel like I'm going to be abducted to the Otherworld and robbed of my innocence..." Felix said uncertainly.

Sunshine grinned, took his hand, and pulled him out the door. Borderline giddy and barely contained, Sunshine could not keep his hands to himself. He kissed Felix at every given opportunity, on the cheek or knuckles, on the temple, or right beneath his ear. He felt like a child with a puppy, desperate to snuggle every moment of love out of him.

He didn't, for once, worry what the Devil had planned, or what was happening with Sarai. He didn't give two shits about office politics or Emil's attitude. He sincerely hoped he'd never have to feel the aching uncertainty that had clouded his life in recent months.

The days moved slowly but the weekend ended in the blink of an eye. A few jaunts to dairy farms, breweries, and scenic outdoor locales and this small reprieve concluded.

Monday morning, they returned to the office and Felix headed upstairs without a word to anyone.

Sunshine heard him cooing gently to the stray. While Felix did that, he checked in with Jen and made sure to ask Emil how things were, since he'd come into work that day.

"Uh. Things are kind of looking up. We think. The doctors say it'll be slow, but that she'll recover as long as she can rest."

Sunshine nodded.

"Being home helps a lot, I think. Makes it easier on her, not trying to do everything for herself and the kids."

"I'm glad to hear that. Take the time you need, Emil. Really."

"I will. Thank you. I, uh..." Emil glanced towards the stairs. "I've been out of line..."

"I'd leave him alone if I were you. Maybe start with just a nice 'hello' in the mornings," Sunshine advised.

"Yeah, yeah, makes sense."

When he made it upstairs, Sunshine found Felix flat on his stomach sweet-talking the stray. He did that for a while, then hovered around Sunshine, reading emails over his shoulder and offering unsolicited advice.

He paced the office as Sunshine filled him in about what Sarai's mother had studied in her undergrad and grad programs. Her graduate work agitated him the most.

"Ghettos, Sunshine, those people are trying to make ghettos. Ones that would be literally inescapable. Fucking Christ."

"It kind of opens up the options on who killed her. Sarai said her dad's friends did it."

"I wouldn't get mixed up in this," Felix advised.

"Why not?"

"Cause once you're in it, I'm in it, and I don't want to deal with people who think I should be in a concentration camp."

Sunshine tried not to look guilty.

"But I know you're going to goddamn do it anyway, aren't you?"

"It's really starting to feel like we should find out who killed these two. And why they took all the arcane texts in the entire house."

Felix groaned. He opened his mouth, then turned towards the door.

Rose stood there with a mug of coffee.

"Who the fuck is this?" Felix demanded of Sunshine, slinging a thumb towards the young fairy.

Rose turned colors. "I, I, uh, Mr. Sunshine, I brought up a coffee." He eyed Felix nervously and did not come in to place the mug on Sunshine's desk, which he had previously made a habit of doing.

"Ignore him, Rose. Specter, this is our new office assistant. Behave yourself."

"Don't ignore me," Felix snapped.

"Oh, god forbid you should get anything less than everyone's attention," Sunshine said. "Rose, this is Mr. Felix Specter, the other half of Sunshine and Specter Paranormal Detective Agency. He is always this, if not more, unpleasant. I'm terribly sorry."

Sunshine stood to take the mug from Rose.

"I'm not unpleasant!" Felix growled. He stalked over to his desk and threw himself into his chair.

Quietly, Sunshine told Rose, "He's actually incredibly tolerable once he feels he's sufficiently established himself as erratic and morbid."

"Uh, I. Well. I'm sorry, I just…Enjoy your coffee."

Felix said, "I can *hear you*."

Rose glanced towards Felix.

His back fully turned to Felix, Sunshine continued, "Honest to god, he's harmless. How was your weekend?"

"Busy," Rose answered.

"Do I know you?" Felix called. He stood up and looked over Rose.

Rose edged out of the door. "I should go, Jen has something for me to do, I'm sure, I'm sorry."

Felix came over to the door and watched Rose rush downstairs. He squinted after him. "So."

"So what?"

"You hired a high-end escort as an office assistant."

"Pardon?"

"Oh, yeah, I've seen him around mage-y society events. You know, the ones that Reinharts get invited to," Felix shared haughtily. "Or. Well. I used to see him. I guess transitioning kind of does a number on your client list if you're mainly catering to old straight guys."

"Are you sure?" Sunshine asked.

"Incredibly."

"Hmm." Sunshine pulled the door to their office closed.

"This is why we should interview people together."

Not quite sure where this would end, Sunshine asked, "So we can exclude sex workers from our hiring pool?"

"So we can make sure we hire them, you dipshit. Poor kid. It's hard to build a client list. Must suck to lose it."

Sunshine thought of the night job Rose had alluded to previously. "Should we say something?"

"How would you feel if your new boss asked you if you were a hooker?" Felix asked.

"Fucking…you know that's not what I meant."

Felix plucked the Robinson casefile off Sunshine's desk. "I'm going to look into the dad some more. I'm sure you missed something."

"I thought we agreed no flirting at the office."

"First of all, I would never agree to that," Felix began but never finished. He opened the Robinson file and dove deep into his research.

He surfaced at the sound of the world's most timid knock.

"Come in," Sunshine called.

Rose barely came inside. "I was wondering if you had a lunch order?"

"Come inside," Felix said. "Close the door."

Rose did both but didn't leave the foot-wide strip of hardwood in front of the door before the rug began.

"Like, actually come inside, I'm not going to do anything to you." Felix gestured to the chair across from his desk.

Rose sat, his hands twisted together and his knuckles pale. "I'm sorry, I just, you know, I thought I'd bring up coffee for Mr. Sunshine, it was never a problem before, but I guess I—"

"Don't be sorry. I'm sorry. I was a prick. You were doing your job. Your name is Rose?"

"Rosewood, but just Rose is fine."

"That's a good fairy name," Felix offered.

Rose smiled. "Thanks. My mom was worried about it. She tried really hard to make sure it wasn't, uh, too human or too fey."

"What court?"

"Western."

Felix nodded. "And what about you? Are you pledged to a court?"

"No, I, uh. I do better on Earth, for the most part. I'm not good at lying but I'm also not good at obfuscating, which is pretty much the same as breathing in the Otherworld."

"I understand."

Sunshine sipped his coffee and returned to his work. Felix always balked at new people; if Sunshine had mentioned it, he would have gotten worked up about it the whole time he'd been away. A day or two, maybe even sooner in this case, and then he'd have Rose tucked securely under his wing, as odd of a place as that could be. Felix's way of mentoring and caring about people never manifested itself exactly as expected, but Sunshine genuinely believed that Felix wanted to help people more than he wanted anything else.

Felix dismissed Rose with their lunch order and a fistful of cash that he'd dredged up from a winter jacket hanging behind his desk.

May 11
Wednesday

Felix threw a jacket at Sunshine. "We're going to talk to that girl."

Sunshine bundled up the jacket and set it aside. "I'm in the middle of something."

"Less important."

"It's employee reviews." He still had the rest of the month to work on them, but he liked to give people the right balance of praise and critical help during their reviews. The June ones were most important since those were the ones used to determine how much of a raise someone received.

"Less. Important. Everyone passes. No one's fired," Felix said, waving his hand towards Sunshine's computer. "Come."

Sunshine stood and followed without a second thought. He wondered, briefly, if he should have second thoughts about following Felix so blindly and before he knew it, he'd followed him all the way to Woodlawn Heights.

Felix grabbed him by the jacket sleeve to stop him from walking past the apartment building. "I thought you were ignoring me, but you're seriously spacing out."

"Sorry."

"What's on your mind?"

"Am I stupid?"

Felix scoffed and rolled his eyes. "Listen, can we not do this right now? I told you, I was trying to be nicer, but this is a home conversation, not a work conversation."

"No, not...I didn't mean it like that. I just...I obey. Without thinking about it. Anything anyone tells me to do."

Felix looked him over. "You don't listen to anyone."

Sunshine's brow knitted.

"You listen to people you trust, Sunshine. You wouldn't just go traipsing off after some rando. You wouldn't do something just because some scumbag said to do it," Felix said. "And you used to never listen to me. You fought me tooth and nail on shit for a while."

Heat crept across Sunshine's cheeks.

Felix tugged on Sunshine's earlobe. "Trust and loyalty don't make you stupid."

Sunshine smiled.

"Not knowing that Macon is in Georgia makes you stupid."

Sunshine scowled. "I'm not even from here, you can't give me a hard time about geography."

"I'm not from the US either," Felix reminded.

"And you do have the benefit of formal education at a prestigious school," Sunshine pointed out. "And Canada is still on this planet."

Felix rolled his eyes as though such advantages were a matter of opinion. He grabbed the railing of the staircase and swung himself onto the steps. He jammed the intercom.

"Who is it?"

"Specter, of the Sunshine and Specter Paranormal Detective Agency."

"Go away."

He frowned at the intercom. He pressed the button again.

"I said go away."

"Let me up or I will let myself up. I'm here to speak about your father."

"Felix," Sunshine scolded.

Felix ignored him.

When the door didn't open, Felix let himself in, exactly as he'd promised he would. He strode up the stairs and pushed open the apartment door.

"Fucking Dracula," Sunshine accused quietly as Felix's long

coat flared behind him when he swept into the room.

"Get out!" Sarai demanded.

"Careful, she—"

A hissed chant and small zip of lightning cut off his warning. Felix parried it easily and twiddled it between his fingers before he squashed it in his fist. "Sit down," Felix said.

Sunshine followed him in and eyed the state of the apartment. It had started to edge into filthy.

Sarai didn't sit until Felix sent a chair swooping in behind her.

"First of all, you're going to clean this place up before I leave," Felix said. "Second, you're going to tell me what your parents were up to because I'm pretty sure it got them killed."

She gaped at him.

He sat across from her.

Sunshine hovered a foot or so behind, feeling like hired muscle.

"We are not a codfish, Michael," Felix told her.

She frowned.

"Close your mouth," Felix translated. "And stop staring, it's rude."

"You cast without a spell."

"Of course I did, I'm a demon."

She shook her head. "There's no such thing as demons."

Felix let out half a laugh, "Fffffucking okay. Sure. Then I'm a level ten wizard from the planet Xerxes. We need to talk about your parents. You told Sunshine that friends of your father's killed them?"

She nodded sullenly.

"Which friends?"

"I don't know."

"You don't know the names of your father's friends."

"They weren't that kind of friends. I didn't hang around when they were talking. It was all first names and..." She shrugged. "They kind of all looked the same."

Felix leaned back in his chair. "So, what, like are we talking golf buddies or coworkers or what?"

"I don't know."

"So then why do you think they're even friends?"

"Because they sounded friendly. They came over a lot. Stayed for a long time. They'd go into my father's office and talk for hours."

Felix rubbed his cheeks. A hint of fuzz had appeared on his face; he didn't need to shave more often than every few days and he couldn't have grown a beard to save his life. Once he'd tried to grow a mustache and he'd looked awful. "So tell me what they look like."

She shrugged. "White, uh. Usually wore suits. Two with dark hair. One was, uh, kinda a redhead."

"And they looked the same like brothers look the same or like white people look the same?"

"Like brothers," she confirmed.

"Tell me about their faces."

She shook her head. "I don't want to talk about this."

Felix leaned forward, his elbows on his knees. "I don't want to talk about it either and normally, if you didn't want to find these people, I'd leave it alone, cause you're not paying me. However, turns out your dad contracted with the private prison company that handles supernatural criminals on this coast. He specialized in security and containment."

"So?"

"So that doesn't make you a teensy bit nervous? Cause it makes me nervous, especially since all the arcane texts in your house were stolen."

She crossed her arms. "What are you getting at?"

"Books are big and bulky and heavy. Your parents didn't get found for hours after the break-in, which means you didn't call the cops and you didn't tell anyone. You just ran."

"I was scared."

"For four months you were scared?" Felix demanded. "Or are you just smart enough to know that opening your mouth is going to get you killed, too?"

She stared at him.

"I read your dad's thesis. He was smart, too. If anyone could figure out a way to keep a prison full of mages and creatures on lockdown, it was him. And if anyone could figure out a way to keep creatures in designated locations..." Felix shrugged.

Sarai shook her head. "No, he...Dad wouldn't do that. He did security for prisons, yeah, but he...You're making him sound like he wanted to make concentration camps, but you can't put things that don't exist in camps!"

"Then you tell me what he did study."

For the first time, Sarai looked at Sunshine.

"You know more than you're telling us," Sunshine said. He

gestured to all the papers she'd gathered. "And you need help finding who did this."

"I'm not trying to find them," she admitted quietly. "Finding them won't bring my parents back."

"Then what is all this?"

She clenched her hands, then stood. She went into the bedroom and came back with her backpack. She took out a thick, leather-bound folio. "This is what my father was working on. I knew it's what they came for, so I took it when I ran. But this...this is some advanced shit. I've been trying to figure it out but, you know, it's like trying to translate quantum physics with an algebra book."

"Can I see it?" Felix held out a hand.

She hesitated but placed it in his hand.

With the respect that only an academic could have for paper, Felix opened the folio and examined the first sheet. His eyes moved over the runes.

Sunshine knew better than to ask what it said.

"I'd like to take this," Felix told Sarai.

"No, I..."

"You and I aren't going to make head or tails out of this. But I know someone who can."

"Who?"

"His name is Georg, he's the Master of Records for my father. He's also a huge nerd."

"And then you'll give it back," she said.

"As long as it doesn't violate the Ethics Code," he agreed.

"Fine."

Felix stood and gestured towards the kitchen. "You two start cleaning."

"Where are you going?" she demanded.

"Hell." He slipped his phone out of his pocket and scrolled through his contacts.

She glanced at Sunshine.

"Dad? Hi. No, yeah, I'm great. Everything is fine. No, no, Dad. No. I don't need you to come here. I actually need to get to where you are," Felix said. "I need to talk to Georg." He winked at Sunshine, a gesture of assurance. "Yeah, now works for me."

He disappeared without a sound.

Sarai recoiled from the sudden absence.

Sunshine headed into the kitchen. "You know, it gets hard to scrub the gunk off the longer you let it dry." He piled her dishes into the sink and began to fill it with water, adding a healthy dollop of soap. "There's a vacuum in the closet."

"Where did he go?"

"Hell."

"There's...There's no such place."

"Then he vanished to some other location that you do believe in. Maybe...Sarasota?" Sunshine guessed. "The vacuum."

"How can you fucking expect me to vacuum right now?" she demanded.

"Is there a reason why you can't?"

"What the *actual fuck* is happening? Where did he go? Where did he take my dad's research?"

Sunshine leaned against the counter. "There are a lot of things that parents never tell their children. Maybe because they don't want them to know or maybe because they know they aren't ready. Your mom had a bad run-in with a vampire in college. She might have thought not knowing about creatures would keep you safe."

Sarai shook her head.

"And I'm willing to bet that your dad felt the same way. He saw the worst that the Community has to offer, the ones so bad that we couldn't police them ourselves. Your parents wanted to keep you safe, didn't they?" Sunshine asked. "Nice quiet town in a nice quiet neighborhood. Homeschooled. Your mom stayed home with you. Didn't let you go out with too many people. It had to be someone they trusted, someone whose parents they'd met. Nice kids."

"They were just strict."

"Sure. Lots of parents are strict," he agreed. "Maybe your dad's research is, uh, I don't know. A really good egg substitute for the vegan bakery he's going to open when he retires. Does that sound good to you? Get the vacuum."

She got the vacuum.

Sunshine tidied up while she cleaned the floor. He called her in to help with the bathroom, which needed a good wipe down but wasn't as bad as the rest of the place.

Halfway through spraying the bathtub, Sarai threw down the cannister of Scrubbing Bubbles with an awful clatter, crouched on the floor, and started to cry.

Sunshine finished wiping down the mirror, tossed the paper towel, and turned around to watch her. "Sarai."

"Fuck you," she sobbed.

He sat beside her. "I know you feel alone, but you don't have to do this on your own. We can help. We can get in touch with your family—"

"No! Leave my family out of this."

"Alright."

"I don't need them dead too."

Sunshine pulled an arms' length of toilet paper off the roll and handed it to her. "Blow your nose."

She blew her nose and sobbed into the soggy toilet paper.

"Tell me about your father's friends, Sarai. So we can get you home."

She sniffled.

He took her by the arm and helped her stand. "Let's get out of the bathroom, too, huh?"

She went with him.

They sat together on the couch.

"My mom didn't like them. She always sent me up to do homework when they came over," she began. "She hated them. But my dad always seemed happy to see them."

"Did she say why?"

"She." Sarai sighed. "She said they took things too far. I figured they had to be other security contractors. Dad was always." She rubbed her nose.

He scanned the room for tissues. He found only take out napkins. He handed her one.

She blew her nose again. "Dad always traveled to conferences and stuff like that. I figured he had to know them from one of those."

"Did you know their names? Or what they did?"

"I think, uh. I think they were related. Talking about kids and aunts and stuff like that. They had, uh."

"Go ahead," he urged after she'd gone quiet for a while.

"Their names. It was like...Three B names. You know, like that Duggar family? They all had the same first letter. Bill, Bob, Brad, Betty, Becca. Everyone they talked about had a B name. I thought it was fucking weird. My mom made fun of them. She called them the B-list. Dad didn't think it was funny."

"Okay, that's good. That's helpful." He took out his notebook and jotted a few things down. "You'd know them if you saw them?"

She nodded.

"Do you know if they were mages?"

"Yeah, I think so. I never saw them doing any magic, but they always seemed to know what Dad was talking about." Her eyes remained puffy and red, but she'd stopped sniffling. "I'd know them if I saw them, though. I would."

He got her a glass of water, then resumed asking her questions, prying out a few more details. Eventually, he had to ask, "How did you know to take your father's research when you ran?"

"He told me to. I...they hadn't been around for a while. I saw them pull up when I came home from Shaniala's. I waved, but when I went inside, they sort of...they sort of rushed in before the door could close. My dad was right there, he was...getting ready to take the dog out. Bubbles—that's our dog, he was barking like crazy. My dad grabbed his bag and gave it to me and told me to run." She licked her lips and took another desperate sip of her water. "So I ran." Her face went gray. "Oh. Bubbles. Is he...Did they...? I heard him barking still, and my mom screaming and I just ran."

"Your dog is with your uncle. He was hurt pretty badly, but he's alive," Sunshine shared. He wished he had better news for her.

She started to cry again.

He patted her shoulder. When she stopped crying, he told her to go lay down for a little while.

She went.

He scrubbed the dishes. He didn't know how long Felix would be gone, but it didn't feel right to leave her alone. When he'd cleaned the apartment and she emerged, he said, "Why don't you come down to the office with me?"

"Why?"

He shrugged. "You won't be alone. We can get in touch with your uncle, too. He's got to be desperate to know you're okay."

"I don't want him to get hurt."

"You know you're only a kid, right? He's supposed to be the one worrying about you," Sunshine pointed out.

"Uncle Josh isn't even done with college yet. He lived with Nana until she died."

"Regardless. He's your closest family. We should let him know you're alive. I won't make you call him, but..." He glanced around. "Don't you at least want to get out of this place? When was the last time you went outside?"

She looked at the floor. "I should shower."

He nodded and tried not to look too emphatic about it. He texted Felix to let him know their plan. He didn't expect an answer—Felix would be too involved in whatever he was doing. He got an answer, though.

Felix says he'll see you there! A picture of Felix flipping off the camera accompanied the message. *It's Ira, by the way. Hi!*

Sunshine smiled and texted back and forth with Ira until Sarai was ready to go.

The journey back to the office was full of quiet, half-started sentences. Neither of them knew what to say, especially not to each other.

At the office, Sunshine showed her around. She didn't seem to know what to make of the place.

She knew less what to make of Rose. She stared at him as he painstakingly typed up some invoices.

He twisted side to side in his rolling chair as he worked and eventually realized he had a spectator. He blinked once, unsettled, then smiled at her. "Hi."

She wrinkled her nose at him. Eyes narrow and mouth turned down, she scrutinized the fairy without returning his greeting.

Discomfort spread over Rose's face. He squared his shoulders and tilted up his jaw.

Sunshine saw this going sideways in about ten different ways. He strode over, blocking Rose from her view, plucked a takeout menu from Rose's desk, and handed it over to her. "Here, go figure out something for lunch. My office is upstairs."

She went, still scowling suspiciously.

Rose stared after her.

Sunshine took Jen's chair and rolled in close to Rose. He kept his voice soft. "It isn't you."

"Yeah, considering all I did was say hi," Rose grumbled.

"She's never seen a fairy before."

"Doesn't mean she has to give me the evil eye."

"Her parents told her creatures don't exist. It's...it's been a point of contention, especially given that they recently passed away," Sunshine explained. "Please, don't take it personally and bear with us."

Rose tucked a stray piece of hair back into his braid. "Alright." He cast a baleful glance towards the stairs.

Sunshine gave the fairy's arm a quick pat. "Thank you."

Rose raised an eyebrow. "Doesn't mean I'm happy about it."

"I don't expect you to be."

"Just quiet?"

Sunshine tilted his head. "I'm sensing a deeper issue here."

Rose shrugged.

"You don't have to tell me, but you can if you'd like."

"No, it's just…" He sighed and rubbed his face. "Getting asked to keep things quiet is not unfamiliar territory. I'm just…I'm not a fan!"

"I'm not asking you to keep quiet about anything. Just make a concession for a homeless fifteen-year-old orphan."

"No, I get it. I do. I'm sorry, Mr. Sunshine. I am." Rose sighed. "Just. *That* was the kind of look I got used to."

"I understand."

"Yeah?" Rose asked.

"Well, I do sparkle. Especially in the sun."

"It's much more subtle than a sparkle. More of a shimmer," Rose said.

"Sparkle, shimmer," Sunshine said with a shrug, "I've been hanging around with Specter for decades and God knows he stopped trying to reel it in years ago. Imagine the two of us walking down Broadway in the seventies. I know what it's like to be looked at."

Rose sniggered. "Yeah, I can imagine."

"I'll find a picture. If you've ever wondered what it would look like if an evil warlock moonlighted as a pimp…"

The fairy covered his mouth and giggled.

Sunshine stood up. "But, you know, in a good way."

"Oh, sure, I bet," Rose said with a tone of indulging Sunshine rather than believing him.

Sunshine headed upstairs to make sure Sarai hadn't gotten into anything.

"That guy was blue," she said as soon as he entered the room.

"He's fey."

"Bullshit."

Sunshine sighed. "I'm going to do some work. Try not to touch anything."

She went over to Felix's desk.

"Don't touch anything on his desk," he warned.

"Can I at least sit?"

"If you want to fight the cat for the chair."

She pulled out the desk chair.

The cat hissed.

Sarai backed away and took the chair on the other side of the desk. "So what do you do?"

He looked up at her.

"Paranormal detectives. Are you like those ghost hunters?"

"We take any case that involves the supernatural, whether it's just that the clients belong to the Community or that there's actual magic involved. Sometimes it's tracking a vampire around to see if he's cheating on his wife. Other times it's hauntings, or hexes gone wrong. Uh." He glanced around and spied the album. He pulled it down from the shelf and checked the spine. "These are thank-you letters from clients."

She flipped through the book. At first, she flipped through with a polite yet feigned interest, but after a while, she seemed to actually read the letters. "This one's from nineteen forty-nine."

"That's the year we opened."

"You inherited it or something?" she guessed.

"No. Specter always wanted to be a detective. I also think he was ready to move out and he had to go and do it as dramatically as possible." Sunshine found another leather-bound book, this one a photo album. He turned it towards her and opened it to the first page. "See? That's us."

The black-and-white photo showed him and Specter dressed in suits and standing in front of the same building their office currently occupied. They stood beside each other, not nearly as close as they would have stood even a few years later.

The closeness in their relationship had not happened all at once, but it snowballed, growing at a normal, steady rate and then spiraling over a few years into their odd brand of intimacy, codependence, and camaraderie.

Sunshine recalled, "Bibi insisted on taking a photograph. I think Specter about died of embarrassment, but he's never been able to say no to his parents, not in any meaningful way. He is, I believe, a very nice boy at heart."

Sarai wrinkled her nose. "The one who says he's a demon?"

"The very same."

She stared at the photo.

He waited for her to tell him it was a fake.

She took the photo album out of his hand and pored over it for a while.

Sunshine left her to it and returned to writing employee reviews.

Rose rapped on the door then let himself in. He usually let himself in if he knew Felix wasn't around. "Were you guys getting lunch?"

Sarai shrugged when Sunshine glanced at her. "I could eat I guess."

Rose eyed the photo album.

She handed it to him. "You some kind of demon, too?"

"Fairy," he corrected.

She shook her head. "Does this shit ever end?"

Rose glanced at Sunshine, a gently quizzical expression on his face.

Sunshine waved him further into the room. "Maybe you can explain it to her."

Rose came further into the room, scooped the stray out of Felix's chair, and made himself comfortable with the cat on his lap.

Sunshine stared. No one had gotten that close to the stray, not even Felix.

"I'm good with animals," Rose said with a shrug.

The cat purred and kneaded his chest.

He winced a little. "So you don't believe in creatures?" Rose asked Sarai.

"Of course I don't. They're bedtime stories and boogeymen."

"So what do you believe in?"

"Things I can see," she answered.

"You see me right now. You see him, too, don't you? If we aren't what we say we are, then what are we?" Rose asked.

"I don't know."

"Then why can't we be what we say we are?"

Sunshine appreciated what Rose was doing. Fairies had a knack for twisting things just so and tended towards asking questions instead of giving answers. Sunshine hadn't understood how someone who blurted out every thought would ever be able to function in any capacity as a paid companion, but he saw it better now.

"What's more likely? That he and Mr. Specter and I are sharing a delusion? That we're in some kind of cult?" Rose asked.

"A hundred years ago people thought the mentally ill were possessed," Sarai countered. "They just didn't understand what was really happening."

Rose scratched the cat's head. He told Sunshine, "You can't make someone believe."

"No," Sunshine agreed. "Not without holding them captive and administering a lot of drugs."

Sarai straightened up a little.

"Dark," Rose noted.

"And effortful. It's easier if people don't believe in us anyway."

"Oh, tell me about it. Sometimes I like to go to those comic conventions just so I blend in for once," Rose said.

"God help me if I ever set foot in one of those again. Specter goes every year and I'd rather peel off my skin," Sunshine said.

The crush of bodies, the endless lines, the lights and sights and, dear God, the *smells* of comic book conventions overwhelmed him.

"Maybe you should go with him this year," Sunshine suggested. "They had a ghost one year and Specter about wet himself with excitement when he got invited to solve their case."

"The Javits Center is haunted?"

"Cursed artifact at one of the booths, actually. Uh, it was..." Sunshine tried to think back to recall it exactly. "One of those Japanese cartoon statues with the big..." He glanced towards Sarai, knowing he should watch his language around her, though she'd made no effort to watch hers.

"Tits?" she supplied for him.

Rose giggled.

He shrugged. "Yeah. Super spooky stuff, though."

Rose remained upstairs; he showed far more interest in the photo album and letters than Sarai.

Part of Sunshine knew he should dismiss Rose back to his actual work, but Sunshine liked having him around.

They ordered take-out from a Middle Eastern place that Sunshine adored.

Halfway through their meal, Felix appeared to Sarai's left and said, "Your dad's not a Nazi."

She yelped and raised her hand to cast a spell.

Felix placed a hand on her wrist and lowered her arm. "None of that." He peered into the take-out bag. "Is this mine?"

"No, it's for the cat," Sunshine told him.

Felix frowned. "Cats don't eat falafel. What a stupid thing to say." He sounded almost offended.

"Stupid answer for a stupid question."

Felix glared at Sunshine, snagged his lunch out of the bag, and warmed it up. He eyed Rose and the cat. "That's my chair."

Rose glanced at the sleeping cat curled up on his lap, then back up at Felix. He opened his mouth, then glanced at the cat again.

"She's sleeping," he offered nervously.

Felix narrowed his eyes at him.

"Don't be a bitch, Specter," Sunshine warned. "Come sit with me."

Felix glanced at their audience cagily.

"Don't make it weird."

"You already made it weird," Felix growled. He came around to Sunshine's desk and shooed him out of his seat.

Sunshine stayed put. He took Felix by the arm and tugged him onto his lap. He rested his cheek against Felix's back. He carried the ashen tang of Hell with him. "Did you see your father?"

"No, he was working. Ira says hi though."

"How is Ira?"

"He looks like shit, but he's pretty perky overall."

Sunshine looped an arm around Felix's waist. He liked Ira, despite him being companion to the Dark Prince Himself. He couldn't fathom what Ira saw in a creature like Satan, other than the guess that maybe Lucifer treated Ira better than people had previously. Ira had a dicey, borderline depressing story to tell, but he told it like being sold into indentured servitude as a child was a normal but unpleasant thing anyone might have to go through. Like a bad divorce or sick sibling.

A bit of falafel fell out of Felix's mouth and landed on Sunshine's arm.

Felix wiped it off with a napkin. "Sorry."

"Where's my father's research?" Sarai asked.

"I left it with Georg," he mumbled around his food.

"Why?"

"He wasn't done reading it, we didn't know if it was dangerous yet."

Sarai stood up. "My father *protected people*. How could it be dangerous?"

Felix set down his food and wiped his hands but remained seated on Sunshine's thigh. He went quiet, probably studying Sarai.

"I'm a hundred and two," he told her. "And I've met a lot of people who've done awful things. Most of them never thought they were doing awful things. They always have a reason, a strong, thought out reason that makes sense to them and to the people that work with them. You know what your dad was doing?"

"You know I don't."

"He was trying to find a way to keep creatures out. Keep them from entering a certain location. My guess is he meant to market it as a, uh..." Felix made a gesture in the air near his head. "A home security sort of deal. You know, vamps and wolves and all we other beasties can't get into your house, so we can't hurt you."

"And that's not dangerous," she insisted.

"Not in and of itself, no," Felix agreed readily. "People can do what they want with their own homes. But it could be flipped. Making places creatures can't leave. Or put on public places. Starbucks decides it doesn't like vamps hanging around, doesn't want any more fairies applying to be baristas." Felix shrugged.

Sarai didn't say anything for a long time.

Sunshine leaned around Felix to see the look on her face.

She looked upset, not sad but somewhere between disappointed and irritated. "You're talking about segregation."

"I've *been* talking about segregation," Felix pointed out.

"My father wouldn't—"

"I'm not talking about your father anymore, sweetheart," Felix said, not catty but uncharacteristically gentle. "I'm talking about whoever killed him. Three men who've already proven themselves to be dangerous. Your father knew what they were after. He sent the two most precious things he had away from them."

She sighed and leaned back heavily in her chair. "I can't take you two seriously like that."

Sunshine glanced up at Felix.

"Why not?" he asked calmly.

"Just..." She sighed. "Look at you."

"Look at me," he repeated. "I mean, honestly. When has the world ever taken a person like me seriously?"

Sunshine nosed him in the back, the smallest gesture of comfort but hopefully enough of one. Felix had once upon a time tried to squeeze himself into the world's expectations but had thankfully given up.

"Should I go home and put on a suit? Buy a house? Get a tenure position at a university? Adhere to whatever arbitrary socio-economic markers we've decided represent respectability and believability?" Felix asked. "Or can I just talk to you like we're both reasonable people? I know this is hard and scary and just plain fucking awful, but we're here to help if you let us."

Sarai didn't answer.

"I love you," Sunshine murmured.

Felix looked at him out of the corner of his eye and gave a

small smile. "You may kiss me."

Sunshine kissed his palm.

Felix gripped Sunshine's hand.

Rose and Sarai glanced at each other.

Sunshine wrapped his arms around Felix and squeezed him tight. He gave him a pat on the thigh. "Up."

Felix stood. "Where are you going?"

"The bathroom, if that's alright with Your Majesty."

Felix waved him away as if granting permission.

May 13
Friday

After a day of likely processing new and relived traumas, Sarai agreed to come back to the office and give more details about her parents' killers.

Sunshine's chest loosened at the sight of her. He had waited beside Jen's desk with his heart in his throat for Jen to come back to the office with their charge. He had mail clutched in his hand. He'd picked it up half an hour ago but had only managed to open one envelope and make terse small talk with a few people in that time.

The sooner the Devil released him from this favor the better.

Sarai wrinkled her nose when he waved to her.

"Specter's upstairs with Tate."

"You aren't coming?" Her voice warbled the slightest bit.

"I'll be up," he assured her. He held up the mail.

Sarai started up the stairs but paused halfway up.

"Listen, he's honest-to-god harmless," Sunshine assured. "I'll be up."

"He's nuts."

Sunshine tried not to bristle. It didn't do him any good to take offense to things on Felix's behalf. He tried to have empathy for people who didn't know Felix, or more specifically, people who didn't understand him. Only so many things could be said in defense of a person like Felix before they started to sound like excuses.

Maybe Sunshine did make too many excuses for him, but how could he not?

"I'm right behind you," he assured.

He handed over the mail to Jen and followed Sarai.

She didn't seem any happier to have him tag along. She barely looked at or spoke to him while she went over the finer details of the men she had seen.

He listened with one ear and started to think about dinner. It wasn't far off. Another hour or so at work, maybe a trip to the store, and then he'd be home, cooking dinner.

Specter would come over. He'd read his comics or possibly a novel at the island counter. They'd have a few drinks. Not too many.

Felix had been trying to have fewer drinks.

"My new motto is harm reduction," he'd declared one morning over breakfast. The concern must have shown on Sunshine's face because Felix had immediately said, "I don't mean like needle exchanges or anything! I'm not doing heroin yet. I just, you know. I'm not going to get to *no* booze or drugs, but maybe I'll do...less booze and drugs."

"What do you want for dinner?" Sunshine asked during a lull in the conversation.

"Do you think about anything but food?" Felix asked.

"Uh. Yes. But you have to eat like three times a day."

"You could always just eat one huge meal a day," Tate suggested.

Sunshine didn't love that idea, so he didn't acknowledge it. "I was thinking chicken and asparagus."

"It is in season," Felix agreed. "You should make risotto."

"You know that's a pain in the ass to make."

"It sounds really good," Tate chimed. "You should make risotto."

Sunshine looked between the two of them, then at Sarai who sat sullenly in the chair before Felix's desk. He made some considerations, then finally said, "Fine, but I need to go to the store if you're all coming over for dinner."

Felix smiled. "Then go to the store."

He gave a delicate wave goodbye as Sunshine left.

Sunshine walked out of the office with a bounce in his step

and wandered through the grocery store with a blissful smile on his face. He bought enough for dinner and dessert.

How long had it been since he'd had people over for dinner? Not just a single friend, but multiple friends.

Well.

A friend, an employee, and an orphaned child.

He bought perhaps too much asparagus, but it was in season.

By the time the others arrived, he had cookie dough in the fridge and the meal divided between stove top and oven.

Felix let himself in, pulled a bottle of wine out of the fridge, and popped himself up onto a free corner of the counter. He wiggled the cork out of the bottle and said, "Tate, there's glasses in that counter. Uh, Sarai, I think there's soda in the fridge."

Tate pulled down three wine glasses and brought them over to Felix. He filled them and passed one to Sunshine.

"I can't, I'm stirring."

"You don't need two hands to stir," Felix said.

Sunshine waved him away.

"Do you have a turkey baster? I could baste it right into your mouth."

"Get plates," Sunshine said.

"Tate, the plates are in the cabinet next to the glasses."

Tate pulled them down.

Felix took a sip of his drink.

Sarai lingered on the other side of the island. "So you two are like...dating?"

Felix and Sunshine glanced at each other.

"Or something?" she asked, looking over them again.

"We're engaged to be married," Felix announced casually.

Tate raised an eyebrow and leaned against the counter by the stove. She peered at the risotto. "I thought it wasn't like that."

"Thought it wasn't like what?" Felix asked Sunshine. "What did you tell her?"

"Not...Not a lot," Sunshine assured. "Are we engaged?"

"Would you like to be?" Felix asked.

"Would you like to be?" Sunshine countered warily. He could not tell sometimes when Felix was being serious or when he was leaning too hard into a joke.

Felix took a sip of wine. "Would it be terribly tragic of me to put ice cubes in this? I feel like it will keep me sober longer."

"You could be especially tragic and put Sprite in it."

"No so wait," Tate said. "Are you two dating now?"

"I..." Sunshine glanced at Felix, who had slunk off the counter and over to the freezer. "I think so."

"We're certainly doing something," Felix agreed unhelpfully. He added a handful of ice cubes and a healthy glug of Sprite to his wine. "Is this awful of me?"

"I think it's absolutely reasonable."

Felix mulled over the tragedy of his drink for a while longer but forgot about it when Sunshine placed a loaded plate in his hand.

They all settled in around the kitchen island.

Sarai picked at her food.

"Eat it before the rice overcooks," Felix advised.

She took a forkful but sighed at it.

"Later we should—" Felix began.

"No, no board games. You get too competitive," Sunshine warned.

As an explanation, Felix offered, "You've played Scrabble with my parents."

"Can I ask," Tate began.

When she didn't finish, Felix said, "You may ask."

"What, exactly, is the deal with your parents? Isn't the Devil your dad? But also the cat? And those other two. I only met them a little bit at your birthday."

"Oh. That." Felix drained his glass and poured himself an undiluted and rather full glass of wine. "I think we have to start at the beginning, which I *think* means starting with how Papa and Bibi met, right?" He eyed Sunshine inquisitively.

"Good of a place as any," Sunshine agreed. "That cat is just a stray though."

Felix flapped a hand at Sunshine and shushed him, then launched into the story of how Phaedrus and Hiram had become his parents, how his biological father and mother had conceived him, where Ira figured into things, and how June sort of played into the whole story.

Tate appeared to follow what he said, despite his many tangents.

Sarai went from sullen to melancholy as they ate.

"Don't like asparagus?" Sunshine asked.

She pushed a spear around on her plate. "I don't know."

"It doesn't taste how you'd think it would," Sunshine

suggested.

"I like the end bits," Felix said.

Sarai sighed.

"One bite."

She pushed her plate away. "I want to go home." She looked so incredibly young and exhausted.

Sunshine wanted to do something to make her life right again but nothing within his power would fix what had happened to her. He couldn't. No one could. Finding those men would make her safer but it wouldn't bring her parents back or heal her pain.

"I can take you back," Tate offered gently.

"Thanks."

"Uh. Or." Tate glanced at Sunshine and Felix. "If you don't want to be alone, you can come back to my place. If you want."

"I don't know."

"Well. Think about it. Let's clean up," Tate said and began to gather their plates.

Sarai sluggishly stood to help her.

They scraped the plates and loaded them into the dishwasher.

Sunshine stored the leftovers. "I made cookie dough," he told Tate.

"Oh, I..." She looked at Sarai. "Do you want to stay for cookies?"

The girl shrugged.

He took the mixing bowl out of the fridge. "I'll send you home with some, how's that sound? You can make them later tonight if you want."

"That's sweet, Sunshine," Tate said.

He scooped out half the dough and stored it in a Chinese food Tupperware. He scribbled baking instructions onto a scrap of paper and taped it to the lid. "Here you go."

"Thank you." Tate turned to Sarai. "You ready, kid?"

"Yeah."

Tate put a hand on Sarai's shoulder.

"Get home safe," Sunshine called.

Felix loaded his glass with ice cubes and did a backward sign of the cross towards the two of them. "The despair of Satan be upon any who affront ye."

"Felix, that's not funny!" Sunshine scolded.

"What? That's never worked," Felix scoffed.

"You don't know that!"

"Well, fuck it, if someone's going to mug them, they deserve whatever happens." He waved. "Bye, girls. Be safe."

"Bye, Specter," Tate said with puzzled fondness in her voice. "Thanks for the cookies, Sunshine."

Sunshine walked them to the door and closed the door behind them. "Tate's such a nice kid."

"Big heart," Felix agreed as he wilted onto the couch.

"You doing alright over there?"

"Oh, I'm so fragile these days, Sunshine, I really don't know."

Sunshine rolled his eyes. "You're not fragile."

"Why can't I be?"

"What?"

"Why can't I be fragile?"

Sunshine leaned over the back of the couch. "Do you want to be fragile?"

"Of course I don't *want* to be!"

"No, I mean...Are you fragile, Felix? Should I be worried?"

"I don't know." Felix licked his lips and swallowed. "I really don't. But can't I be fragile? If I need to be?"

Sunshine leaned further over and took his hand. "Of course you can."

"You don't mind?"

"No."

"Come lay down with me."

Sunshine wedged his way onto the couch with him. He gathered Felix close and kissed his neck. "You would tell me, right? If you need something."

"I hope so." He laced his fingers with Sunshine's. "But you know how I get."

"Is Dr. Reza helping?"

"She helps."

Sunshine kissed his temple. "You know I'll do whatever I can."

"I know. I know *now*. I don't know if I'll know then. I don't know...I. I get caught up in my head sometimes." His voice thickened. "I think something's wrong with me. It didn't use to be so bad."

"I'm sorry."

"I." He sighed and sniffed.

"What?"

"I'm scared, Sunshine."

Sunshine tightened his arms around Felix. "You've had an

awful fucking year. Honestly. A lot has happened and none of it has been easy. Give things a little time to settle. I mean, keep going to therapy and keep using fewer substances, and keep talking to me about it too. And let me help when I can. Okay?"

"Okay," Felix conceded miserably.

"I think it will get darker before it gets lighter. But hold on through that."

Felix didn't answer. He gripped onto Sunshine's arm so hard his fingers dug in.

"I love you."

Felix sniffed. "You fucking better, we're engaged." He chuckled weepily to himself.

Sunshine kissed his cheek. "You're a bit of a beast, you know that, don't you?"

"Isn't that why you like me?"

"Well, yes, but it's also that you're an absolute freak of nature." Felix laughed.

"And you're wonderful."

"Oh, shut up, Sunshine."

Sunshine pulled in a deep breath. "A perfectly marvelous girl," he began.

Felix twisted to face him and placed a hand over his mouth. "No."

Sunshine wrapped his hand around Felix's and kissed his palm. "Are you sure? I know all the words."

"Please no."

Sunshine kissed his inner wrist. "I love you." He nuzzled against his neck and kissed him there too.

"You already said that," Felix whispered.

"So what should I say next?"

"How about...how about let's take this to the bedroom?"

"Would you like to?"

"I think it's about time we try. What spiral into depression would be complete without erectile dysfunction and agonizing failure?"

"I..." Sunshine didn't know how to say what he felt.

"What?"

"It won't be like that with us."

Felix snorted. "Yeah? Your love's so strong you're gonna make my dick work? You think I've never loved anyone before? Or are you just special? Is that one of your super-soldier powers? You and all your buddies rock hard on the battlefield?"

Sunshine rolled them so Felix lay on top of him. "Nothing that happens between us will be a failure." He looped his arms around Felix. "And you said it yourself, didn't you? That it just takes you a little longer."

"Or sometimes not at all," Felix reminded, sour and hurt.

"How often is sometimes?"

"I don't know."

Sunshine raised an eyebrow.

"I don't know! No one ever gives me enough time to figure it out. It used to be...occasionally. Once in a blue moon that I couldn't get it up. But it used to be people, uh...I actually had a chance. A nice night out. Something...romantic. Lots of time to get from A to B without anyone rushing me. But now, I don't know if it's them or me, some kind of culture shift or if I actually used to, to date."

"I can safely assure you that people have been casually hooking up for longer than your lifetime," Sunshine said. "But your dating life has been a little..."

"A little what?" Felix pressed.

"Don't get mad."

"I won't."

"A little desperate. Forced."

Felix sighed. He stretched out over the length of Sunshine's body. "What's the point in dating if everyone's just going to feel threatened but how weirdly close you are with your best friend? All the girls think you're in the closet, all the boys think you're cheating. And honestly, anyone who *isn't* threatened just doesn't really care."

Sunshine shifted beneath him. He wanted to wiggle a lot more but knew that he'd have fewer opportunities to hear unguarded emotion and truth from Felix than he would to rub up against him.

"They were all right to be threatened anyway. But what else should I have done? Been alone all the time, never let anyone touch me because the person I wanted couldn't? When he became so important to me that I couldn't even think about doing anything to risk it." He scoffed and rolled his eyes. "*He.* You, Sunshine, you fucking idiot. When *you* became so important to me. And then I kissed you and I...Christ, Sunshine, I thought I'd fucked it all up."

"You didn't."

"Jury's still out on that."

"Come on, Felix, don't be a shit."

"No, I mean it, Sunshine. I really am frightened."

"Presently or in a more ongoing sense?"

"Ongoing."

"Alright. Well. It's eight thirty on a Friday night and we don't have any plans tomorrow morning. Plenty of time to give things a try," Sunshine suggested.

"Hands and mouths only," Felix warned.

"Fair."

Felix pushed himself up, raked his hands through his hair, and let out a shaky, nervous breath. He looked around.

"We don't have to."

"No, no, I want to. I want to try. Just no promises. Okay?"

"Understood."

Felix stood and headed to the bedroom without waiting for Sunshine. As he went, he said, "Honestly, I don't fucking know, my nerves might give out."

Sunshine caught up with him and slung an arm around him. He kissed his throat. "You can always try being mean to me, you're already very good at that," he purred.

"Christ," Felix breathed. "Christ, Sunshine."

Sunshine pressed close and kissed him.

Felix slid his arms around Sunshine's neck. One hand nestled in his hair. He tightened his grip, tentative at first, but then harder when Sunshine moaned.

They didn't make it to the bed. They hardly made it inside the bedroom, locked together, insistent but not hurried.

Felix pulled back first. He swallowed and ruffled his hair, then asked, "Would now be a good time to tell you what to do?"

Sunshine nodded, not exactly trusting himself to make a coherent sentence.

"Get undressed." There was a tentative note to the command, not unsure of what he wanted, but unsure of how forceful he should be.

Sunshine raised an eyebrow and waited.

"Get undressed, Sunshine," Felix repeated, irritated, but this time without any hesitance.

Sunshine started to peel off his clothes.

"And don't make me repeat myself. You know I fucking hate that," Felix warned. He slipped his shirt over his head and tossed a glance Sunshine's way. "Did I goddamn say you could look at me?"

Sunshine averted his eyes. He stared at the floor. Things did not feel exactly right, but they had never done this before. It would take practice.

He heard Felix's shoes hit the floor, the rattle of his belt.

God, they had never done anything before. Maybe this would be too much at once. Maybe they should have stuck to something they'd both done. Sunshine thought about lifting his eyes, especially when Felix stayed quiet for a long time after they'd both undressed.

Before he could get the chance, Felix said, "Kneel." His voice held no room for argument. This was more than just his usual bossiness.

Sunshine instinctively knelt on one knee and kept his head bowed.

Felix stepped closer, close enough that Sunshine could see his legs and smell his skin. He placed a hand on Sunshine's head and gripped his hair. He tilted Sunshine's head back, not exactly gentle, but not forceful either. Just firm. "Look at me."

Sunshine lifted his eyes, scanning over Felix's body, and met the other man's eyes.

They gazed at each other.

Something inside Sunshine withered, something deep in his core began to dissolve. In its place bloomed something else. Something loving and adoring. Something worshipful. He stared up at Felix and knew that he would follow him to the ends of the Earth. He would follow him to Hell, or anywhere else Felix wanted him to go.

He would do anything for him, follow any order Felix gave in earnest and follow with such confidence that Felix would never ask him to do anything bad.

He was, without a doubt, the best person Sunshine knew. Deeply flawed and utterly perfect.

Something about Felix changed as he stared down at Sunshine. His face, not the shape, but the expression transformed into something focused and heady. His breathing had evened out. He placed his hand beneath Sunshine's chin. Curious but sure of himself, he said, "You will do anything I tell you."

"Everything," Sunshine vowed.

Felix breathed in deep through his mouth as though he could pull Sunshine's promise into himself.

He might have been able to.

Some tether inside Sunshine reached toward Felix. He could

have let everything in himself, every ounce of grace and divinity, seep out of himself and into the demon. He could give all the vastness of Heaven over to him. With him, Felix could do anything.

Felix's eyelids fluttered. He sighed, then pulled in a sharp breath. "Stand up," he insisted. "Right now, get up."

The moment, the connection between them dissolved. Its departure left Sunshine cold and confused.

He stood and wanted to cry.

Felix threw his arms around him and hugged him tight, skin against skin. "Don't give me that much of yourself, I don't know what I'd do with it."

"I'm sorry."

"No, no, don't be sorry. Don't. It wasn't your fault."

Sunshine couldn't help but feel it was his fault. His chest tightened.

Felix cupped Sunshine's face in his hands. "It was such a beautiful thing you tried to give me, Sunshine, it was, but I can't take it."

Sunshine nodded.

Felix kissed him, careful but warm. He melted against him. "Let's try something else."

"Okay."

Felix kissed him again and took his hand. He brought him to the bed and cuddled up to him. "You're so beautiful, Sunshine. Do you have any idea?" He didn't wait for an answer before he kissed him again.

Sunshine didn't feel like crying anymore.

They twined together, all sliding palms and long kisses. Sunshine skated his hands over Felix's sides, his thighs, and ribs. He ran his fingers down his back and occasionally brushed between his legs, a caress or two before he moved on to something else. Hunger built within him, not ravenous but determined to savor.

Felix pressed close and every so often, offered a murmur of encouragement.

Sunshine had never moved quite so slowly with anyone before, not even his first time. He almost wished he had. He wished he'd kissed everyone the way he kissed Felix now, intimate and new, but achingly familiar.

After a while of this careful, sweet petting, Felix took Sunshine's hand and conjured lubricant directly into it.

Just a few syllables, the magical equivalent of spitting into his hand. His lips brushed Sunshine's palm.

Some people tossed in other runes. One guy Sunshine knew had made a pretty decent sour apple flavor.

"You might as well," Felix mumbled sheepishly into Sunshine's throat. "Won't get much harder than that."

Sunshine didn't know what he expected, exactly, based on that comment, but what he found was nothing out of the ordinary. It momentarily made Sunshine fear that Felix had somehow been fucking a subset of superhuman men with insistently virile and rock-hard dicks.

He said, stupidly and not without concern, "I don't think it's supposed to."

"No, just...I." Felix pressed his face against Sunshine's chest. He let out a nervous titter. "I didn't know how else to ask. I don't. Just. Shit," he swore when Sunshine wrapped a hand around him. "Jesus."

Felix relaxed against him, letting out quiet, satisfied sounds. After several minutes, he slicked his own hand and began to touch Sunshine in kind.

Never, in all his experience with hand jobs and mutual masturbation, had Sunshine felt so at peace. Being together should not have felt this easy, this comfortable, after so many years of tension.

But then again, it had never really been *just* about this. A thousand years could have passed without another kiss or a single orgasm shared between them and Sunshine would have happily stayed by Felix's side.

The orgasms, though, when they happened, turned out to be a very nice bonus. Not the start or the cause of the bond between them, but a pleasant way to strengthen it.

Felix got the giggles afterward. It seemed like more than just afterglow; he seemed relieved.

They cleaned up and nestled under the covers.

Sunshine wormed his way close to Felix, underneath his arm, and pressed a kiss to his ribs.

"You should put a TV in here," Felix suggested after a long, quiet stretch of time.

"Why?"

"So I'll have something to do while you're sleeping."

"I can't sleep with the TV on."

"Bullshit. You fall asleep to those ancient alien documentaries all the time," Felix told him.

Sunshine yawned. "Or ones about the ocean," he agreed.

Quiet moments ticked past. Sunshine almost nodded off, content and well-fed and soothed by the weight of Felix's arm resting on him.

"Should we talk?" Felix asked.

"About what?"

"About how you almost fell."

It took Sunshine a moment to process. "I didn't…" He didn't actually know what had happened. He had felt something unusual, but it hadn't been bad. Or scary. He had always thought it would be terrifying to fall.

Tender but insistent, Felix explained, "You can't give that to me. I don't want to be what that would make me."

"I didn't know I could."

Felix's fingers brushed over the birthmark on his arm. A smudge, really. The color of coffee with milk, not any different than a birthmark found on any other person. "Mark of the beast."

"Is it…" Sunshine squinted at the birthmark. "It's supposed to be something, isn't it?"

"I don't know. I don't even know if this is supposed to be the same thing as that mark of the beast shit. Some people see it in goddamn energy drinks. I just…It meant something to my dad. It meant something to Heaven, too, or you wouldn't be here."

"What if it's all just a misunderstanding?"

"What?" Felix asked.

"What if it really doesn't mean anything at all? Or what if it's like, uh, pretty much everything with your dad. What if it only means what we believe it means?" Sunshine asked.

"Ah, the wonder of the collective human consciousness." Felix kissed the top of Sunshine's head. "Whatever this thing means and whatever being an antichrist *is*, I felt something there, Sunshine."

"We'll be more careful."

"It was the way you looked at me," Felix confided. "You…" He licked his lips. "You looked at me like I could do anything."

"You can do anything, Felix." He meant it more than he'd ever meant anything.

Felix reached over to cover Sunshine's eyes. Playfully, he warned, "Don't start. I don't know if I could resist twice. Maybe next time I'll blindfold you."

A little shiver ran down Sunshine's spine. He kissed Felix's throat. "I think I'd like that." He yawned again.

"Go to sleep."

"You don't mind?"

"No, stupid. I have books on my phone."

Sunshine pulled up the covers. He curled up against Felix and kept a hand on his thigh. He should have been able to fall asleep, tired and content as he was.

A single thought wormed in through that comfortable fog. A minor but still unpleasant one.

Another followed.

The longer he had his eyes closed, the more restless he became.

"You doing alright over there?" Felix asked when Sunshine had shifted positions half a dozen times.

"I can't sleep."

Felix set down his phone on the bedside table and rested his chin on Sunshine's shoulder. "You thinking about being a mindless hobo on a baby-murder mission again?"

"I am now."

"Think about something else. Where's your birds?"

Sunshine had never mentioned that to Felix and had never played the recording when they'd shared a room. He rolled over and sat up.

"The walls are thin as goddamn paper," Felix offered easily.

"And you might have a few monitoring charms?" Sunshine guessed.

"Not in your bedroom. I do have some concept of privacy. Play the birds."

"You don't mind?"

"I'm not sleeping anyway," Felix said. "Do what you need to do."

With a hair of embarrassment, Sunshine played the meadow recording. He made the volume just loud enough to hear.

"Robin," Felix noted softly. He took up his phone again. "How do you feel about tuxedos?"

"I like the stripe."

"Mmm. How about white tie?"

"Why?"

"Just thinking."

"White tie is too fancy. I've never worn tails."

"Never?" Felix asked.

"No."

"It is too fancy," Felix agreed. "I don't think I'd want anything that formal."

Sunshine didn't ask him to elaborate. If he wanted to be coy, he would be coy no matter what questions Sunshine asked. He closed his eyes and managed to sleep this time.

May 23
Monday

Emil walked in to work with a smile on his face. It was perhaps the first time that Sunshine had seen him genuinely smile in months. Emil looked directly at Sunshine, Felix, and Rose, who had gathered around the printer in an attempt to either fix it or bully it into fixing itself. "Morning!"

Felix looked over at Sunshine.

"Don't be a bitch," Sunshine warned under his breath.

Felix pinched him. "I'm not." He looked over at Emil. "Good morning, Emil."

"How are you?" Sunshine asked him.

"Good." He smiled again. "Good news from the doctor."

"That's wonderful," Sunshine said.

"Really great," Rose added as he started to flip open parts of the printer. He looked over at Emil. "How's she feeling?"

"We went out last night," Emil said. "First time in a while. She got, uh..." He gave a bashful smile. "She got dressed up and everything."

They murmured a series of appropriate platitudes.

Emil headed to his desk.

Felix looped an arm around Sunshine's waist and cuddled up to him. He placed a kiss on his cheek then said, "Fix this bullshit.

I'll be upstairs doing something better with my life." He peeled away and went upstairs.

Rose watched him walk away, a small expression of concern, or perhaps confusion, on his face. He jiggled something out of the printer and peered at it.

"Sometimes the paper gets jammed through here." Sunshine pointed to a part of the printer. He pried off a panel and squinted into it.

"Yeah, but it won't even turn on."

"Is it plugged in?" Jen asked from her desk.

Rose blinked several times. "Jen, tell me that wasn't a serious question."

"That's what was wrong with the coffee maker last week," she reminded.

Rose took a breath and made a point of not responding to her.

Sunshine continued to stare into the printer as though it would help.

It didn't.

An hour of taking apart and peering at different pieces didn't help.

Felix came back downstairs and made a face at the two of them sitting on the floor and the disassembled printer. He said, "I called someone to come fix the printer. You can stop wasting your time now."

"I swear we've almost got it," Sunshine insisted.

"You actually don't," Felix assured. "And I would like you to come down to the library with me."

Sunshine examined a few printer pieces and picked up a screwdriver. "Why?"

Felix crossed his arms. "The trio of homicidal and possibly genocidal maniacs we're after?"

"Oh."

"Wait, what?" Rose asked.

"Don't worry about it," Felix said. He nudged Sunshine's butt with his shoe. "Come on."

Sunshine fiddled with one more piece.

Felix went from nudging to one solid kick.

Sunshine glanced up at him. He smiled.

Felix scowled. He jutted out his hand and, when Sunshine took it, hauled him to his feet with strength Sunshine always forgot he possessed.

Sunshine bounced up. "What's at the library?"

"Information, specifically old newspapers. I've got a few ideas who these guys might be, but they've gotten shady the last few decades. I want to check out the old society papers."

"Oh, the old society papers," Sunshine agreed in his swankiest voice, "Of course, how could I forget about those?"

Felix flicked his ear. "Don't be fresh."

"Or what?"

"Or I'll turn you over my knee," Felix threatened snootily. A beat later, he added, "But you'd probably like that, wouldn't you?"

"I don't know, can you throw in a Mary Poppins impression while you're doing it?"

"Absolute deviant," Felix accused. He gave Sunshine a push toward the door.

"What exactly are we looking for at the library?" Sunshine asked.

Felix twisted his fingers with Sunshine's. "Uh, there's an old mage family that Papa knows of. They used to be big shots, sort of...rivals to the New York branch of the family."

"The Reinharts have rivals?"

"All the best families do," Felix answered. "But they've been keeping out of the limelight after a, uh, well, after quite the scandal if I do say so."

Sunshine hadn't investigated the leads Sarai had provided. Felix had taken over, as was his way, but Sunshine should have helped more. As they descended into the subway, Sunshine asked, "What sort of scandal?"

He started to feel warm. He usually got nervous taking the subway recently but tried not to think much about it.

Felix dug around in his pockets for his MetroCard. "Imagine with me, Mr. Sunshine, if you will, the Upper East Side, nineteen twenty-four."

Sunshine had a lot of time to imagine it as Felix argued with the turnstile.

Once they'd gotten aboard the correct train and Felix had finished cursing out the MTA, Sunshine prompted, "So you were saying?"

"Oh, fuck, right," Felix said. "Uh...Right. Brewster Goodethorn is the first son of a first son, heir to all the fortunes and wonders of an arcane dynasty. He marries, quite against his father's wishes, a Timberton. A Timberton third or fourth cousin, but enough of one that she's part of society."

"Bad blood with the Goodethorns and the Timbertons?"

"The whole society scene is one vicious mess, Sunshine. So Brewster marries Priscilla. They reproduce, four little ones in as many years. Barton, Blakely, Brianne, and Blithe." He counted the names on his fingers. "Priscilla manages the children and the household, firm but loving. Finest schooling, trips to the Continent. The daughters marry, one son becomes an advisor to Ashley I, and the last one stays home, inherits everything."

"Why do we need to go to the library if you already know so much?" Sunshine asked.

"Shush, I'm expositing. That son, Barton, marries, because God, don't they all? Except he *really* ruffles some feathers with it. He marries a girl from outside the Community. What a mess, everyone thinks. One must be born into it or one will simply go mad. The girl is a sweet thing, young and innocent. They pop out their spawn and seem quite happy. The girl becomes a woman, obedient and polite. A perfect hostess for all their events, a caring mother, a respectful wife. She adjusts to the world of mages. And then."

"What?" Sunshine asked because Felix had intentionally paused.

"And then, ten years in, Barton up and leaves poor Violet with two children, Braxton and Beryl, and another, Brandy, on the way. He takes the maid, *and* he takes the nanny, and they're off to some tropical Latin American paradise with a fat bag of cash and not a single word of farewell. Just divorce papers. It's, uh, just about nineteen sixty when this happens. Violet Goodethorn closes up the house. No more events. She's tightfisted and harsh. She hardens, not a whisper of that sweet girl Barton had married. She raises her children, but they disappear from the papers, the society scene, all of it."

"Ah." Not much of a scandal in the days of reality TV but divorce and single motherhood had carried more heft in decades past.

"So it is my intention to find some old pictures of them, maybe dig through the records and see what the children of Violet and Barton got up to, as far as marrying and reproducing goes. Where, or if, they went to school. If they're still a mage family."

Sunshine rubbed his nose. He went quiet for the rest of the ride, trying to sort out his feelings. He needed to decide if it was guilt or just discomfort with being underground. Finally, when they'd returned to the surface and he'd had a few gulps of fresh air, he said, "I should have been helping you more with this."

"No, goodness, I've barely been doing anything. I just mentioned it to Papa and out he comes with this story."

"Still."

"Still. We are chasing scraps of men and chasing them figuratively. I imagine your role will become apparent when we need to chase them physically, strapping lad that you are."

Sunshine's cheeks warmed.

"Such a big, strong man, here to protect all of us," Felix simpered. He wrapped himself around Sunshine. "What would I do without you?"

Sunshine rolled his eyes and extracted himself from Felix's entanglement. "So why do I need to tag along, if you're not planning a footrace?"

"Because despite that dullest-knife-in-the-drawer persona you insist on maintaining, you are both fully literate and capable of research," Felix informed him. He softened the insult by smoothing out Sunshine's collar and fixing a few of his curls. He even added a kiss for good measure.

Sunshine kissed him back. He wound his arms around Felix's ribs and drew him in as close as he could. They stopped in the middle of the sidewalk and people had to jostle them to get around.

One person jostled them particularly hard.

Felix's teeth clicked against Sunshine's and he jerked back, blood on his lip. "Fucking watch it," he snapped at the man who had bumped into them. He sucked his lip, then touched it and checked for blood.

"Get a fucking room," the man returned.

Sunshine settled a hand on Felix's shoulder.

"Prick!" Felix shouted. He wiped the speck of blood from his mouth.

The man whirled around. "Listen, bud, I'm not the one standing in the goddamn middle of the sidewalk sucking face." He jabbed a finger towards Felix.

Sunshine didn't think. He stepped in front of Felix. "Don't."

The stranger looked Sunshine over. He scowled but didn't seem to want trouble. He grunted and turned away.

Felix put his chin on Sunshine's shoulder and said, "You don't have to do that."

"I don't have to keep you from getting into a street fight

outside the New York Public Library?"

"I just meant I can take care of myself."

"Yeah, and you taking care of yourself ends up with me having to drag your ass out of every concert hall in Manhattan and several in Brooklyn. Three in the Bronx, that one on—"

"Shut up," Felix snapped affectionately. "And they're not called *concert halls*. What year did you get stuck in?" He kissed Sunshine's cheek. "How do you feel about public sex?"

"What?"

"You wanna go fool around in the bathroom?"

"What, like we're homeless?"

"I was thinking like teenagers," Felix said. "But you do know how to suck the romance right out of a moment."

"Not the only think I know how to suck."

Felix let out a cackle. He leaped onto Sunshine's back. "Carry me into the library."

Sunshine secured Felix's legs and gave him a piggyback ride the rest of the way to the library.

Felix told him, "We'll figure out how much you know later."

"I'm not going to fuck you in the bathroom."

"You could blow me, though," Felix suggested quietly into his ear.

"You're such a fucking...degenerate." He set Felix down before they crossed the library threshold. "Your father would be ashamed."

"I don't know about that. I've always suspected Papa might be a bit of a rascal."

Sunshine rolled his eyes.

Felix pushed in front of him. "The collection is this way." He took off without checking to see if Sunshine followed.

Sunshine did follow, of course. Up to the first floor, to the Milstein Division. Sunshine had been here before, probably. He'd accompanied Felix to the library often enough over the years that he'd likely visited every room.

They passed the desks staffed with librarians and tables filled with patrons. Felix slid down an aisle to a corner. He gave Sunshine a look, one that had long since come to mean 'I'm about to do something sketchy, make sure no one sees me.'

Sunshine adjusted himself to block Felix mostly from view and so that he could keep an eye out.

A few minutes past before Felix tugged on Sunshine's sleeve.

They slunk into the passage Felix had revealed. They entered a small, cozy, windowless room lined with books from floor to ceiling.

The wall sealed shut behind them.

Sunshine glanced back, uneasy.

Distinctly, deeply uneasy.

He touched the wall, just to see if it would open.

It didn't.

It shouldn't have. It wouldn't be a secret annex if it did.

No windows, no doors.

He looked around. That unease settled deep in him.

Felix had already made for a section of the stacks. He had a book in his arm, his fingers trailing over the spine of another one.

"...help you, sir?" a woman asked.

Sunshine barely caught her words.

Felix said, "No, we're fine. Thanks."

"Your friend..." she began and continued speaking to Felix.

Sunshine ran his hand over the wall, checking where a seam should have been.

No seam.

He couldn't see any runes, either.

Not that he could have used them if he'd seen them.

He could die here.

No way out.

"Sunshine."

Sunshine tried to orient himself toward the voice. Toward Felix. He couldn't move much. His head, his body, had gone sort of fuzzy.

"Hey, you doing okay?" Felix asked.

His face felt numb. He tried to breathe. "I."

Felix touched his face. "Alright, bud. You want magic or meds?"

Sunshine shook his head.

Calm and gentle, Felix informed him, "You're having a panic attack. I'm gonna get you settled. Try to breathe. I'll take the edge off. Pick your poison."

He swallowed. His tongue didn't fit in his mouth. He tried to breathe, tried to do what Felix said. He glanced back toward the wall that should have been a door, the exit he couldn't use, the only way out.

He could die here.

He shook his head. "I don't know."

"You trust me."

He nodded.

Felix dipped his hand into his pocket and came back out with a small, round pillbox. He selected a pill and said, "Take this, we'll go sit, okay?"

Never had Felix sounded so agreeably calm.

Sunshine parted his lips after what felt like a lifetime of debate and waiting for his body to obey his will.

Felix pushed the tablet past his lips.

It dissolved on his tongue.

Felix stroked his cheek. "Come sit." He took Sunshine by the hand and brought him to an armchair. He settled him in and pulled another chair over so he would be close by. "Doing okay?"

Sunshine shook his head.

"Alright, we'll wait." Felix kept his hand on Sunshine.

His hand, his knee, his hair. He moved it every so often but didn't stop touching him.

Slowly, Sunshine came to realize Felix worried he might bolt.

Felix bolted sometimes. He got squirrely and took off.

Had Sunshine ever done that?

He didn't think so.

He settled after a while.

He settled more deeply than he ever had, all his emotions melting away to leave him as some sort of core being made of coolness and calm.

"What'd you give me?" he asked.

"Oh, I don't know, some kind of benzo. Valium, I think. Don't drink for a few days." Felix took his hand and drew it up to his mouth. He kissed Sunshine's knuckles. "You okay?"

"I think so."

"What happened?"

Sunshine should have felt embarrassed, but he didn't feel anything. "There's no windows."

"Oh," Felix said as though it made perfect sense. He glanced around the room. "It is a little cozy. Do you need to go?"

"I'm okay now."

"Okay." Felix squeezed his hand. "I would have used a spell, fewer side effects that way, but I...I know how you get about my dad. I thought magic might have made it worse."

Smart.

"I'm going to get a few things. Look at some stuff. Then we'll go."

"Sure."

"But tell me if you need to go sooner. I'll open the door I just...it takes a few minutes. I wanted you settled first."

Sunshine repeated, "I'm okay now."

Felix let out a sigh. He looked like he was going to stand, but instead, he just looked right at Sunshine and stared at him.

Sunshine frowned, not sure why Felix looked at him like that.

"I love you." Felix stood and kissed the top of Sunshine's head.

He brought over an armful of books and sat beside Sunshine as he looked over them. He kept his chair close to Sunshine's and leaned forward in his seat, elbows on his knees, as he read. He took careful photos with his phone every so often.

He had an awfully nice phone. The categorically the best one that he could purchase, Sunshine assumed. It took nice photos, crisp and clear, highly detailed.

He used it for selfies and snaps, Instagram and all the other image-oriented forms of social media, as would any modern man of this age.

He also used it for work. He took pictures relentlessly.

Sunshine reached out and took him by the wrist.

Felix looked up, eyes wide. "What? Are you okay?"

"I love you, too." He tightened his grip. "A lot."

Felix smiled. He put his hand over Sunshine's. "We can still go fool around in the bathroom."

Sunshine smiled, let out a small, gentle chuckle that was really more of an exhale.

Felix returned to reading and taking photos.

An hour passed before he returned the books to the librarian and held a hushed conversation with her.

Sunshine didn't have to strain his ears to know it was about him. He knew just by the tone in his voice.

Felix returned, nudged Sunshine's foot with his toe, and nodded towards the exit that didn't presently exist. "Let's go home."

Sunshine frowned.

"You're practically asleep."

"I'm just...calm."

Felix smiled. "Let's go."

Sunshine stood and followed him.

Felix brought them home, to Sunshine's apartment to be precise. He poured Sunshine a glass of water, placed it in his hand, and nudged him towards the couch.

"I'm honestly fine, Specter."

"Yeah, that's the Valium, sweetheart," Felix assured.

Sunshine sunk into the couch.

Felix left and returned with his laptop.

"I kind of feel..."

Felix glanced his way.

"I feel super zen. I don't think I've ever been this relaxed in my life."

That didn't exactly feel true. He hadn't been this relaxed since he'd come to Earth. In Heaven, he had existed blanketed in a warm, gentle world of shared consciousness, outside of time and therefor outside of fear.

"Please don't become addicted to prescription drugs. One of us needs to be able to maintain some level of long-term sobriety."

"Maybe you should try it this time."

Felix, without looking up, informed him, "I haven't used in two weeks."

"That's..." Sunshine knew he should work up the right level of enthusiasm, but he couldn't presently. "Felix, that's so good."

"Yeah."

"No, I mean," Sunshine insisted, "That's *really* good."

"Mhm."

"I'm proud of you."

Felix didn't indicate he had heard. He didn't look at Sunshine or make a sound. His lips twitched and he blinked, twice. A moment later, he touched his nose. He continued to click and tap on his laptop.

Time passed, about twenty minutes Sunshine guessed based on how far they'd gotten into an episode of *Forensic Files*, before Felix even paid attention to Sunshine again. He said, "I'll be back." He made for the door.

"Where are you going?"

"What the fuck do you care? Maybe I need to take a shit," Felix snapped.

Sunshine rolled his eyes.

He didn't come back for hours and Sunshine didn't ask where he had gone. He didn't bother to make a joke, though the situation did sort of call for one.

Felix informed him, "I just came back for my stuff. I'm going out."

"Oh."

"Yeah, I made plans the other day. Forgot to mention it. Kiki's in town."

Sunshine wrinkled his nose. "Don't say hi for me."

"The fucking two of you need to grow up."

"Maybe you need to stop hanging out with the woman who fucking robbed me and made me strip at gun point," Sunshine suggested as mildly as possible.

"To be fair, you were withholding evidence from a police officer."

"A crooked fucking cop," Sunshine reminded. "I don't know why—"

"Cause Kiki's a bridge I can't afford to burn."

Sunshine couldn't really begrudge him keeping the peace with her. She did have evidence that could tie him directly to a series of cold cases along the Jersey shore. They'd come to the agreement that exorcism of a possessed corpse was not the same as murder, even if it did end vital signs. If Kiki ever changed her mind about that, Felix would be up the creek.

She was human and that meant she would die and take her blackmail with her, Sunshine assured himself.

"Be careful," he told Felix.

"It's just drinks. She wants info about banshees for something. I'll be fine." He made like he intended to leave on that note, but he doubled back and kissed Sunshine's temple. "You should be in bed by the time I get home."

"I'm surprised I'm not in bed right now."

Felix left and didn't come back.

Sunshine remained on the couch long after the Valium wore off. He didn't know what else to do with himself and felt entitled to a night of nothing. He spent a decent amount of time reading up about panic attacks because he'd never had one before and certainly didn't want to have one again.

He had obviously experienced fear before but never so suddenly or over something so small as a windowless room.

Panic attacks didn't make for a good soldier.

A dreadful thought crept through his mind, one he'd tried to avoid for a while. Was he becoming weak?

Maybe he had spent too much time away from Heaven. Satan had alluded to it. Angels, as a rule, did not stay on Earth. Many of the Fallen did, but their ties to Heaven and God had been replaced by something else.

Sunshine had not fallen, he knew that much, but he also knew that he did not have contact with God the way that the Fallen had contact with Satan.

Should he start going to church? Should he pray?

Should he fall?

No one could fault him for finally cutting ties with the place that had sent him to kill a newborn baby. At least, he didn't think anyone could. Another angel would, but Sunshine never saw those.

Still, the idea made him queasy. He did not want to fall. He did not want to serve the Devil.

He changed the channel.

Around midnight, as he worked his way through a sleeve of Oreos, he heard Felix come home.

When Felix didn't make his way back over, Sunshine went to bed.

He went over the next morning to wake up him for breakfast and found his bed unslept in. He doublechecked the couch to make sure he hadn't walked by him, then checked the bathroom. He found the demon passed out on the bathmat with vomit in his chin, one shoe off, and his pants half pulled down.

Sunshine rubbed his face, looked down at Felix, sighed, then began to fill up the bathtub.

The sound of churning water didn't wake him.

He pulled off Felix's other shoe and started to pull up his pants because waking up to someone pulling down your pants while you were blackout drunk wasn't a good experience.

Felix groaned.

"You alive?"

Felix sat up with urgency and dry heaved into the toilet.

His hair, now a washed out orangish-pink, stuck up on one side and had gotten matted to his face on the other.

"What happened?"

Felix flipped him off.

"Are you at least sober?"

"I think I'm sober." Felix hung over the toilet. "I think I'm dying."

Sunshine peeled him off the toilet and, with his permission, out of his clothes. He flushed and wiped down the toilet, then escorted Felix into the bath. He left him to soak as he made tea. Upon his return, he handed over the mug, sat beside the bath, and asked again, "What happened?"

"I don't know."

"How much did you drink?"

"Just a few."

Sunshine shook his head.

"Sunshine, I feel like fucking *shit*," he insisted weakly. "I don't remember anything."

"What do you mean?"

"I mean...I. I was talking to Kiki and then it cuts out."

Sunshine pressed his lips together.

Felix stared at him, eyes red-rimmed.

"Does anything hurt?" Sunshine asked.

Felix shook his head. He swallowed. "Not...not like that."

Sunshine glanced towards the pile of clothes, trying to subtly check for anything out of place. Tears, stains, fluids, garments turned inside out...He didn't notice anything. "Do you need a minute?"

"Can you get my phone?"

Sunshine had to scour the apartment. He finally found it on the floor next to the couch. He had a missed call from a telemarketing scam and a few texts. One from Kiki, asking if he'd gotten home alright, and one from Hiram.

Felix dictated a series of questions for Sunshine to send to Kiki.

She assured him he'd left alone when he'd started to feel strange and said she'd even walked him to his station.

The pinched look eased off Felix's face. He sunk further into the bath. "I feel like I have the flu."

"You've never had the flu."

"I did! Forty-seven. Don't you remember?"

The memory bobbed to the surface. "Well, you were miserable. Let's hope it's not the flu."

"I don't know, what's worse? Being roofied or the flu?" Felix asked. "Fucking..." He scoffed. "Fucking *people*, man. What a bunch of shit bags."

Sunshine took the washcloth and wiped Felix's chin. "At least you got home safe."

Felix grumbled and rattled off a few facts about random drink spiking, which Sunshine interpreted as a way to say 'thank god I was only drugged, thank god Kiki walked me to my train, thank god no one found me on the train like this' in the most roundabout way possible.

"We're going to be late," Felix said finally.

"We can work from home."

Felix sank lower into the bathtub, all the way up to his chin. He huffed and a little bit of water splashed him in the face. "Do you think you could ask Kiki what we talked about?"

Sunshine leaned against the tub and took up Felix's phone. He requested a recap of the night's conversation and received vague answers about banshees in return. When he pressed for further details, she mentioned she had to get to work or her boss would be on her ass.

Talk later, she wrote.

Sunshine did not recall Kiki as particularly concerned about workplace appearances or what her boss thought.

He dragged over Felix's shirt. No buttons. "Did you wear a jacket last night?"

"Mmm. No. Why?"

"Looking for a button recorder."

"Why?"

"Cause I don't trust Kiki for shit," he answered. He grabbed his pants and examined the button. He murmured the spell to activate it and the sounds of a bar filled the bathroom.

Quiet voices hummed in the background, a few clatters and rustles of fabric. Sunshine immediately recognized the smoke-and-whiskey voice of Kiki Baldwin asking, "So how about that trafficking ring?"

"I told you I didn't want to talk about it. I thought you wanted to know about banshees."

Felix sat up in the bathtub. "God, is that what my voice sounds like!"

"Yeah, sure, you told me about banshees." The sound of a glass sliding over the table. "I got you another drink while you were in the bathroom. Figured we had more than one's worth of catching up to do."

Felix snorted, both in real life and on the recording.

A bizarre sort of lust temporarily overwhelmed Sunshine; he would have climbed fully clothed into the bathtub to kiss him if Felix hadn't looked so spectacularly hungover.

They listened as the voices on the recording trade small details about their personal and work lives, punctuated with the sounds of sipping drinks and awkward silences. Soon enough, Kiki steered the conversation back to the trafficking ring.

Felix was much more forthcoming with answers this time. He told her who was and was not implicated when she asked about specific people.

Sunshine and Felix exchanged looks.

"That bitch fucking roofied me," Felix growled. He sloshed up out of the water and stepped out of the tub. He faltered a little once on his feet as he aggressively dried himself.

Sunshine stood and steadied him. "Don't be rash."

"I'm not."

"You're in no state—"

"I'm pissed off, Sunshine, not stupid. But I'm gonna burn this fucking bitch alive if it's the last thing I do."

Sunshine could not be sure if he meant literally or figuratively. Felix was, as a rule, mostly harmless, but that didn't mean he was incapable of being otherwise. "What are you going to do?"

Felix snatched his pants off the ground. "I'm going to wait. This is...this is less important than the Goodethorns. Get the button off these for me."

With undue savagery, Felix brushed his teeth.

Sunshine herded him into the bedroom and provided him with sweats and a t-shirt.

He yanked the clothes on and glanced around the room like he wanted to destroy something.

Sunshine embraced him. "You said you were going to wait."

"I know."

"So wait long enough that you'll be careful, too."

"I'm careful."

"With everyone except yourself," Sunshine reminded. "Come show me what you learned yesterday."

"Fine."

Sunshine tightened his arms.

"We're a fucking mess," Felix grumbled.

"We are."

They stood together, arms locked around the other, for several long minutes. "At least," Felix said finally, "We're in it together."

"Mmm."

Felix took his hand and brought him out to the living room, where he proceeded to go through all the pictures he had taken at the library yesterday.

May 25
Wednesday

Felix called Tate and Rose up to the office and handed them both manila file folders.

Tate appraised hers immediately.

Rose stared at his like it might be dangerous.

"You're Millennials," Felix told them.

"I...I think I'm actually Gen Z," Rose answered weakly.

"Even better."

"Who are these people?"

"Those are the names, dates of birth, and recent genealogy of the last scions of the Goodethorn family. Find what you can on them. Check everything from...you know, from Myspace to LinkedIn."

"God, you really are old, aren't you?" Tate asked.

Rose continued to stare at the folder.

"Also you're promoted," Felix told him.

Sunshine raised his eyebrows. They hadn't discussed that.

"I..."

"Tate, give him the Junior Detective badge," Felix instructed.

"But it's got my name on it," Tate protested quietly.

"Fine, tell Jen to order a new one," Felix said with the most severe eye roll Sunshine had seen in a while.

Rose's eyes opened very wide and he stared at Tate. "I don't...I don't think I can be a detective."

Felix confirmed, "Legally, no, you can't, but I know the right people to bribe. Consider, this, uh, a trial run."

Rose looked on the verge of tears.

Felix shooed Tate away, then approached the young fairy. "What's wrong?"

"I can't do this."

Felix put a hand on his shoulder. "I'm literally just asking you to stalk some people on the internet. You're like, twenty, so I figured you'd be good at it. Okay?"

"Okay." Rose swallowed.

"I'm not putting you on fieldwork or anything. It's a little research."

Rose nodded.

"Is that okay with you?" Felix asked, all compassion and gentleness.

"Yeah, I just...I don't do well with surprises, I'm sorry."

Felix gave the fairy's shoulder a squeeze. "Thank you for telling me. I'll be more careful next time."

Rose nodded. "Thanks."

"I am paying you more, though." Felix gave his back one last pat before he moved back towards his desk.

"You don't—"

"Allow me my caprices, Rosewood, especially when they benefit you," Felix advised.

"Specter, you are actually the creepiest person I know," Sunshine told him.

"I'm not creepy, I'm beneficent."

"You're a huge fucking creep," Sunshine said. "Come here."

"Rose, you're dismissed," Felix said.

Rose scampered out of the room looking mildly ill.

Felix approached Sunshine's desk with deliberate slowness and sway to his walk. He slid onto Sunshine's lap and draped his arms over his shoulders. "You had something to say to me?"

"Yeah, don't freak out our employees. Especially not the ones I hired."

"But it is sort of fun."

"It's not very nice."

"I thought you liked it when I wasn't very nice," Felix said. He leaned in close but didn't kiss Sunshine.

He looked better than he had yesterday. Still slightly tired, a hint of shadow under his eyes, but somehow that worked for Sunshine, especially in combination with his usual haughty flirtations.

It really worked for him.

Maybe there was something wrong with him.

Was he supposed to be attracted to signs of illness, to dark clothing, a washed-out dye job, and self-destruction? Was he supposed to think that a simmering potential for violence, a tenuous relationship with reality, and delicate mental health were sexy?

Probably not.

And that wasn't the whole of it.

It was that the violence hardly showed its face and never towards anyone who hadn't done their best to draw it out of him. It was how he never intentionally harmed anything but himself. It was that his strange grasp on the world made him see things differently than everyone else.

Felix could have destroyed everything that crossed his path if he'd wanted. He could have been truly, recklessly cruel instead of just kind of a bitch. He had that power, that potential, but he never had to fight with himself to avoid it.

He simply didn't *want* to hurt anyone.

Well.

Almost anyone.

"Why are you looking at me like that?" Felix asked.

"Because you're beautiful and I love you."

"Well, it's creepy."

"I adore you," Sunshine insisted.

"That's even creepier."

Sunshine kissed him.

They kissed for a long time.

Sunshine let his hands wander more than he should have in a room into which any of their employees could enter at any time.

Felix pressed close, frantically so, kissing and caressing with a determination Sunshine had never felt from him before.

Sunshine responded, at first drawing him closer, then pushing him back so he could lift him and seat him on the desk. His fingers sought the fly of Felix's pants. He drew him out of his pants, not yet hard, but he'd known that already.

He lowered his head and tried to coax a little more readiness out of him.

Nothing happened.

At a certain point, he started to feel silly and uncomfortable.

He didn't know exactly where to go from here.

Maybe they should kiss some more.

He drew back and glanced up to find Felix staring down at him.

Quiet tears had dribbled down his cheeks. "I'm sorry," Felix said.

"It's alright."

"I...I really tried."

"It's fine." Sunshine straightened up and arranged Felix's clothes for him, a stupid, useless, and awkward thing to do, tucking someone's dick back into their pants for them. He did it anyway, not sure why or what else he should have done.

A few more tears spilled from Felix's eyes. He sniffled. "I can do you though."

"No, that's...that's alright, Felix."

"No, it's fair, that's fair. Let me suck your dick," he insisted sadly.

"I don't really want you to," Sunshine pointed out.

It was the wrong thing to say.

Felix started to tremble. Thickly, he promised, "Just let me, it'll be really good, I promise."

"Hon, you're *crying*."

"I'm sorry but I can make it okay."

Sunshine didn't know what to do.

His face wet and his voice strained, Felix told him, "I'm really sorry, I told you it happens sometimes, I just. I'll do you. It'll be fine."

"It *is* fine," Sunshine insisted. "You don't have to do anything." He grabbed a box of tissues from the shelf behind him and pressed it into Felix's hand. "Okay?"

Felix sniffled and wiped his face on his sleeve instead of the tissues.

Sunshine plucked out a few tissues and placed them in his hand.

He blew his nose. "I can—"

"I swear to God, if you ask to blow me one more time, I'm going to start crying, too," Sunshine warned.

Felix let out a weepy, nervous laugh.

Sunshine wrapped his arms around him and crushed him close.

"I really tried."

Sunshine tried not to think of him having this conversation with someone else or of how other people might accept his offer. He tried not to think of how he had misinterpreted his desperation for enthusiasm. He gathered him even closer and settled them both on his office chair, which wheeled back and spun slightly as he did so.

"It happens sometimes, I told you," Felix reminded sullenly.

"I know." Sunshine scooted the chair back, so he didn't have to stare into the corner. "It happens to other people, too."

Felix let out a wet snort that probably got snot all over Sunshine's shirt. "I'm sorry," he whispered.

Sunshine tried to think of something to say to make him feel better.

Felix sat up and wiped a wet patch on Sunshine's shirt. "That was gross, I'm really sorry."

"It's okay. It's one of the less gross bodily fluids you've gotten on me."

"Alright, I barfed on you *one time*. You're really never going to let that go, are you?"

"You have directly vomited on to me once. I have had to clean up your barf far more often than that," Sunshine reminded. He smoothed his thumb over Felix's cheek.

"What?"

"Your eyes look really pretty when you cry."

"You're an idiot."

"Your eyes look really pretty all the time," Sunshine amended. "But somehow you make looking awful look amazing."

"Is that supposed to be a compliment?" Felix demanded.

"I don't know what it is, it's just how I feel."

"He makes 'em kind of screwy up in Heaven, doesn't he?" Felix asked. He wrapped one of Sunshine's curls around his finger and laid it down carefully among the others.

"Maybe God is kinky." The words should not have left the mouth of an angel and it felt like sacrilege to say them, but Felix laughed so that made it worthwhile.

"I'm starting to think there's no other explanation. I'm going to start breaking into churches and dressing the statues in leather."

Sunshine ran his fingers through Felix's hair, ruffling it back to its usual disarray. It had gotten flattened in their embrace.

Felix drew in a deep, slow breath. He patted Sunshine's cheek when he stood. "I really out to check out that Preston case."

"Do you need help?"

He shook his head. "No, I'll just go uptown to talk to her. She's got money, she'll expect that."

"Should I come with you?"

Felix looked him over.

"If she's important, won't she expect both of us there?"

"She's rich, she's not important," Felix corrected. "But I don't mind the company." He tossed the casefile on Sunshine's desk. "Missing boyfriend. Wouldn't be surprised if he's just shacked up with someone else, but we get paid for evidence, not assumptions."

"Oh, get that printed on the business cards next time."

Felix flipped him off.

An hour later, they left to meet with Katy Preston, a thin and pretty socialite who described herself as a fitness influencer. She doled out heaps of information about her missing boyfriend. She handed over photos and bank statements and receipts, anything she thought might be useful.

Felix gave most of it back to her. He poked around her room, asked for the boyfriend's address, and widened his eyes when she said, "He lives here."

Sunshine glanced around the room again.

Not a single hint of a man's permanent presence. The entire apartment was perfectly organized and styled, not a speck out of a place, not a single dog hair on the hardwood floor, despite the Shiba Inu that slept peacefully on a cream-colored bed beside the couch.

They asked a few more questions about Gavin, about his friends, his job, his family, and promised they would get back to her as soon as they knew anything.

On the train ride back, Felix lost himself down the rabbit hole of fitness models on Instagram. He showed multiple pictures of taut and toned people to Sunshine, who had passing little interest in the bodies of perfect strangers.

Felix seemed consumed with a repulsed envy.

Sunshine looped an arm around Felix's shoulders and kissed his temple. He closed the app on Felix's phone for him.

Felix let out a disgusted sigh. He sagged against him. "What's it like to be perfect, Sunshine?"

The question twisted his belly. He had never felt perfect, only adequate and generic. He had no good answers, so he asked, "What's it like to be extraordinary?"

Felix shook his head, a half-smile on his lips. "You lay it on so thick sometimes, that good guy act." He kissed him.

People looked at them.

People usually looked at them, given their unusual appearances and their open affection for each other.

Usually, it was frank curiosity, mild discomfort, or confusion. Sometimes people beamed at them. Depending on where they were and the time of day, the stares could get hostile.

Frequently got hostile.

People shouted things at them.

Sunshine did his best not to notice any of the stares and to ignore the shouts, but he knew that Felix felt every second of every gaze, heard every word. Even the mildest of looks made him squirrely; he'd learned that from Bibi, Sunshine felt sure.

Today, a gaggle of young men watched them from their section of the train car. Teenagers or early twenties, tittering and whispering among themselves. They threw looks towards them.

Felix noticed first. He sat up straighter, pulled out of Sunshine's arms. He glared at them but mostly kept his eyes trained on his boots. He shrugged off Sunshine's hand.

Immediately, Sunshine knew they had to get off the train. He doubted the youths represented any physical danger to them, but he also knew that Felix would not be able to tolerate anything they might shout, not with the year he'd had and not after what had happened at the office. Whether he would explode or collapse, Sunshine didn't want to find out.

Sunshine had always thought of his outbursts as reckless, the product of a short emotional fuse, but he thought of Felix asking, "Can't I be fragile?"

He took Felix by the elbow and urged him out of his seat. Wordlessly, they passed between cars, ignoring the signs telling them expressly not to do so.

In the new car, they sat correctly, facing forward, their legs and arms carefully held to be away from each other.

People still looked at them, but more mildly.

A small girl waved at them.

Sunshine waved back.

Felix conjured a small figure made of smoke and lights. A tiny cat, three inches high, pranced about for the girl.

She laughed, delighted, and reached for it.

When her mother looked over, Felix dispelled the illusion, and when the woman turned away, he winked at the girl and pressed a finger to his lips.

"It's a secret," he mouthed.

He spent the rest of the train ride amusing the girl while her mother stared down at her phone.

Mother and child got off before them. Felix sent the illusion chasing after them for a moment. The girl grinned one last time when it faded.

They didn't talk about how they'd fled the other train car.

They didn't talk much at all.

Sunshine couldn't guess how Felix felt. Fear, anger, guilt, shame, and embarrassment all swirled through Sunshine, shame the strongest of all. He should have said something.

But he had never been brave or confrontational.

Head down, follow orders.

He tried to bury himself in work. Felix managed it better.

By the end of the workday, they had half a dozen solid ideas as to where Gavin might have gone.

By the end of the week, they had found him holed up in a hotel room surrounded by junk food, laxatives, and diuretics. Gavin cried when they told him why they'd come and instead of escorting him back to his apartment, they brought him to a center for the treatment of eating disorders.

They told Katy Preston only that her boyfriend was safe and that he would be able to contact her whenever he pleased.

She paid their fees without hesitation, seeming truly happy that he wasn't dead or kidnapped.

Sunshine counted it as a win.

"I thought she would make a bigger fuss," Felix said for the dozenth time since they'd gotten paid. He glanced up from where he sat on the toilet seat cover.

"If you keep moving, you're going to end up with dye all over your face," Sunshine warned him for the third time.

Felix had a towel draped around his shoulders and thick, pale blue dye spread over half his head so far.

Sunshine, perhaps the most uneasy and unqualified he'd ever been in recent years, had a bowl of dye and a brush in his hands.

"At least we didn't have to bleach it," Felix offered.

"God help us if you ever make me apply chemicals to your

body." Sunshine carefully spread on a little more dye.

The process took a while and it took even longer to let the dye set.

When Felix had finally rinsed his hair to reveal a pastel blue with hints of pink, Sunshine couldn't help but think of cotton candy.

Felix surveyed himself in the mirror, frowned, then said, "It'll do."

Sunshine nuzzled up against his throat.

Felix stepped away. He'd done that a lot since Wednesday.

Sunshine understood why but he didn't like it. Selfishly, of course, he wanted to be able to snuggle up to Felix whenever he wanted, but he also worried that Felix had thought about that misstep too much.

"It looks nice."

"Mmm."

Felix flopped onto the couch and took up all of it.

Sunshine wiggled his way next to him.

Felix sat up and relegated himself to one side, his legs tucked up near his chest.

This time, Sunshine kept his distance. He sat on the other end of the couch but turned so he faced Felix. He debated the best way to start a conversation but knew no way to do it that wouldn't send spikes of panic through the other man.

Finally, he had to say, "We can talk about what happened if you want."

"There's nothing to talk about."

"There absolutely is."

Felix glared. "I told you it happens sometimes, it's not my fault you thought you were special."

"That's..." Sunshine didn't rush to defend himself. "The thing you were worried about happened and I think we should talk about it."

"I was worried about!"

Sunshine nodded.

"That's fucking nice. Blame me for worrying about it!"

"I'm not blaming you."

"I told you I tried!" Felix snapped. "And I said I'd fucking blow you. I don't know what else you want from me."

"I want you to believe that I meant it when I said it was okay."

"Okay for who?" Felix demanded.

"What?"

"Okay for who? For you? Sure, whatever, it's okay for you. Find someone else who can actually do what you want with you. What about for me? What about I'm like this no matter who I'm with!"

Sunshine waited.

"Because I've got a beautiful fucking man with his mouth on my cock and I can't even enjoy it. Years and years of trying to make things up to people, trying to get them to like me by doing whatever they want and here you goddamn are trying to..." Felix faltered. He rubbed his eye with the heel of his hand. "Trying to do something for me. And I can't even have that. Because I want you, Sunshine, so fucking bad and you're right here like you've always been and I *still* can't fucking have you."

"I think you've been sleeping with assholes, Specter."

"Excuse me?"

"That or you're an idiot."

"Fucking. Excuse. Me," Felix managed.

"Do you really think that was your one opportunity? You have texted me in the middle of the night at least once a week for as long as we've had cell phones and I come over every time to make you tea or watch TV or play fucking Scrabble. Do you really think that I wouldn't drop what I was doing, whatever it was, to come blow you at any given point in the day?"

Felix stared at him, somewhere between horrified and concerned.

"I want what we have to be right and even though it isn't about sex, we decided to make sex part of it, so that means I want to do that right, too."

"So...what, then?" Felix asked carefully, his dark eyes narrowed.

"So if you want me to blow you, then we'll make it work, however we need to. I want to give you what you want, Felix, and I want you, too. I want you to grab me by the back of the head and cum in my mouth, I want you to scream when you do it and I want to be so full of you I can't make a sound, and I'm not going to give up just because one time things didn't work out exactly."

"That's...that's both really sexually aggressive and super sweet of you," Felix answered quietly.

"Sorry. I've just been thinking about it for a couple days."

"Apparently. Christ, Sunshine."

"Sorry."

"No, it's..." Felix looked him over. "I have been sleeping with assholes. No one's ever talked about me like that before."

"Ever?"

"I'm not beautiful like you are, Sunshine, no one ever wants me like that. I won't deny that I dress incredibly well, and I do have my own unique sort of attractiveness that appeals to certain people, but I'm also a scrawny, bitchy femme who relies on money and promiscuity to get attention."

"If you want to be highly reductive, I suppose that's what you are," Sunshine said.

"I'm sorry, did you just call me reductive?"

"If you're going to narrow the entire scope of your life to how society categorizes your sexuality, appearance, and the manner in which you interact with gender constructs, then I would say you're being reductive."

Felix frowned. "You've been talking to my parents," he accused.

"I don't have my own to talk to."

"So you thought you'd call up my parents and say, 'hey, your kid can't get hard, how explicitly should I tell him I want to suck his dick?'"

"Not in those words exactly."

Felix smiled but shook his head.

"All I said was that you wouldn't talk to me. They said to be honest first and hope you'd be honest with me."

"So the details were your own personal touch."

Sunshine shrugged. "They were honest."

Felix crawled across the couch and gave him a peck. "I usually wake up with a pretty good one, so if you're serious you should probably stay the night."

Sunshine wrapped an arm around his waist and tugged him closer. "So are you done being mad at me?"

"I wasn't angry, I'm insecure and sexually frustrated."

"That's harder to conceptualize."

Felix pecked his check once more, then twisted in his arms, and laid down with his head on Sunshine's thigh. He took Sunshine's hand and rested it on his chest. He played with his fingers. "Tell me you adore me again."

"I adore you, Felix."

He smiled up at him. "Say it again to me tomorrow. Whisper it in my ear right before you wake me up with that beautiful mouth of yours around my cock."

Sunshine's heart quickened.

Felix turned on the TV and acted like he hadn't suggested something so spectacularly salacious.

In the morning, Sunshine did as Felix had asked, a whisper of adoration and then he turned back the sheets to expose him. He slid on top of his legs, kissed the pale skin of his stomach, and lowered his head.

Fingers brushed through his hair.

He raised his eyes.

With a lazy smile, Felix asked, "Go ahead, what are you waiting for?"

Felix made the loveliest sounds, sweet and demanding all at once. He rolled his hips and gripped hard onto Sunshine's curls. He did it almost forcefully, teetering on the pleasanter side of aggression.

Sunshine enjoyed every moment, every last one, even when Felix bucked and pushed himself in deeper without any more warning than a subtle push on the back of his head.

He didn't scream when he came, not exactly, but he did let out a toe-curling groan that the neighbors must have heard.

"Holy shit," he gasped. "Oh, fucking..."

Sunshine slid up to kiss him.

"No, morning breath," Felix protested and tried to cover his mouth.

Sunshine kissed him anyway, despite the taste of his breath.

Felix slid a hand between his legs. He nipped at Sunshine's throat. Hard.

Sunshine moaned.

Felix barely needed a few caresses to finish him.

Sunshine panted into Felix's shoulder, eyes closed, undone entirely.

"I want pancakes," Felix said.

"What?"

"Make me pancakes."

Sunshine drew in a deep breath. He kissed Felix's shoulder. "Okay."

Felix squeezed him. He pressed a kiss to a sore spot on Sunshine's neck, then rubbed at it with his thumb. "I got you a little bit here."

Later, Sunshine checked the spot in the mirror. Felix had left a bruise.

The sight of it, the idea of Felix leaving a mark on him, made him warm.

He slipped into the shower with Felix.

"Did I fucking invite you in?" Felix demanded.

"Be nice or I won't make you pancakes."

Felix slithered around him. "Yes, you will."

Sunshine squeezed him.

The pancakes came out perfect, fluffy and tender.

Felix poured a mug of coffee and placed it in front of Sunshine. "Pick a date."

"Hmm?" Sunshine asked.

"What's your favorite date?"

Sunshine shrugged. "I don't know. I've always liked Wednesdays."

"Why the fuck do you like Wednesdays?"

"I don't know, you asked me."

"I said *date*, not day, and Wednesday is still a stupid day to like," Felix said. "I like Sundays."

"Saturdays are pretty good."

"I'm always hungover on Saturday."

"You're not hungover today," Sunshine pointed out helpfully.

After a lapse in conversation, Felix pointedly said, "I like Sundays."

Sunshine looked up from his phone. "Okay. What's it matter?"

Felix scowled at him and slapped his phone out of his hand. "Do you pay attention to anything?"

"Yes, but not to the right things apparently." Sunshine picked up his phone and easily parried Felix's hand when he tried to smack it again. "What is it you want me to pay attention to?"

"Me, obviously."

Sunshine glanced up. "I thought you were talking to Dr. Reza about this codependent stuff."

"Yeah, apparently, it's not pathological enough."

"Is that...good?"

"It's better, I guess. I don't know." Felix shrugged, gathered up their plates, and brought them to the sink. He poured them both another cup of coffee. "It's good because it means I haven't turned it into an essential part of my ethos."

"Oh."

"I just wish Dr. Baum hadn't died. I'd already gone through this whole unpacking thing with him and we'd gotten to the point where he believed me when I talked about the crazy shit in my life. It's really hard to get accurate treatment when your doctor thinks your primary diagnosis should be schizophrenia instead of, you know, what's actually wrong with me."

Sunshine set down his phone.

"I brought her all my old paperwork, too, you know, but," here he rolled his eyes, "It was a little out of date."

"Just a hair."

"I had one from, like, fifty-four and it listed me as pathologically homosexual with psychotic tendencies. She didn't think it was as funny as I did."

"Why don't you see someone from the Community?" Sunshine asked.

"Cause they all specialize in vampire shit and they all want to talk about my dad," Felix said. He sat back down. "I'll do the dishes in a minute. So now we're at that weird impasse when I've got to stop avoiding topics if I want to get actual help, but I can't talk about anything without her thinking I'm experiencing some severe delusions."

"What's vampire shit?"

"Intake management, addiction, and eating disorders. Drinking disorders? You wouldn't believe how many vamps end up with anorexia."

Sunshine did believe it. "So what are you actually looking to get out of this?"

Felix shrugged. "I don't know. Therapy evens me out."

"What, uh, what about diagnosis-wise?"

"Oh, that, well, I'm pretty sure I'm bipolar. I've been diagnosed manic-depressive a few times but that's not what it's called anymore." Felix paused to study his nails, which had a little bit of stain from the dye lining the beds. "I also might just be like, regular depressed with too many drugs. But what the hell do I know? You wanna know about like, monsters or ghosts or magic, hit me up, I've got degrees in that stuff. I took one psych class in my undergrad and that was in, shit, what? The thirties?"

Sunshine sipped his coffee.

"But I like Dr. Reza. I think getting her comfortable with the Community will be worth it. She's like...early thirties, so if she stays around and in practice for a while, that will work out for me."

"You should do magic for her."

"I don't want to scare her."

"I didn't say fireballs, I said magic. A nice illusion. Or a little baby conjuration."

"Maybe. But I don't think I should conjure a baby."

Sunshine rolled his eyes.

Felix grinned.

"Do you...?" Sunshine sipped his coffee and put the thought aside.

"Don't do that."

Mostly into the coffee mug, Sunshine said, "People do family therapy."

The mumble echoed off the ceramic and the liquid, giving the statement a strange tenor.

Felix put an elbow on the table and rested his chin on his hand. "Yeah. They also do couple's counseling. Is that what you're talking about?"

"Uh. I don't know. If you ever wanted me to go with you."

"Do you want to go with me?"

"Uh. I want you to have space that's your own, a place you can go to talk about anything. But, uh, if you wanted me there. I would go. If you needed me. If it would help."

Felix fluttered his eyelashes. "That's sweet. I'll keep it in mind." He draped himself over the table and took one of Sunshine's wrists with both his hands. "You know I meant it, right?"

"Meant what, Specter?"

"Everything. All the time. And none of it. Ever. And only some of it, sometimes."

Somehow Sunshine understood what he meant. "I know."

"I really do." Felix smiled at him.

Sunshine smiled back.

May 30
Monday

Sunshine stopped short on the sidewalk and put out his arm to stop Felix. Before the apartment building where Sarai stayed stood the Devil.

Or an abnormally tall and pale woman with terrible dental hygiene.

"You didn't tell me you'd called your dad," Sunshine hissed. He went warm just at the sight of him.

Felix stepped around Sunshine's arm. "I didn't." He approached his father, looked him over, from the pencil skirt and blouse to the messy bun into which he'd gathered his hair. "If I was supposed to start calling you Mom, you'd tell me, wouldn't you?"

The Devil gathered Felix into a hug and kissed the top of his head. "I would, little one."

Felix squirmed out of his arms after a moment. He rubbed the back of his neck and glanced up at his father. "Why are you here?"

Lucifer's eyes slid towards Sunshine. "I have business."

"Dad!"

"With him and the mage girl both."

Sunshine wanted to flee.

"What kind of business?"

Lucifer plucked the manila folder out of Felix's hand. "This kind of business." He crooked a finger toward Sunshine.

Sunshine found himself compelled forward with a heavy stone of dread in his stomach.

Felix stepped between them. He drew himself up as tall as he could stand, which wasn't much in the face of the Devil himself. He snatched the folder back from his father. "He's stupid enough to cut a deal with you, but I'm smart enough to fuck you harder than you've ever been fucked if you do a *single* thing to him."

Lucifer blinked slowly down at his son. "I don't think I'd like that."

Felix frowned.

"Even I have lines I won't cross."

"I meant it figuratively."

"I know you did." Lucifer stroked Felix's cheek. "Will you start a war over him?"

"If you make me."

Bright-eyed, he beamed. His teeth glittered like obsidian, solid black and shiny. "If I make you. You don't know how that tempts me. If I make you." He peered around Felix. "Are you hearing this, angel?"

Sunshine shifted.

The Devil oozed around his son and took Sunshine's face into his hands. He drew Sunshine up to an uncomfortable height, one that didn't lift him but strained his posture. "If. I. Make. Him. What do you think? Should I make him?"

Mild and almost sweet, Sunshine felt the Devil's breath on his face. If he'd breathed in, he would have tasted it.

He had tasted it before, felt it on his ear, felt him twisted around him like a snake.

"I'd like it if you didn't," Sunshine whispered. He wanted to be free of the Devil's grip but a small and hideous part of him wanted Lucifer to...to do something.

To do something awful to him.

To spit on him or bite him.

Sunshine's guts writhed. He looked at Felix, who looked irritated but also peered at Sunshine with a strange suspicion.

Lucifer kissed Sunshine's forehead and released him.

He could breathe again.

His face felt cold where the Devil had touched him. His hands had been warm and soft.

"You're freaking him out," Felix insisted.

Sunshine licked his lips and stepped away.

"You're gonna give him a fucking panic attack and if I have to dose him that means he can't drink, which is going to *fucking ruin* our dinner plans."

"I'm okay," Sunshine assured.

"Better be." Felix took Sunshine by the hand and marched towards the building, towing Sunshine along behind him. He let himself into the door.

"Listen, maybe we should give the kid a heads up," Sunshine suggested.

"She knows we're coming over."

"Does she know he's coming, too?" Sunshine glanced back to see the Devil on their heels.

Felix sighed and stopped. He rubbed his eyes. "She likes you better. You go in first."

"So he gets panic attacks now?" Lucifer asked.

"I had *one*."

Lucifer looked him over. "It's going to get worse."

"What?"

"Earth does horrible things to a body. Absolutely awful place. That fucking sun? *Kills people*, you know," Lucifer confided with a furtive glance upward.

"Dad, can you please reel it in for point five seconds?" Felix asked. "This girl is having a rough time and she's not good with strangers and she doesn't really believe in creatures."

"That's fine."

"Dad. She's an actual child. Please be *good*," Felix urged. "Please."

Lucifer looked at him, lugubrious and slightly wounded. "Of course."

Felix raked a hand through his hair and sent it in wild directions. He closed his eyes, drew in a breath, and said, "I've been having a rough fucking year. I need you to just...to be my father first, for a little while. I know business is business and all that. But I need him and I need you to let me have him. I don't want to...to fight with you, Dad, I don't."

Lucifer stared.

Sunshine stared, too.

"You're a good boy, Felix. You really are," the Devil said. "I'll do my best."

"Thank you."

They proceeded up to Sarai's apartment in uneasy quiet.

Sunshine rapped on the door and announced himself.

Sarai peeked out, then let him in. She eyed Lucifer.

"We can talk about him a second."

Lucifer, to his credit, had shrunk down to nearly normal size.

"Him?" Sarai asked.

"Uh. Or her. I don't think it matters." Sunshine glanced back.

"No preferred pronouns, correct," Lucifer confirmed cheerily.

Sarai frowned. To Sunshine, she said, "*You* can come in." She opened the door a little wider and stepped back.

Sunshine practically had to squeeze through.

She fidgeted morosely as he explained a pared-down version of what they'd learned about the Goodthorne family and how they might be related to her parents' murder. She showed passing interest.

"We want you to take a look at a few pictures," he said finally.

"And then you'll give me back my father's research?"

"Uh." Sunshine hesitated. He didn't think he had any control over whether Felix would give that back. "We can talk to Specter about that."

She wrinkled her nose. "Kay."

"Uh. So. Specter's father came with us."

"Why?"

"I honestly couldn't tell you. I believe he wants to ask you about something or has something to tell you. I don't know."

"Whatever."

Sunshine took that as permission to let the other two in, so he opened the door.

Lucifer hung back and lurked around while Felix showed Sarai the half dozen suspects Tate and Rose had dug up.

She flipped through the photos they'd gleaned from the limited social media of the Goodthorne family. A lot of the pictures had come from a single person, a teenaged girl named Blake who seemed not to care that she belonged to a reclusive family.

Sarai plucked out three photos and handed them over. "That's them."

"You're sure."

"Yeah. Those were my dad's friends. Or business partners, or whatever."

"Thank you."

"Whatever. Can I have my father's research back now?"

Felix opened his mouth, but the answer came from Lucifer. "No."

She looked towards him.

He oozed forward. "You're Sarai Robinson. I'm Lucifer."

She let out a long scoff.

"Oh, shush, sweet thing, let me talk. You'll want to hear what I have to say."

"More crazy bullshit?" she guessed under breath.

"Goodness, teenagers never change, do they?" Lucifer breathed. He sat beside Felix. "My Master of Records has deemed your father's research...not suitable for the current climate on Earth."

"What's that supposed to mean?"

"You are experiencing a, uh, *fun* rise in nationalism and right-wing nonsense, which does not necessarily bode well for the creatures for which I have assumed responsibility, namely my children and the Fallen," Lucifer explained. "The gentlemen, who you've been kind enough to identify, represent a portion of mages who've..." He floated his hand through the air as if searching for the right words. "Who have...taken considerable efforts to...Well. They've really got it out for creatures. Earth for the humans and all that. They've taken enough action to be on my radar, but this is their group's first foray into violence."

"You said my dad wasn't doing stuff like that," Sarai said to Felix.

"He wasn't, but he got mixed up with people who wanted to," Felix said.

"I've come here with the intention to offer you something," Lucifer said to the girl. "I am in need of something, too. We can benefit each other."

"Dad."

Sunshine went cold and hot all at once.

"I can return your parents to you—"

"Dad!" Felix cried. "You can't bring people back—"

"No, I wouldn't bring them back to life, but they aren't dead. They're in induced comas following the attempts on their lives."

Sarai covered her mouth with her hands.

"If you can help to draw out these gentlemen, I will return your parents to you. Healthy as I can make them and fully alive."

The girl let out a harsh sob. "You're lying."

Lucifer withdrew a folded and sealed piece of parchment from within his blouse. "This is the address of their current location, with the appropriate papers to get you into them. Sunshine will bring you. You make contact me with your decision from there.”

“There’s no way.”

“My source among the first responders says that if they’d been called sooner, your parents might have survived altogether. They spent so long unattended...” Lucifer shrugged with his eyes fixed on Sarai’s face. “A coma was the best the mage who responded could do. You know how carefully they guard medical magics.”

The girl dissolved.

“It’s lucky that city even *has* magic workers to respond.”

“Dad, you’re really a fucking bastard sometimes,” Felix said.

Lucifer raised his eyebrows. “Should I not have told her?” he asked with genuine wonder.

It startled Sunshine how often the Devil’s emotions seemed real. All the actors that had ever graced the silver screen didn’t hold a single candle to him.

“It’s about how you do it,” Felix pointed out.

“I did it much differently than I would have if she wasn’t a child,” Lucifer reminded. “I’ll see myself out.” He touched Felix’s shoulder and Sunshine’s back on his way out.

It took some time to calm Sarai. When she stopped crying, she tore open the parchment and stared at it as if it could answer her questions. It couldn’t, of course, so she launched into a barrage of inquiries that was both desperate and infuriated.

Finally, she shoved the paper towards Sunshine. “You have to take me.”

“It’s not a good idea,” Felix advised softly.

“Take me to see my parents!” she screamed. She grabbed on to Sunshine’s shirt. “Take me!”

Sunshine looped an arm around her when she raised her hands. He crushed her against his chest. “Okay.”

She didn’t struggle against him. She begged, “Please.”

“I will,” he promised.

“I have to see them.”

“I know.” He didn’t know, not at all, what it meant to lose your parents, and he never would, but he understood how badly she hurt. The pain radiated out of her and seeped into him.

She shook in his arms, her fists balled in his shirt.

Not sure what to do, but feeling strongly he must do something, he turned his restraint into a hug. “I’ll take you to see them. Okay?”

"Please."

"Try to breathe."

"You want me to give her a Valium?" Felix offered.

Sunshine glared at him only to find that he had a warm expression on his face, an unusual calm and kindness about his eyes.

Felix said, "Or maybe just put on your shoes, Sarai."

She pulled out of Sunshine's arms.

"And wash your face," Felix added.

She went without a word. She looked miserable when she returned, her eyes puffy. She shoved her feet into her shoes and waited by the door.

Felix packed her bag for her, shoving a change of clothes into her backpack. He handed it to her.

As they walked out of the building, Felix said, "Listen, my dad...if he couldn't bring your parents out of it, he wouldn't have said anything. He doesn't come up short on his end of deals."

She looked up at him with hollow eyes.

Sunshine placed a hand on her shoulder. "One thing at a time."

"I'll meet you at the office," Felix said.

"Where are you going?" Sunshine asked.

"To pack an overnight bag. You're going to rent a car."

"Oh." That made sense.

They parted ways.

Sarai trailed behind him, seemingly numb to everything around her.

Sunshine tried to talk to her. It felt important to engage her in some way. He offered her everything he could think to offer.

Finally she accepted his offer of a drink when he stopped to get himself a coffee.

She ordered an iced coffee that consisted more of sugar, milk, and flavoring than actual coffee.

When Felix met up with them at the office and found them both sipping iced coffees and sitting on the stoop, he called them basic. He took the drink Sunshine held out to him and swooped down for a kiss.

"Where's our car?"

Sunshine nodded towards a white Forrester parked on the street. "Heated seats."

"Beautiful boy. Are we ready to go?"

Sarai stood up and slung her backpack over one shoulder.

Felix sipped his coffee. "Oh! Is that caramel?"

"Dulce de leche."

"Beautiful, beautiful boy." He kissed Sunshine once more, his mouth the flavor of coffee and sugar.

Sunshine glowed. He liked it when Felix picked on him, but he liked it even more when he did something right and Felix said something nice.

The first hour of the drive passed in an uncomfortable quiet. Sarai made so little noise that Sunshine forgot she was in the car a few times.

As they moved into hour two, Sarai started to ask questions. Questions about the Devil and the Community and what they'd learned about her parents.

Felix doled out patient and accurate answers.

Sunshine helped when he could.

She lapsed back into quiet after a while.

They had fast food for lunch.

Felix grumbled about the state of his stomach for a while afterward. "I think that curse permanently fucked up my insides. I can't eat the same shit I used to."

Sunshine gave him a look.

Felix flicked his ear, then took his hand. "Are we there yet?"

"A few more hours."

Felix huffed and sighed.

"Listen, are you going to be sick or something? Do you need me to find a rest stop?" Sunshine asked.

"No, I just…" Felix rolled his eyes. "Ugh, I'm bored."

"Put on that awful podcast you listen to."

"It isn't awful!"

"It's the *driest* thing I've ever heard," Sunshine said. "I can't listen to anyone talk about runes for an hour straight."

Felix huffed.

"Anyone but you," Sunshine amended.

"Should I start a podcast then? *Arcane Theory for Big Dumb Idiots.*"

"Put on music or something," Sarai suggested from the back. "Radio sucks anyway."

Felix handed over his phone to her. "Pick something."

After a brief scroll, she said, "I don't know any of these bands."

Felix turned around to tell her, "I didn't say pick something you liked, I said pick something."

She scowled.

"Well, what music do you like?" he asked.

She shrugged. "I like Panic!"

"Did you hear the new album?"

"Haven't really had the chance," she pointed out.

He plucked his phone out of her hand. "Okay, well, listen to the whole thing first and then tell me what you think, because I have feelings and I'd love to get your perspective on it."

Sunshine had little to add to their discussion of a variety of pop-rock bands. He was finally able to chime in when Felix decided to give Sarai a lesson on the history of punk. He also provided a rather scathing review of several Blink 182 albums.

"You can't say they're shitty just because you don't like them," Sunshine pointed out.

"They fucking grew up and got boring."

"People do that, Specter. Frequently. Johnny Rotten sold out like a motherfucker and you still listen to the Sex Pistols."

"Shut up. Anyway. Two thousand three was the end for them, so don't listen to anything after that, but the first few albums were a lot of fun."

The conversation almost felt natural, but disquiet still hung over them. It wouldn't take much to punch through the veneer of normalcy.

Taking an actual child to see her comatose parents, to set her on a path towards a deal with the Devil, sat wrong with Sunshine. He didn't know what else he could do at this point, though. He'd gotten himself in too deep.

All he could do was keep her safe, which he really had no choice in anyway. He would do that to fulfill his favor whether he liked it or not.

He glanced towards Felix.

Of all the stupid and misguided things Sunshine had done, trafficking with the Prince of Hell might have stood alone as the stupidest.

Absolutely worth it, he thought. He shouldn't have, but the thought came on its own and Sunshine couldn't argue.

"Eyes on the road, Sunshine," Felix warned.

"I'm watching the road."

"So you guys are really engaged?" Sarai asked.

"I'm thinking of a fall wedding," Felix confirmed. "Too bad

Sunshine doesn't have anyone to walk him down the aisle." Felix pouted and traced a finger down his own cheek, a mock tear trail. "So sad."

"You could walk down the aisle," Sunshine said.

Felix dismissed the suggestion with a wave of his hand. "No, I'm going to come down on a wire. Big lights show. Lots of sequins."

The idea was so utterly tasteless that Sunshine knew immediately that everything about being engaged had been a joke. "What about doves?"

"What *about* doves?"

"I don't know, it feels like there should be doves," Sunshine said, "If you're gonna be doing the whole David Copperfield thing."

Felix narrowed his eyes. "Don't be a prick."

"You started it."

The demon's face softened. He took Sunshine's hand. "We would walk down the aisle together. I couldn't bear to wait up there all by myself. My nerves would give out."

Now did not seem like the right time to ask if Felix really was serious about all this. He would get offended if he was and he would mercilessly tease Sunshine for years if he wasn't. The kind of teasing that stung instead of making Sunshine warm and fuzzy.

Sarai huffed. "Y'all are weird."

"Deeply," Felix agreed.

"Abidingly," Sunshine confirmed at the same time.

They didn't talk about much else for the rest of the drive.

They reached the hospital and stood outside of it together. Sarai had the bundle of papers the Devil had given her clutched in her hand.

She shook.

"It'll be alright," Sunshine assured. He put a hand on her shoulder.

"I can't."

"It's alright."

"No, no, I can't. I can't see them like that. *I can't.*"

"Okay. What do you want to do?" Sunshine glanced at Felix, hoping for guidance.

The other man had his phone out, typing away. He didn't meet Sunshine's eyes.

"I need them back," she said, her voice low and scratchy.

"He'll be here in a minute," Felix said. He stowed his phone then stretched his arms above his head.

"I don't know if we should..." Sunshine glanced towards Sarai. He sighed. "This seems dicey."

"Letting a distraught child make a literal deal with the Devil. What seems dicey about that?" Felix asked.

"It's my fault they're like this," Sarai said. "I don't care what it takes to fix it."

"It's not your fault."

"If I hadn't run away!" she said. "Or if I'd called the cops. If I'd done *something.*"

"You were scared," Sunshine reminded.

She shook her head. "It doesn't matter. I need them back. I need my life back."

Sunshine looked at Felix.

"Look I'm not any more comfortable with this than you are but I think we're kind of between Scylla and Charybdis here."

"What does that mean?" Sunshine asked.

"Uh, rock and a hard place."

"But what were those other two things?"

"Oh, sea monsters. Greek shit. You're, like, two thousand years old, aren't you? Shouldn't you know that?"

Sunshine shrugged. He didn't know exactly how old he was and he hadn't paid much attention to humanity while he'd been in Heaven.

"Then again, you weren't even literate when I got ahold of you."

A feather-light hand fell upon Sunshine's shoulder; he screamed and danced away from it.

Lucifer tittered.

Felix pressed his lips together and covered his mouth. His eyes crinkled from the effort it took for him not to laugh. He came over and put his arms around Sunshine, his forehead against Sunshine's shoulder. "I'm sorry, sweetheart, I am. Your face though!"

Lucifer approached Sarai, nearly a normal human size. He asked, "Are you ready to discuss things?"

"I don't care," she said. "Whatever it is—"

"No!" Sunshine and Felix interrupted.

"No, no, specific terms," Felix insisted. He peeled away from Sunshine and went to Sarai's side. He gestured towards a Dunkin Donuts. "Let's sit and hash this out reasonably."

Sunshine followed behind the trio and fetched their orders.

Lucifer toyed with the straw in his iced coffee, swirling the ice around in the perfectly black liquid. Not a hint of milk or cream, not a sprinkle of sweetener. "Make it known that you are alive, that you have your father's research," he instructed, "And those men will come to find you."

"They're dangerous," Felix pointed out.

Lucifer gestured to Sunshine with one long, spidery hand. "He is here to keep her safe."

"They're dangerous for him, too."

Lucifer raised his eyebrows. "Are they dangerous for you, angel? Do you fear the strength of mortal men?"

Sunshine didn't. He'd never met a human he thought could do him real harm. Of course, he'd never met anyone with an assault rifle. Idly, he started to plan what, exactly, he would do if he did come against someone with high-powered weaponry.

Lucifer snapped his fingers in front of Sunshine's face.

"Oh. Sorry. No."

"But they're mages," Felix insisted.

Sunshine did worry more about magic. "Are they good mages?" he asked.

"Oh, I don't know," Lucifer said. "What's a good mage?"

"One against three isn't good odds," Felix said.

"Two against three," Sarai corrected quietly. "I can defend myself pretty well."

"I mean, honestly, Felix, shouldn't it be three against three?" Lucifer asked pointedly. "Or are you going to send your, uh...whatever he is out there alone?"

Felix's cheeks turned pink. "No."

"So what's the issue? Seems even to me."

Felix let out a sullen grunt and crossed his arms. He slurped his drink as loudly as possible.

"Then is it sorted?"

"No! What are we even supposed to do with these guys when we get them?" Felix asked.

Lucifer shrugged. "What do you think we should do with them?"

Felix looked at Sunshine. "I don't know. Call the cops?"

"Call the cops," Sunshine agreed.

"Or," Lucifer said.

"No, no, whatever you're going to say—" Felix began.

"Or, you could call me."

"Why? So you can eat them?"

Lucifer's face split into a grin. "Why? Do you think I should?"

"No!" Felix said so loudly that half the Dunkin Donuts turned to look at him. He scowled at those who'd looked over, then hunkered lower in his seat.

"I do have a dungeon. Lots of cell options, too. Ranging from bleak to absolutely miserable."

"What do you want them for?"

"I do like to ask questions," he shared coyly.

Felix rolled his eyes. He turned to Sarai. "Do you care what happens to them?"

"No."

"Alright, fine. Dad, you can have them."

Lucifer grinned. "Lovely. Call me." He stood and slid his hand through the skin of reality, then passed through it all together until he'd gone.

People began to murmur to each other about what they'd seen. Some seemed transfixed with quiet wonder but at least one person demanded, "What the fuck was that!"

"Let's go," Felix said.

The three of them all but fled the coffee shop.

The following few days passed in a blur of cops and tears. They contacted Sarai's uncle, brought her to the police, and arranged for an interview that they would lace with details to let the Goodethorns know where she was.

The police had a lot of questions for Sunshine and Felix, but they danced around them with ease that came with decades of dealing with law enforcement under circumstances that shone unfavorably upon them.

June 3
Friday

Texting with a fifteen-year-old girl on a burner phone felt fundamentally wrong in so many ways that Sunshine couldn't keep track of his unease.

Lurking around her uncle's house felt even more wrong.

Felix had fallen asleep in the backseat.

They'd been staked out for about two days, which did nothing for their relationship or the smell in the car.

Felix snored.

Sunshine threw a balled-up napkin at his face.

"Shithead," came Felix's voice, muffled by the seat cushion.

"Wanted to make sure you were alive."

Felix rolled over, then crawled gracelessly into the front seat. He rinsed his mouth out with a swig of flavored seltzer then spat it out the window.

It was, unfortunately, something Sunshine had seen him do before. He hadn't seen it in a while, and the sight brought back memories. "Remember Charlie Matos?"

Felix slouched in the passenger seat. "My drug dealer?"

"He was your dealer?"

"Yeah, how did you not know that?"

Sunshine shrugged. "I don't know, I thought you just liked

him."

"Yeah, I liked how he sold me drugs."

"He always seemed so nice."

"Yeah, real fucking nice guy," Felix said.

Sunshine went quiet, then had to say, "Remember Oscar?"

"Banks? Of course I remember Oscar Banks!" Felix sounded offended.

"No, Lopez."

"Oh. Poor fucking Oscar," Felix murmured.

Oscar, like a lot of their friends and acquaintances, had died an awful death, alone and far from home.

"I remember all of them."

Sunshine took Felix's hand. "Sarai's heading to bed. Says her uncle locked all the doors."

Felix nodded.

The street stayed quiet for hours.

Sunshine nodded off. He didn't know for how long. Eventually, a hand covered his mouth, startling him awake.

Felix hissed, "Shhh. Don't scream."

"I won't scream," Sunshine mumbled into his palm.

Felix dropped his hand to Sunshine's shoulder. "You've been so fucking jumpy lately." He jabbed a finger up the street towards a tree.

Well. Not the tree. A car with no lights on rolled to a stop.

The engine cut.

The light inside the car flicked on temporarily, illuminating three figures. Not a couple pulling over to park and neck, three solid figures.

Felix's fingers dug into his shoulder. In less than a whisper, he breathed, "Vewy quiet. Wabbit season."

Sunshine bit his tongue to stifle a giggle. He sent a quick text to Sarai to give her a heads up. He didn't like involving her in this plan, but she'd pointed out that she'd be sixteen soon. It hadn't changed his perspective, but she'd been insistent that she could help and wasn't a little kid.

They oozed out of the car in opposite directions. Felix headed towards Sarai's house, nothing more than a shadow that Sunshine's eyes couldn't track.

Sunshine looped around and came up behind the car. He waited a few houses down, hunkered beside a lilac bush.

The figures stayed inside the car for a while.

They seemed to be discussing something, hands moving here and there. Pointing.

A bright blue glow lit up the car for half a second.

A ringtone jangled then was immediately stifled.

An eruption of hissed arguments.

Sunshine didn't move, not an inch. Every so often, his eyes flicked up the street towards Sarai's house.

No movement other than a few small animals. Someone up the street had surround sound and Sunshine thought he recognized the movie.

The car doors opened. The men inside emptied out.

Two of them were heavy on their feet like men who'd once been fit but had eased into a soft middle age. The last one moved like he'd done a lot of sneaking, light and smooth and low to the ground. He moved like a character in a video game, one of those shooters over which young boys liked to cuss each other out.

Sunshine kept his eyes on him.

When they moved towards the house, Sunshine followed, quieter than a kitten.

He dipped his hand inside his pocket and snapped the small disc of glass Felix had enchanted.

Up at Sarai's house, the disc in Felix's hand would break, too, and let out the tiniest rush of power to alert Felix to the incoming threat. Quieter and quicker than a text.

The one that Sarai had would break.

She would, if things went to plan, sneak out the back door and meet up with Felix.

Sunshine followed behind the men as they moved up the driveway. Two of them moved so loudly that Felix mightn't have even needed a warning.

Sunshine hadn't brought his sword, but he wished he had.

A huff of air and a dim flash of light encircled one of the men, sending him to his knees. He let out a hard wheeze.

The second man, the sneaky one, stopped short at the sound, and then dropped to the ground. The second spell missed him.

A crack of lightning took out the remaining one; he dropped, maybe unconscious or maybe just dead.

Sarai didn't look concerned either way, standing on the porch.

The last man standing took off running, back towards his car.

Toward Sunshine.

It was too easy.

All he had to do was wait for him to get a little closer.

Except he didn't keep running. He dodged behind a car parked on the street and crooked his fingers, his lips twisted to form a spell.

Sunshine hesitated.

No, he didn't hesitate. He evaluated. Better than rushing in.

If he approached the man from his current direction, he'd see him coming.

In order to get to a place where the man couldn't see him, though, he'd have to take his eyes off him.

He didn't like that idea.

He'd have to do it, but he didn't like it.

Without sacrificing silence for speed, Sunshine crept around to a place where the man wouldn't see him.

He caught the man's spell, low and ugly.

Sunshine didn't know what would happen when he finished, but he didn't want to find out, now when his target was probably Felix.

Or Sarai.

A slick queasiness wormed through him at the thought of her harmed, of what it would mean to fail the Devil.

He made himself stay calm.

By the time he had the man in his sight again, he'd finished his spell. It bloomed between his hands, about the size of a beach ball, fiery red. Like magma.

It grew legs and arms, ears and a stupid little face.

It dropped to the ground, waggled and waited.

An elemental. It had stubby legs, a broad, flat head with nubby hears and a stout body. Its skin solidified and darkened, a pebbled, leathery hide in a shade somewhere between brick and clay.

Sunshine pounced on the man before he could give the elemental an order.

The mage grunted.

Sunshine clamped a hand over his mouth and looped an arm around his throat. Choking him out wouldn't be pretty, but it probably wouldn't be lethal.

The elemental skittered back a little, watching with stone chip eyes and a flat little mouth.

As the mage writhed and bucked in Sunshine's arms, Sunshine watched the funny doggish-lizard looking thing watch him. It didn't seem to mind.

The man thrashed.

"Sunshine!" came a hiss.

"Over here," he called back, "I've got him but..."

The man redoubled his efforts, his legs kicking wildly.

Sunshine shifted his grip and squeezed a little tighter.

The mage went limp in Sunshine's arm.

Sunshine released him right away and he oozed onto the pavement.

The elemental sat on its haunches.

Felix jogged over. "You kill him?"

"No. Did you kill yours?"

"No." He surveyed the scene a little longer. He crouched down and held out a hand to the elemental.

It sniffed cautiously.

Felix fished out the broken glass from his pocket and held it out.

The element nibbled delicately out of his hand.

Felix stood and nodded his head towards the house. "Bring him over with the other two."

Sunshine obeyed.

The elemental trotted along behind them, making raspy yips as it stared up at Felix's hand. It stood on its hind legs to snuffle his hand.

Sunshine placed the third man among his brothers. Only one of the three had retained consciousness, though he didn't seem to have retained control of his bladder.

The conscious Goodethorn had a rag shoved in his mouth and he wiggled ferociously against the spell that bound him.

Sarai's uncle had come out of the house and argued with her in a hushed, uneasy tone.

She told him, "Go back inside, Uncle Josh. This is...it's going to get taken care of."

"Sari, come on. This is *not* cool," he insisted.

"It's about to get a lot less cool," Felix warned. He held out his hand to Sarai. "Can I use your phone? I left mine in the car."

"Oh, mine's...mine's upstairs." She looked at her uncle.

Sunshine held out the burner phone.

Felix took it. "Go get the one we gave you. Break it, burn it, whatever. Get rid of it."

"Why?"

"Because three men are about to go missing and we don't want to be connected," he offered easily.

Josh gaped.

Sunshine wondered if Josh would become a problem.

The elemental parked itself at Felix's feet as he dialed and lifted the phone to his ear.

A short conversation brought Lucifer to them. He looked uncharacteristically put together tonight, his hair intricately braided and his clothes appropriately sized.

"Going somewhere nice?" Felix asked.

"Georg is getting a commendation for years served." Lucifer looked over the men. "Baldwin, Bradley, and Blane, correct?"

The conscious one seethed and writhed. His breath came out in hard puffs through his nose and around the rag in his mouth.

Lucifer tugged the rag out. "Which one are you?"

"Fuck you."

Lucifer placed a finger under his chin. "Which one are you?"

A dribble of blood worked its way down the man's throat. "Brad."

"Good. Brad, I'll tell you and you can tell your brothers when they wake up. I am the Devil, I'm sending you to Hell, and you're going to answer my questions. I'll see you again in the morning." He paused and smiled. "Well. Maybe later in the afternoon. I do plan to have a busy night."

He returned the rag to Brad's mouth, then drew something gossamer from the nothingness between worlds. He twisted the strands around the men and sent them through the in-between places.

He turned his eyes to Sarai. "We have business."

She stepped forward.

Felix fed a little more glass to the elemental.

It...purred. Maybe. It made some kind of sound.

"My parents."

"Sari," her uncle protested.

"Shut up, Uncle Josh!" she snapped.

"Yeah, Uncle Josh," Lucifer chimed. "Your parents are at home, in bed. Asleep. They will wake up in the morning like it's any other morning. Your father's lungs and left leg will never be quite right. Your mother will struggle with her short-term memory for the rest of her life."

"I don't care."

"You're going to have to take care of them, especially when they get old."

"You said you'd bring them back!"

"Peace, child, I will. I only wanted to give you fair warning of what, exactly, it is I'm giving you."

"Bring them back."

"They're already back."

She stared at him, then turned to her uncle. "Take me home."

"Sari—"

"Goddammit, Josh!" she shouted.

He hurried inside and came back with his keys.

"I like her," Lucifer said once Josh and Sarai had backed down the driveway.

"You would," Felix said.

Lucifer slung an arm around his son and pulled him close. He kissed the top of his head.

Felix leaned against his father. "You didn't even do anything awful this time."

"I thought about it."

Felix smiled.

Sunshine watched.

"Come here, angel."

Sunshine walked over.

Lucifer slid his hands around Sunshine's face. He pressed a feather-light kiss to Sunshine's lips. "The girl is safe. Your favor is fulfilled."

The feel of the Devil's lips against his own made Sunshine mildly nauseated and uncomfortably but almost pleasantly warm.

"That's. Mine," Felix warned.

Lucifer released him. "Of course he is." He brushed his fingers through Sunshine's hair. "I'll see you soon, angel, dear."

Lucifer left.

"Hey, did you get their car keys?" Felix asked.

"No."

Felix slid his hands into his pockets. "That's alright, I'll hotwire it. Get the rental. I'll meet you at the motel."

"Where are you going?"

"I'm going to go light their car on fire in a vacant lot somewhere."

"Oh." Sunshine didn't go towards the rental. "I could come with you."

"No. I'll see you at the motel. Take a shower. God knows you need it."

Sunshine scowled.

Felix reached over and flicked his ear. "Maybe find something for us to eat."

"Alright."

"And give me a kiss."

Sunshine moved in.

"No tongue, I know you haven't brushed your teeth recently."

Sunshine pecked him on the lips. "I'll see you soon."

Felix smirked and walked off, feeding conjured bits of glass to the elemental.

He returned to their hotel room a few hours later reeking of smoke and gasoline.

The elemental followed him into the bathroom and made itself at home sprawled on the tile of the bathroom.

Felix emerged from the shower, scarfed down the Italian takeout Sunshine had procured, and fell asleep face down on the bed, on top of the covers.

Sunshine tried his best to peel back the covers without waking him.

Felix groaned and peeked open one eye. "Hey."

"Sorry."

"Turn up the AC. It's too hot for covers."

"It's *freezing*."

"AC."

Sunshine cranked up the AC as far as it would go and burrowed under the covers.

A few minutes later, Felix slid in beside him, his skin like ice. "You turned it up too much."

"Deepest apologies, Your Highness. I am a worm before you. Crush me beneath your heel."

"You'd like it too much." Felix snuggled closer. He oozed his way into Sunshine's arms and hooked a leg around him. "Garfield is very good at burning things."

"Who?"

"Garfield. The uh, the dog lizard."

"Oh. Right."

"Nothing left to that car but shell." Felix yawned. "He was really good."

"The elemental?" Sunshine wondered if he meant to keep the creature. He'd never heard of anyone keeping an elemental as a pet, but he'd never met anyone like Felix either.

Their lease did allow for one small dog or cat.

"No, Dad. He didn't even make her do a real deal with him or anything. And he didn't do the smile."

"Oh."

"Don't you think he was really good?"

"He did molest me a little."

Felix opened his eyes. He smiled. "Well, with a mouth like that, you're sort of asking for it." He scooted in further.

If he moved any closer, he'd be on top of or possibly inside Sunshine.

"I'd have kissed you too."

Sunshine sighed.

"Did it bother you?"

He sighed again. "I figure it was harmless."

Felix twisted one of Sunshine's curls around his finger. "I'll tell him to leave you alone. I don't think he'll do it, but I'll tell him."

"No harm, no foul, I guess." He knew the Devil needed to do something to seal transactions, usually a kiss or a piece of hair or a bit of blood. Something intimate and personal. He didn't know if a kiss was the worst way to do things. "At least that favor is over with."

"Mmm," Felix agreed. "I think he likes you."

"Great."

"No, I mean...I think he approves. Of you. Of us. I think he likes you, Sunshine. I think he's happy for me."

"Oh. Well. Good?"

"I mean, I hope he does, it would be terrible to have a disapproving parent at our wedding. Don't you agree?"

"It probably would be."

"I was sort of considering spring."

"It might rain," Sunshine pointed out idly.

"Mmm, you're right. You are. But I was thinking of the flowers..." Felix sighed wistfully. "That's alright. I'll figure something out."

"Sure." Sunshine didn't dare ask if he was joking.

"Do you think Heaven would get frightfully mad if we got married in a Church?"

"No, but I think you might burst into flames if you tried to set foot on an altar."

"Maybe that's how the apocalypse would start," Felix suggested. "Do you, Sunshine, take this demon to be your bride? And then a big *whoosh* and the whole place is on fire and there's the horns going. Big Rapture moment, all that. Talk about drama. It would *ruin* the reception."

"I don't think anyone we know would get Raptured. The reception would probably be okay."

"You know, you're right." Felix kissed his cheek, burrowed back into the bed, and closed his eyes.

This time he stayed asleep.

They checked in on Sarai in the morning, as discretely as they could, given the relatively delicate state of her parents.

Felix brought the elemental back to New York.

ABOUT THE AUTHOR

Dan is an author and educator who has lived in Connecticut for their entire life. They received a degree in education and later wrote their Master's thesis on representation of women in same-sex relationships in contemporary Spanish literature and cinema.

More from Dan Ackerman

What Everyone Deserves

2017 Rainbow Awards Honorable Mention

"Although the story deal with some real 1950s issues – discrimination, homophobia, interracial couples and hate crimes – it did it in a way that perfectly suited the characters and the story." - Divine Magazine

In this 1950s period drama, Junius is a New York City fertility demon with a crush. Ever since falling from heaven he's been alone. Except for the mothers and children he watches over.

James Kelly Rosenburg, a black soldier with snowflakes in his hair, walks right into his life with a big problem. James Kelly, turned vampire during the war, is new to New York and its prohibition against vampire killing in city limits.

Junius offers to teach him to overcome his bloodthirsty instincts and live a proper Manhattan life. Their growing friendship leaves them both conflicted as they explore a city both welcoming and alienated by their kind.

That Doesn't Belong Here

2018-2019 Rainbow Awards Honerable Mention

"I liked the ... atmosphere that he created, alongside the paranormal creatures that roam the street. I liked that he wrote characters I could emotionally care for. If Ackerman writes another LGBT fiction, I will give it a try for sure." - Ami, The Blogger Girls

That Doesn't Belong Here begins when Levi and his friend Emily discover an impossible creature in an abandoned pick up. The thing is wounded, frightened and the two friends cannot leave him to the mercy of rubberneckers and tourists. This novel explores what it means to be a person, as the creature, Kato, begins to display not mere intelligence or friendliness but what can only be explained as humanity. The question of who we are allowed to love arises for Levi and Kato, as they are not just crossing the boundaries of gender or sexuality, but of species.